RESTORATION REVIVALS ON THE BRITISH STAGE (1944-1979)

A Critical Survey

Retta M. Taney

UNIVERSITY
PRESS OF
AMERICA

LANHAM • NEW YORK • LONDON

Copyright © 1985 by

University Press of America,® ınc.

4720 Boston Way
Lanham, MD 20706

3 Henrietta Street
London WC2E 8LU England

Printed in the United States of America

Library of Congress Cataloging in Publication Data

Taney, Retta M., 1942-
   Restoration revivals on the British stage, 1944-1979.

   Bibliography: p.
   Includes index.
   1. Theater—Great Britain—History—20th century.
2. English drama—Restoration, 1660-1700—History and
criticism. I. Title.
PN2595.T36   1985   792'.0941   85-7389
ISBN 0-8191-4696-X (pbk. : alk. paper)
ISBN 0-8191-4695-1 (alk. paper)

TO MY MOTHER AND FATHER

AND NENNE

CONTENTS

APPENDIXES

PREFACE

At the very end of <u>Stage Directions</u> John Gielgud has a word about the critic and his effect on actors who cannot love him, for, "even when he gives praise, they are disappointed to find that he has missed entirely what they consider to be some obvious point of excellence in their performance, and if he writes adversely they decide that he is unfair (or has dined unwisely) belittling honest effort and perhaps ruining the chances of a new author or an enterprising management." So it has always been. But to approach the drama through the critic seems still a valid way, for the good critic brings to his theatregoing a sense of the past, the tradition which inspires or bedevils revivals and, though his words might need the pinch of salt, he has the advantage of being the eyewitness, of consciously travelling the road Pepys and other enthusiasts went before him. Therefore, in this study of revivals of Restoration drama, the words of the critic are significant.

Using reviews, biographies, theatre history, and some available scripts, this work brings together thirty-five years of British stagecraft treating forty-five productions of the work of ten authors of the late seventeenth and early eighteenth centuries.

Basically the book is divided into three parts: the introductory section, the revivals, and the concluding material. The introductory section, which begins with the death of Charles I, establishes a time frame for the plays, and describes the state of the theatres before and after the Restoration. There is also an attempt to give an idea of the physical structure of the early theatres, the audience and the actors. Two short essays, one on Restoration acting in this century and the other which views all the revivals under consideration, complete the section.

The central section of the book deals with the revivals themselves. Here, each chapter is devoted to an author, the earliest considered first and the rest moving chronologically along. The plays of each author are placed in the sequence in which they were originally produced (e.g., Congreve: _The Double Dealer_, 1693; _Love for Love_, 1695; _The Way of the World_, 1700). Twentieth century productions of the individual play follow each other chronologically (e.g., _The Double Dealer_, Old Vic Company, 1959; _The Double Dealer_, Royal Court, 1969; _The Double Dealer_, National Theatre Company, 1978). Obviously chapters vary considerably in size as some playwrights are much more revivable than others.

The treatment of each play begins with a plot summary and historical background. The revival itself is viewed in terms of the theatrical climate in which the play was revived, potent dramatic influences on the theatre at the time of the production, and general audience expectation. When it is relevant, the physical structure of the theatre is described. Setting and costume are treated in relation to the directorial emphasis. Consideration of performances in major roles includes: the approach of the individual performance, the quality of the effectiveness of the approach, and the influence of those rare, definitive performances on other interpretations. Other noteworthy secondary performances are dealt with in terms of their value to the individual production.

The concluding material consists of six appendixes. The first three, _The Way of the World_ (1924), _The Way of the World_ (1976) and _The Country Wife_ (1936), offer a view of productions of major importance which lie outside the scope of this book but whose influence is so pervasive that the reader should have access to them. The fourth appendix treats textual emendations and rehearsal techniques for the Brecht-influenced production of the National Theatre Company's

The Recruiting Officer (1963). The fifth appendix is devoted to cast lists and the last to an annotated listing of libraries and theatre archives plus a list of theatre addresses. There is also an annotated selected bibliography.

No book can recreate performance, but it can provide information--salient bits and pieces which add a dimension to the study of this elusive dramatic period. For Gielgud gives the critic his due: he may be able "to record a moment of magic, may describe some piece of business, some cry of emotion, with a vivid phrase of re-creation." It is those moments which we seek, moments which, when coupled with the background of original productions and early interpreters of these plays, provide a link, a throbbing continuum which makes first nights live for centuries.

In addition to the late Aline Taylor, who proposed this study, Professor Joseph Roppolo, who continued to direct the dissertation when Professor Taylor's health failed, and my University Press of America reader, I would like to thank those who offered me both hospitality and encouragement during the research period. In London, Jill Robinson; in Virginia, Carlotta and Jacques Abadie, Jr.; in New York, Martin Ferrand, M.D. and in New Haven, Linda Mosely, M.D. In the deepest South, Professor John David Eatman has my gratitude for his ability to reason with computers. And from the family, Professor Thaddeo K. Babiiha and my aunt, Hilda Taney, have shown faith in me far greater than I deserve.

The following have generously given permission to use extended quotations from copyrighted works: From Robert Waterhouse, Terry Hands and Timothy O'Brien, "A Case of Restoration," Plays and Players. Copyright 1971 by Brevet Publishing Ltd. Reprinted by permission of the publisher. From Stage Directions, by John Gielgud. Copyright 1963 by John Gielgud. Reprinted by permission of the author.

Theatrical Conditions: An Overview

The State of the Stage During the Interregnum

On Tuesday morning, January 30, 1649, Charles Stuart, clad in two shirts for fear of shivering in the cold and giving his enemies cause to denounce him as a coward, went from St. James's Palace to Whitehall. About two in the afternoon the windows of the Banqueting House of the palace were opened and Charles stepped out upon the scaffold. A Puritan noted that it was remarkable that the king "should end his days in a Tragedie at the Banqueting-house, where he had seene, and caused many a Comedy to be acted upon the Lord's Day." At the end of the terrible ceremony, which took less than fifteen minutes, as the executioner raised the severed head of the king and cried, "Behold the head of a traitor!" the crowd responded not with cheers and insults but with a deep, dreadful groan. It would not be surprising if some of those moaning were actors.

Even before the Civil Wars, acts of God like the plague (1635 and 1637) and acts of foolishness like mocking the church (1639) had closed the doors of the London theatres. In February 1642, when Charles fled north and Parliament prepared for war, the playhouses were still in operation and Parliamentary Puritans were protesting. By September the storm had broken and a resolution was passed against sports and stage plays which were considered "Spectacles of pleasure, too commonly expressing laciuious Mirth and Levitie." When war broke out in 1642, the players, particularly the King's Company of the Blackfriars and the Globe, enlisted in the Royalist cause. Indeed, their dramatic talents were used at the king's Oxford headquarters where they were called upon to act before him to keep up his spirit even through the last year of the war.

At the height of the First Civil War (1642-1646) plays were still given at the public playhouses in

London as the actors continued to defy the ordinance, risking the entrance of soldiers to disrupt the play and confiscate the costumes. For example, players at the Fortune in 1643 were suddenly joined onstage by a "strong guard of Pikes and muskets . . . [who] unexpectedly did presse into the Stage upon them, who (amazed at these new Actors) it turned their Comedy in to Tragedy, and being plundered of all the richest of their cloathes, they left them nothing but their necessities now to act, and to learne a better life."

By 1647, the year the Scots delivered Charles up to Parliament, the Globe had been destroyed but the Cockpit, the Fortune and Salisbury Court were all ignoring the 1642 ordinance, managing to survive so adroitly that the government passed a stronger ordinance that all players caught, so to speak, in the act were "to be punished as Rogues, according to law."

On February 11, 1648, an even stricter ordinance was passed which affected the actors, their theatre, the admission money and even levied a fine on those who had had the temerity to attend the performance. By March 1649, the government hit upon the most expeditious measure of suppression: the interiors of the Fortune, the Cockpit and Salisbury Court were dismantled. The Fortune was not to survive this onslaught, but the other two revived while the Red Bull, which had the least benign reputation, continued to function. When the playhouses were unavailable or too dangerous, the actors performed privately and occasionally located in Knightsbridge which was then several miles from the city. By 1654, performances were sufficiently frequent to jog the elbow of the government again, and in 1655, the Red Bull saw another raid. But by this time Sir William Davenant's influence was about to be felt and The First Day's Entertainment at Rutland House was given on 23 May 1656. Davenant's success in driving in the wedge of legitimate productions led to increasingly bolder

ventures, and he was there at the Restoration to gather
the yield of his investment.

The Restoration

On May 25, 1660, King Charles II anchored at
Dover. About noon, a barge went from the ship to the
shore. The king climbed out and fell to his knees on
the sand. The response was tremendous, and Pepys, who
had followed the king in another boat, gloried in the
show: "Infinite the Croud of people and the gallantry
of the Horsemen, Citizens, and Noblemen of all sorts."
The guns and cannons echoed from Dover to London as
bonfires sprang up across the hills. Making his way
slowly to Canterbury, then Rochester, the king entered
London on May 29th, celebrating, on the one day, his
thirtieth birthday and his restoration. He crossed
London Bridge, still clogged with houses, and in the
Strand, John Evelyn, who had known the pain of exile,
recorded in his diary that he beheld the great event
and "blessed God." The pomp of the king's entrance
which included a visual blaze of cloth of silver,
scarlet gowns, velvet coats, gold chains, silver lace,
purple liveries and sea-green uniforms coupled with
jubilant noise heralded the return of a new way of
life: a wholesale release from sensual deprivation for
those with a zest for living and, more particularly, a
release from famine for the long oppressed actors.

The sad state of Whitehall, reduced to a "raw sent
of moist walls, and all as silent as midnight" was
rectified. During the days of decay, the Cockpit
Theatre, which was part of the palace, had deteriorated
into a kind of museum where one could "goe in without a
Ticket or the danger of a broken-pate" and view the
stage and the machinery and bemoan the loss of
entertainment. Now it was ordered made ready. It was
not alone.

3

The State of Things Theatrical

At the king's return, there were several theatres which dated from pre-Commonwealth times, as did some of the actors. The Red Bull, which housed the veterans led by ex-Major Mohun, was the oldest and bore the closest resemblance to the inn-playhouse structure, which meant that it was commodious but unroofed and suffered accordingly from the difficulties of exposure to inclement weather and boasted an even greater disadvantage in that the size and poor acoustics forced actors to deliver lines at the top of their voices, driving away the more genteel ears in the audience.

The other Cockpit--or Phoenix--in Drury Lane had been used during the Interregnum, indeed, even repaired after the interior had been destroyed in 1649. At the Restoration John Rhodes was already installed as manager. Davenant drew principally from the Rhodes group to form the Duke's Men, which were led by a former apprentice to Rhodes, Thomas Betterton.

Like the Cockpit, the interior of the Salisbury Court Theatre had also been wrecked by order of law in 1649. It too was renovated for some sporadic acting between 1652 and 1659 and William Beeston had a company there. The theatre was in good enough shape to house Davenant's fledgling company from November 1660 until June 1661 when they moved to Lisle's Tennis Court.

Gibbon's Tennis Court Theatre, which dated from 1633, belonged to the Elizabethan tradition. It had survived the Commonwealth by attracting patronage by dint of tennis, bowls and very good dinners. It was sufficiently preserved at the Restoration to house Killigrew's company and bear the weight of the new title, Theatre Royal. Pepys lauded it as the "finest playhouse, I believe, that ever was in England."

Less than two hundred yards from Gibbon's and jutting out into the fields was Lisle's Tennis Court which was rechristened the Duke's Playhouse and housed Davenant's company from June 1661. The productions at this playhouse ushered in the new use of scenery and eventually Lisle's eclipsed its neighbor.

Sir William Davenant

As early as 1639, a new theatre was already a gleam in the eye of Sir William Davenant, who was granted a patent which authorized him to build a playhouse which could be used for music, scenes and dancing. Naturally, the deposition of Charles I hobbled his plans, if not his imagination. Probably active before 1656, Davenant came out of the dramatic closet with discreet boldness when he presented the first English "opera," The Siege of Rhodes, at the "back part of Rutland House [Davenant's private residence] in Aldersgate Street." The site of the mansion, previously the home of the Countess Dowager of Rutland, was a fortunate one for the audience as it was located near Charterhouse Yard, which was a magnet to the fashionable. This monument to dramatic strategy was no play; Davenant was too clever for that. Rather, the title page to the printed version reassured the suspicious that the offering had the "Art of Prospective in Scenes, and the Story Sung in Recitative Musick." Though it lacked machines and engines, the production boasted designs by John Webb, nephew and pupil of Inigo Jones, who introduced the innovation of representing crowds and armies on his canvas.

By 1658-59, Davenant was putting scenes, machines and costumes into the Cockpit of Drury Lane. There in July 1658 The Cruelty of the Spaniards in Peru, written for public viewing and containing delightfully dreadful scenes of torture, was on view "At Three after noone punctually." Capitalizing on this success, Davenant produced The History of Sir Francis Drake in the winter of 1658-59. By December of 1658, the Lord Protector was dead and Richard Cromwell was casting baleful looks at the "operas." Davenant always had his ear to the ground and shortly before the Restoration must have gone back to France in order to return in the train of the king.

The Rise of the Companies

When Pepys was busy hobnobbing with "persons of Honour" at Dover on the day of the king's return, he took a walk on deck with Thomas Killigrew, "a merry droll, but a gentleman of great esteem with the King." Killigrew had every reason to be merry; he must have been planning his bid for a dramatic monopoly. Despite the Commonwealth ban on plays, the king found three companies in London on his return. There was Rhodes and his company who had begun to use the Cockpit after Davenant's departure for France. At the Red Bull were the older actors led by Major Michael Mohun. And there was a group at Salisbury Court.

Davenant was in advance of Killigrew as the old patent from 1639 might not have been current but had accrued the interest of his Royalist leanings. Killigrew had to beaver away to get a royal warrant, but he managed; and on 21 August 1660 the joint grant was passed giving Killigrew and Davenant control of the performed drama in London.[1]

The Duke's Company

Under Davenant's management, the Duke's Company played briefly at Salisbury Court while remodeling Lisle's Tennis Court in Portugal Street near Lincoln's Inn Fields. Lisle's combined forestage and innerstage and delighted the public with the use of perspective scenery. The rear stage owed its origin to the picture stage which Inigo Jones had developed to enhance the court masks. Both public and private playhouses knew the forestage. Davenant was instrumental in uniting these two forms and making them successful and, in so doing, set the basic form for British theatre through the eighteenth century.

The company remained at Lisle's from 1661-1667. By April of 1668, Davenant was dead. Pepys payed his respects by going to Davenant's house which adjoined the theatre: "Up and down to the Duke of York's playhouse, there to see, which I did, Sir W. Davenant's corpse carried out towards Westminster, there to be buried." In 1671, the Duke's Company moved into the more elaborate structure built at Dorset Garden. The proscenium was gilded and adorned with statues and carving. Dorset Garden was more capacious with an overall length of 140 feet and a width of 57. This was the largest of the Restoration theatres and when the Duke's Company and the King's Company merged in 1682, it was retained for more elaborate presentations while the Theatre Royal, Drury Lane, of the King's Company did duty as the regular playhouse.

The King's Company

Under the management of Thomas Killigrew, the King's Company played first at the Vere Street Theatre then moved into the first Theatre Royal which was located between Bridges Street and Drury Lane. It opened May 7, 1663 and was destroyed by fire January 25, 1672. The overall measurement of the Theatre Royal was a length of 112 feet and a width of 58 feet. A noble Italian visitor was impressed by the interior which was

> surrounded, in the inside, by boxes separated from each other, and divided into several rows of seats . . . a large space being left on the ground-floor for the rest of the audience. The scenery is light, capable of a great many changes, and embellished with beautiful landscapes.[2]

In February 1666-67 Pepys met Killigrew who was not above a little boasting:

> T. Killigrew and I to talk: and he tells me how the audience at his house is not above half so much as it used to be before the late fire [the Great Fire of London, September 1666]. . . . That the stage is now by his pains a thousand times better and more glorious than heretofore.

After the 1672 fire, the King's Company went temporarily to Lisle's Tennis Court while Christopher Wren designed a new Theatre Royal. The new building had the same width as its predecessor, but the addition of a scene-room in the rear lengthened it. This simple playhouse opened March 26, 1674, and Dryden's prologue for the opening noted the contrast between the earlier Theatre Royal, the ornate Dorset Garden and the present simple structure:

> A Plain built House, after so long a stay,
> Will send you half unsatisfy'd away;
> When fall'n from your expected Pomp, you find
> A bare convenience only is design'd.

But, simple or not, the theatre functioned successfully, outlasting the company it housed.

The United Company

The United Company, which performed principally at Drury Lane, was formed after the collapse of the King's Company. In 1682 the Duke's Company was doing well while the King's Company, which had a long history of mismanagement and internal disagreements, finally collapsed. By 1693 the United Company was under the control of Christopher Rich. Colley Cibber, who knew the slippery Rich, has painted the portrait of this theatrical tyrant:

8

He gave the Actors more Liberty, and fewer
Days Pay, than any of his Predecessors: He could
laugh with them over a Bottle, and bite [deceive]
them, in their Bargains: He kept them poor, that
they might not be able to rebel; and sometimes
merry, that they might not think of it: All their
Articles of Agreement had a Clause in them, that
he was sure to creep out at . . . which in effect,
made them all, when he pleas'd, but limited
Sharers of Loss, and himself sole Proprietor of
Profits.[3]

Eventually the situation became intolerable, and,
in 1695, the older players revolted against Rich who
had consistently abused his position. The rebels, who
included Mrs. Barry, Mrs. Bracegirdle, Underhill,
Williams and Dogget, were led by Thomas Betterton, who
was sixty at the time. The renowned actor obtained a
license from the Lord Chamberlain to move his little
company into Lisle's Tennis Court Theatre. On April 30,
1695, they opened with Congreve's <u>Love for Love</u>.
Popular sympathy for the rebels is indicated in the
anonymous <u>Comparison Between the Two Stages</u> in a
lengthy dialogue between three gentlemen--Ramble,
Sullen and a Critic:

Ramble. You know the New-house opened with an
extraordinary good Comedy [<u>Love for Love</u>], the
like has scarce been heard of.
Critic. I allow that Play contributed not a
little to their Reputation and Profit; it was the
Work of a popular Author; but that was not all,
the Town was ingag'd in its favour, and in favour
of the Actors long before the Play was Acted.[4]

The struggle continued with the older, more
experienced players holding forth at Lincoln's Inn
Fields and the younger ones trying hard at Drury Lane.
After a while, the audience knew where to go and when
to go:

The Town, not being able to furnish out two good Audiences every day; chang'd their Inclinations for the two Houses, as they found 'emselves inclin'd to Comedy or Tragedy: If they desir'd a Tragedy, they went to Lincolns-Inn-Fields; if to Comedy, they flockt to Drury-lane; which was the reason that several Days but one House Acted; but by this variety of Humour in the Town, they shared pretty equally the Profit.[5]

However, internally things were not smooth in either group. Despite the talent of his company, Betterton had to battle low morale, while Rich maneuvered constantly to get the upper hand of his players.

Cibber reports that the Betterton group "having only the fewer, true Judges to admire them, naturally wanted the Support of the Crowd, whose Taste was to be pleas'd at a cheaper Rate, and with coarser Fare."[6] So a project was formed to lure the crowds to a new location: a theatre was to be erected in the Haymarket designed by Sir John Vanbrugh who, along with William Congreve, was given a patent by Queen Anne to establish and manage a new company. The lavish Queen's Theatre, which opened April 9, 1705, rivalled its continental counterparts in splendor while easily surpassing the simple Drury Lane and cramped Lincoln's Inn Fields. Originally, it was intended as a home both for plays and for the increasingly fashionable Italian opera. Although it did house, briefly, some excellent dramatic fare, Cibber describes how Vanbrugh had sacrificed the acoustics to the splendor:

> This extraordinary, and superfluous Space [the large interior] occasion'd such an Undulation, from the Voice of every Actor, that generally what they said sounded like the Gabbling of so many People, in the lofty Isles in a Cathedral--The

Tone of a Trumpet, or the swell of an Eunuch's
holding Note, 'tis true, might be sweeten'd by it;
but the articulate Sounds of a speaking Voice were
drown'd, by the hollow Reverberations of one Word
upon another.[7]

Within several months, Congreve gave up his share
in the theatre and public life generally, and in 1706
Vanbrugh eventually turned the running of the theatre
over to Swiney.

The Publick Voice

The return of Charles II to the throne signaled the reinstatement of the drama as part of the daily round and made licit the provincial, but popular, lesser entertainments. One could go across the river for the delights of dog fighting and bull and bear baiting or to Bartholomew and Southwark Fairs for circus-type amusements including rope dancers, puppet shows and the incredible sight of an elephant. Those in search of diversion from every class could go from a fair to Charing Cross for an execution and thence to a playhouse.

When the king returned and let loose his court, the playhouses welcomed him with the avaricious joy one reserves for a star; for Charles provided the major draw. And his playgoing enthusiasm would have induced even the most reluctant satellite, and there were few of those, to attend. But the concept of a predominantly court-oriented audience has latterly been viewed as more and more of a fiction.[1]

The capacity of the playhouse cannot be determined with exactitude. A round, generous figure is 1,000; a more conservative one is 400. Even using the conservative estimate and allowing for returns for a second viewing, it is unlikely that the upper classes could have been the sole target of the theatrical offerings for any extensive period. And it is more likely that, at one time or another, representatives of virtually every class appeared there.

The structure of the playhouse divides into four seating sections and gives some idea of who generally sat where. The upper gallery accommodated servants and the poorer of the vizard masks. The middle and lower galleries were a favorite with citizens and their families as they lacked the claustrophobic elegance of the boxes and, if there was a ruckus, it was most likely to occur in the pit. Audacious servingmen and apprentices could also make their way down to that slightly more expensive section. The boxes were particularly interesting. One box was reserved for the king and another for the Duke of York. Originally they were at the back of the house giving a full view of the stage. When royalty did not attend, they were sold with the rest. Those in the side boxes near the top of the U had a limited view of the rear stage, but then they had come to eyeball their neighbors in the same location across the house and to converse with those in the pit. The pit seems to have accommodated almost everybody with the stamina to sit there. Certainly both men and women, high and low,legitimate and suspect went there. And for those interested in using the flexibility of the theatre's admission policy, it was the ideal place. One could see one act without charge, and a determined spectator could elude the money gatherer by dodging from the pit to the boxes to the gallery and possibly see--though with very little concentration-- the whole performance.

The prices of admission were steep for someone with a very modest income, but a theatrelover of means would be able to attend performances regularly without risking bankruptcy. The prices, which remained notably stable, were: 4/- for boxes, 2/6d for the pit, 1/6d for the gallery and 1/- for the upper gallery. Despite the prices, the theatres were rarely full, and Pepys's snobbish complaint of 1 January 1668 that he was jostled by a "mighty company of citizens, prentices and others" in the pit is probably a holiday complaint. Citizens frequently found themselves the butts of Restoration comic jests, but they kept coming, and there seems to have been, even before the Union of the companies in 1682, a leaning toward the citizen audience in Davenant's productions while Killigrew's company focused on the elite in the pit and the boxes.

13

There is a whole body of anecdotal literature of playhouse commotion which illustrates the various disturbances, physical and vocal, which kept things humming. Although opinions differ about degree and frequency of pandemonium, it is certain that the Restoration playhouses were not known for the church-like atmosphere that is the hallmark of the twentieth-century theatre. After the heavy midday meal, the audience went to the play in full daylight. There was a nucleus of playgoing regulars who knew each other and who talked, jested, called out approval or disapproval of the work in progress and, on occasion, brawled.

Since the playhouses let in light, the audience was almost as visible as the actor, causing contortions of courtesy. Pepys applauded a little local drama: "But it was pleasant to see how everybody rose up when my Lord John Butler, the Duke of Ormonde's son, came into the pit toward the end of the play." One wonders if the actors shared in Lord John's delight. In 1667, within a decade of the official reopening of the playhouses, the Duke of Buckingham and Henry Killigrew quarreled very physically in a playhouse. Buckingham nearly killed his opponent. As time went on, things warmed up even more. In 1679, Thomas Otway, just returned from the army, challenged John Churchill--not yet Duke of Marlborough--to a duel when Churchill unchivalrously beat one of the orange wenches at the Duke's playhouse. Churchill got the worst of it. Among accounts which show an awesomely low level of audience manners this 1682 report has appealing panache: "Mr. Vaughan and Mr. Charles Deering fought . . . and the last dangerously hurt--on the playhouse stage." Another account of the same incident says that in their eagerness to skewer each other, the gentlemen brushed the players aside and went to it.

If there were distractions to be expected from the pit, the actors were not beyond creating diversions of their own. The handsome Cardell Goodman, who did a brief turn as a highwayman and a longer one as an exile when he was involved in the assassination plot of 1696, was one of the lovers of Barbara, Duchess of Cleveland, whose favors had also been lavished on her royal lover, Charles II. Inspired by love and/or insolence, Goodman narrowly missed insulting the queen in his eagerness to insure that Barbara was around before the play commenced:

> One night when the Queen [Mary II] was at the Theatre, and the curtain as usual was immediately ordered to be drawn up, Goodman cry'd, "Is my Duchess come?" and being answered, "No," he swore terribly, the curtain should not be drawn till the Duchess came, which was at the instant, and sav'd the affront to the Queen.[2]

Then there was always the danger of the injury one player might do another. Farquhar left acting because he had accidentally wounded another player on the stage of the Smock Alley Theatre in Dublin. Much more deliberate is an account of the duel between Mrs. Barry as Roxana and Mrs. Boutell as Statira during Lee's Alexander the Great. Before the play, the ladies had an argument about a veil which Mrs. Boutell had gotten hold of "by the partiality of the property-man." This good fortune enraged Mrs. Barry and the ladies took the fray before the public:

> They were so violent in performing their parts, and acted with such vivacity, that Statira on hearing the King was nigh, begs the Gods to help her for that moment; on which Roxana hastening the designed blow, struck with such force, that though the point of the dagger was blunted, it made way through Miss Boutel's stays, and entered about a quarter of an inch in the flesh.[3]

Players could also be used for the public embarrassment of a rival. Lady Castlemain, a veteran of

15

many playhouse disturbances, persuaded the excellent comedienne, Mrs. Corey, to gild her performance of Sempronia in Cataline with an imitation of Lady Harvey. Lady Harvey then used her influence to have Mrs. Corey arrested. Lady Castlemain had her released, and she went back to play the role with the offending embellishments "worse than ever where the King himself was." The offended Lady Harvey gathered a claque "to hiss her and fling oranges at her." Pepys records, somewhat redundantly, "it seems the heat is come to a great height, and real troubles at Court about it."

A disappointed audience could express instant disapproval and thus censure a play even as it was in progress. The Black Prince, which premiered on October 19, 1667, with Pepys looking on, contained some exposition which the audience, which included the king and the Duke of York, found tiresome. Hart came on to reveal the central plot by reading a long letter. The audience found the bulk of the epistle so unnecessary that they "frequently began to laugh, and to hiss twenty times, that, had it not been for the King's being there, they had certainly hissed it off the stage." The chastised management was up to the occasion. A printed version of the letter was made available to patrons of subsequent performances, and the relieved Hart had only to make "some short reference to it . . . in the play, which do mighty well." So much for popular editing.

Even the tiring rooms were public. Orange wenches carried messages back and forth between the players and the patrons, and, for a fee, a gentleman could enter to talk with actors or dally with an actress.

Pleas in prologues for better conduct do not seem to have produced any miracles of decorum; and if duels were the exception, it is likely that talking (and, since the plays were performed after the day's heaviest meal, a buzz of gentle snoring) was not in the least exceptional. It is a moot point whether or not members of the audience sat on the stage. Assuming that some of the chosen occasionally did, they could only fit on the forestage, where much of the action took place. In that strategic location, they were in the way even if they were as silent as the grave; for they would have been blocking at least one of the two exit doors on either side. All in all, audience activity was as considerable a factor to the player as audience taste was to the playwright.

But it would be foolish--and depressing--to argue that playgoers spent all their time socializing and fighting to the complete neglect of the performance. Although educational tracts are very cautious about encouraging wholesale theatregoing, courtesy books give a gentleman levelheaded advice about how to attend and attend to a play. Samuel Vincent, who has the odd serious moment in The Young Gallant's Academy (1674), advises that the "true-bred Gentleman sits the Play out patiently." This courteous behavior enables him to take mental notes, and "if he observes any thing that is good or ingenious, he turns it into practice; and after the Play is done, home he goes to his Lodging, and can there laugh at the Fopperies of some Persons that were presented."[4]

But the leisured gentleman as audience was on the decline; and if proper reception of high comedy and tragedy was wanting, John Dennis attributed it to the rise of the younger brother, the nouveau riche and the foreigner. The reign of Charles II had produced an audience whose education qualified them to judge a comedy, and they kept in practice:

> In their Closets they cultivated at once Imaginations and Judgments, to make themselves the fitter for conversation, which requires them both.[5]

These practiced judges were being elbowed out by three sorts of people with no education. There were the younger brothers, "Gentlemen born, who have been kept at home, by reason of the pressure of the taxes."[6] Then there were those who had made their fortunes in the war with France (1689-1697), but despite their newfound condition of "distinction and plenty" had not altered their taste which inclined to "Tumblings and Vaultings and Ladder Dancing, and the delightful diversions of Jack Pudding." The third sort, foreigners, were, in terms of the theatre, aesthetic dunces whose demands were being met to the harm of the drama. Some of them

> not being acquainted with our Language, and consequently with the sense of our Plays, and others disgusted with our extravagant, exorbitant Rambles have been Instrumental in introducing Sound and Show, where the business of the theatre does not require it, and Particularly a sort of soft and wanton Musick, which has used the People to a delight which is independent of Reason, a delight that has gone a very great way towards the enervating and dissolving their minds.[7]

These groups did display a kind of influence, which increased with the change in the habits of the once leisured, upper class gentlemen. Dennis mourns the fate that causes this cherished, appreciative audience to keep businessman's hours. In the age of pleasure they had plenty but now

> want throws them upon employments, and there are ten times more Gentlemen now in business, than there were in King Charles his reign. . . . They come to a Playhouse full of some business which they have been solliciting, or of some Harrangue which they are to make the next day; so that they meerly come to unbend, and are utterly uncapable

of duly attending to the just and harmonious Symetry of a beautiful design.[8]

The lifestyle of the court had altered, and now time was important to the men who could once while it away as courtiers:

'Tis true, there may be several Gentlemen in it [the court] who are capable of setting others right, but neither have they leisure to do it, nor have others time to attend to them.[9]

The gentleman no longer relished the turn of phrase, for he came to the theatre with a head crammed with matters of great weight, which the influence of the stage could not dissipate. So the gentleman was still in attendance, but, as he had other things on his mind, he was losing control and, with that, influence.

As the gentleman's grip weakened, the grasp of the citizen tightened. The citizen was a more moral man and didn't want to have to constantly winnow lewdness for values, and he craved some down-to-earth gymnastics to offset the more aristocratic fencing. His was the age which saw the founding of the London Stock Exchange and the beginning of the national debt, not high comedy matters. The age of the Restoration "original" man vanished as in a cloud of mercantile glory the age of the businessman arrived.

The Theatre: Sights and Sounds

Roughly, the interior of the Restoration theatre was U-shaped. There were benches in the pit, sometimes hinged to allow for passage then put down to provide extra seating. There was a level of boxes above the pit--seven boxes at Dorset Garden held twenty people each--and then a level or two of galleries. At the top, the "paradise."

In form, the stage looked backward and forward: there was one stage but two distinct acting areas cut in half by the proscenium. The inner stage, the "house," was enclosed by a back scene, side wings and borders. There were grooves along the floor of the stage and machinery below, to the sides and above to move the complicated scenery. Wings and shutters were used to create scenic pictures, which often gave the illusion of distance. The wings ran in the grooves part of the way across the stage and the shutters could be closed to create a complete back picture. The wings might decrease in height to enhance the effect of perspective as they approached the back of the stage. Borders--blue sky, clouds, treetops, architectural designs--which matched the wings in an elaborate production gave the full effect to the picture. This picture could include furniture and even people painted on the scenery. What movables there were on the stage were spirited off by ropes attached to the legs of the pieces.

The closing of the shutters was very important as scenes could be prepared behind the shutters and then revealed in all their glory, or actors could be discovered in prearranged settings simply by drawing the shutters apart. In this instance, the shutters took the place of an entrance door. Here is a scene change in action:

> The prompter blew his whistle and the scenemen immediately removed a downstage set of wings and

> shutters . . . to disclose a new set ready . . . further upstage, or slid on a downstage pair, which masked the deeper set of the preceding scene.[1]

But this shift of wings and shutters was only part of the full picture:

> Simultaneously the borders above the wings and shutters were changed. An occasional accident or case of negligence on the part of the sceneman, allowing the clouds of an exterior scene to serve as a ceiling for an interior one, for example, emphasizes the importance of a swift, smooth, coordinated shift.[2]

The wing and shutter combination dominated the English stage for more than a century with additional visual variety being provided by "releeve" scenes. This in-depth effect was achieved by placing a number of cut-out ground-rows set one behind the other which drew the eye to the back of the inner stage where the back-scene was mounted in the farthest spot available, well past the area occupied by the grooves. For a divine view, the borders could provide rows of cut-out clouds, which would draw the eye to a heavenly figure situated above the world of the stage.

Ultimately, the actor began to suffer from the overuse of these effects which, however ingenious, had limitations. The most deadly one in terms of visual variety was the case of the actor vs. the perspective:

> The convergence of wings on back shutter or drop, the predilection for a central vanishing point resulted in a fixity of design. The part of the stage behind the proscenium was ultimately inhospitable to the actor, who could not move up or down it without threatening the perspective.[3]

Although scenery and stage effects were powerful audience magnets, the scenic spot was not the main acting area. Stage directions abound which call for the actor to leave the "house" and move to the "stage," an oval apron jutting far out into the audience in front of the proscenium, flanked on either side by a pair of doors for entrances and exits. Above the doors were balconies or boxes which could seat members of the audience but were more likely to be used for the upper levels needed in the play; thus the forestage had two acting levels always available. The doors themselves showed great versatility:

> Characters might pass through the proscenium doors as from the outside to the inside of a house and vice versa. They might pretend to enter a house by leaving the stage through a proscenium door and immediately reenter through the same or the adjacent door or from the wings: The proscenium wall and/or stage would now represent an interior.[4]

The proximity of actor to audience encouraged considerable intimacy which remained part of the dramatic tradition until the proscenium doors, balcony and forestage became obsolete, and the actor was forced behind the curtain line with the entrance doors being moved behind the proscenium.

Until the forestage was shortened, it was the focal point. Here most of the great speeches were made and, if possible, the great deeds were done in full view of the audience. It is estimated that even in the large Lincoln's Inn Fields Theatre the playgoer sitting on the bench in the pit farthest from the stage had only about 45 feet between him and an actor close to the footlights.

In 1696, Christopher Rich, who was managing Drury Lane, made alterations designed to increase the size of the audience by reducing the forestage and enlarging the pit to accommodate more benches. Colley Cibber remarked on the destructive result of this modernization, the loss of intimacy:

> The Area, or Platform of the old Stage, projected about four Foot forwarder, in a Semi-oval Figure, parallel to the Benches of the Pit. . . . By this original Form, the usual Station of the Actors, in almost every Scene, was advanc'd at least ten Foot nearer to the Audience, than they now can be. . . . When the Actors were in Possession of that forwarder Space, to advance upon, the Voice was then more in the Centre of the House, so that the most distant Ear had scarce the least Doubt, or Difficulty in hearing what fell from the weakest Utterance: All Objects were thus drawn nearer to the Sense; every painted Scene was stronger, every Grand Scene and Dance more extended; every rich, or fine-coloured Habit had a more lively Lustre: Nor was the minutest Motion of a Feature (properly changing with the Passion, or Humour it suited) ever lost, as they frequently must be in the Obscurity of too great a Distance.[5]

The closer the audience the better the illumination which originated from a variety of sources. Retractable footlights provided the best source of lighting for the actors' faces and could be lowered in a trough to darken the scene even more. The natural lighting from the windows was increased by judiciously placed candles. Some theatres admitted light from a cupola, but this architectural delight also admitted bad weather with the illumination. Originally, the scenes and the forestage were lighted by chandeliers or hoops of candles (12 to a hoop) which were let down "from the cloud scenes, to a sufficient height, so as not to touch the heads of the actors."[6] Though the hoops had some mobility and did help with illumination, they could obscure the view from the gallery. Sidelighting was provided by candles attached to the backs of the wings. These could be shielded and directed to or away from the stage. Darkness was suggested by having the actors appear with candles and torches and grope their way about.

Although the initial outlay for scenery was considerable (the scenery for one opera cost eight hundred pounds), playwrights did not require a change for every scene. In very short scenes, the actors' lines indicated the location, and no scenery was changed. Additionally, much of the action was set in locations which could draw from the available stock. For example, no theatre could be without a wood, a bare heath, an island, a flat rock or a desert, which could, with some mechanical magic, bloom. Other conventional scenes would have been representations of London spots familiar to the audience: the Mall, the pleasure gardens or a chocolate house.

Things and people came from above and below. The stage was well supplied with trap doors through which people could appear--and disappear. The trapdoor could serve as a woodhole, a cellar, a vault, a well, a grave and, best of all, for an apparition.

There were also many machines. The "Vast Engines" which moved scenery and machinery were probably first introduced at Dorset Garden, and machinery became more elaborate as inventiveness increased. They made ascent and descent popular and enabled the production of water effects, with or without ships.

The sounds of the Restoration and eighteenth-century stage were the traditional ones heard by earlier audiences. Most popular were birdsong, for the gentler moments; thunder and wind, for the more dramatic passages; and, for the military minded, cannons and muskets.

The more dulcet sounds of instrumental music and song, coupled with dance, which Davenant had provided even before the Restoration, became more and more part of the dramatic scene. Since singers and dancers, often foreign artists, did not always trouble to harmonize their performances with the dramatic content of the play, the dramatists could be forgiven for being concerned that all this crowd pleasing was draining the life's blood from their works.

Davenant had left the orchestra in its original location--either above or at the side of the forestage. Then Killigrew moved it to the position that it occupies today--either in front of or under the stage. Pepys visiting the first Theatre Royal on May 8, 1663, was concerned about this new location of the orchestra:

> The house is made with extraordinary good contrivance, and yet has some faults . . . the music being below, and most of it sounding under the very stage, there is no hearing of the basses at all, nor very well of the trebles, which sure must be mended.

Along with the development of the orchestra, there was the development of large choruses. This emphasis on music helped prepare the way for the craze for Italian opera in the early part of the eighteenth century.

In addition to hearing the actors, the sound effects, the music and each other, the audience was treated to a variety of bells and whistles which signaled scene changes and other effects. The diversity of bells was considerable: Border Bells, Cloud Bells, Wing Bells, Drop Cloth Bells, Curtain Bells, Trap Bells and Thunder Bells.[7]

With all this activity, little attention was paid to the curtain. There was one, green by tradition and located within the proscenium, which was raised after the prologue and remained aloft, not even being lowered at the end of the play. Only in the latter half of the

eighteenth century did the curtain become more active.
And now we shall draw it.

Costume

Restoration stage dress was a variable. In comedy, the fashion for the upper classes would follow the French style which, with variations, had returned with Charles II and had been adopted by the court. Most actors were supplied with basic suits of clothing, but only a few were saved the expense of supplying their own accessories.

The fashionable male wore a short-waisted doublet and petticoat breeches. The lining fell lower than the breeches and tied above the knee. Ribbons fell half the length of the breeches and decorated the waistband. The shirt hung out strategically. This style dated from a little before the Restoration, and, after 1660, the breeches became the uniform for the fashionable.

The women's clothes were loose and showed a studied carelessness that has been captured in portraits by Peter Lely. Female dress remained much the same during Charles II's reign though the long pointed waists gradually tightened; the tucked-up skirts grew more formal and the general appearance of the figure became stiffer and narrower while the large lace collars disappeared from the fashion scene.

In 1666 Charles seems to have undergone a sort of sartorial epiphany, closely followed, as usual, by the court. On 8 October 1666 Pepys noted that the king had "declared his resolution of setting a fashion of clothes which he will never alter." On the 15th, Pepys went, as it were, to view the body:

> This day the King begins to put on his vest, and I did see several persons of the House of Lords and Commons too, great courtiers, who are in it; being a long cassocke close to the body, of black cloth, and pinked with white silke under it, and a coat over it, and the legs ruffled with

black riband like a pigeon's leg; and, upon the whole, I wish the King may keep it, for it is a very fine and handsome garment.

Charles did, with modifications, maintain this "Eastern" fashion of dress. The wide, falling collar eventually disappeared and the earliest cravat, without bow or knot, came in. The most elaborate neckwear was made of lace.

The periwig came in a little earlier, and Pepys on 15 February 1664 was there for the unveiling of the Duke of York: "To White Hall, to the Duke; where he first put on a periwig today: but methought his hair cut short in order thereto did look very pretty of itself, before he put on his periwig." In April he saw the King in the fashion and, of course, could not resist one for himself. The full-bottomed wig worn by men of leisure and fashion was impossible for active people, and campaign wigs for the military man and travelling wigs for the peripatetic became available.

The ladies wore their own hair simply dressed, but the head supported a frame of wire covered by silk or lace and aptly called the "tower." A major piece of female equipment was the fan.

Gentlemen wore the hat indoors and even at table. With Charles had come the wide brim and shallow crown. Eventually, the brim was cocked, and in the reign of William and Mary the brim was cocked in three places forming the three-cornered hat. The wearing of this style distinguished the gentleman and the professional man from the lower mortals who wore the hat uncocked.

In the early eighteenth century the female silhouette aimed for width and the skirt extended sideways. The sleeve ended just at the elbow with a ruffle of lace falling onto the forearm. The male dress consisted of a coat, a waistcoat and breeches. The coat

28

fitted close to the waist and then flared out, the skirts of the coat varying in length. The size of the cuffs, which at first were very large and buttoned just above or below the elbow, gradually diminished. The ruffle of the shirt was plainly visible. Beneath the coat was the waistcoat, sometimes very heavily embroidered. Breeches were worn throughout the century. Both male and female servants would wear simplified versions of upper class clothes in much less elaborate material.

In tragedy there was exotic garb for extraordinary characters like the "naked Indians" in The Indian Queen or the Moors in The Empress of Morocco, but there was no great attempt at historical accuracy in general; there being no reason in the mind of the playgoers why a character of any period could not justly sport the latest from Paris or a cast gown from the court. The males wore the periwig and the tragic hero sported a hat adorned with lofty feathers known as a shuttlecock. Downes catalogues the costly donations which adorned the actors in Davenant's Love and Honor:

> This Play was Richly Cloath'd; The King giving Mr. Betterton his Coronation Suit, in which, he Acted the Part of Prince Alvaro; The Duke of York giving Mr. Harris his, who did Prince Prospero; And my Lord of Oxford, gave Mr. Joseph Price his, who did Lionel the Duke of Parma's Son. . . . The Play having a great run, Produc'd to the Company great Gain and Estimation from the Town.[1]

In the same vein, Queen Mary of Modena presented her coronation robes to Mrs. Barry for her role of Queen Elizabeth in The Unhappy Favourite.

But all this splendor did not necessarily help the play. In 1711 Addison complained in The Spectator about the distractions of the shuttlecock:

The ordinary method of making a hero is to clap a huge plume of feathers on his head which rises so very high that there is often a greater length from his chin to the top of his head than to the sole of his foot. . . . Not withstanding any anxieties which he pretends . . . one may see by his action that his greatest care and concern is to keep the plume of feathers from falling off his head.[2]

If the perilously balanced shuttlecock was not enough, there was ample distraction from the heroine:

As these superfluous ornaments upon the head make a great man, a princess generally receives her grandeur from those additional encumbrances that fall into her tail: I mean the broad sweeping train that follows her in all her motions and finds constant employment for a boy who stands behind her to open and spread it to advantage.[3]

Until the middle of the eighteenth century, costume had an uneven look. Besides the plumes and trains of tragedy and the traditional look of a ghost or a villain, the audience could hope at best to see an actor sporting elegant cast-offs of the rich and titled or the best that stock had to offer. The idea of historical research for a period piece was suggested by Aaron Hill who designed, but never executed, a set of "old Saxon habits" to be worn for his tragedy Athelwold (1731) and Charles Macklin paid careful attention to his costume for Shylock when the enlarged Drury Lane reopened on 15 September 1747 with The Merchant of Venice. But they were ahead of their time, for the ideal of historical accuracy in costume as a necessary part of a production was yet to come.

The Actors Are Come

When Killigrew and Davenant formed their companies in 1660, Killigrew chose predominantly older men, those in their thirties and forties with pre-Commonwealth experience, for the King's Company. Those in his company included Mohun, Hart, Burt, Lacy, Edward and Robert Shatterell, Wintershal, Cartwright, Clun, Baxter and Loveday. Kynaston, who had been one of Rhodes's actors at the Cockpit, also went over to Killigrew. Davenant chose the younger men: Betterton, Sheppey, Robert and James Nokes, Lovell, Moseley, Underhill, Turner and Lilleston. The already proven actors would have known the traditions of the Elizabethan stage, traditions which were to be continued on the Restoration stage either in revivals or incorporated into the new drama. So, in the very beginning, the older players could mount productions, particularly of revivals, with more facility, while the younger men had to be trained. And then there were the women.

The arrival of women on the English stage had been anticipated publicly by the visit of a French company in 1629 and privately by the aristocratic women who acted in court masques in the early part of the century. In 1656, one Mrs. Coleman played Ianthe in Davenant's semi-public production of The Siege of Rhodes; so the way was paved for the 1660 prologue which introduced the "first Woman who came to Act on the Stage in the Tragedy, call'd The Moor of Venice."

The idea of the woman player appealed greatly to a society which had known the severe discomfort of sexual repression during the Commonwealth, and the actresses were anything but repressed. This new breed of player sought fame on the stage and fortune in a husband or a keeper. In the search, which was anything but subtle, they made their private lives as much public property as the characters they essayed. However, their offstage activities were more than mere grist for the gossip mill; they were, in fact, very important when one comes to see that such goings-on influenced playwrights in the creation of characters and situations.

If the playwrights and the audience were entertained--in many senses--by the actresses, the ladies too were satisfied; for they gained protectors as highly placed as the king himself, a theatrelover susceptible to the charms of both Moll Davis and Nell Gwyn. The amorous arrangements which could be made backstage in the tiring rooms were reflected in most of the comic plots. Another delight was the increased visibility of the shape of the female, now revealed in the breeches parts. The display of calf and ankle, meaningless to the twentieth century, had particular erotic value for the Restoration viewer. This partially explains why the role of Sir Harry Wildair had so many takers among the actresses and why whole plays (Love for Love among them) could boast productions with all female casts.

The players were trained in the nursery, or acting school, which was maintained by George Jolly and accomplices, under the tuition of the established actors or, as in the case of Mrs. Barry, under the very private tuition of John Wilmot, Earl of Rochester. The training included lessons in manners--phrasing, timing and diction--in deportment and in elocution. Additionally, the players learned singing, stance, gesture and walking. From head to toe the player was supposed to be able to comport himself properly. However, the multiplicity of roles and the brevity of time allowed for rehearsal make it not unlikely that looks and an appealing manner coupled with bravado might be able to carry an enterprising player through a difficult moment. Mimicry was also much in demand. A good, nasty imitation on stage could rival a lampoon any day.

Essentially, there were two acting styles, one for the tragic and one for the comic tradition. In the grand tradition, the heroic lover "canted" and "whined" his passion. He also had to master the "rant"--a long monologue during which the actor built slowly and climaxed at the top of his voice. In his final moments he had to bring the gentlest notes into his dying voice and expire in a melodic vein. If he was the hero of the drama, he did all this while wearing the shuttlecock, the traditional hat topped by a substantial arrangement of feathers, balanced upon his head.

The body itself was subject to considerable discipline. The actor was instructed to attend to

> the government, order and balance of the whole body; and thence proceed to the regiment and proper motions of the head, the eye, the eyebrows, and indeed the whole face; then conclude with the actions of the hands, more copious and various than all the other parts of the body.[1]

The head was expected to be upright--not too high nor too low nor hanging down. The right hand bore the burden of the gesture if one hand only was doing the work. When both were in operation, as when the actor was expressing aversion, a little coordination was necessary, "for these things we reject with the right hand, at the same time turning away to the left."[2] The eyebrows required sufficient motion to be of interest. The mouth behaved stylishly (no licking the lips). The hand was lifted in synchronization with the rest of the body and, to preserve symmetry, the actor must not "raise them [the hands] above the eyes; to stretch them farther might disorder and distort the body; nor must they be very little lower, because that position gives a beauty to the figure."[3] Not a little important-- after the body and voice were in control--was the mastery of the smoldering look:

> And this fire of their eyes will easily strike those of their audience which are contin-

ually fixed on yours; and by a strange sympathetic infection, it will set them on fire too with the very same passion.[4]

Obviously Mrs. Barry had learned something about acting (among many other things) from Rochester as she is praised for her mastery of technique, for "Mien and Motion superb" and a well trained voice which was both "clear and strong." She was able to contend with passion and move the audience with her distress by subsiding in the most affecting "Melody and Softness." In her anger, she poured out her sentiments with an "enchanting Harmony."[5]

In the Restoration theatre, various actors were swiftly singled out for a variety of abilities. Betterton, who was the master, could successfully interpret everyone and anything, from the sublime passages of Shakespeare to the comedies of the new writers. Sandford, however, was thoroughly typed as the master of "disagreeable Characters." Henry Harris leaned toward pathos and the angst of the amorous lover. Edward Kynaston, a figure straight out of Elizabeth's reign, graduated from playing the "loveliest lady" Pepys ever saw in his life (which says no little for the young Kynaston's appeal) to male roles which demanded consummate majesty. James Nokes was the grave English fool, while his alter ego, Cave Underhill, gloried in the booby. Among the actresses, Nell Gwyn excelled in the lighter roles while the sedate Anne Bracegirdle let Congreve and Rowe plead their love to her, comically and tragically, through characters they created. Mrs. Leigh was adept at the antiquated lady, while Mrs. Verbruggen cloped about as the hoyden.

The most valuable actors excelled in some particular aspect of characterization. The playwright knew it and wrote to show off the actor's talent. When the audience enjoyed the show and wanted more, the playwright then supplied the actor with more fuel for his comic, tragic, stupid, witty or seductive fire; and the actor fanned it into flame. Since there was a variety of appeal, there must have been lots of little fires blazing away on the stage on a good afternoon.

Although Restoration comedy has been called "artificial" by later critics and by audiences of succeeding centuries, it was not artificial to the original audiences. The actor actually performed both as himself and as actor. The performer was expected to encourage the audience in this double view while clearly enjoying his task; otherwise, his performance was suspect:

> When a man gives us all the wit and drollery of a comic character, without himself sharing in the diversion he affords us, the insipid coldness is easily perceiv'd . . . when the actor can bring himself to share the pleasure with his audience, he is always sure to please.[6]

The actor was expected to be at once both in and out of the role. The very fact that he played predominantly on the forestage put him near the audience, who wished to be as close to him as possible. For the audience could, especially in comedy, associate with him on a double level. He was seen both as the individual behind the character and as the character, and this second persona, the character, could be a comment on the first, the individual. The audience of the Restoration was possibly the most narcissistic in English theatrical history, for, unlike its twentieth-century counterpart, it was not in ceaseless identity crisis. It knew itself--sometimes all too well--and delighted in the pleasure of recognition raised to the nth power. For the upper class audience in particular, role playing was part of the social life; so that when they came to assess the new comedy they were seeing both themselves playing roles (which they were doing even as they sat in the theatre) and the actor playing a role with which he was as comfortable by virtue of natural affinity plus diligent practice as they were comfortable in their daily roles.

This comfort was important both to the actor and to the audience. Each owned his role. An actor's parts were his possessions, literally. Each part was written on a roll of paper--the part only with minimum cues. Continuity was established by having an actor continue in the part he had created or inherited until he was willing to relinquish it. Even if the actor was years too old for the role, his presence was, up to a point, preferable. Dennis vowed that an aging original in a tailor-made role was better than a youthful substitute:

> Most of our Poets having had either the Address or the Weakness . . . to write to the Manners and the Talents of some particular Actors, it seems to me to be absolutely impossible, . . . that any Actor can become an admirable Original, by Playing a Part which was writ and design'd for another Man's particular Talent.[7]

Continuity was also reinforced by having the actors repeat their roles in sequels. For example, in Cibber's Love's Last Shift (1696) and Vanbrugh's The Relapse (1697) Cibber appeared as Sir Novelty Fashion, later Lord Foppington; Verbruggen was Loveless and Mrs. Rogers was his faithful wife, Amanda. In The Relapse, Mrs. Verbruggen was cast as Berinthia, Loveless's inamorata. The audience was conscious that Loveless (Verbruggen)

> in his flight from the restrictions of monogamy, a state he considers contrary to the nature of man, finds himself trying to commit adultery with Berinthia (Mrs. Verbruggen). The nature of the pursuit of sin is exposed . . . as a search after an image of the female which is . . .identical.[8]

36

Thus Verbruggen was placed in the ironic position of leaving a stage wife to pursue a stage mistress who was his real wife. The variations on this theme are obviously infinite.

Most firmly earthed in terms of audience recognition would be a character actor like the professional villain, Samuel Sandford (even the name sounded like a hiss). Everyone loved hating Sandford so much that he was denied the luxury of playing a decent man:

> A new play [probably Crowne's <u>Regulus</u> (1692) in which Sandford played "a noble Carthaginian"] . . . was brought upon the Stage, wherein Sandford happen'd to perform the Part of an honest Statesman: The Pit, after they had sate three or four Acts, in a quiet Expectation, that the well-dissembled Honesty of Sandford (for such of course they concluded it) would soon be discover'd, or at least, from its Security, involve the Actors in the Play, in some surprizing Distress or Confusion . . . at last, finding no such matter, but that the Catastrophe had taken quite another Turn, and that Sandford was really an honest Man to the end of the Play, they fairly damn'd it, as if the Author had impos'd upon them the most frontless or incredible Absurdity.[9]

The range of the Restoration actor may have been more limited than that of the player today, but within the scope of his accomplishments (and who is to say whether or not narrowness of focus did not produce more excellence) he could achieve the most significant results by means which, in the final analysis, always elude definition:

> What talent shall we say will infallibly form an Actor? This, I confess, is one of Nature's Secrets . . . let us content our selves there-

fore with affirming. That _Genius_, which Nature
only gives, only can complete him.[10]

The Restoration Stance Today

In mounting a Restoration tragedy today, the difficulties in terms of presenting a performance which would exactly recreate the original style are enormous. A complaint about Peter Brook's revival of <u>Venice Preserved</u> (1953) that the production "made little attempt to recapture the style of Restoration acting," and instead evoked the "Elizabethan or Jacobean theatre rather than . . . the age of Dryden or Congreve," may only be saying that the production had recaptured the only tragic style acceptable to the contemporary audience.[1] It would take considerable education to prepare audiences to accept the old style and intensive training to ready actors to perform it seriously. But such preparations would hardly be worth the effort, since naturalistic acting has become such a staple of the theatre that only opera or ballet can bear the burden of traditional symbolism.

Tragedy aside, is it possible to play Restoration comedy and make the audience feel that what is seen and heard is a "true reflection of life as it was lived and as it was understood"?[2] Yes and No. The difficulty in reproducing the Restoration situation is grounded in the fact that the present-day actor playing a character created in and by the past is reduced to giving an imitation of a quality of life.

The private life and the public image of the actor as commented on in the character he plays have not the same deliberate ironic connotation today as they had for the less inhibited Restoration audience. Though information about the private life of a twentieth-century player is available today, that knowledge is frequently the cumulative perception of a persona created and cultivated by publicity and is not carried into the theatre by an audience which feels comfortable enough to apply it to a dramatic situation and react to it overtly in the theatre. Nor are there many actors who can capitalize on typecasting with the success of their predecessors; for the playwright writing for the seventeenth-century actor could evoke the memory of an earlier characterization or popular gossip knowing that both actor and audience would relish the evocation.

A case in point is the Mrs. Loveit of Etherege's The Man of Mode (1676). Loveit was created for Mrs. Barry, a lady notoriously crass in the treatment of her lovers and an accomplished tragedy queen. The audience could enjoy the first allusion, the jibe at Barry's activities, simply by virtue of the casting. Furthermore, the top contender for the character of Dorimant in the spot-the-original game so popular with the audience was none other than Mrs. Barry's erstwhile drama coach, John Wilmot, Earl of Rochester. So the spectators were treated to a view of Mrs. Barry, herself an accomplished mistress, playing a stale paramour railing against a champion seducer closely modeled on her own protector, a champion rake. This outstanding libertine was played by Betterton, the preeminent actor, in his most devil-may-care vein. The intensity of the pleasure of recognition must have made everyone delirious.

More important to the dramatic balance, the ravings of Loveit against the unfaithful Dorimant, which create a serious problem for the contemporary actress, would not seem strained in Mrs. Barry's practiced grasp, and the audience, which knew her aptitude at both kinds of playing, would not be distracted by the inclusion of tragic elements in the comedy.

Like Mrs. Loveit, Congreve's Lady Touchwood has been imbalancing The Double Dealer (1693) for the better part of this century. She is confusing on the post-Restoration stage because she too was written for Barry to continue her grand ravings in a comedy ingeniously balanced in casting by the Lord Touchwood of the majestic Kynaston and the Maskwell of Betterton, who could add the dimension of a conniver to this rake-seducer role.

Now, the twentieth century can boast a respectable number of very good tragic actresses, but reigning tragedy queens who can incorporate the more exalted style of playing into the comic context, integrating the artificiality of the tragic interpretation into the more relaxed style of comedy are not to be found easily, even in the most distinguished present-day company.

Furthermore, the early actor played deliberately to the audience, hoping for a double-levelled response, to himself and to his character. The contemporary actor is much more cautious. Rehearsals for The Recruiting Officer (1963) offer a good instance of reluctance to nudge the audience. During the first run-through of the play on the Old Vic stage, it was decided to omit the exchange between Plume (Robert Stephens) and Brazen (Laurence Olivier). In the scene, Brazen asks Plume whether to invest in a privateer or a playhouse. Olivier felt that, as he was investing his career in the embryonic National Theatre, the lines would take on the character of a private joke, and they were deleted. The Restoration actor would rarely have exhibited such deference to the audience and such modesty about his accomplishments.

Also, training for the Restoration actor was the same for all, pre-Commonwealth expertise insuring the continuation of the tradition. The nursery formed a player geared to either revivals of old plays, the current forms of tragedy or the comedies. The techniques used in Theatre of the Absurd, Brecht-inspired productions, Theatre of Cruelty, no matter how far back they trace their lineage, were not even gleams in the actor's eye. His position was, in fact, relatively simple: he was expected to produce a clearly predetermined effect performance after performance. He knew it and so did the audience.

The theatre community had not produced the hydra-headed beast of the multiple theatres of today. There were only two companies performing regularly, and after the Union in 1682, only one for over a decade. So the competition, when it was strong, was nowhere as diffuse or as varied as it is currently. Though there was much outside the theatres that might pass for entertainment and the occasional foreign troupe to give competition, of regular dramatic rivalry beyond the companies there was none at all. The man of leisure cultivated himself, if we are to believe John Dennis, to be fit for conversation, and the conversation for which he was prepared was derived from the aristocratic style of address imported from France along with the fashions. He spoke well, balancing elegance of style with repartee, and demanded that his stage counterparts do the same. The current audience may be more widely read and more instantaneously informed, rarely is it as well spoken and never as completely outspoken.

The contemporary result is that the Restoration style of the twentieth century often reduces itself to the mastery of not completely unimportant but certainly fairly basic accomplishments. There is the wearing of the costume, no mean accomplishment for either man or woman. And this easy wearing must be accompanied by proper gait and a comfortable carriage of the arms. If the costume is mastered, then there is the handling of the obligatory props, particularly the snuff box and the fan. The latter accomplishments become an annoyance only when the more difficult aspects of character-ization are ignored and manual dexterity is all an actor has to offer.

There must be proper use of the voice if not in a consciously musical sense then in attention to the words of the text, which require an interpretation unlike the words of any other period.

The totally successful playing of Restoration comedy is limited to a relatively small number of actors and actresses. It is not possible to excel simply by talent and industry. Interpretation requires that the performer be willing to use his talent to achieve a stylistically acceptable period tone and manner while making the character look as though he has found his feet in the new century. Strained artificiality, except when it is presented as ironic, must be abandoned; but unfamiliar social practices must be made acceptable while, at the same time, the relevance of the dramatic situations is projected to the audience.

Additionally the theatre of the twentieth century is, increasingly, a platform for the director's thesis. The result is diversity of approach to the classics. But the thesis or the variations on a theme do not necessarily integrate smoothly into the narrow confines of Restoration comedy, and it is less easy for the imaginative director to dress up Congreve in modern silhouette than to meddle successfully with, for example, A Midsummer Night's Dream. For the plays of the Restoration are, finally, actors' pieces. The bulk of revivals are mounted by repertory companies, which, as nearly as anything, approximate the set-up of the Restoration companies; for only in such groups do certain actors have comparable niches in terms of characterization. But no twentieth-century cast has, or can hope to have from top to bottom, the unity and strength of their counterparts at Drury Lane or Lincoln's Inn Fields; consequently, even skilled repertory companies are frequently aided by the appearance in the Restoration productions of a guest actor of proven excellence in Restoration interpretation.

Of the many skilled actors Britain has produced, only a fraction have achieved long-lived success in Restoration roles, and that small number has done so by a combination of period stance and currently acceptable stage methods. For example, Miles Malleson was wonderfully adept in realizing doddering dodos, while Richard Wordsworth made a little career of the Restoration dirty old man. John Gielgud and Laurence Olivier have both left their mark, Gielgud more broadly than Olivier. Gielgud can both direct and act in Restoration because he brings to the play a close attention to speeches and to the physical requirements of the role. Olivier uses the approach of the character actor: manipulation of voice, peculiarities of diction, movement and considerable make-up, place a definite stamp on his performance.

Among the women Edith Evans led the way with a combination of voice, movement and that essential quality, manner. And Maggie Smith brought to her Restoration performances a varied background which included revue comedy, a form which has, for some contemporary directors, a peculiar affinity with Restoration comedy.

Others have made good work of a single performance, but these will be found to be more in the line of types which they play with expertise and which pop up in the whole range of drama. Among these, Margaret Rutherford excelled as Lady Wishfort, despite, not because of, her major comic assets which usually stressed the gentle over the grotesque. She proved that to ask any actor to play now as they played then is to ask for a metamorphosis in the theatre structure, the audience and the player's training. The big roles were written to glorify one person; the smaller ones as cameos for particular talents. Generations can play variations on the theme but they cannot play the original tune--perhaps a better one but not the same one.

The contemporary actor has been trained to a more varied stage--physically, intellectually, vocally--than his predecessor. The theatrical climate of the Restoration with the limited number of companies, the playwrights focusing on particular actors, the audience knowing the actors (both in the Biblical and in the social sense) and persistent, particularly in comedy, in their search for the mirror image, is not available today. If Restoration comedy is truly comic, if an actor is truly comic in it, it is because the play transcends the tradition (which is what it was supposed to do all along) and the actor must unearth that transcendent quality or fail.

The Revivals: A Brief Survey

For those involved in reviving period drama, there was an increasing awareness of the relevance of Restoration themes for the twentieth century, and substantial attempts were made to point out connections to the audience. This consciousness of connections, which was not well defined immediately after the war, gained clearer definition in the 1950s and became more explicit in the next two decades.

In the late 1940s and early 1950s the productions were staged in a manner which emphasized their artificiality, although without dehumanization of the characters, and considerable attention was paid to an evocation of the period in which they were written. The 1960s leaned toward the thesis production: a production in which a major idea, like a leitmotif, ran through the play unifying the entire structure.

The productions of the late 1960s and 1970s showed an increasing desire to approach the text from the explicitly modern point of view. Definite parallels were drawn between the stage figures and their modern counterparts so that, in effect, the characters became not only creations of the past but also speakers for the present. The virtue of this trend was that the audience no longer saw the Restoration figures as long-dead types nor the plays as museum pieces voicing the cleverness of an extinct world. The danger was that this modern emphasis could achieve a spurious contemporary relevance at the expense of the text.

The first play considered is by George Villiers, Duke of Buckingham, whose adaptation of Fletcher's The Chances was chosen by Laurence Olivier as one of the three opening plays for the Chichester Festival Theatre when it came into being in 1962. Buckingham is represented in the second part of this obscure play, which Olivier had chanced upon while studying manuscripts in the British Museum. The production emphasized the visual rather than the verbal; yet of the two period pieces given at Chichester in that opening season, this second piece, played as a romp, was better received by the audience than the other, Ford's <u>The Broken Heart</u>, which achieved the lesser status of lurid melodrama.

John Dryden, the butt of Buckingham's parody in <u>The Rehearsal</u>, fared better in this century. In the post-war society, that grand theme of love versus honor, which was prominent in the tragedies of Dryden, was no longer of particular sociological consequence. The stylized idealization of the heroes--often military giants--was not congenial to an audience suffering from the disillusionment of a second World War. In comedy, the partially successful <u>Marriage à la Mode</u> had, at best, an escapist value for 1946. By 1977 Prospect Productions had gained sufficient experience in mounting neglected drama to attempt the blank verse of Dryden on the grand theme. The production of <u>All for Love</u> painted a large canvas with beauty and precision in a production mounted and spoken with a splendor that made the revival more than an historical curiosity.

George Etherege received two productions of <u>The Man of Mode</u>. In 1965 Prospect Productions chose a seemingly ideal location in the recently restored Georgian Theatre in Richmond, Yorkshire. However, the players overacted in the intimate house, originally designed to facilitate direct address. In 1971 the Royal Shakespeare Company presented the play at the Aldwych and attempted to emphasize the sexual in contemporary visual and musical terms, producing a glamorization of almost Hollywood-like glitter. In the two great artificial characters, Fopling and Mrs. Loveit, there were considerable differences of approach which were barely reconcilable. Yet the production succeeded in exploring artificiality if not by Restoration standards then by the standards of the present day.

William Wycherley is represented by five different productions of a single play, The Country Wife. There is a record of a heavily cut production of The Plain Dealer presented as part of a mixed bill in 1948 by the students of the Old Vic Theatre School; but the piece was so beyond their acting capabilities that there was very little critical recognition accorded it, and, beyond the fact of the attempt, there is little other value for the literary or theatrical historian.

In 1936 there was a significant production of The Country Wife. This Old Vic revival broke through the conventions of that conservative theatre by admitting a play by the then disreputable Wycherley and making it a resounding success. Additionally, an American actress, Ruth Gordon, achieved international recognition in the title role, and the production transferred to New York. In 1956 the English Stage Company, an emerging ensemble devoted principally to the encouragement of modern playwrights, was aided, both financially and artistically, by a mounting of The Country Wife, which went from its home theatre, the Royal Court, to continue performances in the West End. By the 1950s the salaciousness of the Wycherley play, which had once shocked audiences, was no longer the principal focus, and the emphasis was on the admitted psychological lure of its dramatization of wish fulfillment for the audience.

The title character, Margery, demanded an actress of definite qualifications: a quaint accent, visual appeal and a comic zest for the forbidden pleasures which her husband would deny her. Such a Margery had become almost a convention accepted by actresses since Gordon in 1936. In 1966 the Nottingham Playhouse Company continued the tradition by offering the play as a vehicle for a young actress, Judi Dench, who successfully mastered the letter-writing scene and projected a suitably humorous view of Margery.

But it was only in the performance of Maggie Smith at the Chichester Festival Theatre in 1969 that the conventions were surpassed and an individual, three-dimensional Margery arose, relevant both to period and to contemporary attitudes. The Country Wife was given a solid production in 1977 by the National Theatre Company. The character of Margery remained centrally focused, this time joined by a stylistically effective Pinchwife and a disappointingly aloof Horner.

Wycherley's single play remains a staple in Restoration revivals, for it may be approached for character motivation, as a study in misanthropy or sheerly for the fun of siding vicariously with the immoralities of the piece.

The second figure represented by a single play is Thomas Shadwell, whose Epsom Wells failed because there was ample critical opportunity to compare the wit of stronger authors with the attempt of Shadwell. In the hands of Shadwell, wit was reduced to verbiage. Also, there was a want of substance in this 1969 production by the Thorndike Theatre: a lack of a central, informing idea upon which the audience could fix, a dearth of something with which they could either identify or argue. The result was manipulation of characters for the very sake of pulling the comic strings.

Along with Shadwell, Buckingham and Wycherley, Edward Ravenscroft makes a fourth with a single production. The emphasis on burlesque rather than interpretation was acceptable in The London Cuckolds, revived in 1979 and sufficiently engaging to justify the revival on more than simply historical grounds.

Thomas Otway is unique in that he is represented twice by a tragedy, both times successfully, and twice by a comedy, which, despite critically debatable merit, had sufficient audience appeal to reappear after only a three-year interval between productions.

In 1964 Otway was unevenly represented by his single comedy revived in these decades. The Soldier's Fortune was mounted by Prospect Productions, and the pander, Sir Jolly Jumble, and the deceived husband, Sir Davy Dunce, dominated in an imbalanced production in which the approach to the comedy seemed strained and excessive. In 1967 The Soldier's Fortune reappeared in its first West End production in thirty-five years. It was mounted by the English Stage Company. Again, it was not a complete success, and some of its failure was attributed to a misanthropy traceable to the disillusioned author, whose heavy scorn could not be lightened by any valid method. Sir Jolly and Sir Davy again held sway, but this time it was because the approach to the roles emphasized the repulsive and the ludicrous.

In 1953 Venice Preserved was presented by John Gielgud. This production was approached with a balanced but grandly dramatic view of a tragedy not acted within living memory. The danger of the adverse effect of the bathetic on the audience was overcome by a judicious handling of the text by a cast which made the neglected drama part of a living tradition. In this attempt, which recognized and proved the playability of Otway, Gielgud had one of his major successes. In 1969 Venice Preserved was presented by the Bristol Old Vic Company with a new emphasis. The shoddiness rather than the grandeur of the conspirators was underlined. Much of the epic greatness was lost, but the play gained a new—if dubious—vitality for audiences now concerned with the realistic, less willing to be caught up in the glory of a production and more taken with analysis of identifiable characters and situations.

Sir John Vanbrugh is represented by three plays in ten productions of varying importance. The most frequently produced of his plays was <u>The Relapse</u>, which had a series of successes. In 1948 Anthony Quayle produced it and offered the post-war audience the performance of Cyril Ritchard as Lord Foppington. The production was reminiscent of the 1940s--stylish and "fantasticated"--leaving Ritchard free to create a character totally out of the modern context. In 1950 Ritchard brought his Foppington to New York. This time his success was limited because he was supported by a principally American cast which could not back him with the effectiveness of the English company; nevertheless, he triumphed in the presentation of a tremendous Restoration characterization.

In 1963 there was an attempt at a musical version using the play's subtitle, <u>Virtue in Danger</u>, which failed despite a significant cast many of whose members were more than conversant with Restoration comedy. Nevertheless, this production served as a bridge between the conventional but successful approach of Ritchard and the later more experimental Foppingtons.

By 1967 the Royal Shakespeare Company presented its first Restoration play, with Donald Sinden as a psychologically complex Foppington. Sinden emphasized the duality of the character, showing him as a petulant child-man crouching pathetically beneath the immense camouflage of his wardrobe. This successful production was recast and remounted in 1968 with Barrie Ingham replacing Sinden and managing to strike a balance between the cheerfully inventive performance of Ritchard and the psychological subtlety of Sinden.

The realistic view of humanity in <u>The Provok'd Wife</u> made it solid material for the modern audience. When it was presented in 1963 by Prospect Productions and brought to the West End, it was judged the most sociologically relevant of the Vanbrugh offerings in its ironic approach to an unhappy marriage, with the added realism that, despite the mismatch, Lady Brute remains chained to her husband. The play showed an impressive relevance to contemporary domestic difficulties, but the stylistic success was debatable. A difficulty had arisen in the reconciliation of movement and speech--the kind of fusion that Gielgud's colleagues had mastered in the 1940s and 1950s--with the desire for immediacy of social comment. Style had become self-conscious artificiality and a distraction from the evocation of any period.

In 1967 the experimental director, Joan Littlewood, presented an adapted version of the play. This adaptation, entitled Intrigues and Amours, was presented partly to spite the then powerful office of the Lord Chamberlain, which had no control over the classics. But Littlewood, whose production of Oh What a Lovely War! had been a stinging social commentary, was completely unsuccessful with the Vanbrugh material. In 1973 the play was produced by Robin Phillips, whose company had gathered around him as an emerging directorial talent. In his production, as in that of Littlewood, the pivotal character, Sir John Brute, received a disappointing interpretation, an error which faulted both the director and the interpreter of the role. Although the Phillips production had intelligent moments, it was, by and large, not a success.

The Confederacy was presented three times, but never in London. In 1951 the Birmingham Repertory Theatre offered a misguided production that emphasized the burlesque. The play was so ill-timed and ill-played that it left at least one critic considering the desirability of remounting Restoration drama at all. By 1964 Prospect Productions achieved a valid success. Although the performance was imbalanced by the excellence of the female over the less decisive male roles, the final product was still closer to the idea of Vanbrugh's comedy than was the Birmingham production. A production in 1974 at the Chichester Festival Theatre was the closest the play got to London. The fact that it did not transfer to the West

End, as others from Chichester had done before, was due to the lack of unification of the actors as an ensemble: the diversity of styles, without even the excuse of a naturalistic approach, resulted in something like histrionic chaos.

Despite the number of revivals, Vanbrugh emerges as a one-play author: his Relapse offered the most amusement for audiences from the late 1940s to the late 1960s. Although his social commentary seemed ideal for the later decades, it was not handled with sufficient restraint to create an effective production; therefore, there is not a completely successful production of either The Confederacy or The Provok'd Wife in the time span under consideration.

Widely represented in twelve productions is William Congreve, whose three major plays, The Way of the World, Love for Love and The Double Dealer were all performed with a degree of success.

There were three revivals of The Double Dealer. In 1959 the Old Vic Company produced the play with an unusually strong cast, which did not diminish the fact that the principal villains, Maskwell and Lady Touchwood, were virtually unplayable to critical satisfaction. However, that company was adept at communicating the importance of the speaking of the lines as opposed to a 1969 production by the English Stage Company, which attempted a verbally naturalistic approach which resulted in a combination of acting styles that were irreconcilable with a unified production. The presentation in 1978 of The Double Dealer at the National Theatre yielded particular dividends in the way of performance. Two conventions were recognized--the satiric and the melodramatic--and a real attempt was made to fuse them without imbalancing the production.

Although Love for Love was revived only twice, it saw more travel than any of the other Restoration plays. Gielgud played it in London, New York and Toronto, and in 1965 the National Theatre Company brought it to Moscow, Montreal and then to London.

In 1947 Gielgud, already a respected figure in the United States, went to New York to present his Love for Love, which had been a success in 1943/44 in London. Although Congreve's language was sufficiently well received by the American audience, the play took second place to Oscar Wilde's The Importance of Being Earnest, which was played in repertoire with the Congreve piece. Even in Britain Love for Love was dormant for more than twenty years, only to be revived under the influence of another major theatrical figure, Laurence Olivier. In 1965 the National Theatre Company, of which Oliver was the director, employed a naturalistic approach to Love for Love, and the production was successful in its attempt to find a special social relevance. There was an effort to humanize dramatic situations by frequent visual inclusion of the lower classes, so that there were always the figures of the poor haunting the periphery of the circle of the elite.

The Way of the World, noted for its failure when first produced in Congreve's time, continued a strange theatrical history in the twentieth century. Because of the exquisite games Congreve played in language of rich sheen, the terrific complications of the plot, though acknowledged by the critics as a performance liability, were cheerfully overlooked. In the early years the emphasis was on characterization and the delight it could evoke. The Way of the World at the Lyric Theatre, Hammersmith, in 1924 was a perfect example of success in this vein. Forming itself around the Edith Evans performance as Millamant, the play succeeded as no other production has done in this century. Character emphasis continued in the 1940s, and when in 1948 Dame Edith played Lady Wishfort against a lesser Millamant, Faith Brooke, the balance shifted, and the Evans character became the center of the play's focus.

In 1953 John Gielgud, now at home both in acting and directing Restoration drama, presented The Way of the World. Gielgud, who in several Restoration plays took roles that were very light for someone of his dramatic weight, followed the same pattern once more. By choosing to set his Mirabell against the Millamant of the expert but miscast Pamela Brown, he inadvertently turned attention again to Lady Wishfort, this time in the person of the arch-comedienne Margaret Rutherford. Her contribution was the individuality of her comic style, and she provided such splendid amusement that she was forgiven for not being in the traditional mode of the character.

It is to Gielgud who produced two Congreve plays and an Otway tragedy that much of the credit is due for establishing, in mid-century, a solid style of performance: a vivid complement of speech and movement that showed others how to attempt the Restoration play so that it would be acceptable both by contemporary aesthetic standards and by acknowledged tradition.

In 1956 another Restoration veteran, John Clements, attempted the play while, amazingly, ignoring the pacing. There was a thirteen-year interval before the play was presented again in London, this time by the National Theatre Company. There were two innovations in this 1969 production: the play became more sexually explicit by correlating stage business with textual implications, and the monetary theme dominated. The business transaction was something that could be relished by an audience, and the play was projected as a witty study in bartering.

In 1977 at Stratford, Ontario, Maggie Smith played Millamant and realized in the gallery of her Restoration interpretations that most difficult of roles which demanded the full stretch of her comic talent.

In 1978 the Royal Shakespeare Company presented The Way of the World with a well integrated cast. The exposition was slow and deliberate; the world was a place of solid objects and the characters and their intrigues plausible.

Of all the Restoration playwrights considered, George Farquhar most easily adapted to the shifting sociological schemes of the three decades under consideration. He could amuse the post-war society; he could influence the socialist in Brecht and he could act as inspiration for productions using both the new and the traditional approaches. He is represented by four different plays and one adaptation in seven productions.

In 1969 the Nottingham Playhouse Company attempted to create a modern-dress musical from Farquhar's earliest play, Love and a Bottle. The theme, though light, still did not tolerate the inept music and lyrics, which neither blended with the period nor appealed effectively to the modern taste.

In 1967 The Constant Couple was revived, and its major contribution, courtesy of Robert Hardy's performance, was the reinstating of Sir Harry Wildair as a significant Restoration comic portrait. In the spirit of Ritchard's Foppington, he remained firmly earthed in period, an early original rather than a figure of immediate identification for the contemporary man.

In 1956 the Berliner Ensemble presented an adaptation of The Recruiting Officer, retitled Trumpets and Drums, which showed Farquhar to be adaptable to modern techniques. This production was not a transient success; for, in 1963, a Brecht-inspired director, William Gaskill, fulfilled the newly formed National Theatre's duty of remounting old classics by approaching Farquhar's own play in rehearsals that were improvisational; attempting to create, through modern directorial techniques, a production which sought a response comparable to the one evoked by the Berliner Ensemble. In 1970 Prospect Productions, still a touring company, presented a generally less successful--because admittedly traditional--production of the play. The production's greatest merit was in the portrayal of Captain Plume by Ian McKellen, who offered an insight, limited but valid both textually and dramatically, into a psychologically complex character.

In 1949 John Clements produced a thoroughly pleasing version of <u>The Beaux' Stratagem</u>, which, at 532 performances, was one of the longest running ventures in Restoration comedy ever mounted. In 1970 the National Theatre Company, again under the direction of William Gaskill, appeared first in Los Angeles and then in London with <u>The Beaux' Stratagem</u>. The play made points as a social commentary by its timely plea for facilitating divorce when new alterations were still pending on the British divorce law. In performance, Maggie Smith's Mrs. Sullen coped with the pathos and the humor of a woman struggling against the stultification of an impossible marriage.

II. Buckingham

George Villiers, Duke of Buckingham, is best known for his contribution to <u>The Rehearsal</u> (1671), which ridiculed selected literary figures, Dryden in particular, and the style of the heroic play generally. The very topicality of <u>The Rehearsal</u> makes it virtually unplayable for the twentieth-century stage, but <u>The Chances</u> is more flexible. <u>The Chances</u> is significant in dramatic literature: the first part, still attributed to Fletcher, shows Jacobean elements, while the Buckingham section with its manipulated situations is an example of an early attempt at a comedy of manners. In performance, Buckingham predominates over Fletcher, for the second part of the play, with its added low-life characters and muscular dialogue is the more roundly amusing section.

THE CHANCES
Plot Summary

I. Don John and Don Frederick have come to Naples in search of a woman whose praises they have heard sung. But their search, thus far, has proved futile. John is admiring the city when he sees a house dark and unattended. He investigates and a strange woman gives him a parcel, which turns out to be a baby. Frederick, in search of John, meets Constantina 1 who begs his protection and asks that he secure her in a safe refuge. Frederick complies while John has to suffer the suspicions of his landlady over the baby.

II. The Duke meets up with the revenge-seeking Petruchio and his followers. John enters and defends the Duke, who is grateful but will not reveal his identity. Petruchio later laments that his sister, Constantina, was drawn to dishonor by the Duke of Ferrara. Upholding the honor of his house, he asks John to carry a challenge to the Duke.

III. When John brings the challenge, the Duke
freely admits that he has a child by Constantina (the
baby John is keeping) but that her honor is unstained
for she is his wife. Naturally, Petruchio and the Duke
are reconciled. John assures them that Constantina is
safe, but when the Duke and Petruchio come for her, she
is gone with the landlady and John and Frederick are
suspected.

IV. Constantina 2 and her mother enter. They
have lightened one Antonio of his gold. Constantina 2
asks John's protection begging him to save her from a
man she hates. When she unmasks, he is impressed and
she is taken with him. John locks her in and, faithful
to his promise, is willing to fight rather than let the
lady be seen. Finally he compromises, and old Antonio
is allowed to view her since he knows Constantina 1 and
is harmless (they think). Abruptly, word comes that
Antonio, who knows a thief when he sees one, has run
out of the house after the woman.

V. Antonio's servant is after Constantina 2 and
her mother, and Constantina 1 is alone out on the
street. She dares not return to her refuge, for the
landlady has spun tales about Frederick. John finds
Constantina 2 and they swear undying love. Antonio
strikes a bargain with Constantina 2: he will trouble
her no longer if she returns his gold. Everyone ends up
on stage and all are reconciled.

Background

The date of the original production of Fletcher's
play is not definite, but it first appeared in the
folio of 1647. The play was revived early in the
Restoration, and Pepys saw it in 1661 both in April and
in October. Probably not long after the revival, the
Duke of Buckingham produced his version which alters
the last two acts. Buckingham's version was printed in
1682, and the title page makes clear that the comedy
acted at the Theatre Royal was "Corrected and Altered

by a Person of Honor." Genest calls the new material the "happiest material alteration of any old play ever made," and Langbaine says that it was acted "with extraordinary applause."

With the exception of Charles Hart as Don John, the original cast is not known. Downes says of the role that it was one of the parts in which Hart excelled and praises his versatility: "In all the Comedies and Tragedies, he was concern'd he Perform'd with that Exactness and Perfection, that not any of his Successors have Equall'd him." Hart retired in 1682 at the union of the two companies. Rymer talks about his accomplishments citing his visual grace:

> The eyes of the audience are prepossessed and charmed by his action, before aught of the Poet can approach their ears; and to the most wretched character he gives a lustre which so dazzles the sight, that the deformities of the poet cannot be perceived.

In a revival of The Chances in 1691-92, Mrs. Leigh played the Bawd and Charlotte Butler was the Second Constantina. That powerful combination, John Wilks and Anne Oldfield, brought their talents to the play in the early part of the eighteenth century: he as Don John and she as the Second Constantina. In 1922 it was briefly revived under the direction of the indomitable Montague Summers.

Critical Evaluations

On July 3, 1962, The Chances by Fletcher, revised by Buckingham, opened at the Chichester Festival Theatre under the direction of Laurence Olivier. The piece was to be played in repertory with Ford's The Broken Heart and Chekhov's Uncle Vanya, and this triumvirate was planned to show how plays of very different periods could effectively utilize the stage facilities of this new theatre in Sussex in its first ten-week season. The cast included: Keith Michell as

Don John, John Neville as Don Frederick, Robert Lang as Petruchio, Alan Howard as the Duke of Ferrara, Rosemary Harris as Constantina 1, Kathleen Harrison as the Landlady, Joan Plowright as Constantina 2 and Athene Seyler as Her Mother.

There was great interest in the new building, and the author of "The Chichester Festival Theatre" noted the innovations in the theatre's internal structure:

> For the first time in this country a theatre is being specially constructed with an open stage jutting out into the auditorium. . . . The non-scenic Elizabethan stage, encompassed on three sides by the audience, has at long last reached fruition in an actual theatre.[1]

The basic design for the theatre was a composite:

> [It] combined the classical lines of the old Greek and Elizabethan playhouses with those laid down by contemporary requirements. This means that the arena has been so constructed that from every part of the auditorium all may see and hear properly.[2]

The appointment of Olivier as director, a step towards his later office as director of the National Theatre, was in the nature of a trial, and he defended the deliberate selection of the disparate plays:

> My plan is to demonstrate the versatility of the stage through a range of styles, conventions and periods to be presented in each season. Fletcher and Ford if successfully produced will be so with no very great surprise to anyone. It has been said that amphitheatre presentation has been to the advantage of any play up until the 18th century.[3]

Nevertheless, Oliver did not succeed in demonstrating that the arena stage was as flexible as he had hoped that it could be. Of the three inaugural productions not one was a complete success. Michael Jamieson judged that "The Chekhov was memorable, while the Fletcher was vapid, and the Ford worthy but misguided."[4] Perhaps the burden that Olivier assumed was, though nobly ambitious, too weighty for him, for he directed all three productions and appeared in both the Ford and the Chekhov. His choice of The Chances was a risky one, for it was not, in itself, a sufficiently reliable play with which to open so significant a playhouse. Neither it nor The Broken Heart had the audience appeal of the Uncle Vanya with Michael Redgrave, Olivier, Rosemary Harris and Joan Plowright.

The content of The Chances made the choice even more inauspicious: "The Chances is a conventional, feeble, and protracted comedy of mistakings, whose great vogue in the annals of our drama was in no way explained by anything that happened on the Chichester stage."[5] Harold Matthews argued that, in the composite work, Buckingham's sharp style came off best:

> Cervantes' original narrative, gently mocking, was never quite dramatic. John Fletcher had much the same temper but how he finished his play is now unknown. George Villiers . . . substituted a coarser development. . . . His work is much more entertaining than one imagines a second course of Fletcher, with or without Beaumont, would have been.[6]

The quick pacing and emphasis on the broad verbal interplay visually spiced with commedia dell'arte bits helped to confirm the Buckingham section as the most appealing. However, it was a physical appeal reinforced by the architecture of the theatre, and the necessity of movement became a liability.

Apparently fascinated by the very wide, open spaces of the new structure, Olivier approached the production as a romp, but the almost constant movement ("the cast, . . . were kept at the double, mounting steps, shinning up posts, sliding down banisters, and being chased along cat-walks"), produced only minor visual compensation.[7]

The first part of the plot deals with the Constantina 1 of Rosemary Harris, her brother (Robert Lang), and their difficulties. The task here was that the Constantina of the Fletcher play had to be established so that the Constantina 2 of the Buckingham section, played by Joan Plowright, would be a real contrast. Except for the fact that she invented a lisp for the occasion, Miss Harris apparently did little to lay the foundation upon which to build this dramatic contrast except to allow a flirtatiousness to peep out from behind her appeals for sympathy.

The weak foundation supported a tottering structure: as the second Constantina, Miss Plowright seemed to rely on accent antics more than on any in-depth consideration of the character. Although she offered vitality, her comic playing was limited to an appeal for laughs made chiefly by the use of a "flat Lancashire accent which was sheer Music Hall."[8]

There was significant support in the appearance of the veteran Restoration actress, Athene Seyler, who made the mother of Constantina 2 a definite forerunner of Mrs. Malaprop. A good companion performance was that of Robert Lang who, as the brother of Constantina 1, was definite about dramatic tone: "The romantic sentimentality of the first half was amusingly guyed and by none more noticeably than Robert Lang as the brother bent on a vengeance of honour."[9]

The most engaging acting was in the interpretations of Don John and Don Frederick by Keith

Michell and John Neville, with Neville slightly in the lead.

Despite the fact that in his direction of this play Olivier used the unadorned theatre structure as fully as possible, the result was still a flat beginning for the theatre: "All Sir Laurence's cleverness couldn't hide the fact, traceable to the script, that The Chances is Much Ado About Absolutely Nothing: a comic libretto in search of a composer."[10]

III. Dryden

In his comedies, John Dryden concentrated on the
manipulation of plot rather than on the celebration of
manners. Marriage à la Mode (1671), considered one of
his best comedies, is in this experimental vein, and
the whimsical view Dryden took of sexual intrigue was
not to be imitated in the major comedies of the type.
The play is concerned principally with romance, and the
psychology of the lovers, which is relatively uncom-
plicated, is dealt with sympathetically, without the
distance and the calculation which were to characterize
later playwrights. The play is essentially a gentle
amusement for a leisured audience of somewhat languid
intellectual acumen, so its revival in early 1946 must
have been a jolt for the post-war audience who would
have had considerable difficulty finding any grounds
for sympathetic identification with the characters and
an even harder time being amused by the brittle banter.

All for Love belongs to a larger canvas than
Marriage à la Mode. It requires acting, especially by
the principals, of an almost titanic scope. Those
tragedies which celebrate love and honor on the grand
scale demand a tone which does not belong comfortably
to the twentieth century, and Dryden's blank verse
requires precision in speaking that challenges even
experienced Shakespearian actors. Consequently, an
effective revival of All for Love is of historical
importance, for it stands with revivals of Venice
Preserved as a rare example of the ability to respond
to tradition with appropriate style.

MARRIAGE A LA MODE
Plot Summary

I. In a walk near the palace, Palamede hears
Doralice singing and introduces himself, praising both
her voice and her beauty. He reveals that within three
days he is to be married, but his wife is a total

stranger and he has accepted her for fear of being disinherited. Doralice agrees to let him serve her for his few remaining days of freedom. Doralice's husband, Rhodophil the captain of the guards, enters. The two men greet each other, and Rodophil admits to Palamede that Doralice has no fault other than one--she is his wife. He describes his choice of a mistress to Palamede: she is a woman who is infatuated with the court and dotes on new French phrases.

Argaleon, the conniving favorite of the usurper king, and Amalthea, his good sister, enter. The scene is given to exposition. The late king, dying in battle, commended his infant son and his queen to the care of Polydamas, his general. The trust was betrayed and Polydamas was hailed as king. But the queen, the prince and Polydamas's own wife fled Syracuse. Two very attractive young people, Leonidas and Palmyra, have been discovered and brought to court, and Leonidas is presented to the king as his lost son, a situation which infuriates Argaleon.

II. Melantha (the lady of the French phrases) is talking about Rhodophil when Palamede enters with an introductory note from her father. She sets the conditions for their civilized marriage then rushes off to see the new prince. Palamede realizes that she bears a close resemblance to Rhodophil's description of his prospective mistress.

Amalthea reveals to Rhodophil that her brother is jealous of the new prince, and he agrees to remain vigilant. Leonidas refuses to court Amalthea and is only just in time to save Palmyra from the advances of Argaleon. The rejected suitor spies on Leonidas and Palmyra as they vow mutual fidelity.

III. Brought before the king, Palmyra refuses to renounce her love; but Hermogenes reveals that Palmyra, not Leonidas, is the king's child. Polydamas does an about-face, demotes Leonidas and raises Palmyra.

IV. Palmyra learns that Leonidas is truly the son of the late king, but when she discovers that he will take the crown by force, she cannot agree to endanger her father's life. The king orders Leonidas seized.

V. Palamede, who is to be married the next day, attacks Melantha in a volley of French and nonsense, realizing that the trouble she is costing is increasing her value for him. The two men admit to the innocence of their women and make a "firm league, not to invade each other's property."

The king sends Leonidas off to execution, but he breaks from his guards, proclaims himself, and Palamede and Rhodophil join him. The victorious Leonidas is reconciled with the justly deposed Polydamas and asks for Palmyra's hand. Argaleon's life is spared for Amalthea's sake, but he remains a prisoner while she retires to a life of chastity and seclusion. Leonidas and Palmyra begin a happy reign, and Palamede resigns himself to the fact that he must get Melantha a place at court.

Background

Marriage à la Mode was produced around Easter of 1672. It was the first original comedy given at Lincoln's Inn Fields by the King's Company which had moved to this location after the Theatre Royal was destroyed by fire. The cast included: Wintersel as Polydamas, Kynaston as Leonidas, Cartwright as Hermogenes, Mohun as Rhodophil, Burt as Palamede, Cox as Palmyra, Mrs. James as Amalthea, Mrs. Marshall as Doralice and Mrs. Boutell as Melantha.

In a letter to The Gentleman's Magazine of January 1745, an old theatregoer praised the original effort, which, he claimed, made its debut "with extraordinary lustre. Divesting myself of the old man, I solemnly declare that you have seen no such acting, no not to any degree, since."

The original cast was a strong one. William Cartwright was originally a member of Prince Charles's Company before the Civil Wars. He began acting immediately upon the Restoration, remained a solid theatrical figure and was appointed one of the directors of the King's Company along with Kynaston and Mohun during the friction between Killigrew and his son, Charles.

William Wintershal had also been an actor before the war and, with Cartwright, had been acting at the Red Bull at the Restoration. He was admired by both Pepys and Dennis and immortalized by Buckingham in The Rehearsal.

Two sisters, Ann and Rebecca Marshall, were both leading ladies in the King's Company. Because of the tradition of using only the surname in the cast list, it is impossible to know which of the two nymphs created the role of Doralice.

Mrs. Boutell created many significant Restoration roles, two of which, Melantha and Margery Pinchwife in The Country Wife, still attract actresses today. The description in Curll's History of the Stage shows her as an attractive woman able to turn her weaknesses to advantage:

> Mrs. Boutel was likewise a very considerable Actress; she was of low stature, had very agreeable features, a good Complection, but a childish look. Her Voice was weak, tho' very mellow; she generally acted the young Innocent Lady whom all the Heroes are mad in Love with; she was a Favourite of the Town.

Boutell was succeeded in the role by Mrs. Mountfort, an actress whom Cibber praised for her considerable range "which made her excellent in characters extremely different." She showed a variety of humor, vivacity and elocution, coupled with an ability to give "many heightening Touches to Characters but coldly written." In choice detail, Cibber describes Mountfort's Melantha reading her father's letter which has been delivered by Palamede, who is being recommended to the lady as a suitable husband:

Modesty is the Virtue of a poor-soul'd Country Gentlewoman; she is too much a Court Lady, to be under so vulgar a Confusion; she reads the Letter, therefore, with a careless, dropping Lip, and an erected Brow, humming it hastily over, as if she were impatient to outgo her Father's Commands, . . . crack! she crumbles it at once into her Palm, and pours upon him her whole Artillery of Airs, Eyes, and Motion; down goes her dainty, diving Body, to the Ground, as if she were sinking under the conscious Load of her own Attractions; then launches into a Flood of Fine Language, . . . still playing her Chest forward in fifty Falls and Risings like a Swan upon waving Water; and, to complete her Impertinence, she is so rapidly fond of her own Wit, that she will not give her Lover leave to praise it.

Edward Kynaston had originally been with the Cockpit Company where as a youth he acted female roles, having particular success as Evadne in The Maid's Tragedy. But his talent was not confined to these parts, and he created a large number of male roles of considerable importance. He is praised in D'Urfey's The Richmond Heiress (1693) as the "last, not least in Love, the only remaining branch of the old stock," Killigrew's Company.

In 1707 a public subscription for three guineas allowed the subscriber three tickets for the first day of three plays of the "best" authors. The plays were: <u>Julius Caesar</u>, Fletcher's <u>A King and No King</u> and a combination of the comic scenes of <u>Marriage à la Mode</u> and <u>The Maiden Queen</u>. The rationale for this pastiche was that "these comic episodes were utterly independent of the serious Scenes." Cibber was delighted with the result: "The Project so well succeeded, that those comic Parts have never since been replace'd, but were continu'd to be jointly acted, as one Play, several years after." This "several years" lasted until nearly the end of the century. The play as a whole was resurrected briefly by the Phoenix Society in 1920.

Critical Evaluations

On 24 July 1946 John Clements both directed and played in <u>Marriage à la Mode</u> with Kay Hammond at the St. James Theatre. Others in the cast included: Robert Eddison, Frances Howe, Moira Lister, David Peel and James Mills. The setting was by Laurence Irving and the costumes by Elizabeth Haffenden.

Although the production was considered a "brave effort," Hope-Wallace viewed it as an "untheatrical affair." What was lacking was a "little more of the true high comedy style."[1] The <u>Times</u> critic estimated that Clements had succeeded in bringing "two-thirds of these two-plays-in-one amusingly to life." In order to blend the two he "'fantasticates' the romantic play as well as the comedy, so that we may smile or sigh at both of them indifferently." The acting, however, was not totally indifferent, and Kay Hammond was dubiously singled out in her role as Melantha, the <u>précieuse</u>, as being "only perfectly at ease in the anticipation scene." Despite a firm beginning and a spectacular second act, the third act revealed how "perilous and gallant the whole adventure has been."[2]

The play opened on the 24th of July. On the 29th, it went into repertory with The Kingmaker, also starring Clements and Hammond. It lasted less than a month. August 20th was the last performance of Marriage à la Mode, and The Kingmaker closed on the 24th.

In trying to combine the romance and the comedy, John Clements, both as director and as actor, succeeded only in stressing that they were distinctly separate entities, and the production unraveled accordingly. Consequently, the production, suffering from the postwar climate which could hardly have been conducive to a widely empathic response, ultimately failed due to the inability of the director to fuse disparate elements into a playable whole.

ALL FOR LOVE; or, THE WORLD WELL LOST
Plot Summary

I.   It is after the battle of Actium.   A despairing Antony, sequestered in the Temple of Isis, laments the loss of his wife Octavia and his friend Dolabella. Ventidius, Antony's general, upbraids Cleopatra and tells Alexas, her eunuch, that Cleopatra's power over Antony is nearing its end. On a more positive note, he encourages Antony to behave once more like a Roman, and they return to the fight.

II.   Although Antony scrupulously tries to avoid her, Cleopatra tricks her way into his presence, but Antony, backed up by Ventidius, rejects her. Cleopatra plays her ace: she reveals that Octavius Caesar had offered her Egypt and Syria if she would join him against Antony. Realizing the political enormity of her sacrifice, he immediately becomes her captive again.

III. Antony successfully attacks Caesar's camp, and Ventidius wisely counsels peace. Dolabella, whose love for Cleopatra has forced him to desert to Caesar's forces rather than rival Antony, comes with an offer of peace.   When Antony asks why Caesar has made this offer, Ventidius brings in the peacemaker, Octavia, with their two daughters. Antony is swayed by the appearance of his family and by Caesar's offer of the Eastern part of the Empire.

IV. Fearing another encounter with Cleopatra, Antony sends Dolabella to say goodbye for him. Dolabella leaps at the chance to pay his own deferred courtship. Under the instruction of Alexas, Cleopatra seems to accept Dolabella and the deception works. Antony's reaction to the news makes Octavia jealous. When Dolabella reappears with Cleopatra, Antony rejects them both.

V. As Cleopatra is debating suicide, word comes that the Egyptian fleet has joined Caesar's forces and that Antony sees the desertion as the work of Cleopatra. In despair, Cleopatra takes refuge in her monument, and Antony determines to die fighting. But Alexas, always ready with a new ruse, brings word that Cleopatra has slain herself to prove her constancy. When he is convinced of Antony's sorrow, he rushes back to Cleopatra with the good news. But Antony takes the opportunity to fall on his sword, and, too late, Cleopatra rushes in to rectify Alexas' lie. Antony dies in her arms, and Cleopatra, always one to grasp the moment, arrays herself as a bride and seating herself beside the dead Antony applies her asp just as Caesar's troops rush in to claim her as one of the spoils of war.

Background

All for Love; or, The World Well Lost was produced at the Theatre Royal, Drury Lane, in the winter of 1677-78 probably in December or January. The cast included: Hart as Antony, Mohun as Ventidius, Clarke as Dolabella, Goodman as Alexas, Griffin as Serapion, Coyash as Myris, Mrs. Boutell as Cleopatra and Mrs. Corey as Octavia.

Dryden had successes in both comedy and tragedy. All for Love falls into two popular categories: love and honor tragedy and renovated Shakespeare. It was popular at the time to "improve" Shakespeare. Davenant had produced a "purified" Hamlet shortly after The Siege of Rhodes. He also redecorated Macbeth and remade Measure for Measure. There were no fewer than eleven of Shakespeare's plays that underwent this kind of refurbishing. In All for Love, Dryden overcame this dangerous tradition by going his own way with a drama which had already received not only Shakespeare's attention but was also the subject of a recent Antony and Cleopatra (1677) by Sir Charles Sedley.

Charles Hart had been an actor before the Commonwealth and was a member of the King's Company from its inception. He was one of the principal tragedians of the Theatre Royal. At the time that he played Antony her was nearing the end of his career (he died in 1683) and by previous experience would have been well suited for the role. He was backed by Mohun, a colleague who could boast the same background: he had been a pre-Commonwealth actor and he too had joined the King's Company at the Restoration. The description of his abilities makes Mohun an ideal choice for one of the magnets in the love vs. honor struggle, for Mohun "from his inferior height and muscular form, generally acted grave, solemn, austere parts."

Thomas Clarke was a much younger actor who joined the Theatre Royal about 1672-73. He had his eye on Hart's buskins and is one of the players who, at the time of Hart's retirement, claimed principal roles for himself. Cardell Goodman led a life that rivalled some of the lesser heroes of the drama. He had definite potential, for he successfully succeeded Hart as Alexander the Great. But Goodman's real histrionics were in his offstage performances which included a brief stint as a highwayman to augment his theatrical salary and another role turning King's evidence to escape execution for his involvement in the Assassination Plot of 1696.

Of Mrs. Boutell, Curll says, "she generally acted the young Innocent Lady whom all the Heroes are mad in Love with." This may not have made her the ideal choice for Cleopatra, but as she was a favorite of the town and had already created Melantha in Marriage à la Mode and Margery in The Country Wife, she would have been a sure crowd pleaser.

Mrs. Corey had gained the nickname "Doll Common" because of her superlative performance of that lady in The Alchemist. Her particular specialty was old women, and her Widow Blackacre in The Plain Dealer (1674-75) was called "the most comical character that was ever brought upon the stage." Her geniality may have enabled her to make the wronged Octavia bearable.

Cibber, reporting on the rise of his company and the granting of the patent in 1718, tells how the company was "emboldened, to lay out larger Sums, in the Decorations of our Plays." Therefore, they revived All for Love and in acknowledgment of the public's renewed interest spent a great deal of money embellishing the production: "the Habits of that Tragedy amounted to an Expence of near Six Hundred Pounds; a Sum unheard of, for many years before, on the like Occasions."

All for Love held the stage for over a hundred years. The last eighteenth-century production in London was at Covent Garden in May 1790. Nineteenth-century productions of Shakespeare's Antony and Cleopatra in 1813 and 1833 boasted "additions from Dryden." It was revived by the Phoenix Society in 1922 with Edith Evans as Cleopatra.

Critical Evaluations

Prospect Productions' presentation of Dryden's <u>All for Love</u> settled at the company's London home, the Old Vic, on 1 December 1977 after being performed at the Edinburgh Festival and on tour. The cast included John Turner as Antony, Barbara Jefford as Cleopatra, Robert Eddison as Alexas, Suzanne Bertish as Octavia, Kenneth Gilbert as Ventidius and Michael Howarth as Dolabella. Frank Hauser directed the Dryden version of the legendary romance, which was costumed by Nicholas Georgiadis after early eighteenth-century paintings of Tiepolo. The impressive result, as J. W. Lambert noted, was the creation of a sartorial world of "periwigs and blazing sculptured cloaks."[1]

The presence of Shakespeare's <u>Antony and Cleopatra</u> in the company repertoire aided the comparison between the two pieces. Vital blank verse of the later play was brought alive by skillful speaking, and Bernard Levin was impressed that the "strength and colour of the lines constantly justify the comparison on which Dryden insisted," noting that "particular speeches are deliberately set parallel to Shakespeare."[2] Additionally, the production emphasized, particularly in the confrontation between Cleopatra and Octavia, Dryden's ability to handle repartee and stressed the play's affinity with the comedy of manners.

The principals fittingly divided the critics. Douglas Blake noted that the revival was overdue if only because it provided an unusually toothsome role for an actress, a fact which Barbara Jefford's Cleopatra grasped "with firm understanding of the inexorable power of her love."[3] J. W. Lambert saw the attention of the play directed by a "series of mirrors held up to an Antony in whom sexual subjection is at war not so much with intelligence as with self-respect." Well equipped in all the essentials, John Turner exploded with "physical and vocal grandeur into a figure of pitiful towering helplessness, especially in the corrosive bath of jealousy which all but consumes him."[4]

There was a counterpoint for each of the lovers in the supporting roles. Kenneth Gilbert's Ventidius was Antony's opposite, a "sardonic executive officer, an inverted Iago, always ready with unflattering loyalty," and Robert Eddison as the meddling eunuch Alexas quivered with "gloating, unhappy malice."

Dryden's magnificent death scene which shows the bodies of the lovers side-by-side on thrones fittingly climaxed Frank Hauser's carefully paced, seriously spoken production and made the revival an object lesson of non-trendy ingenuity.

Interestingly enough, when Jefford and Turner replaced Dorothy Tutin and Alec McCowen as Shakespeare's lovers, the result was, particularly for the unhappy Benedict Nightingale who had suggested the change in an earlier article after seeing the Dryden, disappointing--especially in the case of Jefford who tended "to bring out Cleopatra's majesty rather than her skittishness or her torment."[5]

IV. Etherege

Before its provincial revival in 1965 and its major London production in 1971, <u>The Man of Mode</u> (1676) had suffered the fate of those Restoration comedies which lend themselves easily to discussion but rarely to performance. George Etherege wrote principally for the court and its followers; and, for that audience, the figure of Dorimant was admirable and imitable, and the excesses of Sir Fopling's slavish adherence to fashion were humorously recognizable.

When Etherege was reworked for the contemporary stage, the emphasis was on similarities of thought and behavior in the London of Sir Fopling and Dorimant and the London of the early 1970s. Given the flexibility of the moral code in the London of 1971, the presentation of the play in modern dress by the Royal Shakespeare Company gave Dorimant a new opportunity to appeal to an audience who could relish his amours without having to sublimate them in a period context. Sir Fopling continued his bizarre course, his behavior now motivated by clearly suggested neuroses. Mrs. Loveit and Bellinda remained unsympathetic, surrounded by an aura of artificiality which dehumanized them and precluded compassion.

THE MAN OF MODE; or, SIR FOPLING FLUTTER
Plot Summary

I. Dorimant has two women pining for him: the redoubtable Mrs. Loveit and his current favorite, Bellinda. He has just learned that he has also been noticed by Harriet, a young lady in from the country, but his reputation has gone before him and Lady Woodvill, Harriet's mother, would never receive him. Dorimant confesses to Medley that he plans to have Bellinda enrage Mrs. Loveit and thus give him an opportunity to break with her. Young Bellair arrives and discusses Sir Fopling Flutter, a superfop and would-be darling of the ladies. Young Bellair's news is that his father, Old Bellair, has come to town to force him into a marriage (with Harriet), and that the old man is lodging in the house where Young Bellair's secret love, Emilia, lives.

II. At Lady Townley's house, Emilia reveals that Old Bellair, not knowing of her relationship with his son, has become fond of her.

III. Harriet and Young Bellair happily find themselves in identical positions and agree to join forces: shamming love and outwitting their parents. Arriving in the park, Dorimant sees Harriet and falls in love with her. When Sir Fopling comes in, Dorimant points out Mrs. Loveit hoping that Sir Fopling's attentions to her will give him a new excuse for a fight.

IV. At Lady Woodvill's dance, Old Bellair continues a flirtation with Emilia, and Dorimant, calling himself "Mr. Courtage," outwits Lady Woodvill by impressing her. Trying to match wits with Harriet, Dorimant finds himself bested.

V. Dorimant and Loveit quarrel, and he demands that she publicly repudiate Sir Fopling. Bellinda watches as Mrs. Loveit vows to expose Dorimant's secret love to the world and realizes anew that his treatment of Mrs. Loveit is a pattern of what her own situation with Dorimant will become.

At Lady Townley's, Young Bellair and Emilia have been secretly married, and Dorimant offers Harriet his hand. The parson reveals the marriage and Old Bellair is furious. Dorimant gives up his ladies and, since Harriet sees him as her only possible husband, her mother accepts the situation. When Sir Fopling enters, Mrs. Loveit no longer has any use for him, and she swears off men. Harriet wryly describes life in the country to Dorimant who shows stalwart determination—for a London rake—to wed her anyway.

Background

The Man of Mode was first produced before the King at the Duke's House in Dorset Garden on 11 March 1676. The cast included: Betterton as Dorimant, Harris as Medley, Smith as Sir Fopling, Leigh as Old Bellair, Jevon as Young Bellair, Mrs. Barry as Mrs. Loveit, Mrs. Betterton as Bellinda, Mrs. Leigh as Lady Woodville and Mrs. Twiford as Emilia. Downes reports that "This Comedy being well Cloath'd and well Acted, got a great deal of Money."

Possibly conscious of the opening night failure of She Would If She Could in 1668, Etherege was taking no chances. Sir Car Scroup wrote the Prologue and Busy's songs in the fifth act; Dryden wrote the Epilogue; and Mary of Modena, Duchess of York, accepted the dedication to the printed text. The help was not wasted, for this was the finest of Etherege's three comedies. His playwrighting career began with The Comical Revenge; or Love in a Tub in 1664. This early play was a milestone in English comedy; for Dryden had not yet come forward to make his mark, and Etherege drew his inspiration from the plays of Molière, which he saw as beacons lighting the way to a dramatic interpretation of fashionable foibles. Drawing from Molière's Les Précieuses Ridicules Etherege produced Man of Mode and from Molière acquired, in part, the concept of Sir Fopling. One of the strengths of the play was that it inspired in the audience the game of spot the original. The role of Dorimant drew the most contenders. Dennis voted for Rochester as the most likely subject:

> I remember very well that upon and first acting this Comedy, it was generally believed to be an agreeable Representation of the Persons of Condition of both Sexes, both in Court and Town;

and that all the World was charmed with Dorimont
[sic]; and that it was unanimously agreed, that he
had in him several of the Qualities of Wilmot Earl
of Rochester, as, his Wit, his Spirit, his amorous
Temper, the Charms that he had for the fair Sex,
his Falsehood, and his Inconstancy. . . . Sir
George Etherege wrote Dorimant in Sir Fopling, in
Compliment to him, as drawing his Lordship's
Character, and burnishing all the Foibles of it,
to make them shine like Perfections.

Sir Fopling was so popular that he even made his
way into theological disputes for that year, and he
held the stage well. When Etherege was at Ratisbon as
English Envoy, Middleton, the Secretary of State,
reported: "Every weeke there are plays at Court; the
last time Sr Fopling appear'd with the usuall
applause." Since Etherege was not appointed to Ratisbon
until 1685, Sir Fopling was doing him proud.

Among those in the considerable cast was Mrs.
Barry as Mrs. Loveit. True to the name of the
character, Mrs. Barry, who had been Rochester's
mistress, later became the inamorata of Etherege by
whom she reputedly had a child.

Both Betterton and Mrs. Betterton performed: he as
Dorimant; she, who excelled in serious roles, as
Dorimant's about-to-be-cast-off Bellinda.

As late as 1722, John Dennis, who was acquainted
with Etherege, defended Dorimant and praised his
longevity. Dorimant is an

admirable Picture of a Courtier in the Court of
King Charles the Second. But if Dorimont [sic] was
designed for a fine Gentleman by the Author, he
was oblig'd to accommodate himself to that Notion
of a fine Gentleman, which the Court and the Town
both had at the Time of the writing of this
Comedy. 'Tis reasonable to believe that he did so,

and we see that he succeeded accordingly. For
Dorimont not only pass'd for a fine Gentleman with
the Court of King Charles the Second, but he has
pass'd for such with all the World, for Fifty
Years together.

In the early eighteenth century Wilks was a
popular Dorimant and Colley Cibber flourished as Sir
Fopling. The play lasted for well over half of the
eighteenth century--the last recorded presentation in
London was in 1766 at Covent Garden--and by the
nineteenth century it was ripe for the moralists.

Critical Evaluations

The Man of Mode (1965)

In 1949 the first steps in the restoration of the
Georgian Theatre at Richmond, Yorkshire, were nearly
complete. But by 1960, the work had come to a
standstill because of a lack of funds and was inching
along as money became available. The three major
losses which the theatre had suffered were the pit, the
stage scenery and the original proscenium. Eventually,
the pit was restored, and there was talk of
reconstructing the understage machinery for the benefit
of visiting students.[1] By 1962 the theatre was
operative and, in 1965, participated in the
Richmondshire Festival when Prospect Productions
presented in this 1788 building Etherege's The Man of
Mode in its first professional performance in two
hundred years.

Although restoration of the theatre had reduced
its audience capacity to 230, about half its original
size, the result of the renovation produced an
authentic specimen of eighteenth-century theatre
design. There was a narrow forestage with adjoining
balconies and doors and an inner stage and sunken pit
of equal depth.

Considering the reduced seating capacity, it is easy to see how the building itself was hazardous for actors accustomed to projecting characters in much larger spaces. Toby Robertson's production, which opened on September 3, 1965, did nothing to modify its approach to conform to the interior with the result that "the actors intensify one's feelings of being in a toy theatre."[2] The very intimacy of the house with its invitation to direct address was ignored by all the players but Ronnie Stevens who took advantage of his situation by playing Sir Fopling "almost in revue-style; a figure suggesting an ambulatory lemon-meringue pie, addressing every quiver and contortion of civility straight out to the house."

By contrast, the remainder of the company stuck resolutely to the broader style with an uncomfortably overwhelming effect, "projecting with enough volume for Drury Lane, and sacrificing audience contact to stylistic mannerisms--the florid bowing, smirking, and epicene delivery which have turned so much Restoration production into an empty fetish."[3]

The Man of Mode (1971)

When The Man of Mode joined the Royal Shakespeare Company's 1971/72 season on September 13, 1971, at the Aldwych Theatre in repertoire with Harold Pinter's Old Times, Gorky's Enemies and the circus-like A Midsummer Night's Dream, it was announced that this play had not been seen on stage since 1766. But Irving Wardle remembered the "standard parade of bloodless gallants and simpering mistresses" of the Prospect Productions' version in 1965.[1]

The Royal Shakespeare Company's parade included Alan Howard as Dorimant, Julian Glover as Medley, Terence Taplin as Young Bellair, David Waller as Old Bellair, John Wood as Sir Fopling Flutter, Brenda Bruce as Lady Townley, Isla Blair as Emilia, Vivien Merchant

as Mrs. Loveit, Frances de la Tour as Bellinda and
Helen Mirren as Harriet.

The company hoped to revitalize the comedy, and an
interview with Terry Hands and Timothy O'Brien, the
director and the designer of the production, defined
the approach to the play in terms of a particular
concept of Restoration theatre:

> This play was written in 1676, some 16 years after
> the Restoration itself; it has the label of a
> Restoration comedy but our understanding of
> Restoration drama derives from a tradition of
> playing it, not from a knowledge of the period.
> The little that we do know about the Restoration
> style suggests that it was a sort of cabaret: they
> put in Pop numbers, the latest fashions and
> anything that was exciting on the scene.
> Restoration drama doesn't appear to have been the
> kind of finger twirling mannered performance we've
> become used to.[2]

The program notes included a discussion of
Libertinism as a fashion:

> Perhaps partly a reaction against the
> Puritanism of the Commonwealth. But taking its
> inspiration from a variety of classical sources,
> libertinism acquired its peculiar blend of
> refinement, sensuality and aggression by grafting
> onto these classical sources the ruthlessness
> taught by Machiavelli and the English philosopher
> Hobbes.

This led to a consideration of the activities of
Dorimant:

> There is an element of Rochester's aesthetic
> nihilism in Etherege's Dorimant, but Dorimant, in
> his complex response to Harriet, also conveys

something of the libertine quest for genuine existence.

And the libertine in his ruthlessness was closely related to the villain of earlier dramas:

> For a start the play stands at a fascinating point in dramatic evolution, a post-Jacobean melodrama conceived in terms of early Restoration comedy. In Etherege the Restoration style takes its earliest shape in substituting the pursuit of sex and the acquisition of dowry for the murkier Jacobean motivations of murder, incest and revenge. Dorimant, the play's principal, emerges as a positively Jacobean villain who uses sex as a weapon in a private war against fashionable society, womankind in general, and himself in particular.[3]

As there was little contemporary precedent for interpreting the play, the design possibilities were vast. Hands noted:

> Only about 40 lines of text actually relate to the period. This left us free to concentrate on trying to create the effect on the audience of today that the play might have had upon the audience in its own time rather than presenting an erroneous museum facsimile. We wanted a design concept that would delight the audience, enable them to see themselves in the play like the 1676 audience might have seen themselves, but be sufficiently removed for them to get the satirical points and be amused by the goings on.[4]

However, the attempt to provide an original interpretation and the desire to emphasize variety produced myriad acting styles that were less than congenial as there was "something of a gap between . . . the broad farce of Vivien Merchant's Mrs. Loveit and the more cerebral comedy of Frances de la Tour's

Bellinda."[5] John Barber noted an incongruity between the real feelings exposed by the play and production gimmickry: "So we have a modern hero plunging naked into a bath on the stage. We have girls in modern red wigs and pantaloons. And yet all the talk is of damned dissemblers, sedan-chairs, and orange-women who are really procuresses."[6] Some of this incongruity may have been based in a visual concept of modern "sexual aesthetic" on the part of designer O'Brien, who

> started to develop a costume from his idea of what our men would want to show: chests and arms, if you like biceps. So the sleeves became fuller than modern clothes, the chest area was more distinct-- but not so much that the audience wouldn't understand what was going on. It was a very rich world, too; we wanted to convey wealth, colour, flamboyance. If the play were done in Restoration costume, only the sophisticated half of the audience would respond; there's an enormous new audience which wants to see plays it can relate to.[7]

As the artificial Fopling, John Wood emphasized vulnerability in his performance and made Sir Fopling appealing rather than annoying: "Everyone wants him [Sir Fopling] to do his thing: he is a cause of entertainment, not irritation, to the other characters."[8] O'Brien saw something completely natural in Fopling's one great scene:

> In Scene 8 Fopling comes to Dorimant's house to examine the bed for traces of Bellinda's ruin and is astonished at the urbanity of Dorimant at being able to conceal it. In a passage after that Sir Fopling becomes tremendously alive inside his artificial limits. Someone says, "Look, Sir Fopling's dancing" and he's up on a cloud at the end of a wonderfully successful party where he has felt himself the real comet in the sky, and he's celebrating this so nakedly in his Brandenberg

with its soft colours and weaving about the stage like some marvelous happy moth. Then he explains that he has written a song, which is teased out of him. It's read over and he's persuaded to sing it. He stands on the bed, starts to sing, and suddenly realises it's a much better song than he remembered. Almost with tears of pride he sings. Then he sits down and his friends say: "Of its kind it couldn't be bettered and it's particularly remarkable for being in the French manner." "That's what I aimed at," he says, bursts into tears, and then makes a marvelous gesture: he cries, "Slap, down goes the glass and we're at it." That's not artificial, it's someone so enthusiastic, so capable of enjoying himself, that the artificiality has vanished. At that point the play is really consummate.[9]

The other great artificial was Mrs.Loveit. Vivien Merchant allowed her to participate with relish in the carnival atmosphere of the play. Her first appearance on stage was wonderfully camp: "her entrance . . . voluminously gowned in heliotrope and puce to the strains of a torchy blues, is a moment to treasure."[10] Thereafter, she continued to employ a faded film star technique. But Merchant's interpretation, though it blended with the broader elements, seriously threatened the graver moments:

> As Mrs. Loveit, Dorimant's much-abused mistress, Vivien Merchant invests the character with such high-strung histrionics that she seems about to undertake the assassination of Duncan rather than a mere assignation in the Mall. At the serious level at which Miss Merchant takes the part the play's comedy becomes insupportable and the whole production goes out of the window.[11]

Dorimant, who must bear heavier dramatic weight than his paramours, fared little better. Jeremy Kingston complained that Alan Howard's Dorimant was "overburdened with the details of self-love," an imbalance that boded ill for his final conversion.[12] Despite his authority and a good supply of mannerisms, he did not have sufficient flexibility to suggest the heartless man who finally finds a heart. And his characterization seemed out of the period context: "Howard comes down heavily on the interpretation of Dorimant as Jacobean villain. He is a morose, self-tormented lecher who rasps his lines in a series of extended cadences that lure the ear away from an understanding of the complicated plot."[13]

A dominant feature of the set was the arrangement of six steel balls which were adjusted to different levels creating a variety of angles to signify scene changes. The mobile structure was an inventive addition to the game theme inherent in the sexual intrigues of the play. The gigantic toy recalled Newton's cradle "which demonstrates the law of motion--here extended to sexual intrigues and life itself--that to every action there is an equal and opposite reaction."[14]

Although the language and the framework of the characters' activity had to remain fixed in the Restoration, the basic appeal made was to similarities in modes of thought and behavior in 1971 London. The rationale was that as the plot is there only to support a series of confrontations by means of which intrigue piles upon intrigue and there is nothing of great seriousness in the play and no resolution of outstanding importance, the presentation of Etherege in a modern context does not have to overcome many obstacles. Thus the play was presented as a clever toy which, if operated efficiently, gave much amusement.[15]

V. Wycherley

One of William Wycherley's four plays has had amazing theatrical resilience. It is not The Plain Dealer (1676) which, in his day, was considered his finest achievement; rather it is his most indecent play, The Country Wife (1675), which has been so consistently revived that it is now considered his best.[1] In none of his other plays does Wycherley expose with such misanthropic joy the pretenses and hypocrisy of the society in which he moved, and the play turns on the eventual acceptance, by most of the characters, of degradation with a high surface gloss. In Wycherley's hand, the comedy of manners becomes black indeed.

Although the principal intrigue turns upon the success of Horner's lie about his virility and the lesser intrigue upon Alithea's union with the right man, the focus of performance attention is on the title character, Margery Pinchwife, and the assessment of her interpretation by various actresses is the backbone of most critical evaluations of the play.

Because Wycherley's play is elusive for the director, no directorial concept has achieved any real thematic unity which would draw the varied dramatic situations together. Often, it has become a one-character play: a vehicle, albeit a fine one, for the purpose of exhibiting a tour de force performance by the actress playing Margery at the expense of any sociological views Wycherley may have been rudely propounding.

THE COUNTRY WIFE
Plot Summary

I. Horner has let it be known about town that he has become emasculated by the "English-French disaster," and gloats over the fact that as a supposed eunuch he will have access to any lady's chamber. A round of visitors comes to confirm the report. Sir Jasper Fidget with his wife and sister are Horner's first experiments, and he is so convincing that Sir Jasper feels free to leave the ladies alone with him. Harcourt and Dorilant are also convinced while Sparkish, a pretender to wit, relishes the situation. The prime victim, Pinchwife, arrives and is forced to admit that he has married a young, pretty country girl.

II. The rustic Margery complains to the overprotective Pinchwife that she is not allowed the delights of London. When her husband warns her against the gallants, her curiosity is even more excited. Meanwhile Sparkish, engaged to the reluctant Alithea, arrives with Harcourt, who privately begs her to break the engagement. Now the butt of general ridicule, Horner temporarily drops his pretense to tell Lady Fidget how things really are.

III. Yielding to Margery, Pinchwife agrees to take her out disguised as a boy. When she appears with her husband, Horner and Dorilant follow them.

IV. Pinchwife dictates a letter of rejection for Margery to send to Horner, but Margery substitutes her own. Horner continues to capitalize on the success of his scheme by dallying with Lady Fidget and Mistress Squeamish before the uncomprehending gaze of their relatives. Pinchwife arrives with the letter, and when Sparkish invites Horner to his wedding dinner, Horner accepts on the condition that Margery be there. Pinchwife arrives home to find Margery writing to Horner to help her escape her marriage.

V. Becoming more adept at subterfuge, Margery claims to be writing for Alithea. Pinchwife chooses to believe her and insures his own downfall by complying with her request to bring Alithea (really Margery in disguise) to Horner's lodging. At Horner's, Mrs. Fidget and Mrs. Squeamish boast of the immorality they conceal behind moral airs. Pinchwife appears with the real Alithea whose honor has been jeopardized by Margery's imposture. When Pinchwife threatens Horner, Margery appears and protests her love for him. Just as Pinchwife realizes that all the men have been duped by Horner, Quack, the suspect physician who originally put the story of Horner's lost virility abroad, reappears, and in concert with the ladies, assures the men that Horner is a eunuch. The play closes with the husbands willing to believe the lie and the women encouraging their self-deception.

Background

The Country Wife was produced at the Theatre Royal, Drury Lane, on 12 January 1675. The cast included Hart as Horner, Kynaston as Harcourt, Lydal as Dorilant, Mohun as Pinchwife, Haines as Sparkish, Cartwright as Sir Jasper Fidget, Shotterell as Quack, Mrs. Boutell as Margery, Mrs. James as Alithea, Mrs. Knepp as Lady Fidget, Mrs. Corbet as Mrs. Dainty Fidget, Mrs. Wyatt as Mrs. Squeamish, Mrs. Rutter as Old Lady Squeamish and Mrs. Corey as Lucy.

This company had already had favorable experience with Wycherley's first play, Love in a Wood, in 1671. Among the many talents highlighted in The Country Wife, one particular actor outshone the rest. Hart, who "might teach any king on earth how to comport himself," lent dignity to Horner's weary plan. Kynaston, who could completely command "true Majesty" and "terrible Menace," settled into the refined, satirical elegance of Harcourt. And Mrs. Knepp, who had excelled in the role of Lady Flippant in Love in a Wood, could be safely trusted with Lady Fidget. Knepp, who was large of heart, granted her favors to her husband, "a kind of jockey," Sir Charles Sedley and Pepys, who has immortalized her by many references in his diary. He confirms that she was the "most excellent, mad-humoured thing," which sounds about right for the creator of Lady Fidget.

90

But the triumph of the evening went to Joe Haines, who had already established himself as a top comedian. He was known as an "incomparable dancer" and Pepys allowed that he also "sings pretty well." It is assumed that Dryden created the role of Benito in <u>The Assignation</u> (1672) for Haines. In addition to his comic talent and his musical and dance abilities, Haines was noted for his delivery of prologues and epilogues, and Cibber refers to him as a "Fellow of wicked Wit" offstage. Haines is described, in toto, by Downes as a "very eminent low comedian, and a person of great facetiousness of temper and readiness of wit." If the character of Sparkish was incorrigible, interpretation would have come easily to Haines, whose real life buffooneries and extravagances made his stay in any theatre company a tenuous matter.

<u>The Country Wife</u> enjoyed a long stage life until the middle of the eighteenth century. In 1766 its decline began when David Garrick adapted the play to the more delicate palates of his audience and produced <u>The Country Girl</u>. To sit through his hodgepodge produced "a sensation not easily to be endured." Wycherley's original piece was revived by the Phoenix Society in 1924 with Isabel Jeans as Mrs. Pinchwife, Baliol Holloway as Mr. Horner and Athene Seyler as Lady Fidget. With the same two actresses it was again produced in an edited version at the Everyman in Hampstead in 1926.

Critical Evaluations

The Country Wife (1956)

On April 2, 1956, the first English Stage Company production opened at the Royal Court Theatre. The new company was a non-profit organization founded with the idea of presenting new English plays and contemporary classics from abroad under the artistic direction of George Devine with Tony Richardson as associate director. Within two years of its founding, it presented twenty-eight new productions, seventeen of them the work of British writers. Most significant was the presentation of <u>Look Back in Anger</u> (1956) by the then unknown John Osborne.

In addition to the regular offerings, a scheme was introduced to foster new talent on the basis of Sunday evening performances. The main purpose of the company was to alert the playwright and the theatre to each other and to make the policy of the company as expansive as possible:

> It [the company] does not push any political or ethical dogma, though its morality--and its political sympathies--are usually evident. What is often dismissed as being vaguely anti-Establishment is pro--all that liberated the human spirit and body from social and material pressures of any kind.[1]

The project, which almost foundered in the first operative year, was stabilized by a combination of old and new playwrights. The <u>Times</u> noted that "Future historians of the arts may be puzzled to learn that the turning point [for the Royal Court] was a television excerpt from <u>Look Back in Anger</u>, which fanned that play into a financial success, consolidated by a revival of <u>The Country Wife</u>."[2] It is significant that in the first year of the company's existence, <u>The Country Wife</u> should have been a decisive factor in establishing an organization which had for its chief goal the promotion and preservation of contemporary talents. The stimulus provided at this Chelsea theatre often extended to the West End. There <u>The Country Wife</u> was transferred to give eighty-eight performances at the Adelphi and sixteen at the Chelsea Palace, in addition to those already given at the Royal Court.

When <u>The Country Wife</u> opened at the Royal Court on 12 December 1956, Kenneth Tynan sounded a festive note for this Christmas-time presentation: "This production is a sort of holiday task for the English Stage Company, and there is wit in their choice: having shown us, in 'Look Back in Anger,' the first evidence of virility in English drama since the war, they round out the year with a self-proclaimed eunuch."[3]

Joining Laurence Harvey as Mr. Horner were Nigel Davenport as Quack, Esmé Percy as Sir Jasper Fidget, Diana Churchill as Lady Fidget, Shelia Ballantine as Mrs. Dainty Fidget, Alan Bates as Mr. Harcourt, Robert Stephens as Mr. Dorilant, John Moffatt as Mr. Sparkish, George Devine as Mr. Pinchwife, Joan Plowright as Mrs. Pinchwife, Maureen Quinney as Alithea, Moyra Fraser as Mrs. Squeamish, Jill Showell as Lucy and Margery Caldicott as Old Lady Squeamish.

In addition to playing Pinchwife, George Devine also directed the production. Although his handling of his directorial role was generally praised, there were mixed feelings about his interpretation of Pinchwife. The _Times_ reviewer found him "surprisingly unfunny" in performance because he was "too realistic to be the chief butt of the plot," yet praised Devine as director for the "sureness of touch with which this ribald comedy is organized."[4] In assessing Pinchwife, Milton Shulman found that Devine's portrayal "leans too heavily on Puritan self-righteousness and neglects the lasciviousness of an ex-rake jealous to protect a young wife from men like himself." Nevertheless, he acknowledged that, as director, Devine had recognized that "without style and pace there would be more rough than smooth in The Country Wife. Against a background of rococo charm, it is played with such fastidious grace that . . . modern audiences should be delighted."[5]

Predictably notable was the portrayal of the title character by Joan Plowright. There was precedent for excellence in a 1924 production with Isabel Jeans and the even more famous 1937 production at the ultra

conservative Old Vic with Ruth Gordon as Margery and
Edith Evans as Lady Fidget, which "threw the gallery
into convulsions and the governors of that foundation
into a panic."[6] Against those awesome forerunners, Miss
Plowright's charming performance which balanced rustic
savvy with inquisitive innocence was a study "drawn in
miniature."[7]

If the production had a fault, it was not in the
salaciousness which had once so shocked pre-war
audiences. Now, the more sophisticated playgoer could
boldly seek "the vicarious pleasure of being, for once
in a sad while, on the immoralist's side," delighted in
being able to admit that "bawdry is a wonderfully
liberating exercise."[8]

There was, however, a real flaw. When Philip Hope-
Wallace complained that the audience appeared not to
follow the "elegant double-edged banter with much aural
attention,"[9] he indirectly referred to the chief difficulty of the production noted specifically by the Times
critic:

> The play's over-riding requirement in any revival
> is that the dialogue should be spoken with relish.
> For the central comedy device should have the
> effect of bringing out the insidious slipperiness
> of language when those who employ it have only one
> idea in mind. Words take on unexpected and ambigu-
> ous meanings, and whole scenes are carried on
> strings of double-entendre. The chief fault of
> this revival is that too few of the actors appear
> to savour their lines.[10]

If every word was not relished and the production
was somewhat rushed, part of the reason could be that
the John Clements offering of The Way of the World had
opened six days earlier to hostile reviews which
censured a fatal slowness of pace. As it was, the
success of The Country Wife prompted the English Stage
Company to present other revivals of rarely performed

Restoration plays, which, if not totally successful, at least merited serious critical evaluation.

The Country Wife (1966)

After its founding in 1963, the Nottingham Playhouse Company became one of a select group of British repertory companies "whose standards of production and acting, and whose choice of material, equal or surpass those of London."[1] Its initial plan was to have a full-scale repertoire which included both classical revivals and as many new English plays as possible.

In January of 1966 the Nottingham Playhouse Company presented its first Restoration comedy, The Country Wife, with Judi Dench as Margery. Once again, the play was a vehicle for a recognized but not yet completely established young actress who, like Joan Plowright before her, was to become a leading artist in a London repertory company. Rounding out the cast were Michael Craig as Mr. Horner, John Tordoff as Mr. Harcourt, Laurence Carter as Mr. Dorilant, Harold Innocent as Mr. Pinchwife, Jimmy Thompson as Mr. Sparkish, Patrick Tull as Sir Jasper Fidget, Alfred Bell as Quack, John Nightingale as the Parson, Sara-Jane Guillim as Alithea, Ursula Smith as Lady Fidget, Marian Forster as Mrs. Dainty Fidget, Diana Ford as Mrs. Squeamish, Janet Henfrey as Old Lady Squeamish and Mary Healey as Lucy.

Despite judicious editing by the director, Ronald Magill, the production still ran almost three hours, though the energy and zest of the performers did something to balance the length. The play's prurience was neutralized by a "certain charm in its bawdiness and a distant unreality about its undying quest for making whores and cuckolds that carries it through the 'shock-barrier' beyond offensiveness."[2]

The designer, Stephen Doncaster, employed sliding sets which suggested Restoration scenery and celebrated the rush of Restoration energy in variegated yellow, orange and gold costumes. In his program notes, Doncaster stressed the fact that the styles and the coloring reflected the temper of the times:

> In planning the sets for this production, I have tried to exploit the seventeenth century principles of scene change in which the "flats" slid in grooves in the stage itself, a system which could easily cope with the number of scenes and variety of locations required by Mr. Wycherley. The clothes of the time also reflected the release from Puritan repressions, and were attempting to catch up with foreign modes, especially those of France. This aim was actually achieved some fifteen years later, but in 1675 the styles, although rich and flamboyant, were still essentially English. Our play presents a robust and direct comment on Society, and I have tried to reflect this by emphasizing the line of the fashions of that year, and eliminating some of the more fussy details.

There was additional help in establishing the period: music in the manner of Purcell and the interpolation of some crowd-pleasers: baggy-trousered sceneshifters to make the audience feel like their forefathers whiling away their time at Drury Lane.

In the key roles, Michael Craig's Horner was noted for a "cool dignity" and a "nice touch of sardonic courtesy towards the women he affects to despise."[3] He was balanced by Harold Innocent's severe Pinchwife, looking like a "sour version of the Puritan off a porridge oats packet," who played his broader scenes "with the scowl of a Demon King in pantomime."

Then attention focused on the "deliciously husky" Margery of Judi Dench, who stressed an accent like a "pail of Devon cream" and a scurrying approach that resembled "some delicious little squirrel, squirming through matrimonial locks and scuttling with delight towards seduction."[4] She mastered two important factors in the presentation of Margery: she made a success of the letter-writing scene, and she made it "a real joy to watch the . . . lighting-up of her face as she hears her censorious husband's catalogue of the city vanities she must avoid."[5]

Despite the acceptability of the performances and the appointments of the production, the play was accused of a lack of relevance:

> The trouble with "The Country Wife" is that the theme is taken through so many permutations and so many innuendoes fall on deaf contemporary ears that as far as the audience are concerned it is a question of whether the spelling is "bawd" or "bored." Too often it is the latter.[6]

Nottingham was to continue its policy of bringing in a guest artist, like Judi Dench, to complement the excellence of its resident players.[7] It is worth noting that when Miss Dench joined the Royal Shakespeare Company, she did not, among her many roles, include parts in the earlier Restoration productions of The Relapse or The Man of Mode mounted at the Aldwych. Perhaps, she was saving herself for Millamant.[8]

The Country Wife (1969)

In 1966, John Clements followed Laurence Olivier as director of the Chichester Festival Theatre and delineated the company's policy which was to subordinate directorial theory to acting:

97

The Royal Shakespeare, he [Clements] suggested, had a monopoly of Bard and Sade, the National of international classics and the Royal Court of new writers. But surely there was room for a theatre of sheer old-fashioned performance--he hoped to make Chichester Britain's leading showcase for actors.[1]

In the 1969 season, the Festival Theatre presented Pinero's The Magistrate, with Alistair Sim, which transferred to London; a "somehow un-Brechtian" Caucasian Chalk Circle; Antony and Cleopatra and The Country Wife. The cast of the Wycherley included Keith Baxter as Mr. Horner, Gary Hope as Mr. Harcourt, Christopher Guinee as Mr. Dorilant, Gordon Gostelow as Mr. Pinchwife, Hugh Paddick as Mr. Sparkish, Brian Hayes as Sir Jasper Fidget, Maggie Smith as Mrs. Pinchwife, Renée Asherson as Alithea, Patricia Routledge as Lady Fidget, Hermione Gregory as Mrs. Dainty Fidget, Charlotte Howard as Mrs. Squeamish, Viola Lyle as Old Lady Squeamish, Richard Kane as Quack, Audrey Murray as Lucy, Geoffrey Burridge as Servant to Horner and Richard Denning as Servant to Sir Jasper. Robert Chetwyn directed and Hutchinson Scott designed the production.

The program notes for The Country Wife, the third production of the season, set the tone of frivolity:

In the theatre The Country Wife must always be preposterously comic. Maybe the last word should by Agate's: "One will boldly continue to deny Wycherley any moral impulse, and say rather that his talent lay in lighting a bonfire in St. James's Park. At this he warmed his hands, rejoicing in the glare which it cast upon the fashionable promenaders."

This theory was carried out in the performance, which rather than being self-consciously sociological, was emphatically entertaining. Robert Chetwyn avoided a "sombre social documentary of a by-gone permissive society" substituting a "sprightly dramatisation of a dirty joke."[2] This cheerful approach softened the play by depriving it of any seamy realism. The result was

> a romp, a bedroom farce in which [there is] not one face pock-marked or grimy, nor one dress-hem splashed with the mud of the London streets.
> . . . .
> Mr. Chetwyn's production is indigenous to neither time nor place. Movement and the use of music combine to soften the play's over-riding misogyny; there is no hint of real squalor, either moral or physical.[3]

But the essential capriciousness of the piece could be justified when set against the serious machinery of the other Restoration playwrights: "Compared with The Way of the World, where love is a mechanism in the service of finance, or with The Soldier's Fortune or The Recruiting Officer, which use their comedy as a vehicle for serious comment on the state of society, it's a fundamentally frivolous piece; and Robert Chetwyn has, rightly, given it a frivolous production."[4] Within this framework of frivolity and style, fashion and social pretensions were discarded in favor of "broad farce, shouts and tumbles and pantomime horseplay."[5]

The most original critical reading of the play was in terms of an overriding homosexual theme explored by Harold Hobson:

> Now the director, Robert Chetwyn, appears to set great store by the fact that on the fist occasion that Mr. Horner fondles Mrs. Pinchwife she is dressed, not as a woman, but as a boy. In an age like the present, this circumstance . . . strikes a ringing note of revelation.

At Chichester the first act of Wycherley's foul and funny play is geared to the assumption that though the men in it pay compliments to the ladies, they reserve their kisses, their thumping, smacking kisses on the lips, for each other. They exchange them every time they meet or part, and sometimes even interrupt their conversations to leap at each other, gluing themselves mouth to mouth. My heart bled for the neglected women, frightened though most of them looked, as the men, in full sight of their despised charms, pursued with enthusiasm their amorous goings-on.[6]

Playing the role of Horner was Keith Baxter who, later in July, was to have a notable success as a remarkable Octavius in <u>Antony and Cleopatra</u>.[7] However, the calculating Octavius offers less of a puzzle for the actor than does the impassive Horner whose masquerade may be motivated by revenge or lust. Baxter gave no hint of motivation nor of the "driving, insatiable misanthropy . . . without which the play loses its venom."[8] Hampered by the myriad acting styles, Baxter was forced to join rather than lead:

> Instead of dictating its tone, nearer to Jonson than Congreve, he's forced to fall in with a generalized, stingless bustle and jollity, racing round the vast Chichester platform with the rest rather than dominating it like a fox in a fluttered chicken-coop.[9]

Balancing Baxter's precarious role was the visually-oriented performance of Gordon Gostelow as the deceived husband who registered each shift of mood by a different walk. His great kinetic appeal brought joy to the audience: "his rubbery hangdog visage, Groucho walk, acrobatic rages of jealousy and desperate appeals to the audience to confirm his fragile hopes, raise cuckoldry to a state of grace."[10]

Against the "leering urbanity and nutcracker fury" of Gostelow was the Lady Fidget of Patricia Routledge, who developed her own "tottering walk and a little fainting voice [with which] she telegraphs a lubricity that finally breaks out almost to the point of jazz in the masquerade."[11]

The production was mounted as a showcase for Maggie Smith upon her return to the stage after an absence of several years. She proved, especially in her solo scenes, the validity of the Chichester policy of celebrating a "star" performer. Since the production had been assembled as a vehicle for her with little attempt to fuse the cast's wildly varied styles into a smooth ensemble, she could not make the whole a total success; however, her Margery became one of the great Restoration performances. She reached her full maturity in the letter scene, which offered the "thrill of a great cadenza, executed with masterly skill."[12]

Ronald Bryden made the most technically significant investigation of Smith's comic technique at work in Margery:

Her effects are not of the kind critics can analyse. . . . Their essence is timing, a swift silver surety and lightness. You can describe her reactions, in her first scene, to the barked prohibitions of Gordon Gostelow's Pinchwife on reference to London parks where she might see younger gallants. Tumbling back from his feet like a startled puppy, dropping the slipper she held for him, she beams at the audience sudden, joyous knowledge where the forbidden fruit hangs. . . . She's really too quick and thoroughbred for the naive little bumpkin of Wycherley's dialogues, so she plays instead for gawky garrulity. As she rattles irrepressibly on, trailing a nasal farm-yard drawl about the stage, she makes poor Margery's stifled talent for loving seem like some monstrous escaping vegetable, burying the rest of the play knee-deep in eager, luxuriant greenery. But she's easily wounded to silence, as when Horner hisses "Peace, dear idiot." It's only the cruel sophistication of the others, accomplices in Horner's plot to cuckold every husband in London by pretending impotence, that makes her a monster.

The apex of her performance was her solo in the letter scene:

Panting, hanging her tongue almost to her chin, climbing half on to the writing-table with anxiety, she catches the quill in her hair, her eye, her inkwell, in a marvelously clowned evocation of laborious schoolgirl semi-literacy. Alone on the stage, she holds the audience helpless with laughter.[13]

Somewhat anxious questions that had been raised in 1962 about the unwieldy scope of the Chichester Festival Theatre were answered by observations that the size of the playing area and the shape of the arena stage frequently forced the performers into a quick march. Miss Smith's command of the large area was an additional tribute to her talent and ingenuity.[14]

For all the unevenness of the broad, swirling production, the play produced, in Maggie Smith's Margery, a characterization of the highest order, an actualization of the potential suggested by the success of her Lady Plyant in 1959, her Sylvia in 1963, continued by her Mrs. Sullen for the National Theatre in 1970 and crystallized by her triumph as Millamant at Stratford, Ontario, in 1976.

The Country Wife (1977)

The National Theatre Company's production of The
Country Wife opened on November 29, 1977 at the Olivier
Theatre with Albert Finney as Mr. Horner, Nicholas
Selby as Quack, Robin Bailey as Sir Jasper Fidget,
Elizabeth Spriggs as Lady Fidget, Ann Beach as Mrs.
Dainty Fidget, Kenneth Cranham as Mr. Harcourt, Gawn
Grainger as Mr. Dorilant, Ben Kingsley as Mr. Sparkish,
Richard Johnson as Mr. Pinchwife, Susan Littler as Mrs.
Pinchwife, Polly Adams as Alithea, Helen Ryan as Mrs.
Squeamish, Tel Stevens as Lucy and Madoline Thomas as
Old Lady Squeamish. Central interest was on the staging
by Peter Hall, with Stewart Trotter.

This production followed Hall's Volpone, which had
opened April 26, yielding a comparison between
Wycherley and Ben Jonson as colleagues in a comedy
tradition which revealed a clearly visible moral
strain. Irving Wardle saw Wycherley as Jonson's heir
and Volpone and Horner as two of a kind, a "pair of
confidence men who expose the corruption of their
fellow citizens by outsmarting them at their own
game."[1]

As a director, Hall seemed to be trying to unearth
a style to suit all the classics he produced, but the
result was that, in performance, the two productions
did not balance each other; for as Hall successfully
cultivated speed in interpreting Jonson he failed in
his approach to Wycherley by trying to elevate him to
the dizzying heights of classical dignity. Hall
stripped down The Country Wife to relieve it of the
encumbrances of affectation and produced an ordered yet
macabre reality which reminded the audience of the
"grasping fingers behind the fans, the death's heads
beneath the powdered wigs,"[2] yet so civilized was the
presentation of this terrific reality that Ted
Whitehead was unsettled by a conception of the play

which was "too tidy, too orderly to convey the dizzy amorality of the Restoration world."[3]

John Bury, who designed the sets and costumes, came in for as much, if not more, critical censure. Most notably, the central playing area was marked by a tiled floor, a self-conscious location which produced a kind of dramatic stasis by forcing

> all the crucial scenes [to be] played bang in the middle. This may give the action a fearful Blakeian symmetry but it reduces the sprawling life of drama to the ordered formality of a landscape garden.[4]

This anchoring of the action created hygienic, clean-lined orderliness in the staging and resulted in the failure to suggest any hint of disorder in the society.

Bury's design incorporated--as the program illustration showed--some key features from Wren's Drury Lane, where The Country Wife premiered, onto the stage of the Olivier. The main additions were the side doors, the forestage and an upstairs window, which doubled as a musician's gallery and part of the set. But the tribute to Wren became a liability in performance:

> The side doors, for instance, are situated at oblique angles in the central wall so that entrances have to describe a long looping curve to approach centre stage. As for the forestage, it may be true that Restoration acting had not yet taken shelter behind the fourth wall, but I doubt whether Wycherley's own actors tripped so often downstage to confide in the audience, stranding the rest of the company in paralysed smirks and bringing the action to a standstill.[5]

Albert Finney's Horner came in for disappointed consideration. The character was seen as a "Restoration reincarnation of Volpone, a trickster and lecher whose sacred mission is to show up other people's trickery and lechery."[6] On the credit side, Finney's performance offered "prurient eye rolling and limbs weary with lust." More important, he did not "shrink from the nastiness of a man who confesses he hates women wanting only to 'laugh at 'em and use 'em ill.'"[7] Alas, he did not round out the character. Robert Cushman applauded his vigor but found that he generalized, "missing both Horner's misanthropy and his implicit discomfiture: he neither judges nor is judged."[8] Thus Horner was a lame conqueror, negligently leading the lascivious ladies in their dance of duplicity.

Two other special performances were the Pinchwife of Richard Johnson and the Sparkish of Ben Kingsley. Anne Morley-Priestman saw that these two actors gave the "obverse and reverse" of a clearly dated coin. Their currency was "certainly not a fake but might well be an authorised replica rather than an original."[9] In this production, Pinchwife was considered the play's crucial character, a "first cousin of some of the self-tortured, doubt-riddled heroes of the plays of Molière."[10] While Johnson succeeded in avoiding a stereotypical performance, Kingsley won points for his portrait of a fop "bubbling with piglike snorts of laughter at his own jokes and nervous balletic lunges, working away on his coldly contemptuous companions like a desperate driver cranking a frozen engine."[11]

Hall's production gave a nod to the contemporary scene and the sophisticated audience: "Permissiveness has so far advanced to-day that we may regard it [the play] as pleasant without necessarily being instructive."[12] The production opportunities were sometimes, as in the case of Susan Littler's Margery, taken with gusto and sometimes, as in the case of Finney's surprisingly subdued Horner, sadly missed.

VI. Shadwell

Of the eighteen plays by the commercially if not always critically acceptable playwright Thomas Shadwell, Epsom Wells (1672) is not the best, but it combines interestingly elements more strategically employed by the major playwrights. Shadwell effectively pictures the bourgeoisie and, like Farquhar after him, frequently places his scenes in the country. In Epsom Wells he justifies the sophistication of the major figures by making them Londoners on holiday at a watering place. The difficulty that Shadwell faced was that although he drew his influence from Ben Jonson, he could not produce a specific comedy of humors, and, though he admired Etherege and made use of the social hierarchy by having the higher orders poke fun at the lower classes, he could not afford the luxury of writing for the closed circle of wits and gallants who accepted The Man of Mode. For a twentieth-century audience his particular approach to the comedy of manners needed considerable reworking to make it acceptable.

EPSOM WELLS
Plot Summary

I. At the Wells, Raines and Bevil agree that they take the waters only to prepare themselves for more wild and wooly living. Bevil receives a note from Mrs. Woodly inviting him to her house for the day. Carolina and Lucia enter, and threatened by Cuff and Kick, they successfully appeal to Raines and Bevil for help. Bisket comes to invite Raines to play at cards with Mrs. Bisket. Woodly despises Bisket as a cuckold not knowing that his wife is obliging him in the same vein. A letter comes challenging Raines and Bevil to a duel, and since they may both lose their lives, they are off to their pleasures with gusto.

II. Justice Clodpate presses his suit to Lucia, but when he finds that she hates the country as much as he loves it, he withdraws. Lucia, determined to play a trick on Carolina, paints her as a woman whose aversion to London equals Clodpate's.

Bevil visits Mrs. Woodly, but the return of her mate forces him to hide and, fearing that dodging Woodly may force him to miss the duel, Bevil eventually rushes out. The jealous Mrs. Woodly sends Peg, the maid, to follow and report.

In the field waiting for their opponents, the men encounter only Carolina and Lucia who eventually admit that they themselves sent the challenge.

III. Peg reports to Mrs. Woodly that Bevil met Carolina, and Mrs. Woodly sends a note in Carolina's name to test him. Mrs. Jilt, who suffers under the happy affliction of believing that all men are in love with her, visits Mrs. Woodly. Among a great bundle of Jilt's letters is a rude one from Bevil which indicates a previous intimacy, and the unhappy Mrs. Woodly realizes that Bevil has been juggling two affairs. Peg returns to report that Bevil received the note joyfully, and Mrs. Woodly rushes out. Left alone, Mrs. Jilt and Peg are revealed as sisters. The former is pretending to a higher station and is fixing her sights on Clodpate. When he appears, she does a wonderful anti-London lecture, and Clodpate is a lost man. Bevil comes to meet Carolina and drops the letter. When Mrs. Woodly appears disguised, he takes her for Carolina until she reveals herself. But Woodly has found the note and followed. Because she is masked, Bevil manages to keep her secret.

IV. Bevil pursues Carolina, and both Woodly and Mrs. Woodly hide and listen to their conversation. Bevil admits that Mrs. Woodly pursues him, so Carolina must tell on Woodly. In order to get rid of Clodpate,

Lucia dreams up the tale that Carolina's brother has come to take her to London to force her into a marriage. She will be staying at a house near the church until she leaves. If Clodpate will wait for her in the churchyard at night, she will come to him.

V. Cuff and Kick have robbed Clodpate, bound him and tied him up in a sheet to look like a ghost. Woodly meets Raines and offers to duel with Bevil. Fribble and Bisket get drunk and Cuff and Kick take them away to sleep it off, offering themselves to the wives as escorts. Clodpate enters in his sheet to the general terror of all until his servant releases him and reveals that Carolina was in on the churchyard plot. In revenge, Clodpate tells Peg that he wants to marry Jilt. Fribble and Bisket search for their wives and find them in bed in compromising situations with Cuff and Kick.

Raines and Bevil are pressing marriage to their girls when Clodpate--just married--finds that Jilt is Peg's sister, a thorough London woman and a complete liar. Peg offers to unmarry them, for a fee. When Bisket and Fribble bring in the four offenders, Clodpate is more than ready to exercise his authority as a justice. But the wives beg for mercy and the husbands are compliant. Woodly and Mrs. Woodly agree to divorce; Peg reveals that Clodpate's marriage was a sham and Raines and Bevil are put on trial as prospective wooers.

Background

Epsom Wells was produced at Dorset Garden on 2 December 1672. The cast included: Harris as Rains, Betterton as Bevil, Smith as Woodly, Underhill as Clodpate, Nokes as Bisket, Angel as Fribble, Mrs. Johnson as Carolina, Mrs. Gibbs as Lucia and Mrs. Betterton as Mrs. Jilt. Downes reports that the play "in general being Admirably Acted, produc'd great Profit to the Company."

Cibber has immortalized Cave Underhill whose comic importance was established, in part, by the judicious use of his physical equipment:

> Underhill was a correct, and natural Comedian, his particular Excellence was in Characters, that may be called Still-life, I mean the stiff, the heavy, and the stupid; to these he gave the exactest, and most expressive Colours, and in some of them, look'd as if it were not in the Power of human Passions to alter a Feature of him. . . . A Countenance of Wood could not be more fixt than his, when the Blockhead of a Character required it: His Face was full and long; from his Crown to the end of his Nose, was the shorter half of it, so that the Disproportion of his lower Features, when soberly compos'd, with an unwandering Eye hanging over them, threw him into the most lumpish Mortal, that ever made Beholders merry! . . . In the course, rustick Humour of Justice Clodpate, in Epsom Wells, he was a delightful Brute!

Underhill excelled in low comedy, and his career, like Shadwell's play, had a vigorous run of some fifty years.

Critical Evaluations

On November 4, 1969, the Thorndike Theatre in Leatherhead, Surrey, opened its three-week run of Shadwell's Epsom Wells, adapted by Joan Macalpine.[1] The cast included Robert Cartland as Clodpate, David Weston as Woodly, Teddy Green as Rains, Simon Ward as Bevil, Barrie Rutter as Kick, Mark Nicholls as Cuff, David Goodhart as Roger, Michael Roberts as Toby, Sonia Graham as Mistress Woodly, Josephine Tewson as Mistress Jilt, Celia Bannerman as Lucia, Patricia Shakesby as Carolina, Henrietta Holmes as Peg, Louise Rush as Mab, Liz Moscrop as Mary and Edward Flower as the Musician.

This was the third play presented at this new theatre, which had opened on the 18th of September.[2] It was directed by Anthony Wiles and designed by Sidney Jarvis. The costumes were by Julia Foyle and the musical arrangements by Martin Best.

Miss Macalpine's simplification of the piece included rearranging the dialogue by replacing conversation among several characters by a series of exchanges between pairs. Songs were added, some of them indicating the close of an act and others accompanying the changing of the scenery. Basic plot information was retained, while the dialogue was pruned. Two added characters, Mab and Mary, did much of the singing. An added prop, Bevil's watch, marked the passage of time as he consulted it at crucial moments during his intrigues. The mercantile cuckolds, Bisket and Fribble, were cut completely from the text, as were the scenes in which they appear.

In the general melee which involves Rains, Bevil, Woodly and some ruffians, the girls, Carolina and Lucia, did not take flight, as the Shadwell text indicates, but joined in the scuffle. Great use was made of trees for hiding, and several pages of stage directions were devoted to Clodpate's churchyard scene.

Despite the tightening of the text, the production was not a triumph. Eric Shorter complained that "it bore a superficial resemblance to Restoration comedy," but much of the acting came across "too coyly and self-consciously."[3] Although it was recognized that part of the reason for the selection was due to the geographical proximity of Epsom to Leatherhead, the pleasure of recognition of local references was not considered sufficient motive to mount the production. Although Irving Wardle criticized Shadwell's general dearth of wit, he appreciated the Clodpate of Robert Cartland, "whose characteristic approach is to discharge his flintlock into the flies and offer the severed carcass to the lady of his choice." Cartland, "confidently extending his hand to catch the prize and always missing it," created one of the evening's more diverting figures.[4] And Celia Bannerman's Lucia managed to combine grace with playfulness.

In the Thorndike Theatre production the play was adapted by excising class jokes in favor of a brisk plot and clever conversation. Unfortunately, once the framework of the jokes, the social order, was removed, the humor lost most of its point and much of its fun. Despite added characters, songs and considerable stage business, the play could not work with an audience which was more likely to identify with the middle class than to sneer at it.

VII. Ravenscroft

Edward Ravenscroft, a lawyer turned poet and playwright, flourished principally because of his agility at borrowing from the continental playwrights. His early plays leaned heavily on Molière and stressed physical bustle over characterization. His considerable ability in the hurly-burly of farce made it unlikely that he would be treated as anything more than a lightweight dramatist, but the single revival of his work proved him to have sufficient substance to withstand critical and audience scrutiny after a stage silence of two centuries.

THE LONDON CUCKOLDS
Plot Summary

I. Alderman Wiseacre (near fifty) is marrying a fourteen-year-old girl whom he has bred from an infant to be as uninformed in terms of the world as possible. His friend Dashwell warns him against this course and praises his own wife whom he believes to be a godly woman.

Ramble is pursuing a new mistress, but Townly reminds him that his intrigues have always been doomed. Ramble receives a note from Eugenia, Dashwell's wife. And Arabella, Alderman Doodle's wife, sends her maid with instructions for Ramble. Townly identifies the tablets Engine carries. The woman to whom he gave them is the one woman in the world he most fancies, for it is her wit that he admires. Townly offers to go in Ramble's place to visit this lady, but Ramble wants two strings to his bow.

II. Loveday comes to Dashwell's house seeking employment. Alone, he rhapsodizes on Eugenia. Eugenia is entertaining Ramble, and when they are interrupted by the return of Dashwell and Doodle, Loveday saves Eugenia's situation. The thwarted Ramble now looks for Doodle's house where he impresses Peggy, the bride-to-be. Wiseacre returns to warn Peggy that in London, "They get young folks and bake 'em in pies." Mistaking Townly for Ramble, Eugenia's maid calls him to return to the house.

III. Arabella tries to get rid of Ramble but he is determined. Suddenly Doodle appears; Ramble is trapped and Engine must take him into her bed for the night. When the women are set to change places, Roger, Ramble's servant, cries "Fire!" from outside. Ramble is less than grateful for the diversion. Engine tries to get Ramble back in through the cellar window, but he gets stuck and is tormented by various passersby. When his cries finally raise the watch, he is taken for a thief.

IV. Loveday reveals himself to Eugenia as her beloved of seven years ago. When they hear noise, Loveday retreats under the covers of the maid's bed and Ramble enters seeking delight. While Eugenia is putting him off, Dashwell returns. To save himself, Ramble pretends to be looking for someone in the room and discovers Loveday.

Wiseacre catechizes Peggy on love and duty then tells her to guard his nightcap through the night with armor and lance. Doodle, showing off himself, tells Arabella to answer any questions from impertinent men with "No."

V. Arabella meets Townly and uses her "No's" to advantage. Ramble comes in to rescue Peggy from the fire and offers to instruct her in her lesson before her husband returns.

Eugenia tells her husband that Loveday has made overtures to her. She asks Dashwell to impersonate her and meet him in the garden. When Ramble tries to exit quietly by dropping from the balcony, he drops upon Doodle. Peggy turns the knife by assuring Wiseacre that the duty she learned was "ten times better duty than that you taught me."

Dashwell, disguised as Eugenia, is whipped by Loveday in the garden. Peggy identifies Ramble while Dashwell recognizes his wife's former secretary in Loveday. Ramble hopes for another chance with Peggy; Eugenia and Arabella are triumphant and their husbands have to laugh, ruefully, at their situation.

Background

The London Cuckolds was produced at the Duke's Theatre in November of 1681. The cast included: James Nokes as Doodle, John Richards as Roger and Tom, John Wiltshire as Loveday, Mrs. Norris as the Aunt, Elizabeth Currer as Eugenia, Mrs. Petty as Peggy and Mrs. Osborne as Jane.

James Nokes had created many characters in the popular comedies of the day, and he had a particularly strong line in foolish husbands and silly old men, not to mention the occasional foolish old woman. John Richards had perfected the roles of footmen and valets, which accounts for his double casting. Elizabeth Currer, a popular member of the Duke's Company, is said to have had both beauty and spirit, appropriate qualities for Eugenia. A very young actress when she joined Dorset Garden in 1676, Mrs. Petty would have been well in line for the role of Peggy in 1681.

Cibber had very little use for the play which, he felt, did nothing to lessen the growing licentiousness of the stage:

> These Immoralities of the Stage, had, by an avow'd Indulgence, been creeping into it, ever since King Charles his Time; Nothing that was loose, could then be too low for it: The London Cuckolds, the most rank Play that ever succeeded, was then in the highest Court-Favour.

His opinion was shared by "some squeamish females of renown" who, Ravenscroft complained in the prologue to Dame Dobson, made visits to his play "with design to cry it down." But authors usually relish such ladies: the greater the complaint the greater the publicity.

After its first appearance, the comedy enjoyed continuing popularity for seventy years, being revived annually on Lord Mayor's Day. In 1751 Garrick dropped it from the Drury Lane repertoire in response to the decency of his age, but it was still played at Covent Garden until 1758. The last recorded performance was a Covent Garden benefit in 1782 when the piece had been reduced to two acts. In 1938 it was revived by Raymond Raikes, a radio producer, at his father's private theatre in Dulwich, and it was heard on BBC Radio 3 in 1975.

Critical Evaluations

The London Cuckolds broke its long stage silence on 27 February 1979 when it opened at the Royal Court Theatre. The comedy was presented by the English Stage Company under the direction of Stuart Burge with settings by Robin Archer. The cast included: Alan Dobie as Wiseacre, Roger Kemp as Doodle, Barry Stanton as Mr. Dashwell, Deborah Norton as Arabella, Cherith Mellor as Engine, Michael Elphick as Mr. Townly, Kenneth Cranham as Mr. Ramble, Christopher Hancock as Roger, Stephanie Beacham as Eugenia, Susan Porrett as Jane, Brian Protheroe as Loveday, Nina Thomas as Peggy and Ann Dyson as the Aunt.

Besides the historical interest of the revival, the play provided a cheerful look at farce. Though the characters were predominantly stock comic figures and the quality of ensemble acting was missing, the production boasted good individual performances. Particularly impressive were the three wives who cloaked their infidelities under the guises of hypocrisy, cleverness or simplicity. Hypocrisy ensures that under the mantle of religious devotion one can check out potential lovers in a neighbouring pew; cleverness allows that one can outwit even the most rigorous husbandly injunction; and simplicity entitles one to be there for the taking.[1]

The plot centers around Ramble, a would-be seducer with a sad history of failure, as he sets out on a libidinously greedy night of over-booked assignations with the two older wives. Farce prevails as Ramble scurries from the clutches of early-returning husbands. He loses the experienced ladies but wins the innocent Peggy, a Margery Pinchwife manqué. Although each husband is enlightened as to his fate, "the blow is not desperately severe: for each knows that his mates have been similarly foiled. His pride--his most treasured possession--is left intact."[2]

Visual comedy enriched Ramble's attempts to satisfy his sexual starvation. Benedict Nightingale catalogued the humiliations which leave him "stuck in a basement window, doused with a chamber-pot, and robbed by passing chimney sweeps, who complete their entertainment by blackening his face." Ramble's agonies are contrasted with the Horner-like magnetism of Townly, and the result is an erotic truth: "Those who don't try get, and those who try too hard don't get."[3]

As Michael Billington pointed out, Ravenscroft skillfully employed many of the "stock ingredients of farce,"[4] but Nightingale felt compelled to defend him against critical charges that on the contemporary British scene he would have been turning out television situation comedies or lowbrow farces. The deeper truth was that he showed a "scorn for male pride" and displayed a "pleasure in the female libido" that could not be discovered in the comic froth of the twentieth century.[5]

The only puzzlement was that the English Stage Company claimed a policy of discovering and promoting new talent. How then did Ravenscroft fit in? Nightingale eased into his review with a whimsical answer: "It is always nice to discover a bold new talent, even if that talent is three centuries old."

VIII. Otway

In his autobiographical military comedy, The Soldier's Fortune (1681), Otway deals with the remnants of a disbanded army. This play has not the zest for life shown later by Farquhar in The Recruiting Officer (1706), but its bitter realization of man's position in the social machine and its literary and dramatic burlesques made it the logical if not overwhelmingly successful subject of two revivals.

Otway's literary prestige is based more firmly on his two successful tragedies, The Orphan and Venice Preserved. The former, an extreme study in pathos, is low on the list of potential revivals. By contrast, Venice Preserved (1682) has, besides the pathos, the sensationalism of the Antonio-Aquilina scenes and the political aspect of the plot against the corrupt Venetian senate. Both of these elements had contemporary parallels for a late seventeenth-century audience: the lecherous senator Antonio was a thinly disguised portrait of the Earl of Shaftesbury and the intense plotting called up the machinations in the court during the final years of Charles II.

The great attraction of the first production of Venice Preserved for the twentieth-century London audience was in the quality of the performances, which never lost sight of the powerful emotional appeal of the play. In the second attempt, this appeal was lessened by emphasizing the hopeless situation of the conspirators and by an imbalance in the companion roles of Pierre and Jaffeir.

THE SOLDIER'S FORTUNE
Plot Summary

I.   Beaugard and Courtine, two soldiers returning from the war, rail against their declining fortune. Sir Jolly Jumble, a pander, meets the soldiers and discourses about a lady enamored of Beaugard. Lady Dunce tells Sylvia of her love for Beaugard, whose departure into France had forced her into this hateful marriage with an old husband. Now Lady Dunce has an elaborate scheme to make Sir Davy the unwitting go-between in her affair.

II. Sir Davy is delighted that his young wife has reported Beaugard's advances. He tells Beaugard of Lady Dunce's revelation and protests that she scorns her would-be lover. Courtine has proposed to Sylvia, who, for the moment, rejects him. But when Sylvia leaves, Courtine admits that he is still in love.

Under the auspices of Sir Jolly, Lady Dunce meets Beaugard and reveals herself as the girl he had once been in love with and mentions a ring which her husband was to have delivered to him. When Sir Davy, who had forgotten the ring, reappears and offers it to Beaugard, the penitent lover sends a promise to keep the token as long as he lives.

III. Sylvia and Courtine meet again, and she tells him to be under her window between eleven and twelve midnight. Lady Dunce brings Sir Davy a letter supposedly thrown into her chair and begs him to return it. Sir Davy returns the letter which Beaugard sees is an invitation from Lady Dunce. As the pleasures of the evening are about to begin for the twosome, Sir Davy springs out of the closet. Lady Dunce offers Beaugard's sword to her husband to dispatch her, bemoaning the fact that her "fatal beauty" has been her undoing.

IV. In a tavern, Sir Davy plots with Fourbin and Bloody Bones to murder Beaugard. Beaugard and Sir Jolly learn that the murder has been planned while Courtine keeps his appointment with Sylvia.

At Sir Davy's house, Sir Jolly and Lady Dunce arrange Beaugard to look like a corpse. When Sir Davy arrives, Lady Dunce tells him that since the murder was done at his command, the corpse was delivered to the house. Sir Davy immediately repents of his rashness, and Sir Jolly suggests that life might be renewed by putting the corpse in a warm bed. Sir Davy pleads with his wife to do all that is necessary to revive the deceased while he goes to his closet to pray.

V. At Sylvia's, Courtine wakes from a drunken snooze to find himself bound to a couch in Sylvia's chamber. She teases him by admitting a love for Beaugard and he counters that he loves Lady Dunce, but they finally strike a bargain and agree to be married.

Meanwhile, back at the Dunces' Sir Davy is terrified by visions of the devil while Beaugard adds to his woes by rising up like a ghost. When Sir Jolly offers to remove the body to his house and suggests that he take Lady Dunce with him, Sir Davy is all compliance. However, once they are gone, Sir Davy calls the constable, tells him of a murder next door and points out Sir Jolly's house.

At Sir Jolly's, the loving couple are enjoying a banquet when the constable and the watch come to search the house, but when Beaugard is discovered with Lady Dunce, the watch clears off. Sylvia and Courtine come to announce that they are to be married, and Sir Davy at last realizes that he has been bested by Beaugard.

Background

The Soldier's Fortune was produced at the Duke's Playhouse in Dorset Garden early in March 1680. The King saw the play on 1 March and possibly this was the original performance. In April of 1681 and November of 1682 the King again saw the play. The cast included Betterton as Captain Beaugard, Smith as Courtine, Nokes as Sir Davy Dunce, Leigh as Sir Jolly Jumble, Jevon as

Fourbin, Richards as Bloodybones, Mrs. Barry as Lady Dunce and Mrs. Price as Sylvia.

The Soldier's Fortune was inspired by Otway's experiences as a soldier with the British forces stationed in Holland. Disappointment in his love for Mrs. Barry, who inclined toward men like Rochester, and losing bouts with drink seem to have pushed him into this venture in the service. He returned from Holland with a flourish: producing his two great tragedies (The Orphan and Venice Preserved), this comedy, and fighting a duel with Churchill--before he became Duke of Marlborough.

Downes reports that The Soldier's Fortune, along with The Fond Husband by Durfey, "took extraordinary well, and being perfectly Acted; got the Company great Reputation and Profit."

Cibber vividly describes the comic effect of Nokes, who originated Sir Davy Dunce:

He scarce ever made his first Entrance in a Play, but he was received with an involuntary Applause, not of Hands only . . . but by a General Laughter . . . yet the louder the Laugh, the graver was his Look upon it; and sure, the ridiculous Solemnity of his Features were enough to have set a whole Bench of Bishops into a Titter. . . . When he debated any matter by himself, he would shut up his Mouth with a dumb studious Powt, and roll his full Eye, into such a vacant Amazement, such a palpable Ignorance of what to think of it, that his silent Perplexity (which would sometimes hold him several Minutes) gave your Imagination as full Content, as the most absurd thing he could say upon it.

If Nokes was a powerful comic force as Sir Davy, he could produce a double-barreled effect when coupled with the Sir Jolly Jumble of Leigh:

In Sir Jolly he [Leigh] was all Life, and laughing Humour; and when Nokes acted with him in the same Play, they return'd the Ball so dexterously upon one another, that every Scene between them, seem'd but one continued Rest [returning a tennis ball from player to player] of Excellence.

An interesting figure of lighter weight is Thomas Jevon, who created the role of Fourbin in The Soldier's Fortune. He was a slight man, and tradition has it that he had originally been a dancing master as there are contemporary allusions to his grace and agility. In pantomime, he became the first English harlequin and created a large number of roles in successful plays.

The Soldier's Fortune held the stage for about fifty years, until 1748 when it was reduced to an afterpiece of a couple of acts at Covent Garden.

Critical Evaluations

The Soldier's Fortune (1964)

On July 20, 1964, Prospect Productions presented a revival of Otway's The Soldier's Fortune at the Oxford Playhouse. The production was directed by Toby Robertson and the cast included William Holmes as Sir Davy Dunce, Neil Stacy as Sir Jolly Jumble and Amanda Grinling as Sylvia. The critic for the Times noted the significant fact that in many Restoration comedies "the audience are turned into peeping toms, indulged with immoral fancies, only to be given the jolting corrective of a happy and moral ending."[1] The difference here was that Sir Davy Dunce—played by William Holmes as a "voluble stately slobberer"—is cuckolded and must make the best of it; so that the play, "instead of a sanctimonious shrug, departs with a knowing grin." The playing was dominated by Sir Davy and the Sir Jolly Jumble of Neil Stacy, "a creeping Pandar of great vocal and facial energy."

Toby Robertson's direction caught and kept the play's "mixed tone of flippancy, formality and lightly cultivated seriousness."[2] The only difficulty was that the broadly mannered acting inclined toward farce in what might have been a misguided but understandable attempt to supply the play with comic energy.

The Soldier's Fortune (1967)

After the death of George Devine and the appointment of William Gaskill as director of the English Stage Company, a new repertory policy evolved which stressed premieres of new plays, revivals of contemporary plays for a second airing and the mounting of neglected classics. One of these classics was The Soldier's Fortune (last seen in the West End in 1935 in a carefully edited production directed by Baliol Holloway) which opened at the Royal Court Theatre on January 12, 1967.[1] Peter Gill directed the Royal Court production. The cast included Maurice Röeves as Beaugard, Charles Thomas as Courtine, Roger Foss as Fourbin, Wallas Eaton as Sir Jolly Jumble, Sheila Hancock as Lady Dunce, Elizabeth Bell as Sylvia and Bernard Gallagher as Bloodybones.

The chief problem, one of pacing, resulted in a performance of extraordinary slowness. Philip Hope-Wallace attributed his discovery that there were "nine dozers in the circle . . . not critics either" to the fact that the play seemed both tedious and clumsy.[2] Alan Brien was moved to near violence: "there were many times when, . . . I would have been tempted to carve my way through somnolent spectators to the exit."[3]

Nevertheless, for those who survived the tedium, the play had an essential worth that was still viable. Although misanthropy was too much in evidence--"Otway's heavy, clumsy, rancorous malice-towards-all . . . stems from deep personal feelings which burst disturbingly through the artificial dialogue and the traditional intrigue"[4]--the critics found in Otway a writer of prose who could rival his contemporaries. Harold Hobson saw that the ridicule of Beaugard and Courtine for cheated husbands "is put into speeches which, in their exquisite balance and sense of humorous abuse," gave real Restoration flavor.[5] Ronald Bryden compared this "looser, messier" comedy "full of derivative echoes and parodies," with Venice Preserved and dubbed the lesser play a "joyous, harsh young comedy with twice the vitality" of the more famous tragedy.[6]

Once the critics were assured of the merit of the play, attention was turned to the character of the peacetime soldier whose fortune could now be made only in bed. There was an almost Brechtian slant to the redcoats, who were played as shabby fellows devoid of style of any kind and who despite their bold speeches were really sad creatures. Although they were never intended as sympathetic characters, their situation was a comment on the very society against which they railed. As exiles from their occupation, they lived off the territory "like guerrillas in a conquered province," protected from censure by "the Jonsonian assumption that such is the soldiering-animal's nature, that it cannot be otherwise."[7]

Beaugard emerged as a dramatically idealized self-portrait, living for his creator a dream of wish fulfillment in Otway's hopeless infatuation with Mrs. Barry: "It is notable that Beaugard never achieves his Lady Dunce, but is granted unrestricted admission to her through blackmailing her husband."[8]

Since the audience did not yearn for the consolation of the romantically disappointed Otway, the soldier held a less significant place with the public than did the older figures. Consequently, the triumph of the evening was shared between the Sir Jolly Jumble of Wallas Eaton and the Sir Davy Dunce of Arthur Lowe. Sir Jolly, the grotesque, bisexual voyeur-pander, is a character who once again shows Otway, as did Antonio in Venice Preserved, "as a master caricaturist of the frailties of senility."[9] Paradoxically, he became the most sympathetic character in the play. The scene in which he makes a third at table, "beaming over the adulterers' nuptial breakfast," vindicated him as he looked on "with an adoration which dissolves prurience in innocent worship of their youth and the use they make of it."[10]

Arthur Lowe saved Sir Davy from the standard fate of the stage cuckold by a memorable visual performance as he "sinks his dewlaps into his periwig like an outraged frog, sliding wonderful reptilian stares over his household and its invader."[11] Lowe managed to give comic weight to the most insignificant line and balanced the characterization by evoking pity and humor at Sir Davy's fall: "at the end, where he is humiliated beyond all permissible bounds, his pathos is all the deeper for being expressed in comic terms."[12] At its best, it was considered the most ingenious Restoration performance since Cyril Ritchard's Lord Foppington nineteen years earlier.

His partner, Lady Dunce, was played by Sheila Hancock who made the most of her lines of parody and managed melodramatic bathos in one splendid scene: "[She] is surprised by her husband in bed with Beaugard and makes much play with his discarded sword in a style that sometimes verges, but never unsuitably, on the manner of the Victorian melodrama."[13] This Lady Dunce, "snapping at men as if they were cocktail sausages," may not have approached the character in the manner of a Mrs. Barry, but in her mock-heroic parody of Macbeth, Hancock exhibited a grand desperation worthy of a comic Mrs. Siddons.

Another excellence of the company showed in the handling of the more scholarly references in the language of the play which offered "mock-diatribes which overtly parody Marlowe, Shakespeare and the Jacobeans ('But who hath the rugged Bankside bear . . .')."[14]

Despite the sluggish pace and the fact that the supporting players were not well received, the production had, principally because of the invention of the more seasoned members, a real measure of success.

VENICE PRESERVED; or, A PLOT DISCOVERED
Plot Summary

I. Jaffeir has married Belvidera, the daughter of Senator Priuli, without her father's consent. Consequently, the old man refuses to aid the impoverished couple. Jaffeir's friend, Pierre, also has an enemy in Senator Antonio, a wretched old man who has taken away Pierre's love, the courtesan Aquilina. Pierre tells Jaffeir that Belvidera has been evicted from their home and that Priuli himself signed the order. This outrage convinces Jaffeir to fall in with Pierre's plot against Venice and its corrupt government.

II. When Pierre meets Aquilina, she curses old Antonio but refuses to break with him because she needs him. The friends meet the other conspirators at Aquilina's house and repeat their vow to overthrow the senate, which has acted against the interests of the state. To solidify his position, Jaffeir has Belvidera brought in, gives her into the keeping of another conspirator, Renault, and offers a dagger as a pledge that her life is the price of his honor.

III. Aquilina and Antonio are shown together, and when the old man's attempts at love become too noisome, she dismisses him. Reunited with Belvidera, Jaffeir rashly exposes the plot, which will include the death of her father. Not surprisingly, her sense of honor is activated and she objects to the plan. To give weight to her argument, she reveals that Renault has attempted to force his attentions on her. Now Jaffeir cannot remain in the same room with Renault and leaves the conspirators' meeting in disgust. Capitalizing on his

126

revulsion, Belvidera leads him to the senate emphasizing the terrible distress of the city if the revolt is effected.

IV. At the meeting of the senators, which includes Priuli and Antonio, Jaffeir agrees to reveal the conspiracy in return for pardon for himself and his fellow conspirators. The senate pretends to comply, but once Jaffeir has spoken, the entire group of plotters is arrested immediately. All the conspirators choose death, assuming it will be honorable. Pierre strikes the pardoned Jaffeir publicly and returns the dagger. Jaffeir, torn in the traditional love-and-honor pose, attempts to stab Belvidera; for Pierre has repudiated him and the senate has decreed death by torture for the conspirators. But his love overcomes him and he sheathes the dagger.

V. Belvidera pleads for the conspirators while Aquilina begs Antonio for Pierre's life. On the scaffold the two men are reconciled, and Pierre begs Jaffeir to stab him and save him from dishonorable death. Jaffeir complies and caps that performance with his suicide. Belvidera, seeing the ghosts of Pierre and Jaffeir, goes mad (traditionally in white satin) and dies. Too late Priuli realizes the extent of his losses.

Background

Venice Preserved was produced at Dorset Garden 9 February 1681/2. The cast included Betterton as Jaffeir, Smith as Pierre, Mrs. Barry as Belvidera, Mrs. Currer as Aquilina, Leigh as Antonio, Gillow as Bedmar, Bowman as Priuli, Wiltshire as Renault, Percival as Spinosa and Williams as the Duke of Venice.

In 1680 The Orphan had been produced with Mrs. Barry, the object of Otway's unreciprocated affections, in the title role, and the play had been hailed as a masterpiece. But Venice Preserved, in which he created the role of Belvidera for Mrs. Barry, was reckoned his supreme achievement. Downes in Roscius Anglicanus cites Belvidera, Monimia in The Orphan and Isabella in The Fatal Marriage as the three roles which

> gain'd her the Name of Famous Mrs. Barry, both at Court and City; for when ever She Acted any of those three Parts, she forc'd Tears from the Eyes of her Auditory, especially those who have any Sense of Pity for the Distress't.

> These 3 Plays, by their Excellent performances, took above all the Modern Plays that succeeded.

The Popish Plot had been exposed in 1678, and in 1681, the Earl of Shaftesbury, the leader of the Whigs, had been imprisoned. Dryden had already immortalized him in Absalom and Achitophel, and it is generally believed that the characters of the lecherous conspirator Renault and the lascivious Senator Antonio offer a composite picture of this less than estimable figure. This approach gave the play added spice in the form of powerful satire.

The drama belongs to the tradition of the love and honor tragedy. In this case, the love is twofold: the marital bond between Jaffeir and Belvidera and the love of friendship that unites Jaffeir with Pierre.

There are no contemporary details of the original cast in performance, but Aline Taylor in Next to Shakespeare suggests that Betterton as Jaffeir would have "emphasized the intellectual qualities in Jaffeir and infused a masculine vigor into an otherwise overlush character."[1] And Cibber's description of the actor gives an idea of the appearance of his Jaffeir:

> The Person of this excellent Actor was suitable to his Voice, more manly than sweet, not exceeding the middle stature . . . his Limbs nearer the

athletick, than the delicate Proportion; yet however form'd, there arose from the Harmony of the whole a commanding Mien of Majesty, which the fairer-fac'd . . . ever wanted something to be equal Masters of.

In Anthony Leigh's Antonio there would have been a performance from a master of the comic tightrope. Cibber says that, "In Humour, he love'd to take a full Career, but was careful enough to stop short, when just upon the Precipice." And he had enough variety to excel as Sir Jolly Jumble, Scapin and Pandarus. When Leigh died in 1691, mastery of the character of Antonio went with him. Antonio remained in the play until about 1750 when the role was excised.

Wilks played Jaffeir to Verbruggen's Pierre at the Haymarket, but the play seemed to lose its appeal after the death of Charles II. It returned in the eighteenth century with a dramatic vengeance. In 1721 it was acted at Lincoln's Inn Fields with Lacy Ryan as Jaffeir. In 1748 David Garrick made his first appearance as Jaffeir. He had already played Pierre in 1742, but his success in the Jaffeir role was inseparably linked to the Belvidera of Mrs. Cibber. In 1782 Mrs. Siddons displayed her genius in the role of Belvidera, and, despite the alterations of time, she played it until 1812. In 1786 she played Belvidera to the Jaffeir of her brother, John Kemble, and the popularity of the two made the play a great favorite. In 1805 John Kemble took over Pierre and left Jaffeir free for his brother, Charles, and the preservation of Venice continued to do a booming business. In 1820 Edmund Kean appeared as Jaffeir, but his naturalism was not congenial to the role. But in the late 1820s Fanny Kemble, daughter of Charles, helped keep Belvidera going.

The play had substantial revivals in the nineteenth century, but audiences were less and less inclined to accept the play. A 1920 revival by the Phoenix Society at the Lyric Theatre with Baliol Holloway as Pierre, Cathleen Nesbit as Belvidera and Edith Evans as Aquilina reaffirmed the difficulty of playing the tragedy naturalistically.

Critical Evaluations

Venice Preserved (1953)

John Gielgud's season for Tennant Productions at the Lyric Theatre opened on the 24th December 1952 with Paul Scofield in the title role of Richard II. In February, Congreve's The Way of the World followed. 1953 was Coronation Year, and, on May 6, Tyrone Guthrie presented Shakespeare's Henry VIII at the Old Vic in a gala performance before the Queen and the Duke of Edinburgh. On May 15, 1953, the Lyric quartet of John Gielgud, Pamela Brown, Paul Scofield and Eileen Herlie appeared in the coronation revival of Otway's Venice Preserved. Gielgud played Jaffeir, Scofield was Pierre, Herlie was Belvidera and Brown played Aquilina. In the supporting cast, Richard Wordsworth was Antonio, Eric Porter played Renault, Herbert Lomas was Priuli and Brewster Mason, the Spanish Ambassador. Peter Brook directed the production and Leslie Hurry designed the settings. The play had been neglected for thirty-three years, but Gielgud's leaning towards the classics and the grand occasion of that year lent themselves to this adventurous revival of a Restoration tragedy.

The theatre was also a singularly effective setting. In London's architectural context, the Lyric Theatre was one

of the best examples of the fin-de-siècle theatre interior in Greater London—one designed by a master of the art of theatre building. Matcham, who was responsible for the Coliseum, the Palladium, the Hippodrome, the old Metropolitan and a number of other famous theatres in London and the provinces was perhaps the most successful and experienced theatre designer of his time. If the Coliseum is his masterpiece the Lyric Opera House could well claim to be the most endearing of his works.[1]

The interior offered a perfect performing situation:

> It has superb sight-lines, a unique intimacy, an orchestra pit of exceptional size for so small a theatre, and excellent acoustics; any inaudibility being entirely due to the defective technique of the actors concerned. The existence of an apron seems to help this quite extraordinary feeling of intimacy and it can be used in many ways to break down that "Fourth Wall." In all it does have . . . the essential qualities of an ideal playhouse and . . . no actor has ever failed to acknowledge the pleasure of performing there.[2]

For John Gielgud, the revival of <u>Venice Preserved</u> was significant in three ways. His success as Jaffeir disproved a remark about the limitations imposed on his performance by the cerebral quality of his interpretations:

> Mr. Gielgud cannot make convincing love, and he lacks dash. . . . Flatness, indeed, a Chekhovian flabbiness of spirit and body, characterises all his productions, the best no less than the worst. His supreme need is for an increase of flesh and blood as well as mind and spirit.[3]

Secondly, during the run of that play he gained his knighthood. Finally, he successfully produced a drama long regarded as a museum piece.

Since tragedy of the kind verging on the bathetic suffered from long disuse, the company logically feared misplaced laughter. Overcoming this difficulty was due in great part to the daring efforts of the principals:

> The curtain rises upon the deserted Rialto--one of Leslie Hurry's admirable sets--in a smoky green twilight. Hastening to his momentous rendezvous with the conspirators, Jaffeir enters and passionately whispers "I am here." Well not a titter was heard: Gielgud sold even this staggering piece of bathos without the least difficulty. Presumably he refrained from cutting it quite deliberately, as a little test of his power over us.[4]

Though the Otway play was still considered second-rate by a number of critics, the production was a double success in that it not only brought back a neglected, non-commercial drama--in itself a real achievement--but also brought it back as a first-rate production. Maurice Wiltshire reported the enthusiastic reception:

> The first night cheers were deafening; from the gallery someone called "magnificent." John Gielgud bowed and said he had feared this strange tragedy, written in 1681, was a museum piece; now it was at least a collector's piece.[5]

Otway's use of the vernacular was censured by Ivor Brown:

> Here is a poetical drama largely without poetry. The flow of metaphors and images respects the formula and never deviates into freshness. Swords flash, the words never. Smoothness of rhythm there may be, but not the Shakespearean triumph of mind over metre.

But Brown conceded:

132

Mr. Gielgud takes Otway by the scruff of the neck and forces him at least to be a poet. Under the persuasion of his voice we are carried back from Silver Age to Golden, from the fop-audience of Betterton and Mrs. Barry at Dorset Garden to the Elizabethan connoisseurs of the uncommon touch who sat under Shakespeare and around Burbage at the Globe.[6]

The prime reason for the appeal of the play was the playing of the already successful quartet--Gielgud, Scofield, Brown and Herlie--now worked into ensemble thoroughness. As Belvidera, Eileen Herlie, the Mrs. Marwood of the Congreve offering, found her principal difficulty in the mad scene:

Eileen Herlie has a good shot at it [the mad scene], but tends to force the note and bellow heartrendingly just when a little concentration and a wider gamut of vowel sounds would do the trick better. . . . Miss Herlie wins points in the simpler pathos, however.[7]

It is probable that Herlie's Belvidera, in itself adequate, was less complete when set against the Aquilina of Pamela Brown. A comparison between the two by W. A. Darlington yielded the conclusion that Miss Brown "unleashes greater power with less effort."[8] Miss Brown was referred to variously as "wondrously flamboyant" and a "fine swirling, flaming slut." If the role of Aquilina was arguably unessential except as part of the original satire, then Brown disproved the argument and made the part particularly her own, electrifying the stage during her three appearances.

Richard Wordsworth had a long history of playing aging lechers, a fortunate preparation for the particular depravity of Antonio. His was both a vocal and a visual accomplishment:

He will never play a dirtier [old man] than this slobbering senator--hopping along the floor pretending to be a dog on a lead, demanding to be spat upon and kicked, he positively wallowed in senile depravity.[9]

Brown and Wordsworth were given the scurrilous, frequently omitted Nicky-Nacky scenes to play out in full. These proved sufficiently to the taste of the audience to allow them to appreciate the ribaldry without noticeable qualms. Probably Wordsworth and Brown succeeded more completely as a couple than did Gielgud and Herlie. Brown was playing a role that was congenial to her bold style of attack, and Wordsworth was continuing a line of types well known to him.

The balanced roles of Jaffeir and Pierre still carried equal performance weight in the playing of Gielgud and Scofield. Although the less appealing revolutionary was chosen by the star performer, there was precedent for the choice. Betterton was the original Jaffeir. John Kemble (with his sister, Mrs. Siddons, as Belvidera), and Edmund Kean all played the role. Garrick had experience in both parts. He had begun by playing Pierre, but had fully grasped the difficulties of the other role:

the Part of Jaffeir is a most difficult and laborious character, and will take me up much time, before I have attained what I imagine may be done with it.[10]

Gielgud's leaning toward the more romantic Jaffeir benefited from conscious contrast with Scofield's tougher interpretation, but the audience sympathy remained with Pierre. The critics agreed that Pierre, played by the younger actor who had recently scored in Gielgud's production of Richard II, "sails close to the summit of the most outrageous heroic panache."[11] A comparison between the two roles shows that Scofield, understandably unable to erase totally the memory of the Gielgud Richard, had been able to take complete possession of Pierre:

> This actor came close, at times, to stealing the play's dramatic honours. His Richard II had been a deeply intelligent study, poignant and compelling, though perhaps a little too overlaid by Gielgud's own conception, as former actor and present producer, to mark itself supremely as a great creative interpretation. In Pierre he found a new strength, superb bitterness of tongue, and a virility and fire not surpassed on our stage for some years. This young actor of height and grace not only fitted the part in looks, he sculptured the character to three-dimensional dramatic contours and delved into the sources of spiritual revolt and sense of betrayal. His "Curst be your Senate: Curst your Constitution" sparked lightning; his cannon-shot retort, "Death, honourable death!" at the Duke's "Pardon or death?" had a splendid pride of spirit; and the bitterness of his:
>
> > It will not be the first time I've lodg'd hard
> > To doe your Senate service – –
>
> remains in memory with his gesture of flinging the dagger at Jaffeir. At the end, there was tragic heroism too, and a moving nobility in defeat.[12]

If Gielgud commanded, it was not by the heavier weight of his role but rather by his particular approach. One critic compared his method with that of Laurence Olivier:

> Olivier has an attack and a power to surprise that Gielgud does not command and does not need, since he scores by raising words to a higher power and by portrayal of feeling as the natural basis of

things said and done by a character. His big moments are not startling assaults on the audience: they are always the artist's development of little moments.[13]

His Jaffeir was a Brutus-Hamlet composite, and his interpretation of Shakespeare's prince was still in the critical mind when <u>Venice Preserved</u> was produced. The scene that received the most notice was the final one between the two friends when Jaffeir frees Pierre from the ignominy of torture and himself from the multiple difficulties of his situation. Gielgud's character was well prepared for this moment: "Jaffeir has all the appeal of an impulsive creature whose heroic moments are as ill advised as they are well meant and whose love fatally lacks the power to simulate the cruelty it needs."[14] If his lines were less muscular than Scofield's, he had the tenderness and passion of the text of which he had made himself the instrument:

> It is not Sir John's way thus to subsume the pity and the loveliness of an entire speech in a single carefully chosen phrase. He sees the speech whole, ordered and regular in its music and architecture and he presents it to us . . . in all its unbroken beauty.[15]

The theory was actualized both physically and vocally:

> Gielgud's grief, tenderness and passionate self-laceration were exactly what the part required, together with loftiness of visage to create the illusion of nobility and a voice of such music and range that the verse became an orchestration of sound, pliant with feeling and too genuine in distress to fail to pull at the heart. Dramatically, he could still rise to the level of Pierre and, after the cold douche of his friend's virulent scorn, thrust into the great scene of threatening Belvidera with the dagger without an effect of anti-climax or relaxation of tension.[16]

The particular spell created by <u>Venice Preserved</u> was, for many, unique in playgoing experience, and there were even modern overtones:

Indeed, in these days when underground movements against tyranny have become normal, and the bad faith of tyrants a commonplace, this story of a plot to destroy corrupt government in Venice has almost a modern air.[17]

But this did not dissuade Gielgud from a definite period handling of the text. Under the eye of Peter Brook, a director particularly attuned to the visual, and aided by Leslie Hurry's atmospheric sets, he managed to create some mesmeristic stage pictures:

SIR JOHN GIELGUD . . . as Jaffeir clutched Eileen Herlie as Belvidera to his bosom, raised in his right hand a dagger above their mingled heads, and spouted noble propositions in elevated tones, a living mezzotint. We in the audience sat with bated breath, that we did so was . . . a measure of the actor's greatness. We had in fact abandoned ourselves to a purely theatrical spell unthinkable at any time within the memory of the oldest living theatregoer: <u>Venice Preserv'd</u> brought back the excitement of all that magnified life which, badly done, has for generations been laughed at as "ham."[18]

The formidable style of <u>Venice Preserved</u> was based almost exclusively on the powerful acting, and the company that had partially succeeded in <u>The Way of the World</u> had a full triumph in revitalizing Otway's tragedy.

<u>Venice Preserved</u> (1969)

On February 5, 1969, the Bristol Old Vic Company presented <u>Venice Preserved</u> at the Theatre Royal,

Bristol, for a four-week run. This was the first major revival since the Coronation Year production and it had the advantage of being mounted in the oldest theatre in England with a continuous working history. The cast included Alan Bates as Jaffeir, Antony Webb as Pierre, Ingrid Hafner as Belvidera, Patricia Maynard as Aquilina, Bernard Hepton as Antonio, Richard Kane as Renault and Peter Bland as Priuli. Val May directed and Robin Archer designed.

The major difficulty was the set, an unstable arrangement of "steps, pillars, platforms, chapels, dungeons, all constructed on the dinkiest scale and crowned with a pink-flushed picture postcard of the Doge's palace."[1] Not only did it not enhance the production, the set was also at variance with the formal structure suggested by the very architecture of the Georgian Theatre Royal which housed the company.

The core of the play, as Val May directed it, was the conspiracy, and in the conspiratorial meetings an unexpected shoddiness undercut the greatness of intention:

> A kind of corporate delirium throbs in the lines, in which the various thrusts of spite or personal envy are gathered into great waves of violence and rancour. And yet these furtive, rabid, shabby men, squabbling in a cellar, give off an overwhelming sense of moral squalor. Their actions are pitifully ineffectual, their resolution scarcely less so.[2]

In reviewing the 1953 production, J. W. Lambert had stressed the modernity of the principals, seeing them-- as opposed to their circumstances--as "rather more than counters in a series of strong situations based on Love, Friendship and Honor; though naturally it is (as it always will be) the situations which first carry us away in the theatre."[3] But in emphasizing modernity, the Bristol Old Vic demolished the dramatic structure.

High tragedy gave way to the realistic and the realistic produced the bathetic. Means was substituted for end and violence and lust were synonymous. The fire had burned down to ashes.

The production did manage to establish a link with Otway's lighter plays, for the "bitter honesty" which informs his comedies--and which was so evident in the production of The Soldier's Fortune at the Royal Court two years earlier--"finds its most powerful expression in the moral and intellectual shiftiness of his two agonized protagonists. One finds nowhere else this subtle juxtaposition of the heroic bombast of the period with the bleak, humorous truthfulness character-istic of Restoration comedy."[4]

As Jaffeir, the role made complete by Gielgud, Alan Bates nobly avoided the tendency to "degenerate into a monotonous and maudlin dirge" and maintained a "most judicious balance between Jaffeir's pliancy and the sterner qualities--of timing, pitch, pace and breath control--which make his grand monologues so pleasurably thrilling."[5]

In the conception of Pierre, the excitement generated by the young Paul Scofield in 1953 was subdued in Antony Webb's interpretation by the emphasized link with the squalor of the conspiracy: "Pierre is the only one of the conspirators who betrays an inkling of the seamier sources of their exultation--which he shares with Otway's comic heroes, and which makes him one of the most complex tragic heroes ever penned."[6] Unfortunately, Antony Webb played him as "a trifle thick."

However, in recreating the role of Antonio, which Richard Wordsworth's histrionic lechery had colored so vividly, Bernard Hepton (director of the Birmingham Repertory Company from 1958-1961) rendered a considerable service to this obscene character with a "primness which sits most jauntily . . . on Otway's cruelly contemptuous grotesque."[7]   In the moments with Patricia Maynard's "admirably raucous whore," it was "extraordinary to find this dapper little oddity capering so briskly in scenes of such rank, obscene brutality."[8]

IX. Vanbrugh

Sir John Vanbrugh gained popularity on the late seventeenth-century stage principally by his reworking of contemporary French comedies, but in the twentieth century two of his original efforts received great acclaim. The Relapse (1696) and The Provok'd Wife (1697) fared very well in revivals.

Although The Relapse belongs to the comedies which, like those of Farquhar, stress social problems, it was not the exploration of domestic crises which was responsible for the longevity and popularity of the piece. The public of the twentieth-century revivals were far less interested in the distress of the faithful Amanda trapped between her conscience and the protestations of Worthy than they were in the primping, preening and peacocking of Lord Foppington, the Restoration dandy par excellence, a character with little to say for social reforms of any kind. The Relapse owed its popularity to Foppington who received outstanding interpretations by Cyril Ritchard and Donald Sinden, delighting audiences both in Britain and in America.

The Provok'd Wife is a study in domestic discomfort and shows Vanbrugh less concerned with precision of dialogue and convolutions of plot than with the situations of his characters. In performance, however, the motivation for the other characters relies heavily on clearly defined playing by the actor cast as Sir John Brute. Three revivals of the play, one of them an adaptation, did not yield an interpretation which gave him the significance the play required.

The Confederacy (1705), a translation from Dancourt, had three provincial revivals, but there was never a production which was sufficiently successful to make the transfer comfortably to the competitive West End.

141

THE RELAPSE; or, VIRTUE IN DANGER
Plot Summary

I. In his country house, Loveless, a reformed rake, rejoices in the quiet life while his wife, Amanda, although much in love with him, worries about their coming journey to London.

Young Tom Fashion has come to town to borrow from his elder brother, Lord Foppington. At home, Foppington is dressing up to his newly bought title, and he is so taken with himself that he barely notices Tom's entrance. Coupler, a lascivious old matchmaker, approaches Tom with a proposition no younger brother could refuse: for five thousand pounds, he offers to marry Tom off to Foppington's bride, a wealthy country girl.

II. At Loveless's town house, he tells Amanda of an incident at the playhouse. He saw a character on the stage very like himself "only with the addition of a relapse." Between the acts he had been gazing on a beautiful woman, and only the lesson that the stage was teaching made him shift his gaze from her. When Amanda's relation, Berinthia, appears, Loveless recognizes the lovely lady from the playhouse. Loveless goes off with Worthy, a gentleman of the town, still wrapt in a fog of admiration for Berinthia. Amanda indicates to Berinthia that Worthy has pressed his own claims of love upon her, but that her love for her husband has, thus far, withstood his advances.

III. Foppington is about to go to a play when Tom presents his case for borrowing five hundred pounds. Foppington hems and haws and finally refuses him.

In his garden, Loveless admits his love to Berinthia and follows up the admission with a little demonstration. Worthy spots the two, and, when Loveless is gone, Worthy suggests to Berinthia, now revealed as

142

his former mistress, that they join forces for their respective gratifications.

At the country house of Sir Tunbelly Clumsey, Tom succeeds in passing himself off as Foppington, and Sir Tunbelly releases his cherished daughter, Hoyden.

IV. Well pleased with her groom (with just about any groom), Hoyden looks forward to her life in London.

When Amanda and Berinthia are alone, Berinthia praises Worthy and encourages Amanda's uncertainties about herself and Loveless. Then Berinthia trips to her room, where she finds Loveless hiding, and allows herself to be persuaded into the closet.

At Sir Tunbelly's, Hoyden and Tom have been secretly married by the parson just as the real Foppington, with full entourage, arrives at the gate. Tom takes horse for London. Sir Tunbelly now gives Hoyden to the real Foppington. Quite up to the situation, Hoyden binds the parson and the nurse to secrecy and prepares for her second wedding.

V. Berinthia and Worthy plot to make Amanda jealous so that Worthy can take advantage of her emotional situation.

Amanda returns from spying on Loveless and Worthy takes his opportunity; but, at the final moment, she overcomes her inclination to avenge herself on her husband with Worthy. Worthy, now convinced of her purity, is converted.

In the midst of the second wedding festivities—including a masque—Tom enters and calls the witnesses of his marriage. Foppington must take a philosophical attitude to the loss of his bride "for a philosophical air is the most becoming thing in the warld to the face of a person of quality."

Background

The Relapse was produced at Drury Lane in December 1696. The cast included Cibber as Lord Foppington, Verbruggen as Loveless, Powell as Worthy, Bullock as Sir Tunbelly Clumsey, Mills as Sir John Friendly, Johnson as Coupler, Simson as Bull, Haynes as Serringe, Dogget as Lory, Mrs. (that's right) Kent as Young Fashion, Mrs. Rogers as Amanda, Mrs. Verbruggen as Berinthia, Mrs. Cross as Miss Hoyden and Mrs. Powell as Nurse.

The Relapse was Vanbrugh's first play. He had seen Colley Cibber's comedy, Love's Last Shift, at Drury Lane early in 1696. He then promoted Cibber's creation, Sir Novelty Fashion, to the peerage as Lord Foppington. From Cibber's play he also culled the characters of Loveless and Amanda, but the other characters were his own creations. The Relapse received the dubious honor of being selected by Jeremy Collier for particular attack in his A Short View of the Immorality and Profaneness of the English Stage (1698), and though Vanbrugh did try to defend himself, particularly in terms of Worthy's sudden change of attitude toward Amanda, Collier still made the better case.

Colley Cibber gives an account of his double delight as both author and actor. Though he had enjoyed particularly good audience response both to Love's Last Shift and to his performance as Sir Novelty Fashion, his career received an additional boost when Vanbrugh noticed him and his play and created a sequel: "This play (the Relapse) from its new, and easy Turn of Wit, had great Success, and gave me, as a Comedian, a second Flight of Reputation along with it." Then Cibber praises the skill of Vanbrugh as a writer of lines:

> There is something so catching to the Ear, so easy to the Memory, in all he writ, that it has been observ'd, by all the Actors of my Time, that the

Style of no Author whatsoever, gave their Memory less trouble . . . which I myself, who have been charg'd with several of his strongest Characters, can confirm by a pleasing Experience. And indeed his Wit, and Humour, was so little laboured, that his most entertaining Scenes seem'd to be no more, than his common Conversation committed to Paper.

Cibber admits that Love's Last Shift was inferior and acknowledges the truth in Congreve's observation that it contained "a great many things, that were like Wit, that in reality were not Wit." In The Relapse, he finds the wit authentic: "Yet we see the Relapse, however imperfect, in the Conduct, by the mere Force of its agreeable Wit, ran away with the Hearts of its Hearers."

In terms of performance, Vanbrugh himself, in the preface to the printed edition of the play, gives a sketch of Powell, that champion drinker, terrifying the playwright on opening night:

The fine gentleman of the play [Powell], drinking his mistress's health in Nantes brandy, from six in the morning to the time he waddled on upon the stage in the evening, had toasted himself up to such a pitch of vigour, I confess I once gave Amanda up for gone.

Now Mrs. Rogers was playing the chaste Amanda, and Cibber notes her penchant for carrying a good thing as far as it would go--and then some:

Her Fondness for Virtue on the Stage, she began to think, might perswade the World, that it had made an Impression on her private Life . . . in an Epilogue to an obscure Play . . . wherein she acted a Part of impregnable Chastity, she bespoke the Favour of the Ladies, by a Protestation, that in Honour of their Goodness and Virtue, she would dedicate her unblemish'd Life to their Example. .

. . Her first heroick Motive, to a Surrender, was to save the Life of a Lover [Wilks, with whom she later lived], who, in his Despair, had vow'd to destroy himself, with which Act of Mercy (in a jealous Dispute once, in my hearing) she was provok'd to reproach him in these very Words: "Villain! did not I save your Life?"

Cibber also praises The Relapse for boosting the Drury Lane talent, which was still in a state of evolution:

Tho' we, in Drury-Lane, were too young to be excellent, we were not too old to be better. . . . One good new Play, to a rising Company, is of inconceivable Value. In . . . the Relapse; several of our People shew'd themselves in a new Style of Acting, in which Nature had not yet been seen.

Although the Drury Lane company felt themselves inferior to Betterton's group, they were, generally, younger and had the advantage of being able to stretch their talent into new realms: so being shown to advantage in "quite new Lights," they began to be able to hold their own and "to make a considerable Stand" against the competition.

Critical Evaluations

The Relapse (1948)

In 1948 England saw three Restoration productions (two of them commercial West End offerings) of varying excellence. Anthony Quayle had a success with his production of The Relapse. It was not a production for those who believed that revivals should be devoted "first and foremost to their author's intentions and only in the second place to their present-day public."[1] But the public approved the lively, vulgar interpretation, and the play transferred

146

from Hammersmith to the Phoenix. The cast included Cyril Ritchard as Lord Foppington, Paul Scofield as Young Fashion, Anthony Ireland as Loveless, Audrey Fildes as Amanda, Esmond Knight as Worthy, Madge Elliott as Berinthia, Jessie Evans as Miss Hoyden and Hamlyn Benson as Sir Tunbelly Clumsey.

Two performances which were singled out were those of Madge Elliott and Cyril Ritchard. As Berinthia, the scheming widow, Madge Elliott gave a performance that raised some questions about her up-to-date interpretation: "There are moments in this coarser play, when a Congrevean elegance and calculated modulation would not be amiss. Miss Elliott brings down the house by pointing her phrases in a modern way. . . . But it is not quite what is wanted."[2]

In this performance, the modern bent of Miss Elliott was coupled with her awareness that her role was a direct foil to the one in which Ritchard, as Lord Foppington, scored so heavily. For Ritchard, "like some monstrously funny 'Dame' in a pantomime," both enjoyed the bizarre role and communicated his delight to those who saw him. His performance refreshed those who found contemporary acting too refined to commit itself to honest vulgarity. Ritchard's creative ability was explored by Kenneth Tynan:

> He was chiefly excellent because he was vulgar: he showed us what we had long suspected, that Restoration comedy outside Congreve is not witty and artificial, but broad and boisterous. Foppington is an upstart, ineffectively arrogant, desperately clinging to what he imagines is his dignity. Perhaps the most inventive touch was Ritchard's attempt at dignified locomotion with his ankles tied together: he slunk along in a series of minute shuffling movements, like a dowager in a hobble skirt. The kind of vulgarity this illustrates is social: a man trying to behave

above his class of mind and manners. It made belly and mind laugh together.[3]

Paul Scofield, already a veteran of Restoration drama, balanced off Ritchard as Foppington's plain-spun brother, Young Fashion. Esmond Knight as Worthy, in partnership with Audrey Fildes as Amanda, was praised for the success of Act V, iv, "the most difficult scene in the whole of Restoration comedy, that which begins as a cavalier wooing and ends in a pious duet."[4]

Ritchard's success encouraged him to direct the play and recreate Foppington in New York in 1950. It was an uneven production, but the incredible Foppington with his "Restoration Rhumba" walk still pleased. Historically, Ritchard's successful try was doubly important in that it both delighted audiences and paved the way for Donald Sinden's neurotic Foppington nineteen years later.

Virtue in Danger (1963)

On April 10, 1963, the Mermaid Theatre presented a musical version of The Relapse called by its subtitle, Virtue in Danger. The original was renovated by Paul Dehn and James Bernard. The critic for the Times defined the production's intention: to "replace the romantic verse of the original, leaving the comedy intact . . . while preserving a seventeenth-century melodic line."[1] The attempt was, however, not successful. For one thing, the score was inappropriate because it "neither hits the idiom of the play, nor compensates with the theatrical impact of the modern musical." And there was justified complaint that the constant breaking of that decorum so close to the heart of Restoration comedy was exhibited "every time another graceless accompaniment strikes up and characters give voice to numbers with such titles as 'I'm in love with my husband' and 'Wait a little longer, lover.'" In refurbishing the classic to shape a family show the adaptors sterilized the bawdry, and the cast had to resort bravely to emphasizing innuendo in place of authentic lasciviousness.

The cast included John Moffatt as Lord Foppington, Richard Wordsworth as Coupler, Jane Wenham as Amanda, Barrie Ingham as Young Fashion, Alan Howard as Loveless, Patricia Routledge as Berinthia, Basil Hoskins as Worthy, Patsy Byrne as Miss Hoyden and Hamlyn Benson as Sir Tunbelly Clumsey. The production was directed by Wendy Toye. The patched up result was especially unfortunate because this production boasted many actors who had appeared, or would later appear, in substantial Restoration roles. Jane Wenham (Amanda) would later play Mrs. Marwood to the Fainall of John Moffatt (Lord Foppington) in the National Theatre's The Way of the World (1969). Barrie Ingham (Fashion) was to play Lord Foppington in the Royal Shakespeare Company's remount of The Relapse (1968). Alan Howard (Loveless) would appear in two RSC Restoration productions: as Young Fashion in The Relapse (1967) and as Dorimant in The Man of Mode (1971). Richard Wordsworth (Coupler) was known for playing dirty old men as far back as his Antonio in the Gielgud production of Venice Preserved (1953).

John Moffatt was already a veteran of Restoration comedy on two continents (Sparkish in The Country Wife: London, 1956; New York, 1957) and even in the Mermaid's pastiche production, his Foppington, although unable to free himself from a "cornucopian chestnut peruke," was singularly effective.

Despite critical censure, the play moved to the Strand Theatre in the West End, a sure sign of popular success.[2] After the transfer of the play to the Strand, the London scenes took a longer time adjusting themselves than did the country scenes, and the balance between Moffatt's Foppington and Ingham's Fashion was not established quite comfortably.

The Mermaid's production was another instance--and there were no exceptions--in which the attempt to translate a Restoration comedy into musical terms and, in this case, the family vernacular as well, was soundly defeated by the very nature of the piece.

The Relapse (1967)

Despite the many classical and contemporary works produced by the Royal Shakespeare Company from its founding in 1960, it was not until 1967 that the first Restoration comedy, The Relapse, was staged, closely followed by a revival of that same production in 1968 and by The Man of Mode in 1971.[1] The cast for the first production included Donald Sinden as Lord Foppington, Roy Kinnear as Chaplain Bull, David Waller as Sir Tunbelly Clumsey, Janet Suzman as Berinthia, Donald Burton as Coupler, Frances de la Tour as Miss Hoyden, Susan Fleetwood as Amanda, Alan Howard as Young Fashion, Patrick Stewart as Worthy, Charles Thomas as Loveless and Lila Kaye as the Nurse. Christopher Morley designed and Guy Woofenden composed the music, while Robert Ornbo lighted the production.

The Relapse was directed by Trevor Nunn, who had been praised for his recent production of The Taming of the Shrew for the RSC. Nunn chose a virtually uncut text, which he enhanced with clever effects. This ingenuity added to the detail but resulted in an overlong running time.

The ever-pressing search for contemporary comment in the classical revival could be briefly abandoned, for Nunn eschewed the satiric bent and was content to exhibit a "gallery of comic people, leaving us to pluck out the moral for ourselves if we feel like it."[2] Absence of intrusion was evident also in the production designs, which set the play apart from the traditional as they "exaggerate and vamp up the play to exactly the right degree of affectionate parody without ever sacrificing the writing to the playing."[3] This emphasis on a fair approach to the text was admirable in that the production honored the seriousness of intention in the straight passages and refused to invent needless embellishments. However, the very pace of the action may have been the major factor in keeping the playing straight, as Nunn, following the rhythms of Vanbrugh, accepted the fact that "his characters are too busy planning stratagems and getting out of impossible situations to have much time to spare for sitting down for exchanges of elegant bitchery."[4]

There was an evident directorial concern with the Real vs. Mask theme. The masquerade element reached a fitting climax in the masque of the final scene. The real came into play in the more homely scenes with the women when Amanda and Berinthia, having gotten the men out of the way, dropped their decorous manners to bring out the drink and clay pipes.

Set against these two kinds of reality, the social and the private, were the grotesques, Sir Tunbelly Clumsey and Foppington. As Sir Tunbelly, David Waller added to the traditional brute strain "a streak of courageous manliness . . . that doesn't generally appear in such characters. His like fought at Blenheim and Minden and Waterloo when they weren't bullying their families at home."[5] He was not the traditional country squire but a "genuinely formidable Border baron before whose gates visitors quail when they hear wolves howling within."

In the same plot line of the play, Foppington appears. The performance by Donald Sinden challenged the Cyril Ritchard creation of 1948, and, like his predecessor, the highly versatile Sinden made of it a huge success. His speech, larded with current oaths, "stap my vitals," "strike me speechless," had a ring of narcissistic heartlessness emphasized by his pauses of self-appreciation. He managed to go through the comedy

151

in the highest style without spoiling either the verbal or the visual.

His appearance was, of course, wonderful. He dressed with the help of fifteen adults and two pages, and the effect was like "some enormous, blousy sugar-plum fairy."[6] But it was the unmasked Foppington of the first scene upon which Sinden built his character:

> We first see him in undress, a sour petulant figure gulping his morning chocolate, and only assuming the foppish role as he is taken with voluminous black petticoat and a mountainous rose-pink peruke. The joke . . . is that he remains a powerfully masculine presence.[7]

Lord Foppington took on a valid human presence that, without dampening the fun, intensified the reality of the character. Sinden's performance expanded on the psychology of Foppington:

> He shows us a man, or half-man, with a flaw in the mechanism, such as we all know. His Foppington has presence, intelligence too; but one can feel that he has retreated into foppery, his grotesque egotism is a defense, his petulance a child's cry of rage when the world spoils his fantasy.[8]

The emphasis on the androgynous theme was the factor that invited Donald Burton's Coupler to be a "frighteningly decayed and disturbing ambidextrous" matchmaker serving as a kind of link between Foppington and Sir Tunbelly.[9] The sexuality of the piece was so diffuse that only something almost hermaphroditic could have a binding effect. The performance of Alan Howard added balance by giving a suggestion of asceticism to Tom Fashion.

The three principal women came in for special notice. The Berinthia of Janet Suzman, an actress capable of projecting considerable sensuality, was "kittenish without coyness, sexy and comical in the same breath."[10] She harmonized with the Miss Hoyden of Frances de la Tour, the "gawky, forlorn, passionate tomboy from the backwoods" with her abrupt approach to getting her man: "'never mind what I did then,' she hollers at her old nurse, boring on to a suitor about her infant habits. 'Tell him what I can do <u>now</u>.'"

The asceticism for the distaff side was presented by Susan Fleetwood's Amanda, who managed to be the one area of calm uncertainty in the whirling waters of the production: "she makes a touching thing out of a good woman's agonized trembling upon the brink of adventure, torn apart by unwelcome desire and unwanted revenge, painfully discarding priggishness."[11]

This 1967 production was remounted the next year--a proof of its worth to the RSC repertoire. It remained the single unqualified success of the company in its early dealings with the revival of a rare Restoration comedy.

The Relapse (1968)

In 1968 The Relapse was revived at the Aldwych in August at the close of the summer season, and there were multiple cast changes. Lord Foppington was now Barrie Ingham; Sir Tunbelly Clumsey, Brewster Mason; Young Fashion, Michael Jayston; Coupler, Jeffrey Dench; Worthy, Emrys James and Chaplain Bull, Derek Smith. In the women's roles, Berinthia was Toby Robins, replacing the successful Janet Suzman; and the role of Amanda was rendered less significant with the substitution of Lynn Farleigh for Susan Fleetwood. A major asset to the production was the continuing Miss Hoyden of Frances de la Tour. Also continuing were Charles Thomas as Loveless and Lila Kaye as the Nurse.

The necessity for comparison between the two casts was obvious. Although the new players retained a sense of humor, they had not yet unearthed as much "grace, subtlety and sheer verve" as the original performance displayed.[1] The most negative view was that the production had not yet discovered a satisfactory combination of art and artifice:

> Trevor Nunn's production constantly tends to emphasize artificiality by affected voices, extravagant costume, comical gaits and farcical business. We are offered a none too satisfactory mixture of tedious seriousness and near-pantomime burlesque.[2]

There were also negative views of the Foppington of Barrie Ingham, whose performance was a reminder that Donald Sinden was currently appearing in the West End in a Whitehall farce.[3] In Ingham's Foppington, the breadth of the Sinden performance was substantially narrowed, for the character seemed

> curiously subdued and contrived by comparison. His inability to master the swoop of effeminacy, the abandon of eccentricity, the courage of sartorial egotism, saps this Restoration comedy of much of its natural style and humour.[4]

Although Ingham's interpretation failed to round out the figure, he did manage to find an area of appeal in the curious mixture that is Foppington:

> He [Ingham] shows no edge of meanness and spite in the midst of his folly as did his predecessor Donald Sinden, but comes dangerously near to winning our sympathy as he parades himself in rose-pink satin, a Harlequin's red wig perched on his tall figure.[5]

As Ingham played him, Foppington was not separable from his wardrobe; he existed only when he was "dressed, shod, powered and bewigged," as his great concentration was on the supremacy of the mirror to the exclusion of all else: "beneath the affectations there is, in Mr. Ingham's playing, the feeling that what others might regard as insult and humiliation are irrelevancies to a man whose whole purpose in life is to be fashionable."[6]

Making his second trip to the play, Ronald Bryden meditated at length on the point that the production, now tightened to half an hour less running time, was trying to make. Although the increased pace had stamped out some of the subtlety, the wedding-masque, noted in the earlier production and more tentatively approached then, now became the point at which all aspects of the play converged:

> What Nunn has done is seize the hint given by the wedding-masque in the last scene at Lord Foppington's town house. He's recognized Vanbrugh's comedy as a kind of diffused prose version of "Comus," opposing as Milton did the virtues of rustic innocence and faithful marriage to the elegant, fantasticated vice of aristocratic life. Milton's Lady splits into two—the virtuous, forlorn wife Amanda and the inexperienced Hoyden—but her temper remains a single, emblematic figure: the androgynous Foppington, sequinned eyelids glittering surrealistically beneath the gigantic horned periwig which towers above his retinue. The difference is that Comus triumphs here. One by one the country innocents are drawn into the dance of monstrous urbanity, their homespun costumes becoming webbed with the same silver lacery as those of the London rakes, paramours and panders. At the final curtain they freeze into a tableaux of metallic, suddenly horrifying revelry. Everyone is in the picture now, the innocents initiated into an adult-world of cynicism.[7]

The comedy offered cameos of behavior, "startlingly quiet, painful scenes of innocence being corrupted, sophistication sliding into gleaming

155

cruelty, more in the manner of 'Les Liaisons Dangereuses' than traditional Restoration comedy."[8]

Harold Hobson, in communion with Bryden, noted the beautiful and functional set with its movable furniture and trees, which gave a never-never land quality to the piece. This world was a world of the characters' own making:

> Nothing is cribbed, cabined, confined, or bound in. Everywhere there is a feeling of freedom. The characters--the fop, the deserted wife, the _femme fatale_, the virtuous but impoverished younger brother--move from vanity to sense, from morality to sin, from idyllic peace to anguished jealousy, there and back again, uncased by any building, untrammelled by local habitation. They live in a world of words, and the only bricks they know are those they drop in conversation.[9]

Only two scenes in the play were considered in any critical detail--both involved Michael Jayston's Young Fashion. A bit of athleticism between Jayston and Brewster Mason's Sir Tunbelly claimed some whimsical attention: "Their powers of fielding are indeed remarkable. There is a scene in which Mr. Mason despatches, and Mr. Jayston catches and returns, a mug across a table that will be of interest to any connoisseur of cricket. It is a thing to make one muse and ponder."[10]

Of greater interest was the scene between the grotesque Coupler of Jeffrey Dench and Young Fashion. The suggestion of insubstantiality in the piece, a concern of the director and the designer, aided the actors in making palatable the sexuality of the incident:

> One of the surest, as well as the pleasantest, ways of making "The Relapse" seem savoury is to suggest that it is not quite real. Mr. Nunn's

production contains, and contains without offense, a scene which, even in the most debauched days of the Regency, London theatres hesitated to present. I mean that in which Coupler climbs lecherously up the body of Young Fashion.[11]

Despite its defects the remounting had sufficient invention and zest to make a twentieth-century audience sit up and take note: "As a mirror of its own foppish amoral times, 'The Relapse,' perhaps, has a few points to make for our own peacock day. . . . Its cynical but unhypocritical voice makes out Vanbrugh's time to have been no less a merrier one to live in, but a far less dull and inhibited one."[12]

THE PROVOK'D WIFE
Plot Summary

I.   After two years of dubious bliss, Sir John Brute has proven to be such a failure as a husband that Lady Brute is driven to discuss with her niece, Belinda, the possibility of accepting Constant's attention.

An anonymous letter comes to Lady Fancyfull, who considers all men her captives, requesting a meeting in St. James's Park.

II. In the park, Lady Fancyfull meets Heartfree, who bluntly tells her that her looks, her movement and her language have been warped by affectation, and she is become a laughingstock. When she leaves in a huff, Constant comes in to moan to Heartfree about his two-year pursuit of Lady Brute. The appearance of the callous Sir John serves to banish any vestiges of hesitancy in the young men, and Heartfree decides to help Constant in winning Lady Brute.

III. Sir John leaves Constant and Heartfree in possession of his house while he goes after his drinking companions. Constant is given just enough hope by Lady Brute to make him delirious with joy. Lady Brute and Belinda confide in each other and Lady Brute suggests that while she is making Constant happy, Belinda try to conquer Heartfree.

IV. Sir John and his hell-raising cronies have already attacked one man when they find a tailor with a churchman's gown. Sir John puts it on just as the Constable and the watch come up. Sir John is brought before the Justice, and though he dishonors the cloth he is wearing by his behavior, the Justice is loath to expose him and he is set free.*

In the Spring Gardens, Lady Fancyfull and Madamoiselle, her maid, spy on the group. Sir John comes upon the them, and, thinking the ladies are whores, wants to join the party. But Belinda goes off with Heartfree, and as Constant is about to draw Lady Brute into a private arbor, Lady Fancyfull and Madamoiselle rush out on them and disappear.

V. The group is at home when Sir John suddenly returns. Though Constant is willing to duel, Sir John's natural cowardice keeps him from putting up too hostile a front. When Madamoiselle reports to Lady Fancyfull that there is to be a marriage between Heartfree and Belinda, Lady Fancyfull determines to destroy Belinda's reputation.

---

*In 1725 Vanbrugh rewrote part of the fourth act. Sir John, in robbing the tailor, robbed him not of a churchman's gown but of Lady Brute's dress and cloak. He introduces himself to the Watch as Bonduca, Queen of the Welchmen. When he is brought before the Justice, he introduces himself as Lady Brute, a woman of quality and his behavior evokes the Justice's pity for the man married to such a "woman."

When the men return to Sir John's house, Lady Fancyfull enters disguised and tries to discredit both women, but she is exposed and Constant and Belinda agree to complete their bargain.

Background

The Provok'd Wife was produced at Lincoln's Inn Fields in April 1697. The cast included Verbruggen as Constant, Hudson as Heartfree, Betterton as Sir John Brute, Bowman as Trebel, Bowen as Rasor, Bright as the Justice of the Peace, Mrs. Barry as Lady Brute, Mrs. Bracegirdle as Belinda, Mrs. Bowman as Lady Fancyfull and Mrs. Willis as Madamoiselle.

Cibber reports that *The Provok'd Wife* had been written before *The Relapse*, but Vanbrugh had not been willing to trust it to the stage. He had put the play by, but after the success of *The Relapse*, Lord Halifax, that patron of the arts who had smiled upon Betterton's company, heard the play read to him and engaged Vanbrugh to revise it and offer it to Lincoln's Inn Fields. Consequently, Vanbrugh had the advantage of being interpreted by both companies.

When *The Provok'd Wife* was revived in 1725, Vanbrugh, bowing to the moral bent of the time, rewrote the play to make it more acceptable to the audience. Thus the scene in which Sir John Brute dresses in the clergyman's clothes and behaves scandalously was altered so that Sir John does indeed dress up and misbehave, but now he is garbed in his wife's gown. Thus, quite unconsciously, Vanbrugh in pleasing his age also pleased the twentieth century, which could spend its energies in analysis of Sir John's psychology.

The selection of players for that revival provoked discussion among the actors which is vividly reported by Cibber. The play's revival aroused the expectation and interest of the court and the nobility, but Wilks was complaining about having to play every day; so the

company offered to relieve him of his new assignment.
Cibber recounts his response:

> When the Actors were summon'd to hear the Play
> read, and receive their Parts; I address'd myself
> to Wilks . . . and told him, That as the Part of
> Constant, which he seem'd to chuse, was a
> Character of less Action, than he generally
> appear'd in, we thought this might be a good
> Occasion to ease himself, by giving it to another.
> --Here he look'd grave.--That the Love-Scenes of
> it were rather serious, than gay, or humourous,
> and therefore might sit very well upon Booth.
> --Down dropt his Brow, and furl'd were his
> Features.--That if we were never to revive a
> tolerable Play, without him, what would become of
> us, in case of his Indisposition?-- Here he
> pretended to stir the Fire. . . . This provoking
> Civility, plung'd him into a Passion . . . when
> his Reply was stript of those Ornaments, it was
> plainly this: That he look'd upon all I had said,
> as concerted Design, not only to signalize our
> selves, by laying him aside; but a Contrivance to
> draw him into the Disfavour of the Nobility. . . .
> [Cibber replies] But, Sir, if your being In, or
> Out of the Play, is a Hardship, you shall impose
> it upon yourself: The Part is in your Hand, and to
> us, it is a Matter of Indifference now, whether
> you take it, or leave it. Upon this he threw down
> the Part upon the Table, cross'd his Arms, and
> sate knocking his Heel, upon the Floor, as seeming
> to threaten most, when he said least . . . Booth .
> . . said, That for his Part, he saw no such great
> matter in acting every Day; for he believed it the
> wholesomest Exercise in the World; it kept the
> Spirits in motion, and always gave him a good
> Stomach. . . . But Wilks . . . reply'd, Every one
> could best feel for himself, but he did not
> pretend to the Strength of a Pack-horse; therefore
> if Mrs. Oldfield would chuse any body else to play

with her, he should be very glad to be excus'd. .
. . Here Mrs. Oldfield got up, and . . . said
with her usual Frankness, Pooh! you are all a
Parcel of Fools, to make such a rout about
nothing! . . . She said, she hop'd Mr. Wilks
would not so far mind what had past, as to refuse
his acting the Part . . . she believed, those who
had bespoke the Play, would expect to have [it]
done to the best Advantage. . . . To conclude,
Wilks had the Part, and we had all we wanted.

After Betterton had created the role of Sir John
Brute in 1697, the next century saw five significant
actors in the part. Cibber and Garrick were determined
to emphasize Sir John's essential gentility, and both
played Sir John as "an endearing figure of fun, a
little boisterous on occasion perhaps, but even in his
cups 'a gentleman born.'"[1] They represented one school
of interpretation, while Quin, Macklin and Ryder
emphasized the less civilized aspects of the Brute. In
1786, when Ryder played the role at the Theatre Royal,
Covent Garden, the alteration was significant:

Mr. Ryder, as Sir John, does not dress, nor does
he deport himself so much like a gentleman as
others his most celebrated predecessors have
usually done, but although his manners are rather
less polished he is far from letting the spirit of
the character evaporate. He gives us less of the
rakish man of fashion, but more of the drunken
brute than we have been accustomed to behold.[2]

By the end of the eighteenth century Sir John had
become redundant: a character whom the "improvements of
civilization have rendered quite obsolete." The play
fell on evil times in the nineteenth century, and the
1963 revival marked the first West End production of
the play in a century and a half.

Critical Evaluations

The Provok'd Wife (1963)

On July 24, 1963, Prospect Productions settled into temporary residence at the Vaudeville Theatre in the West End with Toby Robertson's production of The Provok'd Wife.[1] The cast included Trevor Martin as Sir John Brute, Eileen Atkins as Lady Brute, Ann Bell as Belinda, June Brown as Lady Fancyfull, Josephine Woodford as Madamoiselle, Dinsdale Landen as Heartfree and John Warner as Constant. This Restoration comedy was the first of several presented by Prospect Productions within a relatively brief time span. Others included The Confederacy (1964), The Man of Mode (1965), The Constant Couple (1967) and The Recruiting Officer (1970). This impressive selection of rarely performed plays was due to Robertson's happy bias toward Restoration classics.

Despite age and neglect, the comedy was judged relevant by the critics. Milton Shulman thought that notwithstanding the passage of three centuries, "Vanbrugh's cynical wit and ironic sallies against fidelity and marriage still retain a great deal of their freshness and relevance."[2] And Gerald Barry found that, in spite of the heavy-footedness of the play in comparison to more regularly popular Restoration comedies, "both matter and style are astoundingly apposite to current fashionable behaviour both in the theatre and in 'real' life." He found the play most immediate: "startling is the ferocious topicality of subject matter."[3]

The company, however, was not satisfied with oblique references to current events, and there were two updated additions: a dubious prologue and an epilogue containing references to the kitchen sink. However, questionable decorations aside, a pertinent social comedy demands excellence in acting and presentation. The company managed an uninhibited style, but the Times found that externals were too often substituted for stylistic comprehension:

> Toby Robertson's production scarcely projects the action as high comedy. It goes through the ritualistic motions of "style," which compels unoccupied ladies to exhaust themselves by keeping their arms raised and men to bite their thumbs when entering a chamber with some stratagem in mind. But these gestures never pass into the second nature that constitutes true style.[4]

Without the unification of directorial discipline the contending tones jostled each other:

> In one mood he [Robertson] is being frankly artificial; in another he is winking at the audience and sending the whole thing up; in another he gives us straight modern farce such as we might encounter on an off-night on the television.[5]

This stylistic confusion affected the performances of the women, particularly June Brown as Lady Fancyfull, who, although she "ran the gamut of affectation," failed to complete the character by neglecting the "over-refinement that should lie at the bottom" of the creation.[6] Her most obvious handicap was that she relied heavily on visual comedy making gesture Lady Fancyfull's only strong suit. Consequently, the performance "consciously ridicules the character's absurdity instead of inhabiting it."

Though Eileen Atkins' sensible Lady Brute was praised for her wit and resilience and for her managing, with Ann Bell as Belinda, to get "all the comedy and even some submerged pathos out of the exchanges of feminine confidences,"[7] her dispassionate approach made Lady Brute "too cold and scheming a woman to have maintained Constant's affection so long."[8]

The principal acting interest was in the performance of Trevor Martin as Sir John Brute. Since this play was one of the most frequently revived comedies of the eighteenth century, and since the interpretation of Sir John was divided into two acting camps, it would be well to note the side with which Mr. Martin allied himself.[9]

Betterton created the part in 1697 and in the next century was followed by at least five significant actors, the most famous of whom, Garrick, never forgot that Sir John was a gentleman.

Garrick and Cibber represented one school of thought, while Quin, Macklin and Ryder emphasized the less civilized aspects of Brute. This brute side of the coin was the one which Martin chose to show. He was described as "convincingly rude, vulgar and cowardly," with the reservation that "at times his performance, in its gruff villainy, seemed to be borrowing a great deal from Barrie's Captain Hook."[10] Especially notable was the transvestite scene in Act IV, in which Martin showed himself "happily free of the stylistic restrictions that hamper other members of the company," as he played the "unbearable Brute in a true bestial vein particularly in his travesty scene with the J. P. where he passes himself off as his wife."[11] The bestial interpretation found critical support: the scenes in which "this pathological woman hater decides, for no good reason, to don his wife's new dress and let himself be arrested as 'Bonduca, the Queen of the Welshmen' are psychologically revealing as well as extremely funny."[12] Thus the success of Martin's Sir John was heightened by the implications for an audience attuned to the suggestions of his character's perverse psychology.

<u>Intrigues and Amours</u> (1967)

In the early 1950's Joan Littlewood established her Theatre Workshop, which played one night stands throughout Britain in informal, makeshift surroundings. After several years the group found a home in East London at the Theatre Royal, Stratford East. The actor Harry H. Corbett, who worked with Littlewood during these years, described the catholicity of tastes in her choice of material: "We did <u>Twelfth Night</u>, <u>Volpone</u>, <u>The Dutch Courtesan</u> and <u>Hobson's Choice</u>. We did what she considered were the classics, of different periods--we didn't care--we just threw them on, gave them a new slant."[1] Eventually the original group disbanded. Corbett speculated that its end was inevitable: "It was founded during the hangover of the thirties, it existed and drew its blood from the thirties, right up until 1955." By then, the initial motivation was no longer viable.[2]

By 1967, the Workshop was back, and the Vanbrugh adaptation was its second offering of the season, opening on May 24, 1967. The cast included Brian Murphy as Sir John Brute, Bob Grant as Constant, Gaye Brown as Lady Brute, Pamela Jones as Belinda, Edward Bishop as Heartfree, Frank Coda as the Singing Master and Sandra Caron and Myvanwy Jenn as the Maids. Joan Littlewood both adapted and directed the play.

The reason for mounting the play was the refusal of the Lord Chamberlain to license a projected production of <u>Mrs. Wilson's Diary</u>. In its place Littlewood offered her version of the <u>The Provok'd Wife</u> which, as a classic, was not liable to the rigors of censorship. The choice seemed an ideal one because it outwitted the Lord Chamberlain and gave Littlewood ample room for social satire, a favorite theme.

The alterations in the text were consistent with Littlewood's style of invention. Among the amusements provided were "interpolated Cockney-Italian dialogue, some Crazy Gang buffoonery and a saintly musical instrumental trio."[3] The text itself lost large portions of dialogue to questionable additions: "Certain plot lines have been truncated and various tripping, dainty songs have been inserted arbitrarily in the action," with the result that "whatever frail continuity remained has been even more deliberately obscured."[4] In addition to some transposition of speeches and a few colloquialisms spicing up the dialogue, there was the whimsical addition of Treble, the singing master, announcing the intervals in Italian.

Peter Snow's set, a black-and-white engraving of Greenwich from across the Thames, framed by colored lights seemed promising and the music, though possibly intrusive, was admirably varied. The ensemble was composed of an on-stage spinet, cello and flute. Some of the costumes were borrowed from the Théâtre Nationale Populaire of Paris.

Despite the promise, a hint of the effectiveness of the adaptation was a comment by Terry Coleman that the "quietly played music was the best thing of the evening."[5] Periodically, the production manifested significant openness, and it was "refreshing to see the business of cuckolding treated as a game of honest lust rather than fancy-dress scampering."[6] However, there was a dearth of detail in the interpretation of Sir John by a physically slight Brian Murphy who was censured for playing with "youthful petulance rather than ripe boorishness." Gaye Brown, as Lady Brute, "uncertain about whether or not she should be indignant or have the vapours," fared little better.[7]

Harry H. Corbett's assessment of his former director gave some insight into the reason for the failure of the performance:

Joan was nothing apart from the material she worked with, and if ever Joan had bad material,

166

actors, etc., there was very little she could do
with them. Joan was the beginner, the suggester,
the bringer of ideas, but they all found an echo
within the people she was working with.[8]

In this performance, the material was not yet
polished, and Ronald Bryden called the new company a
"fairly blunt instrument" which was "capable of
executing the boisterous half of the production's
intention but not yet its graces."[9] The danger was that
the production became a "sort of Restoration-comedy-
made-easy (how to laugh without knowing why)."[10] The
hazard for the original classic was that Littlewood's
hodgepodge production was capable of entertaining those
unfamiliar with the original without giving them the
least idea of the biting social irony which permeates
Vanbrugh's play.

The Provok'd Wife (1973)

On June 14, 1973, Robin Phillips's Company ended
its season with The Provok'd Wife. The cast included
Fenella Fielding as Lady Fancyfull, James Grout as Sir
John Brute, Sheila Allen as Lady Brute and Linda
Thorson as Belinda. Frank Proud directed and Alan
Barrett designed the production.

J. W. Lambert found the comedy a "pretty black
comedy, a merciless picture of licence, spite and beady
eyes on the main chance,"[1] while Irving Wardle related
the play to later drama in that it forecast the
nineteenth-century problem play. More significant than
the manipulation of his Restoration types was the
searching look Vanbrugh took at their "economic
circumstances thus producing a separate dramatic line
at variance with the standard comic values."[2] The
director, Frederick Proud, wisely treated the play as a
"thing apart from the standard comedy of fans and
smirking innuendoes in the drawing room."

Most dramatically satisfying were the dialogues between Lady Brute and Belinda, who "make their exchanges on the subject of women's oblique powers into delightful duets."[3]

The psychological movement of the performance required "a zig-zagging agility by which actors can move in and out of sympathetic positions."[4] The focus of this is Sir John Brute, who must exhibit "more bestial upper-class behaviour than polite comedy normally admits." In that stop-and-go movement he must be a "repulsive monster at one minute and a speaker of bitter home truths at the next."[5] Oblivious to the complications of the role, James Grout played this complex figure as a conventional, though intelligent, drunk.

In her performance as Lady Fancyfull, Fenella Fielding seemed at odds with herself because her "physical and vocal writhing bury what seems, judging by her last Malvolio-like exit, to be in intention an intelligent shot at piercing to the bitterness beneath the flourishes of this silly woman."[6]

THE CONFEDERACY
Plot Summary

I. Mrs. Amlet, who has been doing business with city and court ladies for years, reports to Mrs. Cloggit that city ladies used to be punctual in their payments, but, since they have "set their minds on quality," they no longer repsect their debts to her. She also bemoans the fact that her son, Dick, has disowned her and is going about as a man of fashion.

Brass, Dick's friend who is passing for his servant, advises him to pursue Corinna, daughter of Gripe, because marriage would assure him a good place in society.

Clarissa, Gripe's wife and Corinna's stepmother, languidly discusses with Flippanta, her maid, her husband's love for Araminta, Moneytrap's wife, but she scorns jealousy as a "city-passion, 'tis a thing unknown amongst people of quality." Flippanta offers a bargain to Mrs. Amlet: a diamond necklace, which Clarissa told Gripe she had lost, will be given in pawn for five hundred pounds.

II. Dick is talking with Clarissa when Brass appears to warn him that there is an action out against him. Araminta comes to discuss Gripe's love for her, and the ladies go off to plot and spend money. Flippanta sounds Corinna on the subject of marriage, and when she finds her both eager and cunning (absolute prerequisites), she shows her Dick's letter.

III. At Mrs. Amlet's house Dick searches his mother's strong box and discovers the diamond necklace.

Brass and Flippanta tell the ladies that their respective husbands have played into their hands: each is in love with the wife of the other. The ladies are delighted and determine to use the situation to coin money from their spouses.

IV. Gripe tries to convince Clarissa to mend her ways; but, when she agrees to comply and stay at home, she makes her own exorbitant conditions: music, balls, card parties and more servants.

Brass tells Gripe that Araminta is so hard pressed by creditors that she will turn papist and take the veil. With this sort of fooling Brass gets two hunderd and fifty pounds from Gripe.

V. Moneytrap appears to find out how his suit is prospering, but Clarissa will allow him no advantage. Then she finds that her own husband has parted with the same amount for Araminta. The two couples meet ("very gay and laughing") while in asides the husbands pity each other's ignorance and the wives pity their husbands' stupidity. In the midst of this jollity, Mr. Clip, a goldsmith, enters with the necklace. Clarissa dodges her husband's accusations by saying that his stinginess forced her to pawn the jewels and that she knows the recipient of his two hunderd and fifty pounds. Araminta reveals comparable information to Moneytrap.

Dick is acknowledged by Mrs. Amlet--in fetching phrases--as her very own, and she offers to back his marriage with ten thousand pounds. Corinna is game to throw in her lot with him, and the money wins Clarissa over. The city wives, having had a little revenge, agree that they must go on with their husbands.

Background

The Confederacy, also called The City Wives' Confederacy, opened at the Haymarket on 30 October 1705. The cast included Michael Leigh as Gripe, Dogget as Moneytrap, Booth as Dick, Pack as Brass, Mimes as Clip, Mrs. Barry as Clarissa, Mrs. Porter as Araminta, Mrs. Bradshaw as Corinna, Mrs. Bracegirdle as Flippanta, Mrs. Willis as Mrs. Amlet and Mrs. Baker as Mrs. Cloggit.

Downes reports on the progress of Vanbrugh's theatre. On 9 April 1705 the playhouse opened with a foreign opera warbled by singers imported from Italy, "the worst that e're came from thence." The opera lasted only five days, the gentry liking it "but indifferently." The singers went home, and the old plays, acted in "old Cloaths," were trotted out with equal success. Downes estimates that the new playhouse required new material: "with a good new English Opera, or a new Play; they wou'd have preserv'd the Favour of Court and City, and gain'd Reputation and Profit to themselves." And, by May, new plays were being offered.

At its first performance, <u>The Confederacy</u> met with considerable approval. Mrs. Barry and Mrs. Bracegirdle gave fine performances, while Dogget was greatly applauded in the role of Moneytrap. He had taken considerable pains with the look of the character:

> He wore an old threadbare black coat, to which he had put new cuffs, pocket-lids and buttons, on purpose to make its rustiness more conspicuous; the neck was stuffed so as to make him appear round-shouldered and give his head greater prominency; his square-toed shoes were large enough to buckle over those he wore in common, which make his legs appear much smaller than usual.

His make-up was so masterly that Sir Godfrey Kneller said: "Mr. Dogget, you excel me in painting. I can only copy nature from the originals before me, whilest you vary them at pleasure and yet preserve a close likeness."

During the eighteenth century, the play attracted many great comedians. Among them: Macklin (Brass), Kitty Clive (Flippanta), Foote (Dick), Peg Woofington (Clarissa), Mrs. Abington (Corinna), Mrs. Pope (Flippanta), "Perdita" Robinson (Araminta), Mrs. Jordan (Corinna) and Munder (Moneytrap). Charles Matthews cornered the market on eccentricity as Gripe and W. Farren excelled as Moneytrap.

The play was produced frequently until 1825. After that, it saw provincial revivals and a London production in 1841. It was revived both in London and in the provinces in the first quarter of the twentieth century.

Critical Evaluations

The Confederacy   (1951)

In 1913, Barry Vincent Jackson, later knighted for his services to the theatre, built the original Birmingham Repertory Theatre in Station Street, which opened with a production of Twelfth Night on the 15th of February. The Rep became famous not only for the actors which it produced but also for its modern dress Shakespeare and its championing of contemporary plays, especially those of Bernard Shaw, for whom in 1923 it premiered Back to Methuselah in Britain. The example provided by Jackson in this first theatre to be built for repertory in England inspired the movement all over the country. Fulfilling its function to serve an artistic rather than a commercial purpose until 1971, it remained one of the most famous theatres in Britain, although physically it was a modest structure seating fewer than 500 people with an auditorium constructed basically as a wide, steeply raked staircase. The list of the Birmingham Repertory Theatre plays from 1913-1970 includes many world premieres as well as British premieres and the entire Shakespeare canon.

On October 2, 1951, the Rep produced Vanbrugh's The Confederacy. The cast included Hazel Hughes as Clarissa, Rosalind Boxall as Araminta, Joan Blake as Flippanta, Christine Finn as Corinna, Olive Walter as Mrs. Amlet, Alfred Burke as Gripe and Paul Daneman as Moneytrap. Douglas Seal directed and Paul Shelving designed the production.

Despite the corporate striving, the running time, a total of two and a half hours, seemed much longer than it was. The critic for The Birmingham Post noted that despite the visual advantage of an ingenious set, "which makes adroit use of a revolving stage," there was in the director's approach a "touch of burlesque mainly on the ladies, which makes them appear conscious of their humour."[1] This touch was serviceable for the Clarissa of Hazel Hughes, who "has the trick of raillery at her fingers' end, and is a mistress of discreet dissemblance." But the liability was that "it makes a grotesque of Corinna, the young girl who should be the sole innocent in a world of intrigue." Araminta unexpectedly became "an awkward hoyden."

The emphasis on broad playing was censured by the _Times_, which praised Seale for going "a long way towards recapturing the spirit of Vanbrugh's comedy" but bemoaned the fact that "there are moments when a touch of burlesque robs the play of some of its humour."[2]

The play was, however, still critically acceptable: "The characters in The Confederacy have not the soiled elegance usually associated with Restoration comedy. They rattle and rail in the contemporary mode, but they rattle to some tune."[3] Though the text was still interesting, the presentation did not offer a sufficient argument for the revival of Restoration plays:

> The acting was neither so good nor so bad as to call for high praise or severe disparagement and my predominant feeling as I left the theatre, was that these Restoration pieces, whatever their interest to the student, are calculated to serve as a soporific rather than a restorative, so far as the average playgoer is concerned.[4]

In the next twenty years, the Birmingham Repertory Theatre produced four more Restoration comedies. If the plays of this period were not a staple of the repertoire at least they were not excluded from it.

The Confederacy (1964)

On September 29, 1964, in celebration of the tercentenary of the birth of Vanbrugh, Prospect Productions presented The Confederacy under the direction of Toby Robertson at the Oxford Playhouse. The cast included Sylvia Coleridge as Mrs. Amlet, Michael Meacham as Dick, Robert Eddison as Gripe, Hy Hazell as Clarissa, Amanda Grinling as Flippanta, Toni Kanal as Corinna, Trevor Baxter as Moneytrap and Gudrun Ure as Araminta.

The set design by Alan Barrett with two proscenium doors on each side and sliding panels evoked the theatrical conventions of Vanbrugh's day. The adaptation of the stage bore a close resemblance to a 1920 production of the same piece by the Birmingham Repertory Theatre in which Paul Shelving had used a comparable approach in his design. The program explained the historical frame: "although scenery had been in use in England for nearly fifty years, the staging was still extremely conservative and retained nearly all the characteristics of the style known to scholars as 'presentational,' the play being presented frankly on a stage, and not represented in a pictorial, semi-realistic setting."

The emphasis in the Prospect production was on the ladies, and the program also noted that the female roles are proven vehicles for actresses: "Clarissa and Araminta, although inferior maybe to Congreve's ladies in art and polish, are infinitely more natural and vastly entertaining, whilst Flippanta's raillery of the two old husbands is kept up with consummate verve and skill."

In Mrs. Barry's role of Clarissa, Hy Hazell alternated between "excruciating 'refeenment' of diction with lapses into the broader accent of a humbler origin."[1] As Flippanta, the role originated by

Mrs. Bracegirdle and recognized as "one of the most exacting and at the same time most rewarding comic parts written for a woman player," Amanda Grinling was found to have "unquenchable verve and unfailing piquancy." The Araminta of Gudrun Ure showed a "comically fearsome, bristling coquettishness." The fact that the males were less well represented--with the exception of the remarkably diverting Gripe of Robert Eddison--indicated that the piece was presentationally imbalanced, but it was, at least partially, a success and very much in keeping with the policy of Restoration revivals inaugurated by Toby Robertson.

The Confederacy (1974)

On May 29, 1974, the Chichester Festival Theatre presented Vanbrugh's The Confederacy during Keith Michell's first season as artistic director of the theatre.[1] The cast included Peggy Mount as Mrs. Amlet, Patsy Byrne as Flippanta, Dora Bryan as Clarissa, Jeanette Sterke as Araminta, Gemma Craven as Corinna, Richard Wattis as Moneytrap and Frank Middlemas as Gripe. Wendy Toye directed and Anthony Powell designed the production.

Anthony Curtis judged that "the fulcrum here is money rather than sex."[2] The pretensions, the confusions, the intrigues all result from a misplaced sense of social aspiration due to middle class economic prosperity.

In this social game, the logical aggressors were the women, while the men were the passive ones "whose weaknesses must be exploited."[3] Despite a formidable cast, the performers tended to ignore the possibility of a common conception of the play. In the men's roles, there were extraordinary contrasts. Gripe was played by Frank Middlemas, "looking like Falstaff dressed as Malvolio, in terms of broadest caricature," while Richard Wattis' Moneytrap received an "utterly realistic treatment . . . looking as if he was on the run from <u>The Alchemist</u>." The composite result was "somewhat like a smoothly-performed vaudeville routine."[4]

The attempt to gallop briskly through the evening in no way contributed to a flexible tone. There was "no bite in the satire, no subtlety in the portrayal of class and character."[5] Of Robert Cushman's terse three-sentence review in the <u>Observer</u>, the final words summarized the bent of the critically mixed reaction: "expertly manoeuvred and thoroughly dead."[6]

X. Congreve

William Congreve is the formalist, the verbal technician and the reformer of the artistic rather than the moral conscience. His heroes do not delight in misdeed for its own sake--though there are misdeeds aplenty--for they are generally after the higher goal, the prize in the game of love. His heroines are wise with the wisdom of their world and enter in the plot with the consoling knowledge that they are the very prizes sought.

Of his four comedies, three still hold the stage, a not inconsiderable feat when it is considered that only one, Love for Love (1695), was a triumph during his lifetime.

Love for Love responds both to traditional and to naturalistic interpretations. By contrast, The Double Dealer (1693) suffers from the tragic element in the principal figures of Maskwell and Lady Touchwood, and it is virtually impossible to establish a unified tone in a production. On the page and on the stage The Way of the World (1700) is Congreve's most popular comedy, yet despite more recent attempts, only the "fantasticated" 1924 offering could boast an outstanding success. Later attempts to emphasize social structure were valid, but the cool prose of the characters eluded conscious manipulation on the part of the directors; consequently, the secret to a unifying concept has yet to be rediscovered.

THE DOUBLE DEALER
Plot Summary

I. Mellefont, nephew to Lord Touchwood, is to be married to his beloved Cynthia, the daughter of Sir Paul Plyant by a former marriage. Only Careless and Maskwell are aware that Lady Touchwood is in love with her nephew, who has repulsed her advances. Fearing retaliation from the lady, Mellefont asks Careless to attach himself to Lady Plyant, Lady Touchwood's sister-in-law, while Maskwell is to watch Lady Touchwood herself. However, when Maskwell and Lady Touchwood are alone, they are revealed as lovers and co-conspirators. Despite Mellefont's approaching marriage, Lady Touchwood still desires him.

II. Lady Froth regales Cynthia with tales of her love for Lord Froth and her literary talents. Left alone with Mellefont, Cynthia ponders the horrors of a union which makes man and wife "one flesh and leaves them still two fools." Lady Plyant and Sir Paul enter and accuse Mellefont of the attempted seduction of Lady Plyant. When Sir Paul and Cynthia exit, Lady Plyant protests her honor, while coming to the happy conclusion that her many charms have been the cause of Mellefont's desire, and she leaves him with a guarded promise of her favor.

III. Lord Touchwood is reluctant to believe evil of Mellefont, but Lady Touchwood allows her husband to force the "truth" from her: she claims that Mellefont has been paying court to her for a year. Maskwell tells Mellefont of his assignation and suggests that Mellefont break in upon them, let Maskwell escape and try to bring Lady Touchwood to terms.

As Mellefont predicted, Sir Paul tells Careless his troubles: his great grief is that he has no son to inherit the estate, and, since he has yet to consummate his marriage (she keeps him trussed up in blankets every night), it is unlikely that he will ever have one.

IV. Careless finally conquers Lady Plyant, and, obeying Mellefont's instructions on how to woo, gives her a note. In order to read it, she borrows a business letter from Sir Paul and is so charmed by Careless's invitation to meet in the wardrobe that she returns the wrong letter. Just as Sir Paul is finally undeceived, Lady Plyant pretends that her dealings with Careless were meant to try Sir Paul's constancy.

When Maskwell comes to Lady Touchwood's chamber, Mellefont leaps out. Maskwell escapes as planned and Lady Touchwood begs for mercy. But when she realizes that her husband is watching, she turns the scene to her advantage by accusing Mellefont of attempted incest.

V. Maskwell muses aloud, discovering his love of Cynthia to the listening Lord Touchwood, who not only promises him the girl but offers to disinherit Mellefont and make Maskwell his heir.

Careless and Cynthia compare notes and realize that Careless's early suspicions were correct and that Maskwell is a villain. Cynthia finds Lord Touchwood and conceals him behind a screen where, finally, he hears Lady Touchwood confront Maskwell. Lord Touchwood promises to add his plot to the multiple ones which are already hatching, and, by the quick wits of Mellefont and Lord Touchwood, the wickedness of Maskwell and Lady Touchwood is finally revealed.

Background

The Double Dealer was produced at the Theatre Royal in November 1693. The cast included Betterton as Maskwell, Powell as Brisk, Williams as Mellefont, Verbruggen as Careless, Dogget as Plyant, Kynaston as Lord Touchwood, Bowman as Froth, Mrs. Bracegirdle as Cynthia, Mrs. Mountfort as Lady Froth, Mrs. Barry as Lady Touchwood and Mrs. Leigh as Lady Plyant.

Of the eleven parts in his second play seven were taken by performers who had been in Congreve's first play, The Old Bachelor. Some were repeating the same type of role, but there were a few important changes and some significant juxtapositions. Two actors were brought in: Kynaston and Bowman. Bowman excelled in playing the pompous but not ignoble fop, and he would have made a good job of Froth's dawning realization of his wife's adultery with Brisk. Also, he would have contrasted well with Powell as Brisk, the rake-hero with which Powell was associated, and Mrs. Mountfort as Lady Froth would have balanced them both.

Brisk is contrasted with the figure of Verbruggen as Careless, a role not unlike the one he had played in The Old Bachelor. However, the playgoers would have known that Verbruggen the actor was challenging Powell and Williams to succeed Betterton. Betterton himself played Maskwell and the role casts back to the good-evil fascination of the rake Dorimant, another of Betterton's creations.

Kynaston had played everything from the title role in Epicoene to the most elevated parts. In his full career, Lord Touchwood is the only cuckold that he acted. This striking departure from tradition would have alerted the audience to the essential seriousness of the character.

Mrs. Barry, Mrs. Leigh and Mrs. Mountfort all offered versions of the promiscuous woman, with Mrs. Bracegirdle set apart as the chaste young observer. Even with her exalted reputation, Mrs. Barry would have had her hands full with Lady Touchwood, whose declamation reaches heights perilous for high comedy; yet she was well equipped both by experience--and by reputation--to come to grips with her.[1]

When The Double Dealer was first produced, a special performance was given by Royal Command of Mary II, who was delighted with the play. In 1698 Jeremy Collier condemned it on the grounds that it encouraged immorality, profaneness and immodesty. When it was revived in 1699, it was advertised as "carefully revised and corrected, by expunging the Exceptionable

Passages." In the eighteenth century the role of Maskwell attracted many interpreters, among them Quin and Kemble. The play was neglected in the nineteenth century, then revived in 1916 at the Queen's Theatre under the direction of Alan Wade assisted by Montague Summers.

Critical Evaluations

The Double Dealer (1959)

On August 24, 1959, the Old Vic Company, according to custom, opened at the Lyceum Theatre with Congreve's The Double Dealer directed by Michael Benthall and designed by Desmond Heeley in a try-out at the Edinburgh Festival prior to opening at the Old Vic in the forthcoming season in London. The cast included John Justin as Mellefont, Donald Houston as Maskwell, Alec McCowen as Brisk, Miles Malleson as Sir Paul Plyant, Charles West as Lord Touchwood, Joss Ackland as Lord Froth, John Woodvine as Careless, Ursula Jeans as Lady Touchwood, Judi Dench as Cynthia, Moyra Fraser as Lady Froth and Maggie Smith as Lady Plyant. Miles Malleson and Ursula Jeans were guest artists. The remainder of the cast belonged to the company.

The play had been seen last on the London stage in 1916, and then only in a well received handling by the Stage Society.[2] As the foremost British repertory company of the time, the Old Vic Company was fulfilling the duties of the not-yet-formed National Theatre. In 1958 it had completed its five-year plan to stage all of the Shakespeare plays in the First Folio. This task completed, it was free to engage in interpreting the works of other eminent playwrights. The difficulties of Congreve in terms of a viable interpretation by a modern company were noted in the Observer:

> [Congreve] is the supreme poet of the corrupt ephemeral, and at the same time he is extremely hard to play without sacrificing the poetry to the

corruption. Indeed, until we have a national theatre adjusted to the style of this most rare approach to play-writing, it would be idle to expect even the best company available to meet the occasion.[3]

At the time, the Old Vic was the best company available.

The difficulties of the plot were notoriously problematical. The _Observer_ noted its "absurd complexity," and W. A. Darlington cited the plot problem as the reason for the infrequent revival of the play: "Congreve, for all his inflated reputation as one of our best writers of comedy, suffered from a very defective sense of the theatre. He could create character, he could write scintillating dialogue; he could not clarify a plot."[4] The critic for the _Times_ ingeniously found a way of approaching the comedy as a form of "witty modern review":

> There seemed to-night no more comfortable way of receiving the comedy than as a series of "turns" in which the characters come on in groups ostensibly to hatch out improbable and complicated plots against the happiness of the true lovers but in reality to exhibit for our delight various phases of their coxcombry, coquetry, gallantry and wit.[5]

However the relevance of the play to a contemporary audience and the motivation for its revival were questioned by the critic for the _Stage_. He was undecided as to "whether it was written as a true reflection of the times or merely as a piece of artificial entertainment;" his final judgment was that "it has little for us today."[6] In contrast, the critic for the _Observer_ stressed the modernity of the play in its lack of poetry: "There is no poetry at all in the plot of a Congreve play, and in this respect the matter of his plays is exactly right for this day and age.

The society which Congreve depicted was as disillusioned as our own."[7]

Despite some rough edges and a need for more polish, the production had a successful opening in Edinburgh. One difficulty overcome was the creation of an environment which would allow for the multiple eavesdroppings. Desmond Heeley produced an intimate atmosphere: the set emphasized pale grey walls with scarlet curtains and tassels which gave the spying plausibility. Less happily, Michael Benthall had used Congreve's verse at the end of scenes as an excuse for having the actors suddenly break into song.

The most notable defect was in the speaking of the lines. In fairness to Congreve, Harold Hobson noted that "the surface of the dialogue is marvelously polished: so polished, in fact, that some of the Old Vic players slip on it."[8] Philip Hope-Wallace complained that "what is as yet not always certain is the intonation, which varies as though no one had given much though to the overall sound of the speaking."[9] Several months before, the Comédie Française had appeared at the Princes Theatre is a revival of Les Femmes Savantes, and the excellence of the speaking of the French national theatre was the most immediate basis of comparison for the Old Vic players, who, not surprisingly, came in second.[10]

When the play transferred to London on September 7, the Times critic, reviewing the play for the second time, resurrected the Edinburgh questions of "the extent to which the players would unify its succession of virtuoso scenes and the degree to which they might with practice achieve a valid Congrevian style." His happy conclusion was that the plot "has become as simple to comprehend as the alphabet" and that "neither direction nor acting go against the grain of the writing."[11] Herbert Whittaker expanded upon this theme:

183

There is a great attention to clarity, a steady glow of high spirits and a keen appreciation of any possible witticisms, which means that the actors have enough integrity to play on the line, not invent funny business to accompany it.[12]

The most successful performances were those of Maggie Smith and Miles Malleson as the ill-suited Sir Paul and Lady Plyant. Miss Smith, who was to become one of the foremost actresses of Restoration comedy, here made an early mark most successfully.

Despite a certain lack of "a sense of period style," she got the loudest laughs of the evening, for "Her performance makes the point again and again with the audience by reason of splendid attack, as when she forces herself upon the reluctant gallants with loud shrieks of alarm."[13] Smith's Lady Plyant was a multileveled character. The critic for the Stage defined the lady as "a creature of strangely biting charm . . . conveying a vivacious impression of satirically enjoying herself."[14] The panache with which she played inspired Herbert Whittaker's praise, which foreshadowed reviews in later years. She was, he said, "downright dazzling as that protesting, avid nymphomaniac, Lady Plyant. Here is guarantee that style will not vanish with such celebrated exponents as Dame Edith Evans and Mr. Malleson."[15]

"Sloping, wavering, quavering" Miles Malleson had his own style, which contributed a sense of contrast in approach. His was the richest comedy, for he made Sir Paul Plyant "not only senilely absurd but a trifle pathetic. His quiet, colloquial style is different from that of the rest, but the absence of exaggeration and the subtle inflexions and timings make him a human figure in an artificial world."[16] Additionally, he effected a physical complement to his performance. John Trewin delighted in him: "He manages to look facially like a classic sculptor's idea of an animated sheep, and to speak in tones like those of a furiously confidential turkeycock. . . . Never has chin drooped like Malleson's, or eyes popped so constantly."[17]

The producer's nightmare of the piece is, of course, Lady Touchwood. The critic for Plays and Players found that, like Maskwell, Lady Touchwood is "a straightforward study in unsmiling evil" and, consequently, ill at ease in the world of the comedy.[18] Ursula Jeans, joining the company for the purpose of playing the role, was as successful as an actress can be who is playing "a battleship among a fleet of gondolas."[19]

From the physical angle, Donald Houston was an unconventional choice for Maskwell. He presented none of the usual externals of the villain: "He looks chubby and charming, where he should look slender and evil. And if you argue that Maskwell would have to appear charming, then the actor playing him must be able to convey the evil beneath the charm."[20] For other critics, the casting of the moon-faced Houston with his fair wig and dark costume was acceptable, imaginative and, at best, genius. His affability made an ideal framework for his duplicity.

The play was not attempted in London again until the English Stage Company revived it in 1969 at the Royal Court Theatre. Although the Maskwell of that later production was more conventional, there were casting difficulties unheard of in the Old Vic production and a lack of ensemble effectiveness not known in the 1959 presentation.

The Double Dealer (1969)

On July 18, 1969,the English Stage Company revived The Double Dealer at the Royal Court Theatre, the first performance of that play in the West End since the Old Vic production in 1959. It was judged "the best of three Restoration entertainments now available in

Chichester and London."[1] The director was William Gaskill, who had made a success of Farquhar's The Recruiting Officer for the National Theatre Company in 1963, and the designer was John Gunter. The cast included John Castle as Maskwell, Judy Parfitt as Lady Touchwood, Alison Leggatt as Lady Plyant, Celia Bannerman as Cynthia, Michael Byrne as Mellefont, Geoffrey Chater as Lord Froth, George Howe as Sir Paul Plyant, Gillian Martell as Lady Froth, Malcolm Tierney as Brisk, John White as Careless and Nigel Hawthorne as Lord Touchwood.

Gaskill moved the company at a calculated pace, and Frank Marcus discovered that the production was "scored as chamber comedy: soft, unhurried, and subtle, with irruptions of frightening violence."[2] The effect was "surprisingly stolid with the witty lines sounding as if they were being delivered for weight rather than polished for sparkling."[3]

Gaskill was obviously striving for a contemporary, naturalistic approach which would dispel the Congrevian environment described by a review in the Boston Herald for the English Stage Society London production in 1916. There it had been emphasized that since "his characters move in a pungently astringent and quite a moral atmosphere of their own . . . Congreve's wit is all head-work . . . never a heart-beat in all his comic theatre."[4]

In attempting to redefine this atmosphere, Gaskill refused to "rely on accepted readings, to let 'style' usurp the place of genuine meanings and relationships."[5] There was praise for this concept of a modern, realistic production. The reviewer for the Stage found a balance in that although "some of the verbal wit is lost" there was an advantage in the "fresh wit coming from characters which are made to seem much nearer to our own way of thought and behaviour, in a social context, than might be thought possible."[6] Philip Hope-Wallace welcomed the contemporary approach for being "without prinking or preening or period affectations and yet [it] manages to get to the heart of the comedy as naturally as if it were a mirror of our own society."[7]

However, John Barber voiced the more conservative view that Gaskill achieved his effects at too great a sacrifice: "Clearly, an attempt has been made to seek a modern style of playing the comedy. But without the superlative speaking, and without the gloss of elegant manners, some of the amusement must be lost. Further, when real passions break through the artificial manners, they cannot shock if they have simply been absent."[8] And Clive Barnes informed New York that Gaskill took

> a firm and bleak look at Congreve's society, there is a cold and calculating motivation to these puppets that the director does not dress up in the frippery of eccentricity and extravagance.
>
> It is a difficult play to stage, and Mr. Gaskill has not been entirely successful in making its mixture of farce, satire and melodrama entirely convincing.[9]

The focal point in the play is, of course, Maskwell. Felix Barker summarized his evildoings:

> Slightly blue about the jowl (always a sinister sign) Maskwell devises enough treachery to make the angels not merely weep but have celestial hysterics.
>
> In his devious pursuit of the virtuous Cynthia he arranges for three husbands to be cuckolded and three wives ravished all under one roof in the two hours between six o'clock supper and eight.[10]

The program notes gave an account from Anthony Aston, a contemporary of Betterton who created the role, that offered an idea of the impact of the original villain: "His aspect was serious, venerable, and majestic . . . his Voice was low and grumbling; yet he could Time it by an artful Climax, which enforc'd Attention." Although John Barber found him the best thing in the English Stage Company production, John Castle, who played the role with "an interesting deep voice not yet quite in control," was hardly a match for the memory of Betterton.[11]

It is essential that since evil rules the plot, Maskwell must reign: "Crouched at the center of the intrigue, advancing himself by contaminating those around him . . . the Restoration Iago who acts on the Shakespearian principle that nothing looks more like truth than studied falsehood."[12] As the character controls much of the plot, so the actor must define that control in performance, making the most of his central position so that "his influence spreads out through the play in indirect chain-reaction."[13] He must be larger than life, yet have the appeal to make the audience relish his villainy while understanding the lesson the character unconsciously teaches: "Maskwell, like Don Juan, is an inverted moralist: his deeds, however disreputable in intention, uncover the truth: only unsullied innocence can defeat him. He is Lucifer--with a fatal longing for original virtue."[14] However, when combined with Lady Touchwood in performance, the results were "deliberately stagy melodrama conceptions" which defeated the naturalistic approach of the director.[15]

Maskwell's paramour, Lady Touchwood, was played by Judy Parfitt. Again, the English Stage Company program noted the majestic presence of the original Lady Touchwood, Mrs. Barry, who had a "presence of elevated Dignity, her Mien and Motion superb and gracefully Majestic; her Voice full, clear, and strong, so that no

Violence of Passion could be too much for her." There
was paradoxical praise for her character from Wardle,
who claimed that "the production is most alive when it
is furtherest from comedy," yet admitted that between
Maskwell and Lady Touchwood "these two might have blown
the comedy to smithereens."[16]

The one clear bit of miscasting was the frankly
over-aged Lady Plyant of Alison Leggatt in the role
with which the young Maggie Smith had had such a
success in 1959 at the Old Vic. Here Miss Leggatt was
forced to play "the 'handsome' Lady Plyant against the
text as a matronly frump whose schoolgirlish fluttering
is crudely contradicted by her looks, especially in the
gracelessly misdirected scene of Careless's attempted
seduction."[17] Understandably, the character became
unnecessarily bourgeois.

Though there was considerable invention in
Gaskill's attempt to stage the play, the performance
did prove that Restoration comedy tended to buckle
under an enforced modern approach.

The Double Dealer (1978)

On September 27, 1978, The Double Dealer was
revived by the National Theatre Company in a well
received production at the Olivier Theatre under the
direction of Peter Wood. The cast, which seemed to have
taken the measure of Congreve, included John Harding as
Mellefont, Dermot Crowley as Careless, Nicky Henson as
Brisk, Ralph Richardson as Lord Touchwood, Michael
Bryant as Sir Paul Plyant, Nicholas Selby as Lord
Froth, Sara Kestelman as Lady Touchwood, Robert
Stephens as Maskwell, Judi Bowker as Cynthia, Brenda
Blethyn as Lady Froth and Dorothy Tutin as Lady Plyant.
Pit, in Variety, noted the "sharp touches and attention
to detail." But, as in previous productions of
Congreve, he saw that the total was not as effective as
the parts when they were taken as a "series of set
pieces."[1]

Wood's look at the play was multileveled. John Barber noted that "Wood loses none of the fun. . . . But he never forgets Congreve's promise to 'paint the vices and follies of human kind.'"[2] And Benedict Nightingale concurred that "the comedy of humours was looking strangely real, at times even embryonically tragical."[3]

The two conventions in the play, the satiric and the melodramatic, were balanced by judicious mixing: "by tempering the cruelty of the satire and gently satirizing and melodrama."[4] The result was a ripened interpretation: "In this play Congreve is fully matured in his elegantly formal style, the elegance and the formality both being ingredients of its almost ceaseless fun."[5] Wood had excavated the play to show, as Gaskill had tried to do, a Congreve of the heart. The digging revealed "levels far deeper than anything in Wycherley . . . and suggests that this author had a vein of feeling that looked forward to the Romantics."[6]

The unification of the ensemble was unusual. Bernard Levin noted the skillful balance: "the chief merit of the production is that they [the players] do not revolve in separate orbits, but move in celestial harmony, giving and reflecting light."[7] Part of this unselfish playing evolved from the variations in style which contributed to increased interest in the characters. Robert Cushman defended the individuality of the performances: "the text invites them [to variety]--some critics seem to want everyone to give the same performance."[8] Part of the variation was arrived at by harmonizing natural and artificial delivery with the balance "beautifully drawn, so that although a character may come right downstage for a soliloquy he might only be talking to some companion in the house."[9] The impressive result of this variety and balance and probing direction was indicated by the audience reaction: "the laughter, being extracted from the quiddities of character rather than the excrescences of cartoon, is kindlier and more humane than one could reasonably have expected."[10] Part of the orchestrated laughter was inspired by "a thousand tiny subtleties--semi-pauses, half-sketched gestures, lightening changes of mind--which give naturalness and life."[11]

A key word, then, was compassion. Congreve was revealed as a cynic whose cynicism did not exclude pity: he could feel deeply and he could inspire genuine sympathy in an audience. To achieve this new response, Maskwell, the Double Dealer himself, was reevaluated. Irving Wardle discovered that "if Maskwell remains the play's mainspring, he is no longer the main character."[12] Robert Stephens gave him a particular twist: "his professions of conscience are not all bluff. . . . As a tragi-comic creation, he almost unifies the play."[13]

The seriousness of Maskwell's predicament was noted by Michael Billington, who saw the character as "no cardboard Machiavel but a thinking villain given to a cawing anguish about his personal problems. . . . Mr. Stephens combines the uncertainty of a Hamlet with the intentions of an Iago and the result is a wonderful study of baffled malignity."[14] Nightingale praised Stephens' detachment as he "humanises the hanky-panky, performing it with a strangely doleful look, as if no one in the world were more overburdened or put-upon than he. At times he watches himself with puzzled fascination, a one-man scientific survey."[15] Another critic noted that Stephens played Maskwell "with an almost sagging despair at the discovery of the well of greed and duplicity he draws from, within his own nature. It is bottomless, and it is as if he would be grateful to find one drop of clear, untainted instinct there."[16] Levin acknowledged the magnetic centrality of his vice: "credible almost to the point of likeability; saturnine, pessimistic, without relishing his cruelty, he becomes a profoundly disturbing figure, a black vortex at the heart of the play, into which every one else is in danger of being sucked."[17]

Except, of course, the Lady Plyant of Dorothy Tutin. Tutin, playing the role which Maggie Smith had played successfully in 1959 and in which Alison Leggatt had failed at the Royal Court in 1969, set Lady Plyant on one side of the comic scale by making her a "breathy vixen who has never let her husband touch her, and cannot keep her hands off any other male."[18] Michael Billington praised the portrait as a "fine comic study of sexual hypocrisy . . . which stays well this side of voluptuous grotesquerie."[19] Because of Tutin's ability to ascend to "high lubricious comedy," her lines revealed "the poetry of double-entendre,"[20] and her vocal skill allowed Lady Plyant to swoop "up and down the octaves in an ecstasy of breathless prurience."[21] She could rail against seduction even while she was encouraging it. She was hypocrisy in full cry: "Dorothy Tutin gives as brilliant a display as I have seen of the female tactic of saying No and acting Yes; delivering high-pressure tirades on honour, with every second word a double meaning and clapping Careless's hands around her salient parts in the act of unhanding herself."[22] Levin summarized the kinetic qualities of an actress whose voice "swooping through 2 1/2 octaves in the space of a single syllable and her eyes growing round and huge as cartwheels, can manage with such needle-fine precision the role of hurling herself at every available man while clamorously insisting on the impregnability of her virtue."[23]

Paired with Tutin's Lady Plyant was the Lady Touchwood of Sara Kestelman. Compared by various critics to Lady Macbeth, Phedre and Medea, the character suggested to Nightingale "a hell-bitch on heat."[24] She was a contrast to the 1969 Lady Touchwood of Judy Parfitt. Miss Kestelman, "her mouth a crimson gash and her voice somewhere between a growl and a hiss," managed to bridge the gap between melodrama and satire.

In 1959 Miles Malleson had played a great Sir Paul Plyant. In 1978 his characterization was equalled by the performance of Michael Bryant, who played against the grain of the text by finding a "skulking, shambling pathos in Sir Paul. . . . He confutes the scoffers with a man of feeling and humble dignity, who lets slip his embarrassment and misery in shy, apologetic monosyllables. . . . Even the sofa-stuffing that quaintly droops over his ears cannot sidetrack us from taking him seriously when he declares, as he does more than once, that his 'heart is breaking.'"[25] Bernard Levin sympathized with Bryant's Sir Paul and praised the realization he elicited from the audience: "even as we laugh, he turns this born cuckold into an almost fully tragic figure."[26] Sir Paul's confidences were sympathetically received, for Bryant presented him as "an inexhaustibly apologetic creature, quietly and amiably confiding his domestic happiness, and profound admiration for his wife, if only it were not for one little thing."[27] This little thing is the fact that his lady wraps him in blankets every night to keep him from her. Billington noted the extraordinary pathos of his restraint: "his crinkled smiles and tentative gestures . . . give you the rich absurdity; but what you remember is the tearful vulnerability of an old man desperate for a son."[28] This longing for a son has provoked a quiet war within him, which manifests itself in the whimsical quality of his speech pattern: "No word can escape him without being gravely weighed. He has one longish speech describing his state of life . . . which Mr. Bryant breaks up into sections of two words each. Each phrase gets a laugh."[29] However, the laughter confirmed Bryant's contribution to the total effect: "Mr. Bryant does not take over the centre of the show; but his performance adds an unexpected kindness and directness of feeling which spread into the surrounding atmosphere, revealing another side of the author."[30]

Finally, praise went to the set of Tanya Moiseiwitsch with its fine sense of period and its ingenious indication of time: "It was a perfect replica of a seventeenth-century gallery, with double staircase, all panelled in light oak. Sunlight streamed in through high windows and . . . moved around the stage with the clock until it was shining in from over our heads through an invisible window."[31]

LOVE FOR LOVE
Plot Summary

I. Valentine, who has been prodigal with his father's money, confines himself to his rooms to avoid his creditors. His father, Sir Sampson, wants the wastrel to sign over his inheritance to his seafaring brother, Ben, in return for four thousand pounds to pay his pressing debts. Pursued by creditors, Valentine's options are narrowing. Mrs. Frail comes to announce that her stepdaughter, Prue, who is intended for Ben, has come up from the country, and Ben has dropped anchor.

II. Angelica, Valentine's love, teases her Uncle Foresight about his shaky marital status. When Mrs. Frail admits to her sister, Mrs. Foresight, that she has an eye on Ben and his fortune, Mrs. Foresight agrees to help. Prue is taken with Tattle, a gossip and kiss-and-tell type, who coaches her in city ways.

III. Meeting Angelica, Valentine is disappointed by her lack of commitment, but she truthfully replies that she never admitted to loving him. When the plain, blunt Ben arrives, he has appreciative looks for Mrs. Frail and harsh words for Prue, who returns the favor.

As Sir Sampson and Foresight plan the wedding, Scandal arrives with the news that Valentine has lost his reason. Then the ever credulous Foresight is induced to take to his bed by Scandal, who convinces him that he looks ill. Scandal takes his turn with Mrs. Foresight, but they are interrupted by Mrs. Frail and Ben, who announce that they are in love.

IV. When Sir Sampson and Lawyer Buckram arrive with the papers, Valentine's lunatic behavior soon drives Buckram away. Now Valentine cannot sign the document legally, and Mrs. Frail, seeing her chances for capturing a wealthy Ben disappearing, quarrels with him. Mrs. Foresight engineers a plot to have the mad Valentine duped into marrying Mrs. Frail thinking she is Angelica. She bribes Jeremy, but he reports the scheme, and Valentine and Scandal plan a countermove: they will substitute Tattle for Valentine. Left alone with Angelica, Valentine admits his sanity.

V. Angelica suggests to Sir Sampson that if they announce that they are in love Valentine will throw off his pretense. Sir Sampson has a better idea: if Angelica will really marry him, he will settle his estate upon their children.

Tattle and Mrs. Frail enter to report that Valentine's trick has worked, and they are indeed married. Since Angelica is to marry his father, Valentine agrees to sign the paper since, without Angelica, money would be of no use to him. Unknowingly, he has passed Angelica's final test, and she tears up the paper and admits her love for him.

Background

Love for Love was produced on 16 April 1695, opening the new theatre in Lincoln's Inn Fields. The cast included Betterton as Valentine, Smith as Scandal, Sandford as Foresight, Underhill as Sir Sampson, Dogget as Ben, Bowen as Jeremy, Mrs. Barry as Mrs. Frail, Bowman as Tattle, Mrs. Bracegirdle as Angelica, Freeman as Buckram, Mrs. Leigh as the Nurse, Mrs. Ayliff as Prue and Mrs. Lawson as Jenny.

Downes describes the situation which led to the opening of the New Theatre:

> A difference happening between the United Patentees, and the chief Actors . . . the latter complaining of Oppression from the former; they for Redress, Appeal'd to my Lord of Dorset, then Lord Chamberlain, for Justice; who Espousing the Cause of the Actors . . . procur'd from King William, a Separate License for Mr. Congreve, Mr. Betterton, Mrs. Bracegirdle and Mrs. Barry, and others, to set up a new Company, calling it the New Theatre in Lincolns-Inn-Fields

Love for Love opened the playhouse with an unusually long run: "This Comedy being Extraordinary well Acted, chiefly the Part of Ben the Sailor, it took 13 Days Successfully." Cibber concurs, and he was on the opposing side:

> After we had stolen some few Days March upon them, the Forces of Betterton came up with us in terrible Order: . . . The new Theatre was open'd against us, with a veteran Company, and a new Train of Artillery . . . the old Actors in Lincolns-Inn-Fields began, with a new Comedy of Mr. Congreve's . . . which ran on with such extraordinary Success, that they had seldom occasion to act any other Play, 'till the End of the Season.

At the time, Congreve's reputation was so exalted that the company, in addition to his profits, offered him a share with them in return for his agreement to write one play for them every year. However, his next play--and his last--was five years in coming.

196

Underhill brought his particular talent to the "blunt Vivacity" of Sir Sampson. As Ben, Dogget gained such tremendous popularity that it seemed to affect his priorities:

> The late Reputation which Dogget had acquir'd from his acting Ben, in Love for Love, made him a more declar'd Male-content on such Occasions; he over-valu'd Comedy for its being nearer to Nature, than Tragedy. . . . [He] could not, with Patience, look upon the costly Trains and Plumes of Tragedy, in which knowing himself to be useless, he thought were all a vain Extravagance. . . . He so obstinately adhered to his own Opinion, that he left the Society of his old Friends, and came over to us at the Theatre-Royal.

Of all of Congreve's plays, Love for Love was the most successful in the eighteenth century despite the fact that it suffered from some neglect by Garrick. It was slowly eclipsed in the nineteenth century, then was revived in 1917 and again in 1921.

Critical Evaluations

Love for Love (1944 & 1947)

In 1924, the year of the Lyric Theatre's great Way of the World, John Gielgud played in Love for Love at the Playhouse, Oxford. In 1944, he brought his own production of the comedy from the Phoenix, where it had opened in 1943, to the Haymarket, making the play a commercial as well as an artistic success. The London cast included Gielgud as Valentine, Leslie Banks as Tattle, Rosalie Crutchley as Angelica, Leon Quartermaine as Scandal, Miles Malleson as Foresight, Yvonne Arnaud as Mrs. Frail, Marian Spencer as Mrs. Foresight, George Woodbridge as Ben, Cecil Trouncer as Sir Sampson, Max Adrian as Jeremy and Angela Baddeley as Prue.

The demands of London alerted Gielgud to certain details which had not been of great importance at Oxford. In Stage Directions he discusses the more complete Oxford production: "We gave the play in a very full version, but as our audience consisted largely of dons and the highbrow intelligentsia of North Oxford, the text was easily followed and understood."[1] In London, the text had to be cut more drastically.

Another considerable innovation was reversing the idea of playing according to the 17th- and 18th-century traditions. With Leon Quartermaine, Gielgud reached a decision about a more contemporary mode of presentation:

> We both felt that if the actors would all play realistically--and were also stylish enough to wear their clothes and deport themselves with elegance--there was no reason why we might not play the play in a naturalistic style, with the 'fourth wall down' as it were.[2]

With greater resources than Nigel Playfair's, Gielgud opted for verisimilitude in the only two settings in the play:

> This was in direct opposition to anything I had ever seen, for, in Playfair's productions, the asides were delivered (as no doubt they were in the eighteenth century) directly to the audience, and there was no attempt at localization in the settings, which were merely drop scenes and wings, and served as a background (but not as a home) for the characters in the play.[3]

Rex Whistler sketched the sets, and Jenetta Cochrane made a designer's holiday of the costumes. Particularly happy for Gielgud, as director and actor, was the casting of the veteran Yvonne Arnaud as Mrs. Frail. Taking the lead more by instinct than seniority of role, she guided the play along the paths most inspirational to the cast:

> [She] brought such skill and experience to the part of Mrs. Frail in my Love for Love, that the whole cast seemed to discover and develop the right gusto and style from her example.[4]

In playing Valentine, Gielgud was not tackling the most rewarding of Restoration roles. Several days before the opening, James Agate summarized the role's potential--or lack of it:

> This is the least good part in the play, and can never be more than a peg for the actor's own airs and graces. But since Congreve lavished some of his loveliest prose on the handsome dummy, and since Mr. Gielgud speaks prose to a wonder as well as verse, it is probable that between the two of them delight will be engendered even if no character is born.[5]

Yet in reviewing the performance the critic for the Times awarded Gielgud points for a "witty grace, a perfect command of the Congrevean prose rhythms and the nicest sense of Shakespearian parody in the Mad scene," a burlesque of Gielgud's own Hamlet.[6]

As a production, the play was completely accepted and individually the actors were well received. But the greatest achievement was in realizing the quality of immediacy that Gielgud had sought:

> Here is a performance of the old comedy which captivates the mind in the right way, lapping it, so to speak, in laughter and delight. . . . When the curtain has fallen--not a moment earlier--we may be tempted to justify our experience in terms of Lamb's pretense that the characters who have amused us are so manifestly unreal that we need not mind having laughed at them and enjoyed their

deplorable intrigues. But why should we so bedevil our sense of Congreve's comedy?

> Valentine, Sir Sampson, Mrs. Frail, Scandal, Tattle . . . Ben . . . are not in the least fantastic; all on the stage fairly palpitate with life. While we are looking and listening we doubt their reality as little as did Macaulay pouring censoriously over their scintillating dialogue.[7]

The transfer of Love for Love from London to New York in 1947 is significant in determining how well Restoration comedy travels. There were a monumental number of cast changes, which were not to the advantage of the corporate play. The New York cast included Gielgud as Valentine, Cyril Ritchard as Tattle, Pamela Brown as Angelica, George Hayes as Scandal, John Kidd as Foresight, Adrianne Allen as Mrs. Frail, Marian Spencer as Mrs. Foresight, Robert Flemyng as Ben, Malcolm Keen as Sir Sampson, Richard Wordsworth as Jeremy, Jessie Evans as Prue and Sebastian Cabot as Buckram. As director again, Gielgud had difficulty in remounting:

> I found I was not able to re-create the spirit of the production successfully a second time. It may be too that the background of the Restoration period was puzzling to an American audience. The behaviour of a corrupt, idle, society, led by a profligate Court, though familiar to every English schoolboy who has read of Charles the Second or the Prince Regent, seems as strange to an audience in the United States as the Molière comedies, so eternally popular in France, which have seldom succeeded in translation either in England or America.[8]

Love for Love was presented in repertory with an enormously successful version of Wilde's The Importance of Being Earnest. The Wilde play was considered the best revival of the season. It both charmed and amused the audience, while the Congreve piece did not. William Hawkins assessed the difficulty:

> The play seems to be done with an awesome fidelity to tradition that would undoubtedly appeal more to a British audience than an American one. Here and now it seems bloodless, and only here and there funny.
>
> . . . .
>
> Since "Love for Love" is a talky play it could do with more physical vibrancy than it gets here. Proof of this lies in the fact that so many of the really memorable moments are those that are pictorial for their agility.[9]

The one performance with almost universal appeal was that of Cyril Ritchard whose vigorous approach to Tattle resulted in "capital fooling."[10] The theory that Tattle was perhaps the fattest role in the play was later to be substantiated when Laurence Olivier elected to play it for the National Theatre Company.

Although Gielgud's production did not fare as well once it crossed the Atlantic as it had done on the home front, its influence was remembered as a powerful force when the National Theatre Company brought their production to Canada in 1967. Reviewing the later production, Nathan Cohen recalled that soon after its premiere in 1695, Love for Love received an all-female interpretation, and he speculated that "perhaps that was when the convention developed of presenting the men in Restoration plays in a manner as far removed as possible from the familiar masculine realism, in a way conducive to a total artificiality of attitude."[11] This convention did not die with the close of the seventeenth century, but "evolved, refined itself, and reached its apogee . . . in the John Gielgud-Pamela Brown-Cyril Ritchard production of Love for Love," which conveyed such an androgynous air that the production managed to be "entirely bawdy yet altogether sexless." Such an approach stressed affectation while infusing the text with life--and fun.

Love for Love (1965)

The first performance of the National Theatre's Love for Love, directed by Peter Wood, was on September 9, 1965, in Moscow, where it was played with Othello and Hobson's Choice. The most complete audience reaction was to Laurence Olivier, whom they had just seen as the Moor, and who, as Tattle, "minces about, falls flat on his face, clambers out of windows and almost plays the harpsichord."[1] Naturally, his variety was impressive. The Moscow audience reacted totally, trooping down the aisles applauding and cheering. The cast, which played in Moscow, London and later in Canada, included John Stride as Valentine, Robert Lang as Scandal, Laurence Olivier as Tattle, Joyce Redman as Mrs. Frail, Miles Malleson as Foresight, Geraldine McEwan as Angelica, Lynn Redgrave as Prue, Colin Blakely, and later Albert Finney, as Ben, Anthony Nicholls as Sir Sampson and Tom Kempinsky as Jeremy. The production was designed by Lila de Nobili.

On October 20, 1965, Love for Love joined the repertoire at the Old Vic. Of particular significance to the critics was "A Note on Love for Love" by the director, which appeared in the program. In it, Wood pointed out that the play was "plainly intended . . . for a wider public than the narcissistic, closed circle of the Court. To reflect the interests of this larger group, it is less about love than about money." Wood accepted Congreve's approach via a monetary route, yet stressed the playwright's "sharp disgust at the materialism of his audience." This disgust plus a "steady humanity" are the attributes that distinguish Congreve from his contemporaries.

J. W. Lambert admitted Wood's success in emphasizing the broader social relevance, thus "what

little there is of warmth and humanity in Congreve is
made the most of."[2] This social alertness was also
revealed in the inclusion of the lower orders of
society to contrast with the upper echelon: "this
constant reminder of the poor, smelly world outside
helps give the artificial comedy of intrigue a welcome
solidity and strength."[3] The style of playing toned
down the mannerisms in an effort to keep the feel of
the time intact. E. Martin Brown observed that "the
'Restoration' manners become the natural expression of
. . . vitality, and the peerless lines are the witty
commentary of real people on their own way of life."[4]

In performance, the character of Ben, long a
favorite of actors, attained critical significance
again. Peter Lewis agreed that Colin Blakely made him a
rounded figure with a walk that was "a joy to watch," a
smile of "Hogarthian vacancy" and a testament to the
"sheer good-nature that comes shining through the
bovine intellect."[5]

In 1966 Albert Finney joined the National Theatre
Company and alternated the role of Ben with Blakely.
Harold Hobson saw in Finney's engaging performance a
comment on Wood's reading of Congreve's view of the
state of society:

He [Finney] sees the plain fact which, for all his
learning, seems to have eluded Mr. Wood: namely,
that, far from being a social instructor, Congreve
had values so unhealthy that he ranked a
worthless, but gentlemanly, ne'er-do-well high
above a coarse, industrious working man. What
Congreve despises and jeers at, Mr. Finney makes
sympathetic and affectionately funny.[6]

The balance between the mask of manners and the
face of humanity in the production was struck by the
staccato-voiced Tattle of Laurence Olivier. The critic
for the _Times_ described the magnificent comic moment
when, at the revelation of his marriage to Mrs. Frail

rather than the desired Angelica, Tattle falls flat on his back:

> It is a moment of comedy at which the very ground seems to shift under one's feet, and it brings forth a line that gives the classic antithesis between the courtly man and the natural man: "Gad, I never had the least Thought of serious Kindness," remarks Olivier suavely: then bursts into tears and adds, "I never liked any Body less in my life."[7]

As Scandal, Robert Lang injected a contrasting note, "stalking through the play like an embodiment of lonely scorn," managing to convey the warning that the great danger of cynical wit is its tendency to ricochet.[8]

Farther down on the list of delights was the Valentine of John Stride who was somewhat tentatively applauded for carrying off "the boring scenes of mock madness with a good grace."[9]

In 1966, the National Theatre Company recorded Love for Love. Thomas Lask paid particular attention to the wooing scenes between Prue and Tattle and Ben and Prue, with acknowledgement of the "wealth of quiet humor" in the meeting between the "mad" Valentine and Angelica. He gave special credit to the speaking of the dialogue: "All that the human voice can do to give meaning to words, add shade and nuance to a phrase, or supply a hint through a cool or heightened tone is done on these records."[10] With Othello, it ranked as an outstanding spoken word recording by the company.

THE WAY OF THE WORLD
Plot Summary

I. Fainall meets the glum Mirabell at a chocolate
house, and Mirabell reveals a recent quarrel with
Millamant, with whom he is in love, and his expulsion
from her house at the request of Millamant's guardian,
Lady Wishfort. Mirabell learns that his servant
Waitwell has married Foible, Lady Wishfort's servant,
and he is happy in the beginning of a plot. Witwoud, a
foppish member of Millamant's entourage, comes in to
complain that his half brother, Sir Wilful Witwoud, is
coming to town. As the act closes, two significant
facts are presented: since she controls Millamant's
fortune, Lady Wishfort is a crucial factor in
Mirabell's plans, and Mirabell's uncle is in London.

II. Mrs. Marwood and Mrs. Fainall, Lady Wishfort's
daughter, both lie to each other about their hatred of
men. Fainall himself is unimpressed; he knows that even
now they both love Mirabell. Trusting that her love for
him is still alive, Mirabell tells Mrs. Fainall his
scheme. Since he can only get Lady Wishfort's consent
to his marriage with Millamant by high-handed tactics,
Mirabell has decided on blackmail. The so-called uncle
come to town is really Waitwell, who will act the part
of one Sir Rowland and court Lady Wishfort. After she
has learned to dote on Sir Rowland, Mirabell will
reveal Waitwell's marriage and threaten the old lady
with scandal.

III. Foible baits the trap by praising Sir Rowland and
encouraging Lady Wishfort to believe that he loves her.
She is so impressive that Lady Wishfort vows to marry
him--though she's not yet seen him. Hidden in the
closet Marwood has heard all.

IV. While Lady Wishfort awaits Sir Rowland, Sir Wilful
botches an attempt to court Millamant. When Mirabell
arrives, their duel of wits becomes the "proviso" scene

in which Millamant lists certain demands she would make if they were to be married. When he leaves, she confesses her love to Mrs. Fainall.

When the meeting between Sir Rowland and Lady Wishfort occurs, Waitwell, who is more than up to the demands of the part, plays skillfully on her weak points. Marwood sends a letter revealing the imposture, but together Waitwell and Foible manage to convince Lady Wishfort that this is another trick of Mirabell's to keep her from marrying.

V. Lady Wishfort cannot remain duped forever, and with Mrs. Marwood and Fainall at work, Foible must admit the truth. Fainall makes his demands: Lady Wishfort is to turn over to him the remainder of his wife's fortune plus six thousand pounds. If she does not, he will make public Mrs. Fainall's continuing affair with Mirabell.

Mirabell counters with an alternative scheme: if he can marry Millamant, he can save Mrs. Fainall's reputation and, what is more to the point, her money. Lady Wishfort acquiesces. Mirabell then produces Foible and Mincing, Millamant's servant, who can testify to the fact that Fainall and Mrs. Marwood are lovers and have as much to hide as anyone else. Then Mirabell produces a paper which had made him trustee of Mrs. Fainall's fortunes while she was still single. Completely overthrown, Fainall and Marwood leave and, at last, Mirabell gets Millamant.

Background

The Way of the World was produced at Lincoln's Inn Fields in early March of 1700. The cast included Betterton as Fainall; Verbruggen as Mirabell; Bowen as Witwoud; Underhill as Sir Wilfull; Bowman as Petulant; Bright as Waitwell; Mrs. Bracegirdle as Millamant; Mrs. Barry as Marwood; Mrs. Bowman as Mrs. Fainall; Mrs.

Leigh as Lady Wishfort; Mrs. Willis as Foible and Mrs. Prince as Mincing.

Downes wasn't sure about the performance:

The Way of the World, a Comedy wrote by Mr. Congreve, twas curiously Acted; Madame Bracegirdle performing her Part so exactly and just, gain'd the Applause of Court and City; but being too Keen a Satyr, had not the Success the Company Expected.

But on March 12th, Dryden wrote to Mrs. Steward, "Congreve's new play has had but moderate success, though it deserves better."

Elinor Leigh, probably the wife of Anthony Leigh, had a great success as Lady Wishfort. Cibber affirms that she had a

very droll way of dressing the pretty Foibles of superannuated Beauties. She had . . . a good deal of Humour, and knew how to infuse it into the affected Mothers, Aunts, and modest stale Maids, that had miss'd their Market. . . . She was extremely entertaining, and painted, in a lively manner, the blind Side of Nature.

Anne Bracegirdle's power over both the audience and the authors was undeniable:

It will be no extravagant thing to say, scarce an Audience saw her, that were less than half of them Lovers, without a suspected Favourite among them. . . . She inspired the best Authors to write for her, and two of them [Rowe and Congreve], when they gave her a Lover, in a Play, seem'd palpably to plead their own Passions, and make their private Court to her, in fictitious Characters.

Her physical attractions were increased by her amiable personality:

She had no greater Claim to Beauty, than what the most desirable Brunette might pretend to. But her Youth, and lively Aspect, threw out such a Glow of Health, and Cheerfulness, that, on the Stage, few Spectators that were not past it, could behold her without Desire.

And she had the dramatic range to make two vastly different characters her own:

If any thing could excuse that desperate Extravagance of Love, that almost frantick Passion of Lee's <u>Alexander the Great</u>, it must have been, when Mrs. Bracegirdle was his Statira: As when she acted Millamant, all the Faults, Follies, and Affectation of that agreeable Tyrant, were venially melted down into so many Charms, and Attractions of a conscious Beauty.

<u>The Way of the World</u> remained popular until the beginning of the nineteenth century. In the middle of the century, 1842, it was unsuccessfully revived at the Haymarket. On April 17, 1904, under the direction of Philip Carr, the comedy was presented at Court. So successful was this revival that a public performance was given at the Royalty on November 7, 1904. It was revived again in 1918 at the King's Hall, Covent Garden, and in the provinces at the Maddermarket Theatre, Norwich, in 1923. Among the distinguished Millamants have been Mrs. Oldfield, Peg Woffington, Mrs. Pritchard and Ethel Irving. Lady Wishfort's interpreters have included Mrs. Saunders, Kitty Clive, Mrs. Mattocks, Mrs. Glover and Mrs. Theodore Wright.

Critical Evaluations

The Way of the World (1948)

On October 21, 1948, The Way of the World was presented by the Old Vic Company at the New Theatre with Faith Brook as Millamant and Edith Evans, then sixty, as Lady Wishfort; Harry Andrews as Mirabell, Robert Eddison as Witwoud, Peter Copley as Fainall, Mark Dignam as Petulant, Nigel Green as Sir Wilfull Witwoud, Medows White as Waitwell, Pauline Jameson as Mrs. Marwood, Mary Martlew as Mrs. Fainall, June Brown as Foible, Penelope Munday as Mincing, Josephine Stuart as Peggy and Margaret Chisholm as Betty. John Burrell directed.

Miss Brook, still laboring under the Evans legend of a quarter of a century earlier, was given full critical treatment by W. A. Darlington as he contemplated the two readings, twenty-five years apart, of Millamant's single line, "I may by degrees dwindle into a wife." Darlington acknowledged that the new social situation of Millamant as a wife did not, despite its essential seriousness, dissipate her charm:

> Though she knows in her newly discovered heart that her career as a coquette is now at an end and that she, who has had hundreds of lovers at her beck and call, must now yield to one of them, she capitulates with a wayward charm all her own.[1]

Therefore, the indifferent reception to Miss Brook's reading of Millamant's capitulation was explained by Darlington's description of her lack of perception:

> Miss Brook says this last phrase . . . all in one piece. She says it without any special emphasis and as if she had no suspicion that there is in these eight words any material with which an

actress may make a comic effect. Consequently, the audience has no such suspicion either.[2]

Contrasted with Miss Brook's somewhat flat reading was a series of selected emphases made by Miss Evans in her earlier performance:

> This effect was made by a whole series of extraordinarily significant stresses in which the actress let her voice dwell on the word she was saying, as if she loved it for itself as well as for the meaning she was coaxing out of it--'I may--by degrees--dwindle--into a wife.'[3]

The particular attention to words which had continued to characterize the performance of Edith Evans gave full weight to her Lady Wishfort,

> who becomes, not a broadly funny caricature of a lecherous old harridan, but a picture of a credible human being seen with an understanding sense of human folly and touched here and there with a pity which does not stifle laughter but gives it depth.[4]

Although the critic for the _Times_ noted that the mid-century audience could now "experience the characters in all their glittering absurdity without judging them," the considerably flawed production did not give much room for enjoyment. It was considered "an uneven performance, sprightly and animated now and then but only at ease when Dame Edith Evans is playing a solo passage, and always wanting the correctness and delicacy of composition on which Congreve depends."[5]

The centrality of focus had shifted from Millamant to Lady Wishfort, who was like a caricature of Elizabeth I, and the shift--though in the direction of the Evans talent--had done nothing considerable in interpreting, clarifying or even enlivening Congreve or his characters. Miss Brook's failure ushered in two, some say three, unsuccessful Millamants.

The Way of the World (1953)

On February 19, 1953, John Gielgud both directed and played in The Way of the World, the second of his productions in his season at the Lyric Theatre, Hammersmith. The success of the production depended upon two elements: the power of Gielgud to draw an audience to support his classics and the successful selectivity of his casting, which preserved playwrights

> such as Webster and Otway, by whom our rather conservative playgoers are not drawn except with the magnetic addition of a much-admired actor . . . he does not "draw" merely because he is himself, but because he insists on judicious casting round about him, gives a major care to the lesser parts, and bestows upon the author's whole intention as much skill and devotion as he does upon his own part. His power to draw the public has a special advantage in that he can guarantee support for the classics of "the fringe."[1]

The cast, which, for the most part, was later to appear in the more successful Venice Preserved, was, and still is, notable for the number of performers of extraordinary merit. Gielgud was Mirabell; Pamela Brown, Millamant; Margaret Rutherford, Lady Wishfort; Paul Scofield, Witwoud; Eileen Herlie, Mrs. Marwood; Eric Porter, Fainall; Pauline Jameson, Mrs. Fainall; Richard Wordsworth, Petulant and Brewster Mason, the elder Witwoud. There could be no quarrel with Gielgud's taste in casting, nor with the general style of the performance. In Stage Directions, Gielgud approximates a definition of style as it relates to the acting of the classics:

> What exactly is style in acting and stage production? Does it mean the correct wearing of

costume, appropriate deportment and the "nice conduct of a clouded cane?" Does it also imply a correct interpretation of the text, without undue exaggeration or eccentricity, an elegant sense of period, and beautiful unselfconscious speaking by a balanced and versatile company of players, used to working together; flexible instruments under the hand of an inspired director?[2]

The answer lay in the critical admiration for the practice of Gielgud's theory. Ivor Brown celebrated the achievement, "At the Lyric Theatre, Hammersmith, we have the finery of phrase, finery of aspect, and considerable finery of casting."[3] Kenneth Tynan defined the sophistication of Congreve and the attributes of that definition on display in the production:

> By sophisticated I mean genial without being hearty, witty without being smug, wise without being pompous, and sensual without being lewd.

He then went on to attest to the particular actuality of the characters:

> Because they speak precisely and with affection for the language they are using, it is usually taken for granted that Congreve's characters are unreal. Nothing could be more misguided. These people do not bare their souls (that would smack of nudism), but they are real enough.[4]

Philip Hope-Wallace enjoyed "a patina of style and grace of speech, not to mention four or five delightfully droll and original performances."[5] The grace of speech doubtless stemmed from the director, who elaborated his approach to the words of a text:

> I try to study the sound, shape and length of words themselves, so as to reproduce them exactly as they are written on the page. In a verse speech (and often in a long prose one too) I am

constantly aware of the whole span of the arc--the
beginning, middle and end of the passage. I try to
phrase correctly for breathing, punctuation and
emphasis, and then, conforming to this main line,
I experiment within it for modulation, tone, and
pace, trying not to drag out the vowels, elongate
syllables, or pounce on opening phrases.[6]

The plot had long been accepted as unintelligible,
and Gielgud admitted that neither cutting nor
transposing eased the complications. (Not until the
National Theatre's production in 1969 did a program
valiantly attempt to simplify matters for the
audience.) But accepting the complexities of the
various situations gave no one any real difficulties.
"Of all plots," said Tynan cheerfully, "none more
closely resembles a quadratic equation than that of The
Way of the World;" similarly, Ivor Brown was content to
remain in the maze of situations for the joy of the
words:

When Sheridan put the very sensible question,
"What the devil is a plot for except to bring in
fine things?" he gave ample defense of The Way of
the World. . . . But the words, or most of them,
will always suffice: the wit and music of
Congreve's prose makes Wilde's volleying of
routine paradox seem a trivial tinkling in the
ear.[7]

Considering the amiability of the audience towards
the complexities of the plot and the impressive list of
performers, the evening should have been a total
success. That it was not was dependent, to some degree,
upon the Playfair production of the same play, in the
same theatre, over a quarter of a century before. This
1924 production was, and to some extent still is, the
single most successful production of Congreve's

elaborate, complicated masterpiece. Gielgud was, of
course, familiar with its success:

> In 1924, Playfair announced <u>The Way of the World</u>
> by Congreve for the Lyric Hammersmith, and the
> décor for this revival was entrusted to Doris
> Zinkeisen, whose painted scenery and vivid
> costumes, in poster style, more elaborate but less
> fastidious than the work of Lovat Fraser, were, to
> the eyes of the playgoers of the twenties,
> distinctly <u>avant-garde</u>. But it was, above all, the
> acting of Edith Evans as Millamant and Robert
> Loraine as Mirabell which brought the public to
> see the revival of a classic which no one had
> imagined could possibly succeed with a modern
> audience. Playfair's direction, despite several
> weaknesses in the supporting cast, showed the same
> skill in simplification that he had already
> achieved in <u>The Beggar's Opera</u>.[8]

The success of the Playfair venture belonged
mostly to the Millamant of Edith Evans, which went far
with the critics toward proving that Millamant was the
play. Still vivid in the critical mind after 29 years,
the Evans performance--as it had done with Faith
Brook's Millamant in 1948--stood in sharp contrast to
Pamela Brown's.

Philip Hope-Wallace defined the opening night
situation of all the actors at the Lyric in 1953:

> But if something stands between us and the full
> enjoyment which we continue to expect . . . it may
> possibly be the unlaid ghost of that legendary
> performance on these boards. The players seemed to
> be anxious--and we with them--to forget that they
> might sound like echoes: that each speech should,
> if possible, seem to fall newly minted from new
> lips.[9]

Ignoring the 1924 production, Cecil Wilson gave the most completely successful survey of the Gielgud offering, yet he could do little more for Millamant than to remark that the "dazzling" Pamela Brown tied Mirabell into knots of obedience "with the rolling eye of a very attractive ventriloquist's dummy"--not the most happy phrase for Congreve's elegant, eloquent lady.[10]

The difficulty of Brown's Millamant was apparently based on the not insubstantial fact that the actress was not in sympathy with the character. The critic for the _Times_ summed up the essence of Millamant's comic spirit and Miss Brown's lack of it:

> The comedy of Millamant is that she is about to be married as a woman and that she talks about her marriage merely like a lady of fashion. She talks with such exquisiteness that every word she utters becomes the studied expression of her personal witchery. Yet exquisitely as she talks . . . she is never required by the comedy to think, not even about Mirabell, whom she regards as one of the more agreeable trappings of life which is hers for the taking.
>
> . . . . Miss Brown has some delicious moments before she submits to "dwindle into a wife." Yet there is detectable in her playing an undercurrent of dissatisfaction with a heroine who, for all her wonderful play with irony and paradox and wit, remains an inveterate trifler, happy to watch her own graceful reflection in the social mirror . . . the impression is that she is unaccountably not in love with the idea of Millamant.[11]

And Ivor Brown, although acknowledging the loquacious eye of Miss Brown, could do little more than engage in a comparison which led to a lauding of the Evans performance:

Pamela Brown's Millamant began with a too fussy use of deliberate gaiety . . . and continued to speak with a rather jerky petulance instead of a smooth rhythm of raillery. Some famous sentences which the Evans delivery has kept echoing in my mind (e.g. "I nauseate walking; 'tis a country diversion: I loathe the country and everything that relates to it") went for little. . . . Dame Edith gave her a dear lady's heart under the fine lady's glitter, but Pamela Brown seems to view her more as a minx with a roving eye.[12]

If Millamant was not completely successful, then Gielgud as Mirabell, a part not really up to his weight, was also in difficulty. Although he knew the value of style and cadence, the crucial proviso scene simply did not come off. The imbalance between them was clearly defined by Tynan: "Mr. Gielgud . . . has Pamela Brown begging for mercy almost before the battle is joined."[13]

After the lovers, the next in line for consideration, Lady Wishfort, received a particularly individual approach from Margaret Rutherford. Sixty-one at the time of the production, she specialized in the whimsical and the fey. She had a generous build oddly at variance with a somewhat soft, musical voice and a face of multiple comic charms: "Bulbous eyes set in deep pouches, an impertinent nose and a fierce jaw that rested on an accordion of chins."[14] Miss Rutherford had the major success of the production by playing the role without emphasizing its absurdities. Gielgud saw Lady Wishfort as "a kind of fantastic monster," but Rutherford's monstrosity was of an eccentrically appealing kind. Although her considerable visual appeal outweighed the delivery of the lines, Tynan's review of her Lady Wishfort at Hammersmith is an engaging kinetic picture of the comic actress in full cry:

Miss Rutherford is filled with a monstrous vitality: the soul of Cleopatra has somehow got trapped in the corporate shape of an entire lacrosse team.

The unique thing about Miss Rutherford is that she can act with her chin alone: among its many moods I especially cherish the chin commanding, the chin in doubt, and the chin at bay. My dearest impression of this Hammersmith night is a vision of Miss Rutherford clad in something loose, darting about her boudoir like a gigantic bumblebee at large in a hothouse.[15]

Nevertheless, John Gielgud's production could not be considered at all a failure. He had let the members of the cast have their way, finding in the individual virtuoso scenes a series of singularly excellent comic turns drawn together by a rather fine, though tangled, plot thread. Doing some of these turns were supporting figures who found their way to the forefront of attention. Among them was the Witwoud of Paul Scofield, previously Richard II for Gielgud's company and later the Pierre of <u>Venice Preserved</u>. He played somewhat against the grain of the text:

Paul Scofield makes Witwoud extremely amusing by turning him into a feeble, mincing fop and no gallant for the fair ones; the rendering is brilliant if the part be developed on these lines. But I doubt whether such a Witwoud could have cared to follow in the wake of any woman.[16]

Scofield's venture into the realm of comedy was a particularly important one for an actor who concerned himself almost exclusively with serious roles. Similarly, Eric Porter as the villain, Fainall, was strong and effective in a role which was to receive particular acclaim when John Moffatt played it in the 1969 production for the National Theatre Company.

In 1956 when John Clements would unsuccessfully produce The Way of the World again, the memory of Evans was even stronger. But by 1969 her performance was obviously not in recent critical memory. Nevertheless, except for the 1924 production, The Way of the World was never to be considered an unqualified critical success.

The Way of the World (1956)

In the first week of December, 1956, John Clements finished his repertoire at the Saville Theatre, an alternative to the classics at the Old Vic, by presenting The Way of the World. Like Gielgud, Clements both directed and played Mirabell. Millamant was Kay Hammond and Lady Wishfort was, once again, Margaret Rutherford. The rest of the cast included Douglas Wilmer as Fainall, Reginald Beckwith as Witwoud, Geoffrey Dunn as Petulant, Valerie Hanson as Mrs. Fainall, Margaretta Scott as Mrs. Marwood, Rosalind Knight as Mincing, Harry H. Corbett as Waitwell, Ann Leon as Foible and Raymond Francis as Sir Wilful Witwoud.

The capacious Saville did not lend itself readily to the minutely orchestrated playing of artificial comedy. Nor did the sets by Doris Zinkeisen enhance what was a roundly censured production. Derek Granger attacked the setting calling the interior of of Lady Wishfort's home "an evacuated South Coast ballroom camouflaged battleship grey for the occupation of the Navy."[1] In their disenchantment with the production, the critics were most concerned with attempting to redefine the idea of style in relation to line delivery.

Milton Shulman was disappointed that the "gliding, polished prose stumbled its way across the footlights; the pointed wit was blunted so frequently in delivery that it more often plopped than pinged."[2] He reasserted the belief that "artificial comedy of this kind needs to be played with mannered naturalness. . . . [It should be] as unselfconscious as high fashion and as uninhibited as good gossip." Derek Granger noted that the style must be a composite which "mixes a brutally aristocratic civility with a shimmering effervescence of effect."[3] Philip Hope-Wallace noted a second problem that had dogged the comedy since Faith Brook's failure in 1948: "when a production lacks style or has an unsuccessful Millamant at its heart the plot can seem cruelly tedious."[4] The play fulfilled both these criteria.

Difficulties multiplied. Because of the pace of the production, the tortuous plot now came under fire. Reduced to a "particularly opaque state of incomprehensibility," it deflected attention away from the maze of situations and onto the Millamant, giving substance to the argument that "Millamant is the play's great creation, and that unless she is brilliantly played all the rest is a jumble of incomprehensible plot, from which Congreve's wit and invention can struggle free only at moments."[5] From a discussion of style, the critics were led, naturally enough, to a discussion, a general condemnation rather, of the Millamant of Miss Hammond.

From previous performances, Miss Hammond seemed suitably equipped to adorn the character by drawing on her stock of pretty airs and graces and her charming drawl. Although she seemed to have already developed a stage personality to fit the part, this persona--however delicious--could not conceal the great defect in her timing. Her method was to exaggerate and, by means of exaggeration, to slow down the delivery of her lines; therefore, the critical concentration was on affectation rather than effect. She delivered each word "as if it were on the end of a long wad of chewing gum she was reluctant to give up."[6] And this retardation of lines made the sparkling dialogue "flow like a slow river of super double cream."[7] Characterization shattered under analysis, for she was "not so much acting Millamant as holding the character up for inspection."[8] This detached air deflated the part, and the play suffered accordingly. Kenneth Tynan bemoaned the lack of glitter and the absence of delight in raillery:

> If Miss Hammond takes the stage, it is by default rather than by storm. In she sulks, she is positively morose. She gives us generously of the lady's langour . . . at times her speeches dawdle to inertia.[9]

It was the _Times_ critic who, noting a double performance, indicated the basic difficulty in Miss Hammond's conception of the role:

> The real point of the comedy is that man is pretending to be civilized. Millamant, about to be married as a woman, talks about her marriage merely like a person in society. She is delicately conscious of holding the reality of life away, but Miss Hammond gives us not only the fine lady posing wittily in the social manner but also the actress imitating the fine lady posing wittily in the social manner.[10]

Caught in the critical cross fire, John Clements was censured for an uncertain touch in his direction, and although his Mirabell could be called admirable, he missed the "pride of the self-assured cynic who is in love in spite of himself."[11]

It was left to Margaret Rutherford to salvage the remnants of the production. Finding her performance definitive, J. W. Lambert conceded the possibility of shifting emphasis from Millamant to Lady Wishfort: "Playing less obviously for farce or for pathos than before, she made the old harpy a most dramatic figure, ridiculous in her vanity, shameful in her moments of all-too-lucid self-knowledge, quite frightening in her anger."[12] This same shift in emphasis was noted when Edith Evans, at 60, transferred her attention from her Millamant of 1924 to her Lady Wishfort in 1948. At the time, Evans had managed to redefine the play in terms of Lady Wishfort by sheer virtuosity: "Such is the power of this actress and so great her instinctive feeling for the magic of words, that in this revival Lady Wishfort is the leading part while Millamant is no more than a pretty little wilfull girl."[13] Rutherford did not have the breadth of an Evans, and her triumph was that of skillful assets over endearing liabilities:

> There is a mild doubt, perhaps, that she is not quite the ideal, suggesting a shade too dearly the substance of an animated Tunbridge Wells tea cosy for any such avid and hot-blooded old schemer. But the manner of it--the thrust of jaw, the moody eye, the little skirmishes of hands and feet like mice at some frenzied minuet--assure that the laughter comes when it should.[14]

Still her admirer, Tynan once again referred in some detail to her celebrated chins and blamed the "bloodless bravura" of the Clements production in which the pathos of her performance, so effective in the Gielgud revival, seemed "markedly out of place."[15] The considerable and consistent appeal of Margaret Rutherford which defied any hidebound analysis of style was defined succinctly by the _Times_ critic: "She is extraordinarily unlike Lady Wishfort . . . but she is extraordinarily like herself."[16]

Ironically, in the light of the earlier work by John Clements, whose many excursions into Restoration comedy made him look denuded without his snuff box, the failure of the production was even more marked and his culpability even greater than that of the average director. After the failure of this production, London did not see another revival of The Way of the World until the National Theatre Company included it in its 1969 repertoire.

The Way of the World (1969)

On May 1, 1969, the National Theatre Company opened its production of The Way of the World at the Old Vic. The cast included Robert Lang as Mirabell, Geraldine McEwan as Millamant, Hazel Hughes as Lady Wishfort, Helen Burns as Foible, Edward Hardwicke as Witwoud, Jane Lapotaire as Mincing, John Moffatt as Fainall, Edward Petherbridge as Waitwell, Sheila Reid as Mrs. Fainall, David Ryall as Petulant, Michael Turner as Sir Wilful Witwoud and Jane Wenham as Mrs. Marwood. The production was directed by Michael Langham and designed by Desmond Heeley.

The actors observed an archaic pronunciation which found an immediate and negative response in critical assessments of the play. The adoption of this system of pronunciation with which the players were not really at home resulted in considerable discomfort for the actors and distraction for the audience. The affectation slowed the pace and endangered the comedy as speech assumed "an appearance of effort, a feeling of slowness, that militate against the play's wit, which should sparkle, and its cynicism, which should wound."[1] The effect on the restive audience can be judged from an observation by John Gielgud on the difficulty involved in holding the attention of an audience made lethargic by technology:

> . . . it has become more difficult to catch their interest with the subtle orchestration of living actors' voices and personalities, just as it is more difficult to emphasize for their benefit the significant look or vital moment of action, when they are lazily used to the forceful device of a close-up on the screen. The problem of projecting a subtle play in a large theatre is more challenging today than ever before.[2]

222

Could such a challenge be met effectively by the utilization of a system of pronunciation which is of no benefit to the play? Not likely.

The play itself, still fascinating and puzzling to the critics, revived the enigma of Congreve: "Was he a snob, dallying wittily à la mode, or a dark visionary, almost a misanthropist, forcing his contempt and disgust into a straightjacket of comedy?"[3] Though the production did nothing to solve these problems, it once again raised them for the acute observer. The two great factors of the play were still money and sex. The economic structure was underlined significantly: "For once, Michael Langham's production looks beyond wit, campery and courtship-display to the comedy's hard economic bone-structure. In heavy bronze-gold settings by Desmond Heeley, it makes clear that the plot's hinge is coin."[4] Money, however, shared place with the reorganization of the social structure, for the production highlighted Congreve's concern with a sexual imbalance which allowed a woman money and freedom of action while at the same time denying her more traditional securities.

But despite the clever theories articulated in the program, in performance the play was still giving problems with the high comedy style difficult to achieve yet essential to interpretation. The least palatable character was the Lady Wishfort of Hazel Hughes. J. W. Lambert gave her dubious praise, for though she "certainly livened the evening up" she did so by means of a performance reminiscent of "a pantomime dame replete with some stupefying vulgarities."[5] Although Milton Shulman applauded her "healthy dose of comic vulgarity," he admitted that "she upsets the rather formal, punctilious balance of the rest of the mannered acting."[6] Miss Hughes, whose face was painted to resemble that of an "elderly bull-terrier," presented an outsized character which became grotesque in its savagery and obvious in its labored attempts at comedy. Her panting, mannered, enlarged performance "undermined all hope of putting any pity or real feeling" into her creation.[7]

Millamant was in the hands of Geraldine McEwan, who, like Kay Hammond in 1956, seemed well suited to the role. Ronald Bryden catalogued her attributes: "the clear, quizzical gaze, the knowing dimple, the swerving, amused evasiveness and gravelly, calculated coo bitten off sideways, like thread."[8] But the critics, familiar with her assets, found no real freshness in them. Her distinctively nasal voice did no great service to the lines, and her overplayed mannerisms reduced Millamant to a "languid, gurgling female casting her witty affectations in all directions with a giggling disinterest in their impact."[9] Although Miss McEwan had scored successfully as Angelica in _Love for Love_ in 1965, she did not sustain the grave weight of the production that the character of Millamant forced her to bear.[10]

Mirabell fared no better. Although Robert Lang gave him a touch of Restoration style, the character was hardly graceful in terms of the tradition established, and continued, by John Gielgud. Lang opted for a kind of dramatic respectability, making Mirabell more acceptable than a close analysis of his behavior would allow one to expect; yet his Mirabell was bland. The performance became a study--objective and passionless--"without the plain, shameless wholeness, the frank sexual effrontery, which redeems Mirabell's self-seeking."[11] Most important, his Mirabell was singularly unattractive--a real defect when one considers that the hero moves in the fast company of rakes and boasts no less than four women in the play palpitating, visibly or otherwise, at the mention of him. This vast attractiveness suggested by the text was replaced by the actor's careful calculation. Lang had already played Scandal in the National's _Love for Love_, but his reading of that role, however well balanced, was hardly preparation for the gallant who conquers the elusive Millamant. The dearth of class consciousness exhibited by the principals was a significant factor in undermining the successful routing of Lady Wishfort and the union of the lovers:

> If these people are not made to seem assured of their position, nothing very much is likely to come from their embarrassments, outrage, or disgust when rude reality breaks through the surface of their superficial lives.
>
> This lack of class conceit in the earlier part of the evening--a lack of elegance and glitter and arrogant oily snobbery--renders the long-drawn ruin of Lady Wishfort especially tiresome.[12]

More tiresome was the contract scene which marks the social coming of age of the pair.

The real passion of the play was provided by the Fainall of John Moffatt and the Mrs. Marwood of Jane Wenham. Moffatt understood the necessity of a high comedy style and produced a Fainall whose "coldly reptilian" presence managed to expose "a core of naked hate" which was matched by his paramour. These two provided the necessary sensuality with a definite piece of stage business: "Locking the doors and starting purposefully to strip at the end of the third act, they bring back into the play some of the sexuality missing at its center."[13]

Although the family tree in the program and substantial program notes from Congreve and critics of the nineteenth and twentieth centuries contributed to audience preparation and to a clearer comprehension of the now traditional plot difficulties, the pace, rhythm and choice of actors still did not approach the Hammersmith "miracle" of 1924.[14]

The Way of the World (1978)

On 27 January 1978, the Royal Shakespeare Company presented Congreve's play directed by John Barton at the Aldwych Theatre on what, for financial reasons, had become a permanent set. The cast included Michael Pennington as Mirabell, Judi Dench as Millamant, Beryl Reid as Lady Wishfort, John Woodvine as Fainall, Nickolas Grace as Witwoud, Roger Rees as Petulant, Bob Peck as Sir Wilful Witwoud, David Lyon as Waitwell, Marjorie Bland as Mrs. Marwood, Carmen Du Sautoy as Mrs. Fainall, Eliza Ward as Foible and Avril Carson as Mincing.

The comedy, which had, by now, withstood some terrifying revivals, was still recognized as "one of the most elaborate, intricate social documents in the whole of drama."[1] Because of the intricacy of this document and the traditional complexities of the plot, John Barton, in an attempt to increase the clarity, opened the play at a different pace from what might have been expected: "the exposition of the immensely complicated plot is presented with a slow deliberation and reverence for the text." Whether or not this was desirable stage procedure was open to conjecture: "the careful placing of matters in context, the setting-up of a tangled web of personal relationships . . . has only a subdued theatrical interest." But the value of the slow untangling of the plot was that it revealed in a stage "close-up" a world of "solid objects, calculating relationships and palpable people who go about their business and intrigues (mostly intrigues) with cool deliberation."[2] Benedict Nightingale concurred, finding that Barton's exposition stressed credibility, "a group of plausible worldings in plausibly domestic surroundings trying simultaneously to hide and fulfill desires both pecuniary and sexual."[3] The emphasis on credibility sounded a curiously modern note: Congreve's world "might be London now, a guileful, wangling place where it's dangerous to display emotional vulnerability, and unsophisticated and embarrassing to advertise any but the most formal affection."

Three major characters richly repaid critical scrutiny. As Lady Wishfort, Beryl Reid gave a particularly compassionate performance, playing that difficult lady not as a "shrieking grotesque but as a simple, gullible fretful creature, silly but brave, and not without dignity."[4] Wardle agreed with a performance that could cope with high style and slippery pronunciation: "There is a certain level of decorum beneath which Congreve's old harridan does not sink. . . . The pathos is there as well as the absurdity: expressed in the precipitous slips of her genteel vowels. The performance is full of robust invention."[5]

Millamant and Mirabell were strikingly individualized. The most notable quality of Judi Dench's Millamant was its well masked defensiveness: "Millamant is a dainty praying mantis, sensual but controlled. Under her arch, venomous wit lurks, just perceptibly, a sense of brittle insecurity."[6] But the insecurity and the affectation did not undercut or obscure the strong evocation of the sensual; for this Millamant was "a piece of high-precision sexual engineering constructed from languishing cries, bubbling laughs, instantaneous mood transitions, always in motion with a train like a matador's cloak, designed at once to exert invincible attraction and evade capture."[7] Commenting on the contract scene, Wardle evoked the Evans reading now half a century old, using the comparison to praise Miss Dench: "One masterstroke among many is her final compliance with Mirabell: 'I hate your odious provisos.' Dame Edith Evans delivered this skittishly: Miss Dench lingers caressingly over it."

The enigma of the piece was the Mirabell of Michael Pennington both in terms of garb and approach. Mirabell was dressed in a costume which combined the colors of sand and faded blue. His sandy hair and pale face blurred into the softness of his clothes. He joined the vocal to the visual by refusing to emphasize his dialogue, adopting a lethargic approach to the character which was deliberately at war with his surroundings. Wardle affirmed the sexual emphasis of the approach: Pennington's Mirabell relaxed into a "cool acceptance of his own powers, and concentrates on the lover rather than the intriguer."[8] Robert Cushman, while denying Pennington's character a masterful personality, affirmed in him "all of Mirabell's controlling intelligence."[9] However, John Peter discovered totality of conception and precision of communication in the Mirabell:

> From the very first sight of Michael Pennington's Mirabell you know that you are in the presence of a hunter: a sensitive and intelligent man, compassionate even, but one whose feelings have been tainted by greed and who knows it. In his famous proposal scene with Millamant he stands, courtly but watchful, head thrust slightly forward, his thoughts clearly focusing both on her body and her dowry. There's not a trace of affection in the air.[10]

Yet, together, Dench and Pennington gave a future to the lovers in the proviso scene: "for once it seems the beginning rather than the end of a relationship."[11]

Despite Barton's care, the production was not watertight. Even the invention that informed the performances and the cleverness bestowed on the final moments served only to reinforce some loose ends:

> Mr. Barton makes final use of the play's confusions in a delightfully tangled version of the dance of celebration. The triumph of laws and masculine wiles is not capped by a perfect, orderly bringing together of all parties in a handsome movement, but is undermined by further

confusion as inappropriate partners first take, then disregard, each other. It suggests an interpretation that might have proved interesting elsewhere in the production.[12]

XI. Farquhar

George Farquhar belongs both to the Restoration and to the eighteenth-century traditions. His characters seem to breathe more freely and express themselves with less deliberate self-consciousness than the creations of his predecessors, and he boldly sets the action of both The Recruiting Officer and The Beaux' Stratagem in the country rather than the town.

The youthful first play, Love and a Bottle (1698), was exposed to a twentieth-century audience in Nottingham in a musical version which was censured not for the musical embellishments but for the lack of quality in these additions. The vividness of Farquhar's creations and the strength of the autobiographically based satire in The Recruiting Officer (1706) invited a politically relevant adaptation by the Berliner Ensemble and a naturalistic interpretation by the National Theatre Company. The rich interaction and variety of effect which the play can produce are visible when the difference in these approaches is considered.

In a traditional, well-acted production, The Constant Couple (1699), another popular offering of its day, allowed for an interpretation which assumed a period stance while still enjoying itself. Less immediately accessible to modernization, it still needed no strained effort to amuse.

The most human and most congenial of Farquhar's comedies, The Beaux' Stratagem (1707), was produced both in England and in America. This play has the appeal of a bustling plot, restrained irony in the clever dialogue and the relevance of a strong plea for divorce on the grounds of incompatibility.

Farquhar presents something of himself with his characters, and, barring his sentimentality, which is not underscored in these popular plays, he is the most congenial of the playwrights under consideration.

LOVE AND A BOTTLE
Plot Summary

I. A very poor Roebuck just arrived from Ireland admits to Lovewell that he tried to seduce Lovewell's sister, Leanthe, but her virtue thwarted his attempts. When Roebuck's former mistress, Trudge, comes in with Roebuck's child, Lovewell stays to encounter her. Lovewell is talking to her kindly when Lucinda, Lovewell's darling, comes in and thinks that she sees Lovewell with his own mistress and child.

II. Lovewell asks Roebuck to court a virtuous lady (Lucinda) whose behavior will convince him of the chastity of women, then tells Brush, his servant, to watch Roebuck's behavior carefully and make a report.

Squire Mockmode has come to London to court Lucinda. Lovewell sends word to Roebuck to call himself Mockmode, hoping to find out Lucinda's inclinations to this rival whose appearance in town, he feels, has caused the quarrel between them.

III. Leanthe, disguised as a page, is serving Lucinda. She is pining for Roebuck when Roebuck himself appears. When Lucinda comes in and Roebuck begins to make passionate speeches, Leanthe recognizes bits from past orations to her.

At Widow Bullfinch's, the widow is upbraiding the poet, Lyric, because of his debts to her. Two other gentlemen are announced, and Lyric borrows a hat and wig and disappears. Two bailiffs enter and arrest the bookseller, Pamphlet, in Lyric's place.

IV. Mockmode comes in with Trudge who is pretending to be a widow, and Lovewell tries to forward the plot of marrying the two off by pretending to be Trudge's suitor. Lucinda, who has come out masked with Pindress, is horrified by what she thinks is more evidence of Lovewell's errant behavior. A porter enters with a note for Roebuck, and Lovewell, pretending to be the man, finds it is a letter from Lucinda asking Roebuck to meet her at ten in the garden. Lyric comes to reclaim a poem from Lovewell, and, in returning it, Lovewell drops the letter, which Mockmode picks up.

V.   Roebuck gropes his way into the house and arrives at Lucinda's bedroom. During the scene, he draws out Lovewell's watch, and Lucinda recognizes her jewel tied to it. Enraged, she asks his name, and Roebuck, getting his lines almost right, says "Roebuck Mockmode." Believing him to be her prospective wooer, Lucinda offers marriage.

Lovewell returns to the house to see Roebuck's hat and sword on the table. Roebuck, "unbuttoned," appears and announces that he is married and praises his wife's virtues. Leanthe takes her cue and reveals herself as Roebuck's wife. Lyric agrees to unmarry Mockmode and Trudge and reveals the widow dressed as a parson. Now willing to marry Lovewell, Lucinda asks that he make over his Irish estates to Leanthe and Roebuck.

Background

Love and a Bottle was produced at Drury Lane in 1698. The cast included Williams as Roebuck, Mills as Lovewell, Bullock as Mockmode, Johnson as Lyric, Haines as Pamphlet and Rigadoon, Pinketham as Club, Fairbank as Brush, Mrs. Allison as Leanthe, Mrs. Rogers as Lucinda, Mrs. Moor as Pindress, Mrs. Mills as Trudge and Mrs. Powell as Widow Bullfinch.

The play, Farquhar's first, met with such a favorable reception that Farquhar, who had quit acting at Smock Alley in Dublin and come to London to make his mark as a playwright, saw his dream become reality. It is possible that Love and a Bottle was written a few years before its premiere. If so, its debut was delayed because Jeremy Collier's vitriolic A Short View of the Immorality and Profaneness of the English Stage (1697-98) was making it difficult to produce plays as overtly licentious as Farquhar's. After its successful opening, it was acted nine times in the first season.

Williams played many important roles and Roebuck was one of his last creations. He was more than well cast for the part as Cibber affirms: "the Industry of Williams was not equal to his Capacity; for he lov'd his Bottle better than his Business." However, Cibber, to be fair, laments the somewhat arbitrary dismissal of Williams from the group which had migrated with Betterton to the Lincoln's Inn Fields theatre. The company would not allow Williams and Mrs. Mountfort to be equal sharers with the rest, and they returned to Drury Lane. Cibber argues that "their Merit was too great, almost on any Scruples, to be added to the Enemy; and, at worst, they were certainly much more above those they would have rank'd them with, than they could possibly be under those, they were not admitted to be equal to." Certainly Williams' presence at Drury Lane was an asset to the young Farquhar.

Of John Mills, who played Lovewell, Cibber recounts his good qualities--diligence and sobriety--as the strongest recommendations he had. But they were sufficient for Wilks, who saw in Mills an "honest, quiet, careful Man, of as few Faults, as Excellencies, and Wilks rather chose him for his second, in many Plays, than an Actor of perhaps greater skill, that was not so labouriously diligent."

Although Love and a Bottle had a successful opening, it languished for want of attention, and the 1966 revival at the Dublin Theatre Festival claimed to be the first production since 1698.

Critical Evaluations

Love and a Bottle (1969)

In 1966 the Nottingham Playhouse Company presented a musical version of Daniel Defoe's Moll Flanders, the fourth musical offering since the 1963 opening of the playhouse in Wellington Circus. The attempt yielded the "slickest . . . production seen on this stage for a long time."[1] Heartened by this musical adaptation of a period classic, the company employed William Chappell as a director, and on May 7, 1969, presented Love and a Bottle. Chappell had revived the play in 1966 for the Dublin Festival with great success. Three years later, with a larger budget and a strong repertory company, Chappell not only directed the Nottingham revival but also wrote the lyrics and designed the costumes. A. P. Haynes composed the music.

The cast included David Sumner as Roebuck, David Allister as Lovewell, Barrie Rutter as Mockmode, Bruce Myles as Lyric, Francis Thomas as Rigadoon, John Manford as Nimblewrist, Richard Harbord as Brush, John Joyce as Comb, Nicholas Clay as Club, Elizabeth Power as Leanthe, Jean Gilpin as Trudge, Sheila Ballantine as the Widow Bullfinch, Cherith Mellor as Lucinda and Penelope Wilton as Pindress.

The jumping off points for the production were defined in the program notes for the play in which Chappell compared the work of Farquhar to that of Feydeau and drew a parallel between the Restoration comic sensibility and the Whitehall farce tradition. In making these comparisons, he implied the need for a tricky, modern pace for the play:

> The form of farce, as we know it, crystallised firmly into a certain shape under the pens of the Restoration playwrights. The pattern has hardly altered since then. The behaviour and representa-

tion of character are almost ritualistic. Embarrassing situations, mistaken identities, unbelievable disguises, sexual innuendo and a dash of transvestism are found over and over again in the plays of Congreve, Vanbrugh, Wycherley and Farquhar, and later in the work of Feydeau and the series of farces which packed out the Whitehall theatre for so long.

He then made contemporary connections with Farquhar's depiction of his society:

The society he depicts so vigorously has an affinity to our own it would be foolish to ignore. Both are permissive, selfish, corrupt, riotous and very lively. Remembering this and also bearing in mind the fact that the protagonists of Restoration comedy are mostly in their teens and twenties, it does not appear entirely unjustifiable to set the play in a Never-Never-Land where visual and musical references can be made to the youth of 1969.

With these observations, Chappell attempted to justify the "whooping-up" of the early Farquhar, a justification which could be effected only in performance.

The main visual point was the costuming, which set the characters in a vague period "at once pop-arty and pre-war Hollywood," with a revolving set providing a type of Ziegfeld staircase to display the costumes.[2] The visual, however inventive, received little help from the songs, which tunefully bled the play of satire. Additionally, the uninspired ditties were warbled by actors of dubious vocal ability. All this melodic activity produced a battle for priority: sound versus exposition. "The characters' opening announcements of their identity were partially drowned by the pop band (they also drowned some of the early lyrics, but that was probably to the good), so it took some time to sort them all out."[3]

Although Chappell faithfully retained most of the lines, there was still an imbalance produced by straining toward a sexual interpretation of even the most innocuous events. "All situations, even that of an exasperated landlady demanding rent from an indigent poet, are translated into sex; with a result as bloodless as the Restoration 'style' of drama schools."[4]

In addition to the chancy costuming and indifferent singing, there was a real critical objection to the sociological emphasis of the play since fortune-hunting--at least by admission--was no longer a prime consideration in the swinging London of the late 1960s: "The 'permissive society' does not correspond at all to the world of Farquhar's play in which the displays of philandering are only top dressing to the serious business of fortune-hunting."

Attempting to balance a production top-heavy with contemporary glances, the actors concentrated on harvesting the maximum fun from individual moments by dint of inventive caricature performances. Despite a brave try, they could not overcome the director's awkward thesis; for while trying to associate the periods in terms of the loose morality and outrageous dress of young London, William Chappell ignored the basic differences between the young people then and now. That oversight, together with the inappropriate songs and costumes, contributed to one of the less successful offerings of the company.

THE CONSTANT COUPLE; or, A TRIP TO THE JUBILEE
Plot Summary

I. Alderman Smuggler, an old, not terribly honest merchant, approaches and compliments his nephew,

Vizard, on his piety, which is bogus. The brave officer Standard appears, having that very morning seen his regiment disbanded. Sir Harry Wildair, a rich, cheerful man-about-town, comes in grandly. He admits that a woman is the cause of his return from France; however, when Sir Harry divulges her name, Lurewell, Standard and Vizard reveal, in asides, that she is the object of their affections as well. Sir Harry asks Vizard to suggest temporary diversion and Vizard, taking revenge on Angelica for rejecting him, suggests Angelica, whom he describes as a prostitute.

II. Clincher Junior, in mourning for his father, appears in London and is exposed to the affectation of his brother, Clincher Senior, who is enjoying his inheritance and now "usurps gentility."

At Lady Darling's house, Sir Harry, under the misapprehension that he is going to a brothel, takes Lady Darling's seriousness for hypocrisy. However, when Angelica appears, he is taken by her and she, in turn, falls in love with him.

At Lurewell's house, Smuggler comes to offer Lurewell the money she needs in return for her favors. She agrees, telling him that he must come at night, disguised as a woman.

III. Vizard reveals to Standard that Sir Harry is still in Lurewell's good graces and that Standard has been duped. Standard sends Sir Harry a challenge by the porter, Tom Errand.

Clincher Senior and Lurewell on her balcony are seen by Standard. She has Clincher change clothes with Tom Errand, telling Clincher that Standard is her husband come home.

Lurewell tells Parly the story of her youthful seduction and her ensuing distrust of men when her first love betrayed her.

IV. Dressed in Tom's clothes, Clincher is hurried away to Newgate for the murder of Tom. At Lurewell's, Sir Harry "accidentally" drops a ring and asks Lurewell to wear it. Smuggler appears in woman's clothes and is hidden in a closet. Vizard, who is hoping to enjoy Lurewell, is brought into the room and, mistaking his uncle in disguise for a real woman, reveals his true nature--he is a villain. After Vizard leaves, the butler enters looking for spoons, which are discovered on Smuggler. He too is hustled off to prison when Lurewell refuses to identify him.

V. Sir Harry continues to press his suit to Angelica and raises the amount to a hundred guineas. When Angelica refuses the money, he decides to do business with Lady Darling, who soon undeceives him.

Clincher Junior enters aping his "dead" brother, until Clincher Senior appears in a blanket; no ghost, but definitely come to chide. Lurewell chastises Wildair for being false, showing him the ring. But Standard proclaims himself the real owner, and is revealed as her first love. Smuggler sends word to Vizard that he has disinherited him. Standard produces a pocket-book which contains a record of all of Smuggler's secret practices in trading and forces Smuggler to return to Lurewell all that is hers.

Background

The Constant Couple was produced in December 1699 at the Theatre Royal, Drury Lane. The cast included Wilks as Sir Harry Wildair, Powell as Standard, Mills as Vizard, Johnson as Smuggler, Pinketham as Clincher, Bullock as Clincher Junior, Norris as Dicky, Haines as Tom Errand, Mrs. Verbruggen as Lurewell, Mrs. Powell as

Lady Darling, Mrs. Rogers as Angelica and Mrs. Moor as Parly.

Wilks had one of his greatest successes as Sir Harry, while Henry Norris scored as Dicky, servant to Clincher Junior. Norris, whose mother--one of the first women on the stage--had been prominent in Davenant's company, gained the nicknames "Dicky Norris" or "Jubilee Dicky" from his performance in the role. Norris had a good set of physical equipment including a "droll" face coupled with a diminutive figure. Although he was adept at declaiming the tragic role, his stature--even encased in the requisite costuming of the period--made him a bad choice for the hero, so he excelled in low comedy.

The new play was such a success that the manager gave Farquhar four third nights. And in the preface to Love's Contrivance (1703), Mrs. Centlivre estimated: "I believe Mr. Rich will own that he got more by The Trip to the Jubilee with all its irregularities than by the most uniform piece the stage could boast of ever since." The play had about fifty performances in its first London season, and Gildon, who would have been a hostile witness, said: "Never did anything such wonders."

The success spawned a second try, Sir Harry Wildair: Being the Sequel of The Trip to the Jubilee (1701), but it suffered the fate of many sequels and did not take.

Farquhar and Wilks had begun at Smock Alley in Dublin together. At Wilks's suggestion, Farquhar came to London where, there is no doubt, each contributed mightily to the talent of the other. In his preface to the play, Farquhar acknowledged Wilks's accomplishments as Sir Harry:

> Mr. Wilks's performance has set him so far above competition in the part of Wildair, that none can

pretend to envy the praise due to his merit. That
he made the part, will appear from hence, that
whenever the stage has the misfortune to lose him,
Sir Harry Wildair may go to the Jubilee.

William Bullock originated Clincher Junior.
Davies says of him that he was an actor of "great glee
and much comic vivacity. He was, in his person, large;
with a lively countenance, full of humorous
information." And Macklin referred to Bullock as a
"true genius of the stage" in his department.

Actors of both sexes have played Wildair. Among
the most famous were Wilks, Elliston, Woodward and
Garrick. The most winning of the female creators, Peg
Woffington, scored one of her greatest successes in the
role. After the first performance, the play held the
boards for over a hundred years being produced at
Covent Garden, the Haymarket and the Theatre Royal.
However, after the turn of the century, it was absent
from the London stage. Its last performance was in
1805, the year of the Battle of Trafalgar, at Drury
Lane. When it was revived by Alec Clunes in 1943 at
the Arts Theatre, it had been unacted for over a
century.

Critical Evaluations

The Constant Couple (1967)

On May 25, 1967, Prospect Productions opened at
the Arts Theatre, Cambridge, in The Constant Couple.
The cast included Robert Hardy as Sir Harry Wildair,
Julian Glover as Standard, John Warner as Vizard,
Timothy West as Smuggler, Charles Kay as Clincher,
Helen Lindsay as Lurewell, Juliet Harmer as Angelica
and Jenny Short as Parly. Richard Cottrell directed.

Advance publicity stressed the play's contemporary
parallels, which were essential to Cottrell's concept
of the production:

It was produced in 1699 when the economic background was one of insecurity and the general outlook rather materialist. There's also the parallel with the clothes of today--the men dressed like peacocks and the working class like flashy, nasty peacocks. It was also a period of great sexual licence and moral liberty.[1]

In the program notes Cottrell continued his argument about this second play of the 21-year-old Farquhar:

This is no narrow circle of ladies and gentlemen, but 'prentices, aldermen, pimps and soldiers as well. This is London 1699 in fact. And in its wit and humor, its people with their outlandish dress and outrageous morals, its accent on youth and its preoccupation with money, it is not so very different from London 1967. However dazzling the comedy, it is possible to see our problems reflected in those of Farquhar's characters and from their foibles and follies become more aware of own own.

Farquhar set out to show his fashionable and would-be fashionable audiences how cheerful cynicism, alert wit and carefully tuned affectation can free the rich man-of-the-world from the insecurities and hypocrisies of the middle class. This attitude found ideal expression in the hero, Sir Harry Wildair, "whose money and ancestry insulate him against all extremes, either of gallantry or piety."[2] Treading the thin line between the jaded fop and the languid rake, Sir Harry manages to be the "sensible hedonist; a man who puts pleasure before honour, but manages to keep both simply by talking better sense than his adversaries." In his merry lack of concern for inconvenient conventions Wildair foreshadows the debonair cynics of Wilde and Shaw. His greatest appeal is that he is a brilliant paradox:

He has the traditional gentlemanly qualities of the hero of romantic comedy, which he uses to ends that no conventional gentleman could approve; and he does this, not because he is a hypocrite, but because he has common sense. He has the air, the grace, the flamboyance, the gaiety, the coolness and the unshakable nerve of a Scarlet Pimpernel. But he is a Scarlet Pimpernel who gets himself, not others, out of danger. When he has no choice he will fight with panache. But when he is challenged in the public street he declines a duel with <u>sang froid</u> and a determination that is as firm as it is cheerful and unembarrassed. Asked if he is a coward, he replies with amusement, "I have £8,000 a year."[3]

In the Prospect Productions offering, Robert Hardy approached the role with a "nicely virile dandyism,"[4] which stressed Wildair's delight in himself and his position. He tickled the audience by flinging roses into the stalls and drenching himself with perfume, always conscious that Wildair is "man enough not to fear looking effeminate."[5]

Supporting Hardy were Charles Kay and Timothy West. Kay, a member of the Royal Shakespeare Company in 1967 and later an outstanding character actor for the National Theatre Company, displayed high camp fireworks as the fop, Clincher, who apes Sir Harry with awe-inspiring lack of success; and Timothy West, as Smuggler, projected "jibbering discomfort as the resident senile lecher,"[6] a character reminiscent of Antonio in <u>Venice Preserved</u>, as he showed an old man "who will risk any humiliation for a grope in the dark."[7]

An interesting portrait was the Lurewell of Helen Lindsay. In 1943 it was pointed out that this role eluded Maxine Audley, who told the story of her seduction with "taste and feeling," ignoring the necessary dimension that "Lurewell should surely be a Millamant manquée who conceals her embitterment under a dazzling surface of coquettish allurement."[8] In this 1967 production, Helen Lindsay made herself mistress of the role as she recognized that the effect of the play depends significantly on the sinister charm of the wounded Lurewell. Lindsay's adroit handling of Lurewell's humorless magnetism completed the balance of the production.

After its tour of the provinces, <u>The Constant Couple</u> settled in at the New Theatre, London, on June 29, 1967. Prospect Productions' success with the revivals of Restoration plays was beginning to establish a tradition:

> [The company] continues their custom of making the plays live, not by irresponsible modernisations, but by working for understanding of the times that produced them. The publicity has perhaps over-stressed parallels with our own day, but this stimulating production brings out the play's own seventeenth century vitality.[9]

THE RECRUITING OFFICER
Plot Summary

I. Kite, sergeant to Captain Plume, is trying to seduce the Shrewsbury locals into joining the grenadiers. Plume's friend, Worthy, enters much dejected. He had been on the point of winning Melinda as his mistress when her aunt died and left the girl twenty thousand pounds. Although Worthy now courts her as his wife, she is not to be easily won. At Melinda's house, Silvia upbraids Melinda for her treatment of Worthy while Melinda speaks ill of Plume.

II. When Plume and Silvia meet, he shows her that before the battle of Blenheim he had made her his heir. Silvia commends him but wryly mentions that he would have done well to have left something to his new son by a local lass. Called to her father, Justice Balance, Sylvia learns that her brother is dying. Knowing that her brother's death will make her an heiress, Balance advises her to think no more of Plume; yet he agrees never to give her in marriage without her consent and asks that she never give her hand without his approval.

III. Plume and Worthy are discussing their ladies when a country girl, Rose, and her brother, Bullock, come in. While Rose is bargaining with Plume for the sale of her chickens, he gets her away to his lodging.

Captain Brazen is introduced. He is the kind who claims to know all the important people and to have been intimate with many women. Brazen lives up to his reputation by announcing that he has an appointment with Melinda. Silvia appears dressed as a man and announces her intention to enlist.

IV. Silvia offers to enlist with Plume if he gives Rose up to her and he agrees. The friendship between the captain and the new recruit develops to the point where Plume admits, "There's something in this fellow that charms me."

V. Rose and Silvia are arrested and brought before Balance. Worthy comes to take leave of Melinda, and they are reconciled. She asks him to follow her coach as she is going to visit Silvia in the country. Brazen visits Plume and shows a letter which indicates that Melinda will meet him secretly to be married, and word is sent to Worthy that Melinda has postponed her trip.

In the court of justice unwilling victims are impressed into service, and Sylvia, whose one desire is to make her father impress her, easily succeeds.

Worthy intercepts Brazen and his bride-to-be only to discover that the masked lady is Lucy, Melinda's maid, trying to trick Brazen into marriage.

After court, Balance learns that Silvia is not in the country and that her dead brother's suit is missing. He remembers her promise that she would not marry without his consent and realizes that, by making him impress her, she has tricked him into giving it. Melinda and Worthy are united as are Silvia and Plume.

Background

The Recruiting Officer was produced at Drury Lane on 8 April 1706. The cast included Keen as Balance, Phillips as Scale, Kent as Scruple, Williams as Worthy, Wilks as Plume, Cibber as Brazen, Estcourt as Kite, Bullock as Bullock, Norris as Costar Pearmain, Fairbank as Thomas Appletree, Mrs. Rogers as Melinda, Mrs. Oldfield as Silvia, Mrs. Sapsford as Lucy and Mrs. Mountfort as Rose.

In 1705 Farquhar went to Shrewsbury to raise recruits for Marlborough's army and was extremely well treated by the important locals. Since this seems to be the closest he got to active service, his cheerful view of the recruiting--which shows clearly the duplicity and brutality involved--still does not warp the essential good humor of the comedy. Its popularity is indicated by its travels. When the company began its next season at Dorset Garden, they opened with The Recruiting Officer. When they removed to Drury Lane it went on again. Almost immediately, it became one of the stock comedies of the theatre. In the autumn of 1706 the leading members of Rich's company went over to Swiney at the new Queen's Theatre in the Haymarket, and the two companies played against each other. Most of the original cast migrated to the Haymarket, but Estcourt remained with Rich. Part of Rich's advertisement for the play emphasized that the "true Sergeant Kite" was on view at Drury Lane.

Richard Estcourt, whose most important creation was the role of Kite, aroused various emotions in critics in terms of his abilities. Cibber, on the one hand, calls him a "languid, unaffecting Actor," asserting that the excellence of his mimicry was not equalled by his invention when acting. It is probable that talent for mimicry was his chief excellence, and there he must have had few rivals. On these grounds, Cibber, who created Brazen, had no complaints:

> This Man was so amazing and extraordinary a Mimick, that no Man or Woman, from the Coquette to the Privy-Counsellor, ever mov'd or spoke before him, but he could carry their Voice, Look, Mien, and Motion, instantly into another Company: I have heard him make long Harangues, and form various Arguments, even in the manner of thinking, of an eminent Pleader at the Bar, with every the least Article and Singularity of his Utterance so perfectly imitated, that he was the very alter ipse, scarce to be distinguish'd from his Original.

Silvia and Mrs. Sullen were two of Anne Oldfield's important creations and the role attracted many other important players as did the parts of Plume, Brazen and Kite.

The "spotting" of Anne Oldfield, whom Farquhar called "this jewel I found by accident in a tavern," comes right out of the Cinderella tradition. The story goes that after Love and a Bottle had provided Farquhar with his first success as a playwright, he went to the Mitre Tavern where he heard the niece of the hostess reading some passages from Beaumont and Fletcher's The Scornful Lady. He recognized a talent for the theatre in the girl and she was, through Vanbrugh, recommended to the manager of Drury Lane. There the fairy tale ends, for Anne Oldfield had to wait patiently for recognition and work hard to deserve it. But in her skillful creations of Silvia and Mrs. Sullen she repaid her discoverer.

After the clamorous success of the 1706 opening, the play was revived constantly throughout the eighteenth century. Peg Woffington made a success of her Silvia. The amateur Garrick, at age 11, played Kite and later (1741-42) appeared as Pearmain and as Captain Plume. On June 4, 1789, it was performed by a cast of convicts in Sydney, becoming the first play to be seen in Australia. In 1943 it was revived at the Arts Theatre with Trevor Howard in the lead.

Critical Evaluations

Trumpets and Drums (1956)

In August of 1956, the Berliner Ensemble opened at the Palace Theatre in London with an adaptation of The Recruiting Officer.[1] The cast included Dieter Knaup as Plume, Fred Düren as Brazen, Norbert Christian as Kite, Hans Hamacher as Balance, Ralf Bregazzi as Worthy, Alfred Land as Smuggler, Wolf Beneckendorff as Simpkins, Lothar Bellag as Appletree, Fred Grasnick as Pearmain, Regine Lutz as Victoria Balance, Annemarie Schlaebitz as Melinda, Anneliese Reppel as Lady Prude and Sabine Thalbach as Rose. The music was by Rudolf Wagner-Régeny, and Benno Besson directed.

Most impressive was the "special interpretation of life" established by the play, but even more absorbing was the "practiced team work of the Berliner Ensemble and the clearness of the speaking."[2] From this company which worked for months rather than weeks on a given production, the result was notable in acting style, set, costumes and music. Particularly impressive in performance was the Captain Plume of Dieter Knaup, "who strikes no gallant attitudes. He knows his world and takes a quiet satisfaction in making it work to his advantage." Plume is the sort of character who can be played either romantically or realistically. In the Berliner Ensemble production realism was the touchstone, and the difference in effect could be calculated by a comparison of the Plume of Knaup with the approach of the Restoration veteran, John Clements: "Captain Plume is the kind of role in which, formerly, John Clements was wont to cut a charming dash. Dieter Knaup plays him realistically, as a sallow and calculating seducer."[3]

Traditionally, the German actor plays with the fourth wall up, seldom playing directly to the audience. However, the acting style, as the program noted, was changed to match the play. It was recognized that the Restoration comedy characters "speak not only with each other, they speak to a third person, that is to the audience. . . . The public takes over the enjoyable role of the confidant and can also act as the referee in the disputes which are carried out on stage."[4]

The most obvious alteration in the text was a seventy-year time shift. Instead of setting the play during the War of Spanish Succession, "a typical cabinet war of the Period of Absolutism," it was set during the American Revolution, "in which human booty was to be meaninglessly sacrificed." The time shift gave a more contemporary and, therefore, a more immediately identifiable background. In investigating the multiple war interests of the bourgeois who use the army "arm in arm with the feudal class for their own interests," not only Judge Balance but also Plume and Worthy are found to be culpable. All but two of the characters, one of them invented for the adaptation, have a real meanness in common:

> . . . at every turn we are made to perceive that the debonair captain is a mercenary fellow and that the graceful heroine is a calculating woman going all out for her man without a trace of

scruple. The motive they share is greed thinly disguised as charm.[5]

The emphasis on economics was particularly notable in the interpretation of the heroine, Melinda: "Implicit here is the power of economics to transform Melinda from potential mistress to potential spouse and the application of supply-and-demand principles to both love and war."[6]

Of real interest was the preparation of the set for the production: houses, trees, doors and furniture were drawn on paper to give the deliberate effect of the insubstantial. The extreme delicacy of the settings did not disturb the actors, who, moving competently within the elegant fragility, managed to "play swiftly together, but with such a relaxed air that they . . . score all their comic points."[7] The program noted a particular motive in the treatment of the background: "We use this antique form to stir recollections. . . . Without being aware that it is reminiscing, the audience should get the impression that the action deals with an earlier period." There was also a practical consideration, an alertness to the flow of the play:

> The scene changes are accomplished quickly and elegantly. The play requires this, it is built on tension and the observer--impatient to follow the further adventures of the lovers and the courted-- may not be gripped by the action of the play if he must endure the tortuously boring intervals of time-consuming and bulky set changes.

The costumes for the Berliner Ensemble production were, by contrast to the set, a little extreme, giving a visual emphasis to the make-believe quality of the play:

> All of them are somewhat stiff, many unreasonably ruffled out or extending out from the body. Felt

is the chief material, a thick, less supple fabric. These soldiers and damsels, these peasant girls and country aristocracy which populate our paper Shrewsbury are dressed as if they had risen out of a toy chest in which they had been carefully packed away in wood shavings.

The music by Wagner-Régeny conformed to the costumes and settings, "tender as the decorations and just a bit stiff as the music of Farquhar's time." Viewing Restoration comedy as a combination of burlesque, vaudeville and operetta, the adaptation was replete with songs by means of which various characters vented their feelings.

The final result was that of a re-relation of Farquhar to the contemporary mind. The intended effect was "to make us laugh a little shamefacedly at our good-humoured bourgeois acceptance of the callous gaiety of Restoration stage intrigue."[8] With this innovative production, the Berliner Ensemble acknowledged a tradition which the Brecht-influenced William Gaskill later honored in his 1963 production of The Recruiting Officer for the National Theatre Company.

The Recruiting Officer (1963)

When it opened in December 1963, The Recruiting Officer was the fourth production in the National Theatre Company's brief history. The inaugural production, the virtually obligatory Hamlet, had been followed by St. Joan and Uncle Vanya, both transferred from the Chichester Festival. Therefore, The Recruiting Officer could be said to be the first representative production of the company. The cast included Robert Stephens as Plume, Laurence Olivier as Brazen, Colin Blakely as Kite, Max Adrian as Balance, Derek Jacobi as Worthy, John Stride as Costar Pearmain, Mary Miller as Melinda, Maggie Smith as Sylvia and Lynn Redgrave as Rose. William Gaskill directed. René Allio designed.

In the program notes, Gaskill emphasized the detachment of this play which "observes social values without criticizing them." Juxtaposed against Gaskill's notes was an excerpt from Brecht on directing the classics:

When we stage a classic . . . we must inspect the work with fresh eyes, ignoring the degraded, time-honoured distortions of a declining middle-class theatre. Purely formal innovations are not what we are seeking. We must bring light to its original ideological meaning; we must grasp its national --and hence international--significance. We need to study the historical context in which it was written, the special nature of the author and his outlook on events.

Although Brecht had collaborated in the German adaptation of the Farquhar play, Gaskill refused the German version, Trumpets and Drums, because he saw no reason to stage an "English translation of a German adaptation of a perfectly good English play."[1] In his notes, he countered a tradition of interpretation which, "at bottom . . . is a tradition of deterioration." But Gaskill's production still owed a considerable debt to Brecht:

Brecht was the great formative influence on my work. I think most of the people who work with me share a kind of approach to theatre which is hard to define. Brecht showed us that theatre could be partly a question of economy; reducing things to their simplest visual statement, with the minimum of scenery, the minimum of furniture, necessary to create an expression in the theatre.[2]

Alan Brien acknowledged that the technique had been effective:

William Gaskill's production of <u>The Recruiting Officer</u> at the Old Vic National Theatre is also an attempt to transform a period piece into a modern morality. Mr. Gaskill is the most dedicated Brechtian among our directors and Farquhar's gaily critical examination of conventional views of war and sex needs little underlining for contemporary understanding.[3]

Inspired by the Berliner Ensemble, Gaskill tried, in five weeks, to mount a play to which the German company had given months in rehearsal. He was faithful to the text in terms of subtraction and addition. There were comparatively minimal textual cuts and two military interpolations. Most significant was the reading of the Articles of War in the last act. The extracts used were from a 1706 version and were intended, the National program notes indicated, "to illustrate the immense variety of offenses for which the penalty was death." Also, the final lines of the play, orders from Brazen to the new recruits, were gathered from a military treatise of the period to "help lift the closing moments of the production."

In characterization, the Plume of Robert Stephens, reminiscent of his German counterpart from the Berliner Ensemble, was played "with the unheroic leering quality of a car salesman on the make."[4] Particular attention was paid to the entrance of Laurence Olivier's Brazen in the third act. He crossed the stage twice and only entered into the action at his third appearance: "This triple entrance helps to establish the man's total vagueness and inability to concentrate on anything for more than a few moments."[5]

There were a number of homosexual references. As early as I.i, there is a hint, which the production expanded, in the first exchange between Plume and Kite, that Kite's relationship with Plume is "close and not unduly deferential."[6]

252

Gaskill never gave any particular explanation for the strong emphasis on the physical, but because of the considerable amount of improvisation in his oblique approach to the text, it is likely that it sprang from motive-oriented rehearsal interpretations.

In contrast to the deliberately fragile set of the Berliner Ensemble, the National provided a three-dimensional work:

> When we came in we saw a very drab set, an empty green room with bare walls . . . the lights went down and . . . walls began suddenly to crack and swivel. In the blink of an eye the stage was transformed into a little town square, made up of several separate and three-dimensional houses, each one a tiny gem of naturalistic construction. . . . I have rarely seen a set which shows off the actors so well. The alleyways between the houses cry out for people to move through them. With simple costumes . . . and clear lighting . . . every scene on this stage acquired an air of sharpened reality, like life on a winter's day with frost and sun.[7]

In both background setting and foreground playing, Gaskill had achieved the immediacy he sought.

If a primary duty of national theatres is to preserve native classics and to acknowledge the works of foreign playwrights and their relation to the dramatic milieu, then the example of the cross-fertilization of The Recruiting Officer with Trumpets and Drums is a theatrical milestone. By reshaping the play--altering the text, adding characters, redefining their motivations and adding songs--Brecht prepared the way for William Gaskill's British production. Gaskill's fidelity to Farquhar's text, coupled with dynamic rehearsal technique, produced a piece of realistic theatre that was very much in keeping with the urgency of the new British drama of that period. Thus, a play of real significance was rescued from the relative obscurity in which it had lain since 1943 and re-established on the British--and the German--stage.

The proof of Farquhar's viability lies in the fact that he could withstand the close artistic scrutiny of his interpreters; the proof of his excellence lies in the fact that because of them--and, occasionally, despite them--his play was a popular success.[8]

The Recruiting Officer (1970)

On October 12, 1970, The Recruiting Officer opened at the Arts Theatre, Cambridge, alternating, in Prospect Productions' repertoire, with Arnold Wesker's comedy about modern army life, Chips With Everything. The cast included Ian McKellen as Plume, Trevor Peacock as Kite, Julian Curry as Brazen and Susan Fleetwood as Silvia. Richard Cottrell directed and Keith Norman designed the production.

It was impossible not to compare this Prospect venture with the National Theatre's 1963 undertaking which had stripped the play of the "usual Restoration extravagance by stressing its earthy provincial realism."[1] While René Allio had employed three-dimensional settings for the National, Keith Norman presented a "one-dimensional cut-out of a provincial town complete with miniaturized houses and prettified churches." The chief flaw in the Prospect set was that it was too general and did not match the dramatist's precise sense of place.

In interpreting the text, Gaskill had stressed a naturalistic style of playing, but Richard Cottrell concentrated on "conventional 18th century wit and foppishness," making the significant points about the misuse of the poor and simple by the rich and clever a secondary theme. The principal focus of this production was on Farquhar's portrait of a "close-knit masculine, military society in which women were regarded as decorative embellishments."[2] This attention was particularly fruitful in the Plume-Silvia relationship, which attained an understated ambiguity that blended into the fabric of the piece more gently than the homosexual motif of Gaskill's production. As Silvia, Susan Fleetwood emphasized this sexual riddle by "being just brisk enough when dressed enough and just feminine enough when disguised as a boy to be a source of sexual puzzlement."[3]

The principal source of interest was the Plume of Ian McKellen, who stood apart from the lesser mortals "grave and contemptuous like a Great Dane at a poodle show."[4] His performance made it clear that "for Plume the enlistment-business is no fun but an urgent professional necessity" cloaked by the pose of his cavalier air.[5] Ultimately, McKellen did not attempt to resolve any ethical difficulties, and when Plume's part in the recruiting was over, "you could sense the relief with which he washed his hands of the whole business."[6]

If the production lacked the edge which should have distinguished this play from its contemporaries, some of the difficulty could have lain with the finer points of the ensemble. For example, there was critical discomfort because very little attention was paid to the bucolic supernumeraries and the smaller roles. It is a valid point, especially if one remembers that a later leading man of the National Theatre Company, John Stride, had appeared as Costar Pearmain in the 1963 production at the Old Vic.

THE BEAUX' STRATAGEM
Plot Summary

I. Aimwell and Archer, playing master and servant, are financially embarrassed London blades who, to save face, have pretended to be going abroad. They have, however, remained in England going from town to town alternating roles and trying to impress the notable locals. They trust their money to Boniface, the inn-keeper, unaware that he is in with three highwaymen led by Gibbet. Boniface has his own suspicions, and he plies Archer with drink while advising his daughter, Cherry, to use her own devices.

II. While preparing for Sunday service, Mrs. Sullen complains to her sympathetic sister-in-law, Dorinda, about her marriage. Sullen's appearance does nothing to spoil his harassed wife's description, and she is convinced that in London she would be able to rid herself of him. Aimwell too prepares for church hoping to find an impressionable heiress in the congregation, and the higwaymen bring the loot from a recent robbery to Boniface.

III. Dorinda and Aimwell fall in love at church. When Dorinda reports home, Scrub, the servant, is sent to the inn to invite Archer, the "servant," to come to the house to drink. Aimwell meets Foigard, an Irishman pretending to be from Brussels, who is chaplain to the French prisoners. Archer is not free with information about his "master," and despite a good try on his part, the ladies guess that he is more than a servant.

Mrs. Sullen plots to arouse her husband's jealousy: Dorinda secretes Sullen in a closet while Mrs. Sullen allows Count Bellair, one of the French prisoners, to press his attentions. When Sullen charges out, his interest is not in his wife's honor but in the protection of his reputation.

IV. Since Lady Bountiful, Mrs. Sullen's mother-in-law, is known for her nursing skill, Archer comes in with the story that his master has been taken ill. Archer and Mrs. Sullen snatch their opportunity and even Aimwell manages to make his affection known to Dorinda. Mrs. Sullen and Dorinda compare their lovers, but Mrs. Sullen's new-found happiness makes her more aware of her marital situation. She is heartened by the fact that her brother is coming to her aid.

Aimwell and Archer force Foigard to admit that he is Irish, and, to save himself from the charge of treason, he agrees to let Archer replace the count in Mrs. Sullen's room. Gibbet and his crew make plans to rob Lady Bountiful's house.

V. Sir Charles Freeman, Mrs. Sullen's brother, arrives at the inn where Sullen has been made drunk by the enterprising robbers. Unaware of his brother-in-law's identity, Sullen offers Sir Charles his wife, erasing any doubts Sir Charles might have had about his sister's plight. Cherry alerts Aimwell to the robbery. As she is preparing for bed, Mrs. Sullen is surprised by Archer but withholds her consent. Scrub comes in to tell of the robbery in progress. Archer overcomes Gibbet and joins Aimwell. Victorious against the thieves, Archer presses Aimwell to sue hastily for Dorinda's hand and press for an immediate marriag using Foigard's services. Hoping for a conquest, Archer returns to Mrs. Sullen's bedroom, but he is foiled by the arrival of Sir Charles who knows both young men.

Instead of continuing his pretense, Aimwell confesses to Dorinda that he has been usurping his brother's title, but his confession convinces her of his honesty, and she rewards him with her hand. Now Dorinda has a surprise: Aimwell in truth owns the title, for his brother has--conveniently--died.

The only remaining complication is the marriage of the Sullens. Sullen agrees to a separation for ten thousand pounds, but Archer is in possession of the loot from the robbery, which includes the marriage settlement. He gives all the relevant papers to Sir Charles and Sullen is cut off.

Background

The Beaux' Stratagem was first performed at the Queen's Theatre, Haymarket, on 8 March 1707. The cast included Wilks as Archer, Mills as Aimwell, Bowman as Bellair, Verbruggen as Sullen, Keen as Freeman, Bowen as Foigard, Cibber as Gibbet, Bullock as Boniface, Norris as Scrub, Mrs. Powell as Lady Bountiful, Mrs. Bradshaw as Dorinda, Mrs. Oldfield as Mrs. Sullen, Mrs. Mills as Gipsy and Mrs. Bignal as Cherry.

The new Queen's Theatre was located in a middle class area which was slowly building up. Designed by Vanbrugh, it was unashamedly grand and had been intended to house Italian opera, but the audiences did not respond; and Vanbrugh contributed two of his plays, The Confederacy and The Mistake, to help the theatre's financial situation. Their success was not absolute, and not until the 1707 production of The Beaux' Stratagem did the theatre stop losing money. Farquhar attributed the success of his piece to his friend and colleague:

> The reader may find some faults in this play, which my illness prevented the amending of; but there is great amends made in the representation, which cannot be matched, no more than the friendly and indefatigable care of Mr. Wilks, to whom I chiefly owe the success of the play.

Wilks, who knew a vehicle when he saw one, had had an earlier success for Farquhar as Sir Harry Wildair in The Constant Couple at Drury Lane in 1699.

As an actor, Robert Wilks's success both at the Smock Alley Theatre in Dublin and in London was more a result of application and industry than overwhelming talent. He had vied with the talented George Powell for prominence as a leading man, and Wilks kept going while Powell's dissipation caused him to abuse his considerable ability. Cibber affirms that "from Nature"

Powell surpassed Wilks "in Voice, and Ear, in Elocution, in Tragedy, and Humour in Comedy." Yet Wilks held the course, while Powell "from the Neglect, and Abuse of those valuable Gifts, he suffer'd Wilks, to be of thrice the Service to our Society." Discussing the proper speaking of a prologue, that most dangerous moment in a Restoration play, Cibber outlines the defects of Wilks:

> Wilks had Spirit, but gave too loose a Rein to it, and it was seldom he could speak a grave and weighty Verse, harmoniously. . . . In Verses of Humour too, he would sometimes carry the Mimickry farther than the Hint would bear, even to a trifling Light, as if himself were pleas'd to see it so glittering.

But in terms of Farquhar's comedy, Wilks, actually invited to do impersonations in the role of Archer, was a delight. Steele's appraisal gives an idea of the effect Wilks produced:

> Mr. Wilks enters into the Part with so much Skill, that the Gallantry, the Youth, and Gaiety of a young Man of plentiful Fortune, is looked upon with as much indulgence on the Stage, as in real Life, without any of those Intermixtures of Wit and Humour, which usually prepossess us in Favour of such Characters in other Plays.

Colley Cibber saw Anne Oldfield blossom as an actress and reports that in one of her first good roles, that of Leonora in Sir Courtly Nice, though the rehearsal went badly (due in good part to Cibber's admitted lack of confidence in Oldfield), the performance was a triumph:

> What made her Performance more valuable, was, that I knew it all proceeded from her own Understanding, untaught, and unassisted by any one more experienc'd Actor.

Oldfield then became the ornament of the company and a good student of her craft:

> She never undertook any Part she lik'd, without being importunately desirous of having all the Helps in it, that another could possibly give her. . . . Yet it was a hard matter to give her any Hint, that she was not able to take, or improve.

Oldfield and Wilks often performed together and Cibber praises the combination of their talents:

> Mrs. Oldfield, and Wilks, by their frequently playing against one another, in our best Comedies, very happily supported that Humour, and Vivacity, which is so peculiar to our English Stage. The French, our only modern Competitors, seldom give us their Lovers, in such various Lights.

This kind of playing was a great asset to the company at the Haymarket where the former members of the Drury Lane Company were appearing under Sweeney's management. They began to draw "an equal Share of the politer sort of Spectators, who, for several Years, could not allow our Company to stand in any comparison with the other."

The popularity of The Beaux' Stratagem was so great that it rivalled, or surpassed, The Recruiting Officer. Among those who played Archer were Ryan, Garrick (it was a favorite with him), Smith, Elliston and Charles Kemble. Sullen had his interpreter in Quin. Scrub was played by Macklin, Garrick (for a benefit), Shuter, Quick, Liston and Keeley. Astonishingly, Scrub also attracted actresses, most particularly Mrs. Abington for her 1786 benefit. With the exception of Mrs. Siddons, the leading actresses of the eighteenth century were drawn to Mrs. Sullen. Among them were Mrs. Pritchard, Mrs. Woffington, Mrs. Barry, Mrs. Abington, Miss Farren and Mrs. Jordan. Cherry attracted Mrs.

Clive, Miss Pope and Miss Mellon. The last nineteenth century revival was in 1879 at the Imperial Theatre.

In 1927 Edith Evans had a major triumph as Mrs. Sullen in a cast including James Whale, Miles Malleson, Carlton Hobbs, David Horne, Winifred Evans and Dorothy Hope. Nigel Playfair appeared as Gibbet. Ivor Brown admitted that it was likely that "years hence we shall bore posterity by quoting this magnificent performance to incredulous youth, as we, incredulous and careless, have been bored by Victorian legends of vanished and, no doubt, authentic magnificence."[1] The popularity of the play made the secluded Lyric Theatre, Hammersmith, the place to go, and Dame Edith was even immortalized by a porcelain figurine of herself in character.

There was a 1947 revival in Manchester to celebrate Farquhar's arrival in England in 1697. Ten years later, Bernard Hepton directed the play for the Birmingham Repertory Theatre with Albert Finney in the role of Archer.

The Beaux' Stratagem (1949)

Three years after his ill-fated production of Marriage à la Mode, John Clements presented The Beaux' Stratagem at the Phoenix Theatre on May 5, 1949. The production, which ran for 532 performances, was one of the most successful productions of Restoration comedy to be mounted. The cast included Robert Eddison as Aimwell, John Clements as Archer, Kay Hammond as Mrs. Sullen, David Bird as Boniface, Lloyd Pearson as Gibbet, Gwen Cherrell as Cherry and Iris Russell as Dorinda. John Clements directed.

Placed in its historical context, the comedy showed Farquhar as a transitional playwright, "looking back to the artifice of Congreve and forward to the sentimental realism of Goldsmith."[1] Directing in that vein, Clements insisted on a variety of pace in the acting, particularly in the Mrs. Sullen of Kay Hammond, whose delivery in IV.ii was loaded with mischief as Mrs. Sullen confides to Dorinda: "Look ye, sister, I have no supernatural gifts--I can't swear I could resist temptation, though I can safely promise to avoid it, and that's as much as the best of us can do."[2] Despite Hammond's ability to make the audience laugh in most of the right places, Mrs. Sullen's famous speech ending, "Hark 'ee, sister, I'm not superhuman" went for very little.

Particularly well received was the "catechism" between Gwen Cherrell as Cherry and Clements as Archer in one of the play's most appealing scenes. This Archer of "measure, tact, and a speaking under-lip" was balanced by the Aimwell of Robert Eddison in a performance "so true in all its trivialities that it seems to have been fetched from the Restoration stage of our imagination."[3]

The longevity of the production was due to the composite efforts of the group and to the consistently diligent attempts of Clements.

The Beaux' Stratagem (1970)

On January 20, 1970, the National Theatre Company opened in Los Angeles at the Ahmanson Theatre with the world premiere of its production of The Beaux' Stratagem. It was played in repertory with Three Sisters, directed by Laurence Olivier, which had first been presented at the Old Vic on July 4, 1967. The cast included Ronald Pickup as Aimwell, Robert Stephens as Archer, David Ryall as Squire Sullen, Kenneth Mackintosh as Freeman, Derek Jacobi as Foigard, Paul Curran as Gibbet, Gerald James as Boniface, Bernard Gallagher as Scrub, Jeanne Watts as Lady Bountiful, Maggie Smith as Mrs. Sullen, Sheila Reid as Dorinda, Louise Purnell as Gipsy and Helen Fraser as Cherry. The production was directed by William Gaskill and designed by René Allio.

Taken at a deliberate pace, the play produced multiple effects in terms of language: "The language becomes resonant, in ways we are barely aware of. The words turn slowly, like mobiles, showing everywhere a new complexity from a different perspective."[1]

A significant contribution by Maggie Smith was the view she presented of Mrs. Sullen, the combination of her "caustic humor, her bawdiness, her innate civilization, her longing for a full life, and the pathos of her wretched marriage."[2] Her presentation of the lady was based essentially in the words and the use she made of them:

> She can make a simple, seemingly artificial little audience address, without any stage movement, into a poignant event. She finds a startling number of changes within a line: (Musing): "It must be so." (Becoming confident): "It IS so." (With determination): "It SHALL be so."

> Always she finds in the words the exact state of Mrs. Sullen's mind at the moment, the sense of her whole sensibility, and the direction her mind is moving. It is a truly awesome performance.[3]

After its success in Los Angeles, the National Theatre Company opened The Beaux' Stratagem in London at the Old Vic on April 8, 1970. Once again, the team of Farquhar, Gaskill, Allio, Robert Stephens and Maggie Smith, which had brought prestige to The Recruiting Officer in 1963, combined their talents for the eager London audiences.

The program notes were of special significance, warning the audience not to laugh too lightly as the focus of the play was the serious matter of the Sullen marriage dilemma. Included in the notes were copious extracts from John Milton's The Doctrine and Discipline

<u>of Divorce</u> with examples of the use Farquhar made of Milton's text as he translated it into dramatic dialogue. The fact that the comedy treated of such a serious subject was, in itself, innovative:

> But how was he [Farquhar] to write dialogue about divorce, this quite new thing in Restoration comedy? It must sound convincing, and he had no experience of it. Now about to write a scene between Sullen and his wife, Farquhar opened his copy of Milton's <u>Doctrine and Discipline of Divorce</u> and read this in Book II: "Nay, instead of being one flesh, they will be rather two carcasses chained unnaturally together, or, as it may happen, a living soul bound to a dead corpse. . . ." These phrases Farquhar thus transcribed:

> Sullen: You're impertinent.
> Mrs. Sullen: I was ever so, since I became one flesh with you.
> Sullen: One flesh! Rather two carcasses joined unnaturally together.
> Mrs. Sullen: Or rather a living soul coupled to a dead body.

A brief background of British divorce legality was given by playwright and lawyer, John Mortimer, who noted that, "Some 263 years after the play was written, English Law has not applied Farquhar's grounds for divorce in their full simplicity." He summarized the situation:

> In 1707 the Sullens would have had a complicated piece of legislation to pass on their way to freedom: they could also have been subject to a sharp term of imprisonment for refusing each other "conjugal rights." They were very far away from what Milton had dreamed of as divorce for incompatibility of character, and still liable to what, in the middle of the preceding century, he

had called "The Bondage of the Canon Law and Other Mistakes."

Tracing the procedure through to 1971, when the Divorce Reform Act would become operative, he considered that legislation in terms of the Sullens:

> The latest change in the divorce law, due to take effect in 1971, recognizes the principle of consent and allows a divorce if the husband and wife have lived apart for two years and the marriage has irretrievably broken down. However, even in 1971, the Sullens' troubles will not easily be over. By the end of the play they have only been married for fourteen months, and the fact that it felt like fourteen years is of no legal significance. There is also no evidence of a two year separation. In fact any sort of final dance would still, as any reputable firm of solicitors would advise the Sullens, be a sign of premature rejoicing: "Consent if mutual, saves the lawyer's fee," it would no doubt be explained to them, is the sort of wild statement to be expected from an actor, a comic playwright, a reader of Milton and a friend of Wilks.

The program also contained brief extracts from that very act which would be operative on 1 January 1971. Irving Wardle made an immediate connection between the approach to the text and this popular piece of legislation:

> The text has been stripped down and reassembled in accordance with sense and living situations . . . no superflourishes, no routine displays of eighteenth-century "style." The production takes the play for what it is: a serious comedy about divorce, and, as such, the last nail in the coffin of Restoration drama and a foretaste of Shaw.[4]

William Gaskill's directorial approach to The Recruiting Officer in 1963 had been based on rehearsal improvisation which concerned itself with character interaction rather than the text, which was not memorized until after the movement had been established. By 1970 when the company had been functioning as an ensemble for six years, he could concentrate more completely on the text. The result was that he tried to create a less self-conscious environment in which the dialogue could flourish. Gaskill discussed the dramatic dealings between Robert Stephens (Archer) and Ronald Pickup (Aimwell), a relationship which had to be reversed from negative to positive:

> I always tried to demonstrate that a particular speech in the play came out of a specific emotional relationship. One speech should be glued to the next by the feeling between people. . . . Robert Stephens and Ronald Pickup . . . often played on objectives of contention at such points--they tried to put each other down or one tried to score off the other. This is a bad basis for the relationship between the two men which should be based on the quality of shared fun, the sense of their mutual pleasure in the idea of finding wives for themselves.[5]

Though Gaskill was not sure of the players' interaction, Milton Shulman applauded an "assured panache that makes avarice excusable and immorality forgivable," for these "playboys of the Restoration world . . . are neither burdened by scruples nor deterred by legality."[6]

In the case of the set, there was a visual departure from Allio's Recruiting Officer settings. Allio made the distinction:

The Beaux' Stratagem is mainly two-dimensional. The Recruiting Officer was three-dimensional with elements that turned. I've always wanted to do a Restoration Comedy in two dimensions because that's how they were originally performed, with sliding scenery. Our stages aren't grooved to carry sliding scenery so we've mainly used flying sets and the furniture is actually brought in on tiny trucks. It creates the sense of the flow of the play as it was originally written to be played.[7]

Irving Wardle followed Allio's line of thought very closely in his review:

Settings and production alike are designed to project high-spirited debate and unimpeded action. Allio's foreground pieces—half-walls and galleries, and a single house facade—both follow through the style of the panorama, and make a tactful compromise with the flat backgrounds of eighteenth-century staging: a two-dimensional environment that projects the living three-dimensional actor forward into the house like a reflecting panel.[8]

Despite the excellence of directorial and visual approach, there was little question that much of the attraction of the production was to be in the performance of Maggie Smith, recently lauded at Chichester for her Margery in The Country Wife.[9]

In a pattern consistent with her particular artistic attack, Miss Smith created a brittle, energetic character, showing

a shell of elegant artifice which is repeatedly smashed by the hungry woman within. This swooping descent from decorum to appetite comes out in innumerable small touches, often made as much with a sidelong look or abrupt predatory gesture as with the lines: as where Archer refuses her money with a bow and she stands, purse still in outstretched hand, her eyes running like zip-fasteners up and down his extended leg.[10]

This was her way of taking "the Stanislavski principle of playing against the character as far as it will go, and the fraction further which makes for comedy."[11] Particularly notable was the combination of comedy and pathos in her witty, unhappy woman:

> She makes something lovely of Sullen's one moment of confession, "Oh, Dorinda! I own myself a woman, full of my sex, a gentle, generous soul, easy and yielding to soft desires." The mocking poise falls into perspective: the play acting of a woman desperately defending herself with humour against tragedy.[12]

Most important to the repertory system within which she worked so successfully, Miss Smith contributed to the setting-off of companion players:

> But the joy of it [her performance] is the way it interplays with the other performances--weaving with fascinated evasion round Robert Stephens' cheerful brutality as Archer, matching honeyed sarcasm against the sweetness of Sheila Reid's Dorinda, off-setting with its complex irony the blunt antipathy of David Ryall's Sullen. It's the performance of a star in the true sense: not a solitary luminary but the bright centre of a galaxy, revolving harmoniously among its planets.[13]

She solidified the ensemble, encouraging the cast to function as a unit.

Gaskill's approach encouraged artifice in performance by evoking various styles for various characters: "It's acceptable in Restoration drama to invoke different acting traditions for different types of characters, just as the Italians kept figures from the commedia dell'arte as actors in comparatively straight comedies."[14]

As Archer, Robert Stephens went against the grain of the text in a performance in the Shavian vein. His approach was comparable to his Captain Plume as he "often places himself initially at a disadvantage and goes on to show technique triumphing over basic equipment."[15]

The most obvious of these artificial creations was the Gibbet of Paul Curran, "with his flickering eyes and pencil-line mustache . . . a pure pantomime figure."[16] Less in keeping with the flow of the performances was the Foigard of Derek Jacobi, who "makes no serious attempt to present [the character] . . . as anything but a purely farcical creation." As Squire Sullen, David Ryall presented a more considerable problem by playing Mrs. Sullen's unappealing partner "simply as a slow-witted country gentleman with a sore head."[17] This approach raised the question of reconciling the union of such opposites—especially as Mrs. Sullen had all the money.

CONCLUSION

A significant result of this study has been a realization of the flexibility of Restoration plays as they have been manipulated to accommodate changing tastes, tastes which can be inferred from the variety of appeals made to the audiences of three decades. In the immediate post-war years, audiences were not expected to draw contemporary parallels. Productions were mounted which had entertainment, escapist, emotional or historical value, but no play was presented as conscious social commentary. Realistic interpretation of a work like <u>The Recruiting Officer</u>, which referred directly to the shoddiness of the motivations for war, was not to be found.

Once the internal social structure stabilized, it was possible to employ more invention, and later decades show a progression from a hesitant tinkering with the text to an out-and-out manipulation designed to make the text come to terms with an audience which demanded some basis of identification with the play. Despite this trend, which enveloped many of the principal characters and reshaped them as contemporary individuals, the frankly period creations like Sir Fopling Flutter, later Lord Foppington, and Sir Harry Wildair remained firmly placed in their Restoration settings, although some psychological incentive was suggested as the reason for their behavior. For there is, in the later audiences, a real interest in the psychological and sociological motivations of the characters; and attempts are made, in later productions, to meet these concerns. Valid realization of this need gave added depth to the comedies without stifling the laughter.

Most of these productions are the products of repertory companies. The most representative in quality of performance and quantity of productions are the Old Vic Company, the English Stage Company, Prospect Productions, the National Theatre Company and the Royal

Shakespeare Company. Besides being adequately funded to absorb the high production costs of mounting these plays, such companies are better able to interpret them because of the unifying factor of a continually working ensemble. There is still a difference between the random assembling of a cast of experts and the essential unity of the repertory company.

What emerges from a study of individual productions spaced over a period of three decades is the emphasis on the various facets of a play as it is interpreted by several different casts over the years. Approaching the plays in the 1940s, Gielgud and his colleagues stressed attention to dialogue in addition to grace of movement: a bearing that was a complement to the words. And even the most self-consciously modern production admitted an attention to tradition that was not slavery to an empty form but an animating principle of the drama and the vehicle for conveying that drama to a receptive modern public.

Attention to the dialogue must still be the prime consideration, no matter the approach, and the actors who have excelled in interpretation--John Gielgud, Edith Evans, Margaret Rutherford, John Moffatt, Cyril Ritchard, Donald Sinden, Laurence Olivier and Maggie Smith--have all been praised for a presence which combined the best of the vocal and the visual.

The plays of the Restoration have survived despite charges, sometimes richly deserved, of immorality and profaneness, and they have weathered adaptations which were no less than complete distortions. The fact that so many contemporary uncut revivals can be considered, so many authors discussed despite the financial and artistic difficulties presented by these plays, is due to a realization in the middle years of this twentieth century of the innate value of these plays for a public still greatly concerned with literature and very much involved in life.

APPENDIX A: THE WAY OF THE WORLD (1924)

Edith Evans at Hammersmith

On February 7, 1924, Nigel Playfair presented Congreve's The Way of the World at the Lyric Theatre, Hammersmith. Great pains had been taken to revive the period atmosphere; even the program was printed in old fashioned lettering. There was a whimsicality which offered servants lighting candles in quartet formation and the players striking attitudes. The musicians were costumed and a harpsichord was numbered among the instruments. The cast included Edith Evans as Millamant, Robert Loraine as Mirabell, Harold Anstruther as Fainall, Nigel Playfair as Witwoud, Norman V. Norman as Petulant, Scott Russell as Sir Wilful Witwoud, Harold Scott as Waitwell, Margaret Yarde as Lady Wishfort, Dorothy Green as Mrs. Marwood, Ruth Taylor as Mrs. Fainall, Hilda Sims as Foible, Kathlyn Hilliard as Mincing and Elsa Lanchester as Peggy.

The Lyric Theatre itself had already made a reputation with the more selective playgoers by offering such specialized pieces as Abraham Lincoln and The Beggar's Opera. This particular production was designed to go beyond those thoughtful few, and, since "all the modernity of the dramatist is in this admirable performance," it was possible that the production might make Congreve popular with a larger audience.[1] Probably to make the appeal the more general, Playfair did allow cuts in the text. For example, the scene with Lady Wishfort and Foible in the fifth act was discarded but the dances were not cut.

The Mirabell of Robert Loraine set the modern note in the acting. Making Mirabell a tweed suit man, he brought him closer to Shaw's John Tanner than Congreve's hero. If he was excessively serious, it could be argued that "Mirabell is the one sincere man in his circle, and sincerity does not vary with the fashion."[2] If he was not "Congreve's Mirabell, on whom so much depends," his was still "a manly and direct performance" not lacking in humor.[3] Much was justified by his speaking of the prose. James Agate praised him for using "only the suavest and most gentle notes in his voice," and when he was not speaking, he "listened exquisitely."[4] In this latter approach he was in line with the theory of comedy contained in the _Morning Post_ review:

> One has to remember that the play is "pure" comedy . . . in which the men and women are for the most part to be regarded as mere formulae, the relations between the sexes being almost as passionless as are those between the kings and queens at chess.[5]

Margaret Yarde's Lady Wishfort was pitched on more broadly comic notes--both cruel and amusing. The performance was masterful in "the way of grotesque, unbridled fancy."[6] However, if the reviewer for the _Guardian_ was correct in his assumption that in a twentieth-century audience "there are no groundlings to be tickled" at a Congreve play, then he was also correct in his judgment that Miss Yarde's "rough-and-ready rendering" miscarried.[7] Thus the flamboyant vulgarity of her Lady Wishfort slightly imbalanced the production.

In contrast, the Mrs. Marwood of Dorothy Green, a rendering that seemed to be "bitten into the plate with acid,"[8] was the product of a beautiful voice and a style of performance "truest to the author's intention and period."[9]

Despite the various contributory talents, it was the Millamant for which this production was to be remembered. When Edith Evans assumed the role she was thirty-six with a twelve-year theatrical past which included roles as diverse as Cleopatra in Dryden's _All_

<u>for Love</u> (1922), and the Serpent and She-Ancient in Shaw's <u>Back to Methuselah</u> (Birmingham, 1923). She had already achieved a respected reputation, and the Millamant was to be among the most skillfully painted of an ever-lengthening gallery of classic comic portraits. Evans was never to have tremendous weight in tragedy; she had neither musical nor dance accomplishments; nor had she the bloom of first youth and loveliness which had endeared Anne Bracegirdle to an audience as she created Congreve's heroines. She did not come to charm daintily but rather to command the stage with a most complete set of comic equipment. Nigel Playfair described the accomplishment of her Millamant:

> The Millamant of that last final surrender to Mirabell is something far more than the Millamant who comes "full sail, with her fan spread, and her streamers out, and a shoal of fools for tenders"; it is a woman wittier, more fascinating, and more tender, probably, than has ever been seen off the stage or elsewhere on it. Here is no "character rendered ridiculous by its affected wit"; here is a character rendered sublime by the poignancy and the sincerity of its wit. . . . And it is a most extraordinary tribute to Edith Evans that she was able to take on her shoulders the weight of such an enormous conception, and play it almost as if the conception were purely her own rather than the author's.[10]

Although the critics had already expected a great performance in the comic spirit, it was left to Dame Edith to remind them of Millamant's humanity, to show her as "a dainty rogue, an imp of mischief." Most famous and carefully delineated of the critical analyses of her performance is the praise of James Agate:

> Her countenance is replete, as was said of Congreve's style, "with sense and satire, conveyed

in the most pointed and polished terms." Her acting is "a shower of brilliant conceits, a new triumph of wit, a new conquest over dulness."

. . . .

Her Millamant is impertinent without being pert, graceless without being ill-graced. She has only two scenes, but what scenes they are of unending subtlety and finesse! Never can that astonishing "Ah! idle creature, get up when you will" have taken on greater delicacy, or "I may by degrees dwindle into a wife" a more delicious mockery. "Adieu, my morning thoughts, agreeable wakings, indolent slumbers, all ye douceurs, ye sommeils du matin, adieu"--all this was breathed out as though it were early Ronsard or du Bellay. And "I nauseate walking," and "Natural, easy Suckling!" bespoke the very genius of humor. There is a pout of the lips, a jutting forward of the chin to greet the conceit, and a smile of happy deliverance when it is uttered, which defy the chronicler. This face, at such moments, is like a city in illumination, and when it is withdrawn leaves a glow behind.[11]

It was the Evans Millamant which was to rule the tradition for over fifty years by combining style of performance with humanity in interpretation. There was no alteration of critical ardor when she resumed the role three years later.

Thirteen years after her Millamant, Sidney W. Carroll gave a general description of her acting which shows the durability of her historical as well as her technical appeal:

In almost every role she undertakes Miss Evans invariably reminds me of 18th century style and modish elegance. Her air of impudence is so engaging, her movements are mannered and yet easy, her speech so rhythmic and Celtically lilted. She has glitter. What subtleties lie in her comedy only the keenest-witted members of an audience can fully appreciate. In mood and pace her variety is endless. . . . So systematic is her mask of artifice that when the cardboard is held aside passion in its sublimest form can and does thrill us with an odd and incongruous integrity.[12]

In 1927 Evans repeated her Millamant. The critic for the Times attacked Congreve's exaggerated sensibility, determining that although "it is quite fitting to conclude that there is beneath Millamant's gaiety a depth of sentiment, a fastidiousness of feeling, which compensates you for the monotony of so harsh a drawing of human frailty," the misanthropy of Congreve is evident in the fact that "Millamant's virtue, like Mirabell's lack of virtue, is no more than one of the many artifices which make up the Restoration comedy of manners."[13] Despite this grim reading of the text, the performance still enchanted; the sparkle and the fascination of Millamant conquered the misanthropy of her creator. Evans saw to it that "she shines and glitters and bedazzles, varying her laughter and the ripple of her voice with superb artistry."

Hubert Griffith attempted a delineation of the basis of her skill:

There are two explanations. It is partly power; partly knowledge. Power on the stage means personality. It is a gift that great actors must have, and that many music hall performers have got. This great gift Miss Edith Evans has.[14]

APPENDIX B: THE WAY OF THE WORLD (1976)

Maggie Smith at Stratford, Ontario

It was not until 1976 that a new Millamant was born who combined all the elements of comic delivery, sense of period and modernity to vie with the Evans performance. The Way of the World was the first production of the Stratford Festival of 1976, and the Millamant of Maggie Smith had taken the actress 14 years of stage work.

Maggie Smith approached Millamant by the most circuitous route of all the actresses of the century. She began her professional career as a revue comedienne both in New York and London. When she joined the Old Vic in 1959, her comic ability was channeled into the classical mold, and she exhibited a definite talent for playing in the rarified Restoration atmosphere.

In 1959 she played her first Restoration role, Lady Plyant, in The Double Dealer at the Old Vic. Shortly before joining the National Theatre Company, she played a consummate Margery Pinchwife in the Chichester Festival production of The Country Wife. For the National Theatre she played Sylvia in The Recruiting Officer, a Brecht-inspired production, in 1963, and in 1970 Mrs. Sullen in The Beaux' Stratagem both in Los Angeles and London.

In these roles she had made her mark as a comedienne of the highest order, but Millamant is a necessity for the actress who wishes to solidify her reputation in classical comedy. When Smith was with the National Theatre Company, she had been passed over in favor of Geraldine McEwan for Millamant in the 1969 production; so the Canadian venture offerd her a chance to display her range, vamping as Cleopatra one night and delighting as Millamant the next. Additionally, Stratford, Ontario, is hardly a backwater as its company has been ranked third, after the National

277

Theatre Company and the Royal Shakespeare Company, in the English-speaking theatre.

In its twenty-first year, 1974, Stratford came under the direction of Robin Phillips, a young British director. Very much a man of the living theatre, Phillips still paid scrupulous attention to the text. There was little cutting of the Congreve play, and the production ran three and a half hours. Despite its length, the result was a staging that "admirably sustained the play, gave it a style and period and, yet--particularly in the key relationship between Millamant and Mirabell--offered Congreve's satirical posturings with a contemporaneousness that at times almost startled."[1] The cast, which mixed British with North American actors, included Jeremy Brett as Mirabell, Jessica Tandy as Lady Wishfort, Alan Scarfe as Fainall, Keith Baxter as Witwoud, Bernard Hopkins as Petulant, Tony Van Bridge as Sir Wilful Witwoud, Domini Blythe as Mrs. Marwood, Jan Kudelka as Foible and Jackie Burroughs as Mincing.

Maggie Smith's Millamant was a triple triumph of movement, line delivery and characterization. She had, by the time of this interpretation, gained a considerable reputation as "custodian of the sardonic side of life,"[2] yet she could also grasp the moments in a text which show "those lovely spots of wit, humanity and compassion."[3] Beginning as arch-comedienne of the brittle, she had "laid waste more living-rooms, chaises longues, lead-men, ottomans, vanity tables and handy bric-a-brac than any other enchantress in the business. She coils herself around things, and they disappear in small puffs of smoke, leaving only her violent red hair and her small, contrite mouth behind as a memento of the holocaust. Usually it's a comic holocaust; Miss Smith makes annihilation funny."[4] Part of her technique of comic mayhem was visual. Her Millamant was "wonderfully vague, her hands fluttering about like confused birds, her eyes looking in one direction while her feet move in another" as she debated the prospect of dwindling into a wife.[5] Combining the visual with the vocal, Smith "half closes those magnificent eyes, looks down her extraordinary nose and sucks in those marvelous hollow cheeks as she tells a suitor, very carefully and clearly, 'one no more owes one's duty to a lover than one's wit to an echo.'"

In line delivery she used a counterpoise technique, "inhaling a line in one breath like a drag on a fresh cigarette and instantaneously tossing it away like a dead butt."[6] But the rhythm of the talking, the prattling almost, was part of the characterization. If she seemed to let "one line breed another indiscriminately, until you think language must have overpopulated the globe," she made it clear early on in the performance that "she talks to keep her composure, that language is her last line of defense, that she's secretly more vulnerable than anyone on stage."[7] She made this vulnerability the basis of Congreve's grand lady.

A most significant moment in the development of the character was in the contract scene. She played for the unexpected, unexpected in terms of line emphasis yet justifiable in terms of her approach:

> She is every bit as funny as she ought to be for the most of it, enjoying herself enormously in a tragedy-queen near-faint as she reacts in shock ("Oh, name it not!") to her prospective husband's monstrous mention of child-bearing. But, without a flick of those heavy-lidded eyes of hers, she alters tone utterly with one seemingly unremarkable remarkable request. Mirabell is always to "knock at the door before you come in." With that—who'd have counted on it?—she is totally touching. During all of the imperiously outrageous terms this early apostle of freedom (1700) has been setting, terms bolder and in spots saner than those demanded today, she's been most deeply

concerned about some small, ordinary, unmistakably human need: the barest minimum of privacy.[8]

Maggie Smith's triumph was in a production much unlike the one by Nigel Playfair in 1924. In the first quarter of the century, Playfair had indicated the desire for farce and had followed the instinct to "jazz" his production. Robin Phillips took a much more sober view. In the decades between the Evans performance and the Smith performance, the audience had come to take the situation--if not the characters--seriously. Part of the importance of the Phillips production fifty years after Playfair's venture was the emphasis on serious moral overtones: "The way of the world, so glittering, is wicked, as we learn. A production that can make us laugh at the glitter while taking note of the dour truth is one that demands to be seen."[9]

APPENDIX C: THE COUNTRY WIFE (1936)

Ruth Gordon in London and New York

In 1924 The Country Wife was presented in London
for the first time in 150 years by the Phoenix Society.
In this excellent production, the letter scene in
particular was "admirably contrived and written, and
the dawn of urban cunning in the country woman's brain
is pointed with a genuine dramatic mastery." The
episode revealed the "quintessence of comic artifice."[1]

On October 6, 1936, The Country Wife was performed
at the Old Vic in a production directed by Tyrone
Guthrie. Its appearance on the stage of that
conservative theatre was an historic one made possible
by the manager of the theatre, Lilian Baylis, who
circumvented the probable objections of the board of
governors by showing, in a special performance for
them, the essential "innocence" of the play. In
addition to Ruth Gordon, who was making her London
debut as Margery, the cast included Michael Redgrave as
Horner, Edith Evans as Lady Fidget, Frederick Bennet as
Quack, Richard Goolden as Sir Jasper Fidget, Iris Hoey
as Mrs. Dainty Fidget, Alec Clunes as Harcourt, Patrick
Harr as Dorilant, Ernest Thesiger as Sparkish, James
Dale as Pinchwife, Ursula Jeans as Alithea, Eileen Peel
as Mrs. Squeamish, Freda Jackson as Lucy and Kate
Cutler as Old Lady Squeamish.

Although the play was censured for a "coarseness
of mind which goes deeper than the fashionable
coarseness of language" and a lack of both style and
taste in Wycherley, there was recompense in the
author's "flair for the characteristic detail" and
"infectious delight in his own rubbishy material."[2]

As Lady Fidget, Edith Evans was a reliable source
of sophisticated delight as she managed to take a joke
"not a point farther than it will go, but always as
far." After her 1924 Millamant and her Laetitia in The

<u>Old Batchelor</u>, the best was expected from her comic flights.

Miss Gordon was praised for a "comically distorted rustic simplicity"--a theme upon which she played her variations throughout the evening. And it was asserted that no one who saw her do the letter scene would ever forget it. Her success was rendered the more remarkable by the fact that she was the first American actress to star at the Old Vic. She played for five weeks--two weeks longer than the usual repertory playing time. The comedy broke all attendance records at the Old Vic in the 1936-1937 season and left the repertoire only because it was booked for performance in America.

On December 1, 1936, the production transferred to Henry Miller's Theatre in New York with Gordon still in the title role. Roger Livesay replaced Michael Redgrave as Horner, Anthony Quayle played Harcourt and Irene Browne replaced Edith Evans. The rest of the cast included George Carr as Quack, George Graham as Sir Jasper Fidget, Edith Atwater as Mrs. Dainty Fidget, Stephen Ker Appleby as Dorilant, Louis Hector as Sparkish, Percy Waram as Pinchwife, Helen Trenholme as Alithea, Helena Pickard as Mrs. Squeamish, Violet Besson as Old Lady Squeamish and Jane Vaughan as Lucy. The production was directed by Gilbert Miller and designed by Oliver Messel.

The only previous professional production of the comedy had been the bowdlerized version, <u>The Country Girl</u>, presented in New York about 1901; so, in effect, the Wycherley comedy was being seen in the United States for the first time in the twentieth century in the original version.

Miss Gordon had had a varied career in the United States. Her featured appearance had been in 1918 in <u>Seventeen</u>, and she had gained prominence in <u>Ethan Frome</u>. Although she had appeared both in lightweight comedy and in more serious pieces, there had been no

282

outstanding successes; so she took full advantage of Margery, the first role to show her comic talents to their fullest.

In New York, the play was seen as a mirror of the mores of modern life: the "morals of our time do not seem to be so vastly different from those of a period in history that we are inclined to look upon as pretty dissolute."[3] The spirit of both ages joined at the performance as there was "no over-playing, or self-consciousness or tendency to patronize either the play or the audience." The gaucherie of the part was a neat fit for Miss Gordon, and she made the most of Margery's confusion; "her elaborate confidences turned straight into the faces of the audience, her falling voice, her alarms and studied raptures are funny and original and resourceful, and quite the best thing in Wycherley's old trollop discursion."[4] She made particular use of the asides, which she delivered with a "wide-eyed innocence which makes them excruciating."[5]

The approach to the play was seen as "a burlesque, a lark, for the blades in the stalls to titter into their lace cuffs."[6] There was the minor problem of extending this idea of burlesque to the "Baby Snooks quality" in the performance of Miss Gordon, but that remained a matter of personal appreciation.

APPENDIX D: THE RECRUITING OFFICER (1963)

Textual Changes and Rehearsal Techniques of
The National Theatre Company

In 1965, the National Theatre Company published an annotated text of its production of The Recruiting Officer, and the notes, though not extensive, are indicative of the bent of the interpretation of the text.[1] The play had not been seen in the West End since December of 1943 in a production at the Arts Theatre directed by Alec Clunes, with Trevor Howard as Plume. The critics lauded the production for its ingenuity ("in two and a half hours The Recruiting Officer does not lose its freshness for a moment") and praised Clunes, who had "introduced some nice moments of miming and buffoonery. . . . In the court scene of Act III, fantasy explodes wildly like a box of rockets."[2] The effectiveness of Clunes's attempt was not forgotten. Reviewing the National Theatre performance twenty years later, Philip Hope-Wallace said that the more recent production was "rather less good" than the earlier, shorter version.[3]

The National's longer production allowed necessary deletions and additions to insure clarity. The major cuts were made in IV.iii, the scene in which Kite disguises himself as a fortune teller. The entire exchange between Kite and the butcher whom he dupes was considered "self-contained and dramatically dispensable" and, therefore, was removed.[4] For purposes of plot simplification, Lucy's speeches about Melinda's handwriting were also removed. Finally, the Brazen-Kite exchange, which adds two more letters to the complicated plot, was deleted.

In his logbook of the rehearsals, Kenneth Tynan noted that Kite's display during the fortune telling scene was "obviously written as a set-piece for a virtuoso clown," which Colin Blakely was not.[5] At first, Gaskill added stage business: for example, Kite speared cards on his sword while telling Pluck's fortune but later decided to delete the activity because of his "unwillingness to 'improve on' the text."

The other significant cut was an exchange between Plume and Brazen in V.iv. Here Brazen debates whether he should invest in a privateer or a playhouse. Olivier was reluctant to play lines which would sound too much like a private joke since he was investing himself in the National Theatre.

There were two military interpolations. Most significant was the reading of the Articles of War in V.vi. The note to the National text gives the stage direction: "As Plume reads--at high speed--the Articles of War, a low and menacing drumroll is heard offstage."[6] The extracts were lifted from a 1706 version of such articles and were intended to make the audience aware of the many and varied offenses for which a man could be condemned to death. Additionally, the final lines of the play, orders from Brazen to the new recruits, were gathered from a military treatise of the period to "help lift the closing moments" of the production.

Particular attention was paid to the entrance of Brazen in III.i. His triple appearance was used to help establish the character:

> Brazen is glimpsed crossing the stage at rear. He disappears R., only to make another "subliminal" entrance and exit crossing R. to L., before re-entering L. and spotting Worthy. This triple entrance helps to establish the man's total vagueness and inability to concentrate on anything for more than a few moments.[7]

In III.ii, two bits of business are given for Brazen in his exchange with Melinda. Making overtures

to her, he lists his conquests and concludes: "Fate has reserved me for a Shropshire lady with twenty thousand pounds.
--Do you know any such person, madam?" He punctuates his question with a slap on her bottom.[8] Shortly after, he takes vigorous leave of her: "My hand, heart's blood, and guts are at your service." He takes her hand, and "instead of kissing it, puts out his tongue and <u>licks</u> it." This somewhat overt behavior had a number of counterparts in visual homosexual references.

In I.i, there is a hint in the first exchange between Plume and Kite that their close relationship is less than formal. When Silvia makes her entrance disguised as Wilful in III.ii, she has a significant exchange with Kite:

> Kite: Pray, noble captain, give me leave to salute you (Offers to kiss her.)
>
> Silvia: What, men kiss one another!
>
> Kite: We officers do: 'tis our way! We live together like man and wife, always either kissing or fighting.[9]

The scene was explicated in this way:

> Since Kite does not suspect Silvia's identity, only one interpretation of this exchange is possible: that for soldiers on active service, as for the sailor in <u>Fanny Hill</u>, it is often a case of "any port in a storm." The Brazen-Plume embraces, on the other hand, are merely salutations, <u>sans</u> sex.

There then follows a chase sequence while Plume and Brazen fight over Wilful. In the standard stage directions, while Brazen and Plume fight, Silvia draws. But Kite takes Silvia in his arms and carries her off. The National production was much more kinetic:

Kite chases Silvia offstage. . . . A switch: Silvia dashes across the stage in hot pursuit of Kite. . . . As they [Plume and Brazen] embrace Kite reappears behind them carrying Silvia off perched on his shoulders.[10]

In IV.i, no directions are necessary beyond the standard one in the text, as Silvia formally enlists:

Silvia: . . . And now your hand, this lists me-- and now you are my captain.

Plume: (Kissing her) Your friend.--(aside) 'Sdeath! there's something in this fellow that charms me.[11]

Again in V.iv, Brazen enters:

Brazen: . . . My dear Plume! give me a buss.

Plume: Half a score, if you will, my dear.[12]

The National company interpreted this literally: "they kiss ten times at top speed."

Gaskill never gave any particular explanation for this strong emphasis on the physical, but, because of the amount of improvisation in his oblique approach to the text, it is likely that it sprang from the motive-oriented rehearsal interpretations.

There was one transposition of scenes: v and vi in Act V. It resolved the Brazen-Worthy-Melinda subplot prior to the court scene and led, naturally, to the untangling of the Plume-Silvia relationship.

In 1965, when Kenneth Tynan published his "Rehearsal Logbook," he paid particular attention to the director's methods. Gaskill viewed himself primarily as a teacher and in previous assignments he had "taught rather than directed."[13] This approach was

287

carried over into The Recruiting Officer rehearsals. In the first week, he dispensed with the traditional beginning read-through and explained to the cast that the lines are the "last stage of a process that must begin with a thorough investigation of character and situation."[14] His first morning was devoted to improvisations which were unconnected with the text. Gaskill's theory is that "a director should [not] tell an actor what to do, that there should be a way of directing where one proceeds by question to make an actor understand, and by understanding, do the right thing."[15] Each scene was approached in four stages:

> (1) Seated, the actors read the text. (2) On their feet, and without scripts, they improvise on the basis of what they know of the scene: e.g., in II, Sergeant Kite's basic "action" is to persuade the local lads to enlist, and theirs is to resist his efforts. (Gaskill makes great use of the terms "action" and "resistance.") This scriptless exercise is repeated several times, with widely differing results. (3) Gaskill quizzes the actors about the social background and motivation of the characters they are playing: What do you do for a living? How much do you earn? . . . (4) They perform the scene again, this time with scripts.[16]

The point of the improvisations was "to establish a sequence of emotions in the actor's mind." For example, Gaskill cautioned Max Adrian that Justice Balance's "bonhomie is not fundamental to his character"; rather, "class interests as a JP and a landowner" direct his behavior. Concerning I.i: though the scene is comic, "recruiting isn't fun to Kite and Plume. . . . They're ruthless about it."[17] Later in the first week, when Laurence Olivier joined rehearsals, he too improvised with interesting results: "he invents things for Brazen to do and say which are perfectly consistent with the character but which, when followed through, bring the scene to a different conclusion from Farquhar's." Since

Olivier's first conception of Brazen was considered "too foppish and perky," Gaskill led him toward a tone of "boorishness and sleazy vulgarity." The performance, which Philip Hope-Wallace called "a compound of unemphatic swagger and wandering attention, with a vacant eye cocked at nothing in particular," was the most critically successful in the play.[18]

The second week dealt with the court scene in V.v, with Gaskill most concerned with the "social sub-text" --the collusion of Justice and the Army to get recruits.

Act II.iii, which ends with the recruiting of Pearmain and Appletree, was "very funny . . . [with an] underlying ruthlessness." That the scene was clearly outstanding was noted in the Times review:

> In a programme note Mr. Gaskill rightly points out that the play's main point of contact with the modern world is its portrayal of the "systematic deception of the ignorant." Certainly the most concentrated scene in the production is the one showing the capture of two reluctant volunteers. The illiterate pair see through the trickery of the sergeant but then fall into the hands of Captain Plume, whose maxim is "those who know the least obey the best," and who conjures up such a glowing vision of the soldiers' life that they capitulate--only to have their ambitions dashed by the point of the sergeant's halberd.[19]

This scene, which reaches its climax when the two dupes are drawn, mesmerized, towards Plume's outstretched hand, took one far beyond the regions of comedy.

In the third week, Maggie Smith discovered a moving moment in the IV.i, enlistment scene with Plume:

> Her voice quavers just perceptibly when she says that no matter what perils life in the army may

hold, "they would be less terrible to me than to stay behind you"--and a twinge of genuine feeling disturbs the façade of badinage and imposture.[20]

The first full run-through was not held until the fourth week. Tynan noted that the strength of the production lay in the recruiting scenes, which had been so solidly grounded that they would determine the success or failure of the production.

One of Gaskill's warnings to the cast was that there was still a tendency, at times, not to put full faith in the text, to "overstress, underline and wink at the audience." That this tendency to appeal to the audience at the expense of the text became one of the liabilities of the production can be seen from the critical reaction of T. C. Worsley:

> In the action Mr. Gaskill and his company catch the spirit of the play, which is eminently good-natured. Where they miss it, with only one exception, is in the handling of the lines. . . . A style of some sort he [Farquhar] does demand in the speaking; the language demands it, cries out for it.
>
> I rather fancy (I hope I am quite wrong) that Mr. Gaskill belongs to a school of modern directors for whom style is a dirty word. He may even have encouraged the rest of the company to pay no attention to the shape of the sentences, to the phrasing and the run of the words. And if he has done so, it would be out of a fear, understandable but ill-founded, that style is something false, an accretion, an over-laid patina. I would sympathize with any attempt to get away from conventional stylisation; from those intonations and gestures which have become standard and accepted clichés of Restoration staginess. But that is not what style means. The style that matters is the shape of Farquhar's

language, the way he uses words. . . . A classical style of acting is primarily a style derived from language; everything else follows from that.[21]

It seems that in his war against the physical flourishes which had debased rather than decorated Restoration comedy, Gaskill had equated them with the verbal embellishments. Worsley maintained that he "missed in the speaking that attention to speech rhythms, which even a provincial Restoration writer requires."

The fifth week of rehearsal showed that, despite the success with the recruiting scenes, a difficulty with the crucial court scene still existed. The blame was placed on Farquhar for "failing to clarify his heroine's motives," for it is in this scene that Silvia tricks her father.[22] But Philip Hope-Wallace criticized Gaskill for

a comic trial which in the playing proved the one dull moment in the present delightful production. I believe that the producer William Gaskill was here trying for some sort of solemn satire of "justice," perhaps in honoured memory of the adaptation of this play which the Berliner Ensemble brought us some years back.[23]

During the week of the opening Tynan had some last minute reservations: "Am I right in suspecting that, here and there, the text is not quite strong enough to stand up to the realistic scrutiny to which Gaskill has subjected it?"[24] But after the opening he felt that his concerns were minor when weighed against the final achievement: "A Restoration masterpiece has been reclaimed, stripped of the veneer of camp that custom prescribes for plays of its period, and saved for the second half of the 20th century."

CONGREVE

THE DOUBLE DEALER

Lyceum, Edinburgh   Old Vic Company
24 August 1959
Old Vic, London
7 September 1959

Brisk   Alec McCowen
Careless   John Woodvine
Cynthia   Judi Dench
Lady Froth   Moyra Fraser
Lady Plyant   Maggie Smith
Lady Touchwood   Ursula Jeans
Lord Froth   Joss Ackland
Lord Touchwood   Charles West
Maskwell   Donald Houston
Mellefont   John Justin
Sir Paul Plyant   Miles Malleson
Director   Michael Benthall

Royal Court   English Stage Company
18 July 1969

Brisk   Malcolm Tierney
Careless   John White
Cynthia   Celia Bannerman
Lady Froth   Gillian Martell
Lady Plyant   Alison Leggatt
Lady Touchwood   Judy Parfitt
Lord Froth   Geoffrey Chater
Lord Touchwood   Nigel Hawthorne
Maskwell   John Castle
Mellefont   Michael Byrne
Sir Paul Plyant   George Howe
Director   William Gaskill
Designer   John Gunter

Olivier Theatre   National Theatre Company
27 September 1978

Brisk   Nicky Henson
Careless   Dermot Crowley
Cynthia   Judi Bowker
Lady Froth   Brenda Blethyn

Lady Plyant	Dorothy Tutin
Lady Touchwood	Sara Kestelman
Lord Froth	Nicholas Selby
Lord Touchwood	Ralph Richardson
Maskwell	Robert Stephens
Mellefont	John Harding
Sir Paul Plyant	Michael Bryant
Director	Peter Wood

LOVE FOR LOVE

Phoenix Theatre 8 April 1943	Haymarket Theatre 1944
Angelica	Rosalie Crutchley
Ben	George Woodbridge
Buckram	D. J. Williams
Foresight	Miles Malleson
Jeremy	Max Adrian
Mrs. Foresight	Marian Spencer
Mrs. Frail	Yvonne Arnaud
Prue	Angela Baddeley
Scandal	Leon Quartermaine
Sir Sampson	Cecil Trouncer
Tattle	Leslie Banks
Valentine	John Gielgud
Director	John Gielgud

Moscow 9 September 1965 Old Vic 20 October 1965 Montreal 1967	National Theatre Company
Angelica	Geraldine McEwan
Ben	Colin Blakely/Albert Finney
Foresight	Miles Malleson
Jeremy	Tom Kempinsky
Mrs. Foresight	Madge Ryan
Mrs. Frail	Joyce Redman
Prue	Lynn Redgrave
Scandal	Robert Lang
Sir Sampson	Anthony Nicholls
Tattle	Laurence Olivier
Valentine	John Stride
Director	Peter Wood
Designer	Lila de Nobili

THE WAY OF THE WORLD

Lyric Theatre
7 February 1924

Fainall	Harold Anstruther
Foible	Hilda Sims
Lady Wishfort	Margaret Yarde
Millamant	Edith Evans
Mincing	Kathlyn Hilliard
Mirabell	Robert Loraine
Mrs. Fainall	Ruth Taylor
Mrs. Marwood	Dorothy Green
Peggy	Elsa Lanchester
Petulant	Norman V. Norman
Sir Wilful	Scott Russell
Waitwell	Harold Scott
Witwoud	Nigel Playfair
Director	Nigel Playfair

New Theatre
21 October 1948

Betty	Margaret Chisholm
Fainall	Peter Copley
Foible	June Brown
Lady Wishfort	Edith Evans
Millamant	Faith Brook
Mincing	Penelope Munday
Mirabell	Harry Andrews
Mrs. Fainall	Mary Martlew
Mrs. Marwood	Pauline Jameson
Peggy	Josephine Stuart
Petulant	Mark Dignam
Sir Wilful	Nigel Green
Waitwell	Medows White
Witwoud	Robert Eddison
Director	John Burrell

Lyric Theatre
19 February 1953

Fainall	Eric Porter
Foible	Jessie Evans
Lady Wishfort	Margaret Rutherford
Millamant	Pamela Brown
Mirabell	John Gielgud

Mrs. Fainall	Pauline Jameson
Mrs. Marwood	Eileen Herlie
Petulant	Richard Wordsworth
Sir Wilful	Brewster Mason
Witwoud	Paul Scofield
Director	John Gielgud

Saville Theatre
6 December 1956

Fainall	Douglas Wilmer
Foible	Ann Leon
Lady Wishfort	Margaret Rutherford
Millamant	Kay Hammond
Mincing	Rosalind Knight
Mirabell	John Clements
Mrs. Fainall	Valerie Hanson
Mrs. Marwood	Margaretta Scott
Petulant	Geoffrey Dunn
Sir Wilful	Raymond Francis
Waitwell	Harry H. Corbett
Witwoud	Reginald Beckwith
Director	John Clements

Old Vic Theatre   National Theatre Company
1 May 1969

Fainall	John Moffatt
Foible	Helen Burns
Lady Wishfort	Hazel Hughes
Millamant	Geraldine McEwan
Mincing	Jane Lapotaire
Mirabell	Robert Lang
Mrs. Fainall	Sheila Reid
Mrs. Marwood	Jane Wenham
Petulant	David Ryall
Sir Wilful	Michael Turner
Waitwell	Edward Petherbridge
Witwoud	Edward Hardwicke
Director	Michael Langham
Designer	Desmond Heeley

```
Stratford Festival          Festival Company
Stratford, Ontario
7 June 1976

Fainall                     Alan Scarfe
Foible                      Jan Kudelka
Lady Wishfort               Jessica Tandy
Millamant                   Maggie Smith
Mincing                     Jackie Burroughs
Mirabell                    Jeremy Brett
Mrs. Marwood                Domini Blythe
Petulant                    Bernard Hopkins
Sir Wilful                  Tony Van Bridge
Witwoud                     Keith Baxter
Director                    Robin Phillips


Aldwych Theatre             Royal Shakespeare Company
27 January 1978

Fainall                     John Woodvine
Foible                      Eliza Ward
Lady Wishfort               Beryl Reid
Millamant                   Judi Dench
Mincing                     Avril Carson
Mirabell                    Michael Pennington
Mrs. Fainall                Carmen Du Sautoy
Mrs. Marwood                Marjorie Bland
Petulant                    Roger Rees
Sir Wilful                  Bob Peck
Waitwell                    David Lyon
Witwoud                     Nickolas Grace
Director                    John Barton
```

DRYDEN

MARRIAGE A LA MODE

```
St. James Theatre
24 July 1946

                            John Clements
                            Robert Eddison
                            Kay Hammond
                            Frances Howe
                            Moira Lister
                            David Peel
                            James Mills
Director                    John Clements
```

ALL FOR LOVE

Old Vic Theatre 1 December 1977	Prospect Theatre Company
Alexas	Robert Eddison
Antony	John Turner
Cleopatra	Barbara Jefford
Dolabella	Michael Howarth
Octavia	Suzanne Bertish
Ventidius	Kenneth Gilbert
Director	Frank Hauser
Designer	Nicholas Georgiadis

ETHEREGE

THE MAN OF MODE

Georgian Theatre Richmond, Yorkshire 3 September 1965	Prospect Theatre Company
Sir Fopling Flutter	Ronnie Stevens
Director	Toby Robertson

Aldwych Theatre 13 September 1971	Royal Shakespeare Company
Bellinda	Frances de la Tour
Dorimant	Alan Howard
Emilia	Isla Blair
Harriet	Helen Mirren
Lady Townley	Brenda Bruce
Lady Woodvill	Elizabeth Tyrrel
Medley	Julian Glover
Mrs. Loveit	Vivien Merchant
Old Bellair	David Waller
Sir Fopling	John Wood
Young Bellair	Terence Taplin
Director	Terry Hands
Designer	Timothy O'Brien

FARQUHAR

LOVE AND A BOTTLE

Nottingham Playhouse   Nottingham Playhouse Company
7 May 1969

Brush	Richard Harbord
Comb	John Joyce
Club	Nicholas Clay
Leanthe	Elizabeth Power
Lovewell	David Allister
Lucinda	Cherith Mellor
Lyric	Bruce Myles
Mockmode	Barrie Rutter
Nimblewrist	John Manford
Pindress	Penelope Wilton
Rigadoon	Francis Thomas
Roebuck	David Sumner
Trudge	Jean Gilpin
Widow Bullfinch	Sheila Ballantine
Director	William Chappell
Music	A. P. Haynes
Lyrics	William Chappell

THE CONSTANT COUPLE

Arts Theatre, Cambridge   Prospect Productions
25 May 1967
New Theatre, London
29 June 1967

Angelica	Juliet Harmer
Clincher	Charles Kay
Lurewell	Helen Lindsay
Parly	Jenny Short
Sir Harry Wildair	Robert Hardy
Smuggler	Timothy West
Standard	Julian Glover
Vizard	John Warner
Director	Richard Cottrell

TRUMPETS AND DRUMS

Palace Theatre   Berliner Ensemble
29 August 1956

Appletree   Lothar Bellag

Balance	Hans Hamacher
Brazen	Fred Düren
Kite	Norbert Christian
Lady Prude	Anneliese Reppel
Melinda	Annemarie Schlaebitz
Pearmain	Fred Grasnick
Plume	Dieter Knaup
Rose	Sabine Thalbach
Simpkins	Wolf Beneckendorff
Smuggler	Alfred Land
Victoria Balance	Regine Lutz
Worthy	Ralf Bregazzi
Director	Benno Besson
Music	Rudolf Wagner-Régeny

THE RECRUITING OFFICER

Old Vic Theatre   National Theatre Company
10 December 1963

Balance	Max Adrian
Brazen	Laurence Olivier
Costar Pearmain	John Stride
Kite	Colin Blakely
Melinda	Mary Miller
Plume	Robert Stephens
Rose	Lynn Redgrave
Sylvia	Maggie Smith
Worthy	Derek Jacobi
Director	William Gaskill
Designer	René Allio

Arts Theatre, Cambridge   Prospect Productions
12 October 1970

Brazen	Julian Curry
Kite	Trevor Peacock
Plume	Ian McKellen
Sylvia	Susan Fleetwood
Director	Richard Cottrell
Designer	Keith Norman

THE BEAUX' STRATAGEM

Phoenix Theatre
5 May 1949

Aimwell	Robert Eddison
Archer	John Clements
Boniface	David Bird
Cherry	Gwen Cherrell
Dorinda	Iris Russell
Gibbet	Lloyd Pearson
Mrs. Sullen	Kay Hammond
Director	John Clements

Ahmanson Theatre, Los Angeles
20 January 1970   National Theatre Company
Old Vic, London
8 April 1970

Aimwell	Ronald Pickup
Archer	Robert Stephens
Boniface	Gerald James
Cherry	Helen Fraser
Dorinda	Sheila Reid
Foigard	Derek Jacobi
Freeman	Kenneth Mackintosh
Gibbet	Paul Curran
Gipsy	Louise Purnell
Lady Bountiful	Jeanne Watts
Mrs. Sullen	Maggie Smith
Scrub	Bernard Gallagher
Squire Sullen	David Ryall
Director	William Gaskill
Designer	René Allio

OTWAY

THE SOLDIER'S FORTUNE

Oxford Playhouse   Prospect Productions
20 July 1964

Sir Davy Dunce	William Holmes
Sir Jolly Jumble	Neil Stacy
Sylvia	Amanda Grinling
Director	Toby Robertson

```
Royal Court Theatre          English Stage Company
12 January 1967

Beaugard                     Maurice Roëves
Bloodybones                  Bernard Gallagher
Courtine                     Charles Thomas
Fourbin                      Roger Foss
Lady Dunce                   Sheila Hancock
Sir Jolly Jumble             Wallas Eaton
Sylvia                       Elizabeth Bell
Director                     Peter Gill
```

VENICE PRESERVED

```
Lyric Theatre
15 May 1953

Antonio                      Richard Wordsworth
Aquilina                     Pamela Brown
Belvidera                    Eileen Herlie
Jaffeir                      John Gielgud
Pierre                       Paul Scofield
Priuli                       Herbert Lomas
Renault                      Eric Porter
Spanish Ambassador           Brewster Mason
Director                     Peter Brook
Designer                     Leslie Hurry


Theatre Royal, Bristol       Bristol Old Vic
5 February 1969              Company

Antonio                      Bernard Hepton
Aquilina                     Patricia Maynard
Belvidera                    Ingrid Hafner
Jaffeir                      Alan Bates
Pierre                       Antony Webb
Priuli                       Peter Bland
Renault                      Richard Kane
Director                     Val May
Designer                     Robin Archer
```

RAVENSCROFT

THE LONDON CUCKOLDS

Royal Court Theatre   English Stage Company
27 February 1979

Arabella   Deborah Norton
Aunt   Ann Dyson
Doodle   Roger Kemp
Engine   Cherith Mellor
Eugenia   Stephanie Beacham
Jane   Susan Porrett
Mr. Dashwell   Barry Stanton
Mr. Loveday   Brian Protheroe
Mr. Ramble   Kenneth Cranham
Mr. Townly   Michael Elphick
Peggy   Nina Thomas
Roger   Christopher Hancock
Wiseacre   Alan Dobie
Director   Stuart Burge
Designer   Robin Archer

SHADWELL

EPSOM WELLS

Thorndike Theatre
Leatherhead, Surrey
4 November 1969

Bevil   Simon Ward
Carolina   Patricia Shakesby
Clodpate   Robert Cartland
Cuff   Mark Nicholls
Kick   Barrie Rutter
Lucia   Celia Bannerman
Mab   Louise Rush
Mary   Liz Moscrop
Mistress Jilt   Josephine Tewson
Mistress Woodly   Sonia Graham
Peg   Henrietta Holmes
Rains   Teddy Green
Roger   David Goodhart
Toby   Michael Roberts
Woodly   David Weston
Director   Anthony Wiles
Designer   Sidney Jarvis
Musical Arrangements Martin Best

THE RELAPSE

| Lyric Theatre | Phoenix Theatre |
| | 28 January 1948 |

Amanda	Audrey Fildes
Berinthia	Madge Elliott
Lord Foppington	Cyril Ritchard
Loveless	Anthony Ireland
Miss Hoyden	Jessie Evans
Sir Tunbelly Clumsey	Hamlyn Benson
Worthy	Esmond Knight
Young Fashion	Paul Scofield
Director	Anthony Quayle

VIRTUE IN DANGER

Mermaid Theatre
10 April 1963

Amanda	Jane Wenham
Berinthia	Patricia Routledge
Coupler	Richard Wordsworth
Lord Foppington	John Moffatt
Loveless	Alan Howard
Miss Hoyden	Patsy Byrne
Sir Tunbelly Clumsey	Hamlyn Benson
Worthy	Basil Hoskins
Young Fashion	Barrie Ingham
Director	Wendy Toye

| Aldwych Theatre | Royal Shakespeare Company |
| 17 August 1967 | |

Amanda	Susan Fleetwood
Berinthia	Janet Suzman
Coupler	Donald Burton
Chaplain Bull	Roy Kinnear
Lord Foppington	Donald Sinden
Loveless	Charles Thomas
Miss Hoyden	Frances de la Tour
Nurse	Lila Kaye
Sir Tunbelly Clumsey	David Waller
Worthy	Patrick Stewart
Young Fashion	Alan Howard
Director	Trevor Nunn

Designer	Christopher Morley
Lighting	Robert Ornbo
Music	Guy Woofenden
Aldwych Theatre	Royal Shakespeare Company
15 August 1968	
Amanda	Lynn Farleigh
Berinthia	Toby Robins
Chaplain Bull	Derek Smith
Coupler	Jeffrey Dench
Lord Foppington	Barrie Ingham
Loveless	Charles Thomas
Miss Hoyden	Frances de la Tour
Nurse	Lila Kaye
Sir Tunbelly Clumsey	Brewster Mason
Worthy	Emrys James
Young Fashion	Michael Jayston
Director	Trevor Nunn

THE PROVOK'D WIFE

Vaudeville Theatre	Prospect Productions
24 July 1963	
Belinda	Ann Bell
Constant	John Warner
Heartfree	Dinsdale Landen
Lady Brute	Eileen Atkins
Lady Fancyfull	June Brown
Madamoiselle	Josephine Woodford
Sir John Brute	Trevor Martin
Director	Toby Robertson

INTRIGUES AND AMOURS

Theatre Royal, Stratford East	Theatre Workshop
24 May 1967	
Belinda	Pamela Jones
Constant	Bob Grant
Heartfree	Edward Bishop
Lady Brute	Gaye Brown
Maid	Sandra Caron
Maid	Myvanwy Jenn
Singing Master	Frank Coda
Sir John Brute	Brian Murphy

304

Director	Joan Littlewood

Greenwich 14 June 1973	Robin Phillips's Company

Belinda	Linda Thorson
Lady Brute	Sheila Allen
Lady Fancyfull	Fenella Fielding
Sir John Brute	James Grout
Director	Frank Proud
Designer	Alan Barrett

THE CONFEDERACY

Birmingham Repertory Theatre 2 October 1951	Birmingham Repertory Company

Araminta	Rosalind Boxall
Clarissa	Hazel Hughes
Corinna	Christine Finn
Flippanta	Joan Blake
Gripe	Alfred Burke
Moneytrap	Paul Daneman
Mrs. Amlet	Olive Walter
Director	Douglas Seal
Designer	Paul Shelving

Oxford Playhouse 29 September 1964	Prospect Productions

Araminta	Gudrun Ure
Clarissa	Hy Hazell
Corinna	Toni Kanal
Dick	Michael Meacham
Flippanta	Amanda Grinling
Gripe	Robert Eddison
Moneytrap	Trevor Baxter
Mrs. Amlet	Sylvia Coleridge
Director	Toby Robertson
Designer	Alan Barrett

Chichester Festival Theatre
29 May 1974

Araminta	Jeanette Sterke

305

Clarissa	Dora Bryan
Corinna	Gemma Craven
Flippanta	Patsy Byrne
Gripe	Frank Middlemas
Moneytrap	Richard Wattis
Mrs. Amlet	Peggy Mount
Director	Wendy Toye
Designer	Anthony Powell

GEORGE VILLIERS, DUKE OF BUCKINGHAM

THE CHANCES

Chichester Festival Theatre
3 July 1962

Don John	Keith Michell
Don Frederick	John Neville
Petruchio	Robert Lang
Duke of Ferrara	Alan Howard
Constantina 1	Rosemary Harris
Constantina 2	Joan Plowright
Landlady	Kathleen Harrison
Mother of Constantina 2	Athene Seyler
Director	Laurence Olivier

WYCHERLEY

THE COUNTRY WIFE

Old Vic   Old Vic Company
6 October 1936

Alithea	Ursula Jeans
Lucy	Freda Jackson
Lady Fidget	Edith Evans
Mr. Dorilant	Patrick Harr
Mr. Harcourt	Alec Clunes
Mr. Horner	Michael Redgrave
Mr. Pinchwife	James Dale
Mr. Sparkish	Ernest Thesiger
Mrs. Dainty Fidget	Iris Hoey
Mrs. Pinchwife	Ruth Gordon
Mrs. Squeamish	Eileen Peel
Old Lady Squeamish	Kate Cutler
Quack	Frederick Bennett
Sir Jasper Fidget	Richard Goolden
Director	Tyrone Guthrie

Henry Miller's Theatre, New York
1 December 1936

Alithea	Helen Trenholme
Lucy	Jane Vaughan
Lady Fidget	Irene Browne
Mr. Dorilant	Stephen Ker Appleby
Mr. Harcourt	Anthony Quayle
Mr. Horner	Roger Livesay
Mr. Pinchwife	Percy Waram
Mr. Sparkish	Louis Hector
Mrs. Dainty Fidget	Edith Atwater
Mrs. Pinchwife	Ruth Gordon
Mrs. Squeamish	Helena Pickard
Old Lady Squeamish	Violet Besson
Quack	George Carr
Sir Jasper Fidget	George Graham
Director	Gilbert Miller
Designer	Oliver Messel

Royal Court   English Stage Company
12 December 1956

Alithea	Maureen Quinney
Lucy	Jill Showell
Lady Fidget	Diana Churchill
Mr. Dorilant	Robert Stephens
Mr. Harcourt	Alan Bates
Mr. Horner	Laurency Harvey
Mr. Pinchwife	George Devine
Mr. Sparkish	John Moffatt
Mrs. Dainty Fidget	Shelia Ballantine
Mrs. Pinchwife	Joan Plowright
Mrs. Squeamish	Moyra Fraser
Old Lady Squeamish	Margery Caldicott
Quack	Nigel Davenport
Sir Jasper Fidget	Esmé Percy
Director	George Devine

Nottingham Playhouse   Playhouse Company
5 January 1966

Alithea	Sara-Jane Gwillim
Lady Fidget	Ursula Smith
Lucy	Mary Healey
Mr. Dorilant	Laurence Carter
Mr. Harcourt	John Tordoff
Mr. Horner	Michael Craig

307

Mr. Pinchwife	Harold Innocent
Mr. Sparkish	Jimmy Thompson
Mrs. Dainty Fidget	Marian Forster
Mrs. Pinchwife	Judi Dench
Mrs. Squeamish	Diana Ford
Old Lady Squeamish	Janet Henfrey
Parson	John Nightingale
Quack	Alfred Bell
Sir Jasper Fidget	Patrick Tull
Director	Ronald Magill
Designer	Stephen Doncaster

Chichester Festival Theatre
9 July 1969

Alithea	Renée Asherson
Lucy	Audrey Murray
Lady Fidget	Patricia Routledge
Mr. Dorilant	Christopher Guinee
Mr. Harcourt	Gary Hope
Mr. Horner	Keith Baxter
Mr. Pinchwife	Gordon Gostelow
Mr. Sparkish	Hugh Paddick
Mrs. Dainty Fidget	Hermione Gregory
Mrs. Pinchwife	Maggie Smith
Mrs. Squeamish	Charlotte Howard
Old Lady Squeamish	Viola Lyle
Quack	Richard Kane
Servant to Horner	Geoffrey Burridge
Servant to Sir Jasper	Richard Denning
Sir Jasper Fidget	Brian Hayes
Director	Robert Chetwyn
Designer	Hutchinson Scott

Olivier Theatre   National Theatre Company
29 November 1977

Alithea	Polly Adams
Lucy	Tel Stevens
Lady Fidget	Elizabeth Spriggs
Mr. Dorilant	Gawn Grainger
Mr. Harcourt	Kenneth Cranham
Mr. Horner	Albert Finney
Mr. Pinchwife	Richard Johnson
Mr. Sparkish	Ben Kingsley
Mrs. Dainty Fidget	Ann Beach

Mrs. Pinchwife	Susan Littler
Mrs. Squeamish	Helen Ryan
Old Lady Squeamish	Madoline Thomas
Quack	Nicholas Selby
Sir Jasper Fidget	Robin Bailey
Director	Peter Hall
	with Stewart Trotter
Designer	John Bury

THEATRE COLLECTIONS AND THEATRES

British Theatre Collections, Archives and Libraries

The British Library, Reference Division
Newspaper Library
Colindale Avenue
London, NW9 5HE   (01) 200-5515

Opening Times: The Newspaper Reading Rooms are open
every Mondays through Friday except Good Friday,
Christmas Day, Boxing Day (December 26), New Year's
Day, May Day and the week following the last complete
week in October.

Hours: Monday through Friday 10 a.m. to 5 p.m.

Regulations for Admission: No one under 21 is admitted
except by special permission. Admission is by pass
only. This pass, which is good for the Newspaper
Library only, may be applied for in person or by post.

Holdings: The Newspaper Library contains about half a
million volumes and parcels of daily and weekly
newspapers and periodicals including London newspapers
from 1801 onward, English provincial, Scottish and
Irish newspapers from about 1700 onward and large
collections of Commonwealth and foreign newspapers.
Many titles are available on microfilm.

Underground: Colindale

The British Theatre Association
9 Fitzroy Square
London,W1P 6AE   (01) 387-2666

Opening Times: The British Theatre Association is open
Monday through Friday and closed during the month of
August.

Hours: Monday-Friday   10   a.m.   to   5   p.m.
Wednesday 10 a.m. to 7:30 p.m.

Regulations for Admission: Membership is required and
the privileges of that membership are available upon
request.

Holdings: In excess of 250,000 volumes on drama and
theatre arts including plays and British and foreign

310

theatre journals. Prompt copies. The William Archer Collection includes press cuttings and programs 1878-1924. Press cuttings are updated daily and reviews of major revivals would be available. All material is indexed.

Raymond Mander and Joe Mitchenson Theatre Collection
5 Venner Road
London, SE26 5EQ   (01) 778-6730

Opening Times: The collection is open by appointment and an initial letter is required.

Holdings: Books, newspapers, magazines, programs, photos and reviews. Plus paintings, engravings, theatrical china, costumes and memorabilia from c.1690 to the present.

The Shakespeare Centre Library
The Shakespeare Centre
Henley Street
Stratford-upon-Avon, CV37 6QW   (0789) 204016
Warwickshire

Opening Times: The library is open throughout the year Monday through Saturday and closed on Sundays and Bank Holidays.

Hours: 10 a.m. to 5 p.m. Monday-Friday, 9:30 a.m. to 12:30 p.m. Saturday

Regulations for Admission: Reader's tickets are available on application to the director. Temporary tickets are available on personal application at the library.

Holdings: Books, journals, playbills, texts and engravings cover the activities of Shakespeare and his contemporaries on the stage from the sixteenth century to the present. The Royal Shakespeare Theatre Archives holds prompt books, photos, news cuttings, articles and books covering any play performed at the Shakespeare Memorial Theatre or by the Royal Shakespeare Company, 1879 to the present.

The Victoria and Albert Museum
Cromwell Road

South Kensington
London, SW7 2RL   (01) 589-6371

Opening Times: The Exhibition Galleries are open from
Monday through Thursday and Saturday and Sunday.
Closed on Friday.

Hours: 10 a.m. to 6 p.m. Monday-Saturday, 2:30 to 5:30
Sunday.

Holdings: The departments of primary interest to the
theatre researcher are the Library and the Department
of Prints, Drawings and Paintings; the Department of
Textiles with its extensive collection of costumes and
fabrics and the Department of Woodwork with its
collection of period furniture and interior decoration.

Opening Times for the Library: 10 a.m. to 5:45 p.m.
Monday-Thursday, 10 a.m. to 1 p.m., 2 p.m. to 5:45 p.m.
Saturday. Closed Friday and Sunday.

Regulations for Admission: Users need a library ticket
issued by the Victoria and Albert Library or the
British Library. Contact: Library Enquiries.

Holdings: Thousands of items on the history of theatre
arts and on design in general. Also contains works of
many English dramatists of the 16th and 17th centuries
plus 40 volumes of the correspondence of David Garrick
and the Piot Collection of books on 17th, 18th and 19th
century spectacle. There is a general catalogue in
Guard Book form, a subject index and a portrait index.

Underground: South Kensington

Westminster Reference Library
35 St. Martin's Street
London, WC2N 9HP   (01)   930-3274

Opening Times: The library is open Monday through
Saturday. Closed on Sunday.

Hours: 10 a.m. to 7 p.m. Monday-Friday, 10 a.m. to 5
p.m. Saturday.

No special regulations for admission.

Holdings: The Performing Arts Collection contains about
6,000 books of which about half are concerned with
theatre, predominantly British theatre. 83 theatre
journals of which 25 are current with varying lengths
of files.

American Theatre Collections and Libraries

Folger Shakespeare Library
201 E. Capitol Street
Washington, D. C. 20003   (202) 544-4600

Opening times: Open Monday through Saturday. Closed
Sunday and legal holidays.

Hours: 8:45 a.m. to 4:45 p.m. Monday to Friday, 8:45
a.m. to 4:30 p.m. Saturday.

Regulations for Admission: Readers usually have a Ph.D.
or are actively engaged in dissertation research.
Special permissions are granted to readers who have
gained appropriate skills and knowledge through non-
academic experience if their project requires materials
not normally available elsewhere.

Holdings: Collections cover the 16th and 17th centuries
and are strongest in all aspects of British
civilization. There is a large collection of the works
of Restoration playwrights plus books, playbills,
prints, engravings and photographs.

Harvard Theatre Collection
Harvard College Library
Cambridge, Massachusetts 02138   (617) 495-2445

Opening times: Open Monday-Friday. Closed holidays and
Harvard commencement (2nd week in June, usually a
Thursday).

Hours: 9 a.m. to 5 p.m. Monday-Friday.

No special regulations for admission.

Holdings: The Theatre Collection is one of the largest
in the world, covering the history of performance
throughout the world with a particular emphasis on 18th
and 19th century English and American stage. Available
are promptbooks, manuscripts, letters, diaries,
newspaper clippings and engraved portraits and scenes.

Hoblitzelle Theatre Arts Library
Harry Ransom Humanities Research Center
Box 7219

313

University of Texas at Austin
Austin, Texas 78713

(512) 471-9122

Opening times: Open Monday to Friday. Saturday requires special arrangements. Closed national holidays.

Hours: 9 a.m. to 4:45 p.m. Monday-Friday. 9 a.m. to Noon Saturday by special arrangement.

Regulations for Admission: A reader's card is required.

Holdings: The library houses various collections which include books, plays, playbills, engravings, photographs, programs, newsclippings, technical drawings, sketches, stage models, film designs, letters, engravings, dance materials, film stills and circus memorabilia.

Library of Congress
1st Between East Capitol and Independence Avenue S.E.
Washington, D. C. 20540

(202) 287-5000

Opening times: The hours and days of service vary for reading rooms and particular services. Some parts of the library are open Monday-Sunday.

Hours: (General) 8:30 a.m. to 9:30 p.m. Monday-Friday, 8:30 a.m. to 5:00 p.m. Saturday, 1 p.m. to 5 p.m. Sunday.

Holdings: The computerized catalogue lists 211 books under the subject heading, ENGLISH--DRAMA--RESTORATION and 124 books under the more general heading, ENGLISH DRAMA--18TH CENTURY. The library also has a microfilm collection of early newspapers. The Francis Longe Collection in the Rare Book and Special Collections Division includes 2,105 original plays, theatrical adaptations and translations credited to over six hundred playwrights and is particularly rich in the works of lesser lights of the 17th century.

Newberry Library
60 West Walton Street
Chicago, Illinois 60610

(312) 943-9090, Ext. 314

Opening times: The main reading room is open Tuesday-Saturday. Closed Sunday and Monday. Major holidays: New Year's Day, Memorial Day, Independence Day, Thanksgiving, Labor Day and Christmas.

Hours: 9:00 a.m. to 9:40 p.m. Tuesday-Thursday, 9 a.m. to 5:40 p.m. Friday-Saturday.

Regulations for Admission: The admissions policy restricts the use of the library by high school, undergraduate and beginning M. A. students. N.B. Newberry is a non-circulating library.

Holdings: The library concentrates on printed plays before 1701. It is strong in runs of periodicals and has a good collection of 18th century serials.

Performing Arts Library
John F. Kennedy Center for the Performing Arts
Washington, D. C. 20566   (202) 254-9803 or
                                           (202) 287-6245

Opening times: Open Tuesday-Saturday. On Saturday the hours are shorter. Closed on Christmas, New Year's Day, Independence Day and Veteran's Day.

Hours: 11 a.m. to 8:30 p.m. Tuesday-Friday, 10 a.m. to 6 p.m. Saturday.

No special regulations for admission.

Holdings: The reference collection, which covers all aspects of the performing arts, consists of about 5,000 volumes and 350 serials.

Billy Rose Theatre Collection
Performing Arts Research Center
The New York Public Library at Lincoln Center
111 Amsterdam Avenue (at 65th Street)
New York, New York 10023   (212) 870-1639

Opening times: Monday-Saturday, but the Winter schedule differs from the Summer schedule. Closed on major holidays.

Hours: Summer hours (Memorial Day to Labor Day) noon to 5:45 p.m. Winter hours: 10 a.m. to 7:45 p.m. Monday and Wednesday; noon to 5:45 p.m. Tuesday, Wednesday and Friday. 10 a.m to 5:45 p.m. Saturday.

Regulations for Admission: Readers must be at least 18 or they must be in college or above.

Holdings: The collection covers theatre in all countries and includes all periods. Types of material: books, performing arts newspapers and magazines, scripts, promptbooks, programs, posters, prints and photographs, original scene and costume designs, caricatures, stage plans and blueprints, newspaper and magazine clippings and correspondence and business papers.

Yale School of Drama Library
222 York Street
Box 1903A Yale Station
New Haven, Connecticut 06520   (203) 436-2213

Opening times: During the academic year the library is open Monday-Saturday and closed Sunday. During the summer and vacation periods the library is open Monday-Friday. Closed Saturday and Sunday. Holidays: Semester Break (22 December-1 January), Thursday and Friday of Thanksgiving week, Good Friday, Memorial Day, 4th of July and Labor Day.

The are no admission requirements, but books circulate to members of the university only.

Holdings: Plays, theatre history, theatre architecture, criticism, stage and costume design, stage lighting, biographies and reference books. Periodicals range from scholarly journals to trade papers. Books on performing arts other than theatre are also represented in the collection. The Yale-Rockefeller Collection contains over 80,000 theatrical prints and photographs. Note: The Crawford Theatre Collection in the Sterling Memorial Library is also worth investigating.

Theatres and Theatre Companies

Arts Theatre
Peas Hill
Cambridge
(223) 352-000

Birmingham Repertory Theatre
Broad Street
Birmingham, B1 2EP
(021) 236-6771

National Theatre
South Bank
London, SE1 9PX
(01) 928-2033

Nottingham
    Playhouse
Wellington Circus
Nottingham, NG1 5AF
(602) 44361

Bristol Old Vic
Theatre Royal
King Street
Bristol, BS1 4ED
(272) 27466

Chichester Festival Theatre
Oaklands Park
Chichester
Sussex
(243) 863333

The Georgian Theatre
Friars Wynd
Richmond
North Yorkshire
(748) 3021

The Greenwich Theatre
Crooms Hill
Greenwich, SE10
(858) 7755

Oxford Playhouse
Beaumont Street
Oxford, OX1 2AG
(865) 47134

Royal Court
Sloane Square
London, SW1
(01) 930-1745

Stratford Festival
    Theatre
Stratford, Ontario
N5A 6V2, Canada
(519) 271-4040

Thorndike Theatre
Church Street
Leatherhead, Surrey
(372) 376211

FOOTNOTES

I. THEATRICAL CONDITIONS: AN OVERVIEW

The State of the Stage During the Interregnum

[1]For a comprehensive picture of this period see Leslie Hotson, The Commonwealth and the Restoration Stage (Cambridge: Harvard University Press, 1928).

[2]Travels of Cosimo the Third Grand Duke of Tuscany through England (1669), translated from the Italian manuscript in the Laurentian Library at Florence (London, 1821), pp. 190-91. Reprinted in A. M. Nagler, A Source Book in Theatrical History (New York: Dover Publications, 1952), p.204.

[3]Colley Cibber, An Apology for the Life of Colley Cibber, ed. B. R. S. Fone (Ann Arbor: University of Michigan Press, 1968), p. 139.

[4]Staring B. Wells, ed., A Comparison Between the Two Stages (Princeton: Princeton University Press, 1942), p. 10.

[5]Wells, p. 10.

[6]Cibber, p. 172.

[7]Cibber, p. 173.

The Publick Voice

[1]An essay, "'Restoration Comedy' and its Audiences, 1660-1776," by Arthur H. Scouten and Robert D. Hume, in Robert D. Hume, The Rakish Stage (Carbondale: Southern Illinois University Press, 1983), pp. 46-81, deals with the audience and provides considerable documentation.

[2]Oldmixon, History of England during the Reign of the Royal House of Stewart. Quoted by Montague Summers in John Downes, Roscius Anglicanus, ed. Montague Summers (New York: Benjamin Blom, 1929), p. 83.

[3]Thomas Betterton [William Oldys or Edmund Curll], The History of the English Stage (Boston: William S. and Henry Spear, 1814), pp. 21-22.

[4]Samuel Vincent, The Young Gallant's Academy, quoted in Peter Holland, The Ornament of Action (Cambridge: Cambridge University Press, 1979), pp. 8-9.

[5]John Dennis, "A Large Account of the Taste in Poetry, and the Causes of the Degeneracy of It," in The

Critical Works, ed. Edward Niles Hooker (Baltimore: Johns Hopkins Press, 1939), I, 292.

[6]Dennis, p. 293.

[7]Dennis, pp. 293-94.

[8]Dennis, p. 294.

[9]Dennis, p. 294.

The Theatre: Sights and Sounds

[1]Leo Hughes, "The Evidence from Promptbooks," in The London Theatre World 1660-1800, ed. Robert D. Hume (Carbondale: Southern Illinois University Press, 1980), pp. 130-31.

[2]Hughes. p. 131.

[3]Colin Visser, "Scenery and Technical Design," in The London Theatre World 1660-1800, pp. 84-85.

[4]Visser, p. 70.

[5] Colley Cibber, An Apology for the Life of Colley Cibber, ed. B. R. S. Fone (Ann Arbor: University of Michigan Press, 1968), p. 225.

[6]Visser, p. 112.

[7]Hughes, p. 131.

Costume

[1]John Downes, Roscius Anglicanus, ed. Montague Summers (New York: Benjamin Blom, 1929), pp. 21-22.

[2]The Spectator, No. 42 (April 18, 1711).

[3]The Spectator.

The Actors Are Come

[1]Thomas Betterton [William Oldys or Edmund Curll], The History of the English Stage (Boston: William S. and Henry Spear, 1814), p. 74.

[2] Betterton, p. 76.

[3]Betterton, p. 92.

[4]Betterton, p. 86.

[5] Colley Cibber, An Apology for the Life of Colley Cibber, ed. B. R. S. Fone (Ann Arbor: University of Michigan Press, 1968), p. 92.

319

[6]'Sir' John Hill, <u>The Actor</u>, quoted in Peter Holland, <u>The Ornament of Action</u> (Cambridge: Cambridge University Press, 1979), p. 62.

[7]John Dennis, "Dedication to <u>The Invader of His Country</u>," in <u>The Critical Works</u>, ed. Edward Niles Hooker (Baltimore: Johns Hopkins University Press, 1939), II, 179.

[8]Holland, p. 69. Holland's Chapter, "Performance: Actors and the Cast," has extensive presentation about casting.

[9]Cibber, pp. 77-78.

[10]Cibber, p. 69.

The Restoration Stance Today

[1]Hugh Hunt, "Restoration Acting," in <u>Restoration Theatre</u>, ed. John Russell Brown and Bernard Harris (New York: Capricorn Books, 1967), p. 191.

[2]Hunt, p. 192.

II. GEORGE VILLIERS, DUKE OF BUCKINGHAM

The Chances (1962)

[1]"The Chichester Festival Theatre," <u>Theatre Notebook</u>, 16(Winter 1961/62), 56. All newspapers and periodicals cited are British publications, unless otherwise indicated. Occasionally it is not possible to give a complete citation because many sources were obtained from clippings in theatre archives and the Performing Arts Research Center in New York, and full publication information was not available.

[2]Looker-on, "Whispers from the Wings," <u>Theatre World</u>, January 1962, p. 21.

[3]"Before Chichester," <u>New Theatre Magazine</u>, July/September 1962, p. 4.

[4]Michael Jamieson, "Two Cheers for Chichester," <u>Encore</u>, 9(September/October 1962), 42.

[5]Jamieson, p.44.

[6]Harold Matthews, "The Plays at Chichester," <u>Theatre World</u>, August 1962, p.18.

[7]Jamieson, p. 44.

[8]Jamieson, p. 44.

[9]Matthews, p. 18.

[10]Jamieson, p. 45.

III. JOHN DRYDEN

Marriage à la Mode (1946)

[1]Philip Hope-Wallace, "Plays in Performance," Drama, 3 (Winter 1946), 5.

[2]"Marriage à la Mode," Times, 25 July 1946, p. 6.

All for Love (1977)

[1]J. W. Lambert, "Edinburgh Theatre," Sunday Times, 28 August 1977.

[2]Bernard Levin, "In Good King Charles's Golden Days," Sunday Times, 4 December 1977, p. 37.

[3]Douglas Blake, "All for Love," The Stage and Television Today, 8 December 1977, p. 11.

[4]Lambert.

[5]Benedict Nightingale, New Statesman, 3 March 1978, p. 294.

IV. GEORGE ETHEREGE

The Man of Mode (1965)

[1]Richard Southern, "Progress at Richmond, Yorkshire," Theatre Notebook, 4 (October-December 1949), 9.

[2]"Etherege's Famous Play Revived," Times, 6 September 1965, p. 5.

[3]Times, p. 5.

The Man of Mode (1971)

[1]Irving Wardle, "The Man of Mode," Times, 14 September 1971, p. 16.

[2]Robert Waterhouse, Terry Hands and Timothy O'Brien, "A Case of Restoration," <u>Plays and Players</u>, 19 (November 1971), 14.

[3]B. A. Young, The Man of Mode," <u>Financial Times</u>, 14 September 1971, p. 3.

[4]Hands, p. 14.

[5]Stanley Price, "Man of Mode," <u>Plays and Players</u>, 19 (November 1971), 38.

[6]John Barber,"Restoration Classic's Irrelevant Nonsense," <u>Daily Telegraph</u>, 14 September 1971, p. 12.

[7]O'Brien, p. 15.

[8]Irving Wardle, "Etherege Drama Staged in London," <u>New York Times</u>, 15 September 1971, p. 40.

[9]O'Brien, p. 15.

[10]Kenneth Hurren, "Hands' Turn," <u>Spectator</u>, 18 September 1971.

[11]Price, p. 39.

[12]Jeremy Kingston, "The Man of Mode," <u>Punch</u>, September 1971, p. 393.

[13]Price, pp. 38-39.

[14]John Walker, "The Restoration of Sir George Etherege," <u>New York Herald Tribune</u> (Paris Edition), 18 September 1971.

[15]A revival of <u>She Would If She Could</u> staged by Jonathan Miller and including Paul Eddington as Sir Oliver Cockwood, Ursula Jones as Lady Cockwood and David Frith as Courtall with design by Bernard Culshaw and lighting by Nick Chelton opened at the Ashcroft Theatre, Croydon, on 23 April 1979. It is not included in this survey, and, if the material had been available, certainly would have been.

V. WILLIAM WYCHERLEY

[1]On May 30, 1948, a short version of Wycherley's <u>The Plain Dealer</u> was part of a mixed bill presented at the Old Vic by students of the Old Vic Theatre School.

The play was presented with <u>Penthesilea</u>, which was written for the school by James Law Forsyth. This original work was too obscure for audience comprehension or enjoyment.

A farce, <u>The Wedding</u>, by Chekhov, directed by George Devine, who was to become an important directorial force in Restoration drama in the next twenty years, had the best success in that the farce was staged, as the <u>Times</u> critic noted in "First Performance by Students," 31 May 1948, p. 2, "with every conceivable piece of invention and without labouring it." However, <u>The Plain Dealer</u>, while completely comprehensible, gave the student actors considerable trouble. Though set and costume were adequate, the playing was "so ragged in timing that it was almost impossible to guess the merit of most of the actors."

The Country Wife (1956)

[1] Tony Richardson, "Past and Future," in <u>English Stage Company: A Record of Two Years' Work</u>.

[2] "Putting the Drama in Touch with Contemporary Life," <u>Times</u>, 19 March 1958, p. 3.

[3] Kenneth Tynan, "Past and Present," <u>Observer</u>, 16 December 1956, p. 3.

[4] "The Country Wife," <u>Times</u>, 13 December 1956, p. 3.

[5] Milton Shulman, "The Fall of Mrs. Pinchwife," <u>Evening Standard</u>, 13 December 1956, p. 3.

[6] Philip Hope-Wallace, "'The Country Wife' in Town Again," <u>Guardian</u>, 13 December 1956, p. 5.

[7] <u>Times</u>, p. 3.

[8] Derek Granger, "The Country Wife," <u>Financial Times</u>, 13 December 1956, p. 2.

[9] Hope-Wallace, p. 5.

[10] <u>Times</u>, p. 3.

The Country Wife (1966)

[1] Jeremy Rudall, "Fresh Sap for the Withered Tree," <u>Tulane Drama Review</u>, 9 (Winter 1966), 137.

[2] "A Question of 'Bawd' or 'Bored,'" <u>Derby Evening Telegraph</u>, 6 January 1966.

[3] Emrys Bryson, "Judi Shines in a Bouncing Playhouse Hit," _Guardian Journal_, 6 January 1966.

[4] Bryson.

[5] B. A. Young, "The Country Wife," _Financial Times_, 7 January 1966.

[6] _Derby Evening Telegraph_.

[7] For example, in 1971, Edward Petherbridge, formerly of the National Theatre Company, appeared in _The Misanthrope_, which was played in repertory with the Hamlet of Alan Bates. The company could, however, function very well on its own, as was shown by the world premiere of Christopher Fry's _A Yard of Sun_, which was played, after its opening at the Playhouse, at the Old Vic for a limited run in 1970.

[8] Miss Dench's early roles for the Royal Shakespeare Company included Titania, Isabella and Viola. In 1960 she had played Juliet for the National Theatre Company; in 1966, Lika in Arbuzov's _The Promise_ and in 1968 she was Sally Bowles in a very successful West End production of _Cabaret_.

The Country Wife (1969)

[1] Ronald Bryden, "Miss Smith in Command," _Observer_, 13 July 1969, p. 23.

[2] Frank Marcus, "Good Marks for Conduct," _Sunday Telegraph_, 13 July 1969, p. 14.

[3] Hugh Leonard, "The Country Wife," _Plays and Players_, 16 (September 1969), 18.

[4] B. A. Young, "The Country Wife," _Financial Times_, 11 July 1969, p. 3.

[5] Peter Lewis, "Maggie Smith in Full Comic Flight," _Daily Mail_, 11 July 1969, p. 21.

[6] Harold Hobson, "Foul Play in Chichester," _Sunday Times_, 13 July 1969, p. 53. However, when the play was presented by the National Theatre Company, Frank Marcus, _Sunday Telegraph_, 4 December 1977, p. 18, noted: "The single innovation is the discovery that men kissed each other by way of greeting without embarrassment, so that Horner's kissing of Margery in the disguise of her brother does not carry any taint of homosexuality."

[7]Ronald Bryden, "Views From Everest," _Observer_, 27 July 1969, p. 23, applauded Baxter's rendering as "a performance, one of the rare ones, which alters permanently our conception not only of a role but of the play containing it. For it alone, this revival would have been worthwhile."

[8]Irving Wardle, "A Robust Revival," _Times_, 10 July 1969, p. 13.

[9]Bryden, p. 23.

[10]Marcus, p. 14.

[11]Wardle, p. 13

[12]Marcus, p. 14.

[13]Bryden, p. 23.

[14]The Chichester Festival Theatre is hexagonal in shape. The stage is arranged at one apex. The side galleries are continuous with the upper tiers at the back of the auditorium. During the opening season, Michael Jamieson, "Two Cheers for Chichester," _Encore_, 9 (September-October, 1962), 41, observed its shortcomings when compared with the playhouse at Stratford, Ontario:

> The auditorium, entered from a light-filled foyer, is a sombre Big Top, hexagonal where the Canadian one is round, and it _looks_ vaster, though it seats fewer--1,360 as opposed to 2,190. . . . The main acting area [at Stratford] is placed high, and since the platform is edged with four steps the level is varied, and masking can be avoided. Chichester's smaller auditorium is ranged round three sides of a deck-like platform, larger, lower, and flat, so that the structure seems to sprawl, and intimacy is lost.

The Country Wife (1977)

[1]Irving Wardle, "The Country Wife," _Times_, 1 December 1977.

[2]Benedict Nightingale, "In Search of Love," _New Statesman_, 9 December 1977, p. 823.

[3]Ted Whitehead, "Licence and Disillusion," Spectator, 10 December 1977, p. 26.

[4]Michael Billington, "The Country Wife," Guardian, 1 December 1977.

[5]Wardle.

[6]Nightingale, p. 823.

[7]John Barber, "Merry Indecency Has Meat in It," Daily Telegraph, 1 December 1977.

[8]Robert Cushman, "The Country Wife," Observer, 11 December 1977, p. 37.

[9]Anne Morley-Priestman, "The Country Wife at the Olivier," The Stage and Television Today, 8 December 1977, p. 11.

[10]Frank Marcus, Sunday Telegraph, 4 December 1977, p. 18.

[11]Wardle.

[12]B. A. Young, "The Country Wife," Financial Times, 1 December 1977.

VI. SHADWELL

Epsom Wells (1969)

[1]Joan Macalpine already had experience as an adaptor when, for the "old" Leatherhead Repertory Theatre, she had adapted Tom Jones, the first play to be commissioned by the Council of Repertory Theatres.

[2]The theatre opened with James Goldman's There Was an Old Woman in which the 90-year-old Sybil Thorndike, for whom the theatre was named, appeared. Epsom Wells was followed by The Seagull, and, for Christmas, there was The Sleeping Beauty. This gives an idea of the variety offered in the 3-4 week seasons by this new theatre.

[3]Eric Shorter, "Plays in Performance," Drama, 96 (Spring 1970), 28.

[4]Irving Wardle, "Shadwell Revival," Times, 5 November 1969, p. 14.

VII. RAVENSCROFT

The London Cuckolds (1979)

[1]Victoria Radin, "Cuckolds at the Court," Observer, 4 March 1979, p. 16.

[2]Radin, p. 16.

[3]Benedict Nightingale, "Dirty Business," New Statesman, 9 March 1979, p. 338.

[4]Michael Billington, New York Theatre Review, April 1979, p. 29.

[5]Nightingale, p. 339.

VIII. OTWAY

The Soldier's Fortune (1964)

[1]"Stylish Restoration Comedy," Times, 21 July 1964, p. 7.

[2]Times, p. 7.

The Soldier's Fortune (1967)

[1]The production boasted Holloway as Beaugard, Anthony Quayle as Courtine and Athene Seyler as Lady Dunce. The critic for the Times, "The Soldier's Fortune," 2 October 1935, p. 12, found that "a real vivacity somehow emerges from characters and situations that would be tame enough on the printed page" and praised the acting for being "without pedantry or period flourishes, and consistently high-spirited."

[2]Philip Hope-Wallace, "The Soldier's Fortune," Guardian, 13 January 1967, p. 9.

[3]Alan Brien, "Pursuit of the Nasty," Sunday Telegraph, 15 January 1967.

[4]Brien.

[5]Harold Hobson, "The Soldier's Fortune," Christian Science Monitor, 25 January 1967.

[6]Ronald Bryden, Digging Up a Treasure," Observer, 15 January 1967, p. 25.

[7]Bryden, p. 25.

[8]B. A. Young, "The Soldier's Fortune," _Financial Times_, 14 January 1967.

[9]_Times_, p. 14.

[10]Bryden, p. 25.

[11]Bryden, p. 25.

[12]Young.

[13]Young. Both Felix Barker and Alan Brien praised her particularly for her mock-heroic reading of the line, "Curse on my fatal beauty."

[14]Bryden, p. 25.

Venice Preserved

Background

[1]Aline Mackenzie Taylor, "The Stage History of _Venice Preserved_," in _Next to Shakespeare_ (New York: AMS Press, 1966), pp. 143-244, devotes a considerable portion of her book to tracing the career of the play from its first performance to early twentieth-century revivals.

Venice Preserved (1953)

[1]B. Ashley Barker, "The Lyric Theatre, Hammersmith," _Theatre Notebook_, 24 (Spring 1970), 119.

[2]Disley Jones, "Open House at Hammersmith," _Encore_, 7 (March-April 1960), 27.

[3]"Mr. Gielgud's Career," _Observer_, 4 June 1939.

[4]J. W. Lambert, "Plays in Performance," _Drama_, 30 (Autumn 1953), 18.

[5]Maurice Wiltshire, "A Harrowing Monster of a Melodrama," _Daily Mail_, 16 May 1953, p. 5.

[6]Ivor Brown, "Otway Preserved," _Observer_, 24 May 1953, p. 11.

[7]Philip Hope-Wallace, "Revival by John Gielgud: 'Venice Preserv'd,'" _Guardian_, 18 May 1953, p. 5.

[8]W. A. Darlington, "Neglected Play Revived," _Daily Telegraph_, 16 May 1953, p. 9.

[9]Lambert, p. 18.

[10]Lambert, p. 19.

[11]Wiltshire, p. 5.

[12]Audrey Williamson, "Coronation Fanfare," in Contemporary Theatre (New York: Macmillan, 1956), p. 18.

[13]"Profile--John Gielgud," Observer, 2 April 1950.

[14]"Venice Preserv'd," Times, 16 May 1953, p. 8.

[15]"Gielgud," Sunday Times, 1 September 1957.

[16]Williamson, pp. 19-20.

[17]Darlington, p. 9.

[18]Lambert, p. 19.

Venice Preserved (1969)

[1]Hilary Spurling, "Venice Well Preserved," Spectator, 14 February 1969.

[2]Spurling.

[3]J. W. Lambert, "Plays in Performance," Drama, 30 (Autumn 1953), 18.

[4]Spurling.

[5]Spurling.

[6]Spurling.

[7]Spurling.

[8]Other productions not treated in this work are a 1970 Prospect Productions revival with Barbara Leigh Hunt as Belvidera, John Castle as Jaffier and Julian Glover as Pierre. In 1972 the play was revived by the Citizens' Theatre, Glasgow, and in 1982 there was a four-handed version presented by the Almeida Theatre, Islington.

On 12 April 1984 Venice Preserved opened at the National Theatre's Lyttleton Theatre. The principles were Hugh Paddick as Antonio, Stephanie Beacham as Aquilina, Jane Lapotaire as Belvidera, Michael Pennington as Jaffier, Ian McKellen as Pierre and Brewster Mason as Priuli. Alison Chitty designed the production and Peter Gill directed.

The production aimed for acting on a grand scale, and, according to Irving Wardle, "Discovering Tragic Passion," Times, 13 April 1984, p. 15, the principles achieved their exalted goal:

Like Gielgud and Scofield in the 1953 production
. . . Michael Pennington and Ian McKellen seize on
the separate characteristics of Jaffier and Pierre
and render them in almost musical terms.

So far as verse speaking goes, this partnership displays a mastery beyond the range of
anything to be heard elsewhere on the
classical stage. And when the teeth of the plot
engage . . . the dramatic impact is
tremendous.

IX. VANBRUGH

The Relapse (1948)

[1]Philip Hope-Wallace, "Plays in Performance,"
Drama, 8(Spring 1948), 5.

[2]Hope-Wallace, p. 5.

[3]Kenneth Tynan, He That Plays the King (New York:
Longmans, Green and Co., 1950), p. 79.

[4]"The Relapse," Times, 29 January 1948, p. 6.

Virtue in Danger (1963)

[1]"Salacious Classic as Show for Family," Times, 11
April 1963, p. 17

[2]Already in residence for some time at Her
Majesty's Theatre was the Fielding-inspired musical
Lock Up Your Daughters, another product of Mermaid
ingenuity and the motivation for the less happy
Vanbrugh offering.

The Relapse (1967)

[1]During the time under consideration, the Royal
Shakespeare Company divided itself between Stratford-
upon-Avon and London, playing concurrently at two
theatres. It appeared at the Royal Shakespeare
Theatre, Stratford-upon-Avon, from April to November
and continuously at the Aldwych Theatre in London
(except in the Spring when the World Theatre season was
presented). Four or five Shakespearian productions
remained the basis of the Stratford season, while the
Aldwych repertoire consisted mainly, though by no means
wholly, of modern works. Thus a link was created
between Shakespeare and the modern theatre.

[2]B. A. Young, "The Relapse," Financial Times, 18 August 1967, p. 7.

[3]Alan Brien, "East of Dunsinane," Sunday Telegraph, 20 August 1967, p. 10.

[4]Irving Wardle, "A Fine Stylish Revival," Times, 18 August 1967, p. 5.

[5]Young, p. 7.

[6]Arthur Thirkell, "Theatre," Daily Mirror, 18 August 1967, p. 14.

[7]Wardle, p. 5.

[8]J. W. Lambert, "The Spirit of Delight," Sunday Times, 20 August 1967, p. 39.

[9]Brien, p. 10.

[10]Brien, p. 10.

[11]Lambert, p. 39.

The Relapse (1968)

[1]David Nathan, "A Relapse for 'The Relapse,'" Sun, 16 August 1968, p. 7.

[2]Anthony Merryn, "Complexity in Aldwych Revival," Liverpool Evening Post, 16 August 1968, p. 4.

[3]On June 23, 1970, Sinden again appeared at the Aldwych in Dion Boucicault's London Assurance, playing Sir William Harcourt Courtly, an overaged, overdressed would-be swain. Again he was a success in a role that was obviously a blood relative of Foppington. He repeated the performance in New York.

[4]Milton Shulman, "Vanbrugh's London--Decadent, Delicious," Evening Standard, 16 August 1968, p. 4.

[5]Rosemary Say, "A Hard Look at Frivolity," Sunday Telegraph, 18 August 1968, p. 12.

[6]Henry Raynor, "Morals and Manners on Parade," Times, 16 August 1968, p. 9.

[7]Ronald Bryden, "Restoration Landmark," Observer, 18 August 1968, p. 20.

[8]Bryden, p. 20.

[9]Harold Hobson, "Let Wit Be Unconfined," Sunday Times, 18 August 1968, p. 41.

[10]Hobson, p. 41.

[11]Hobson, p. 41.

[12]Norman Cox, "Wit to Defeat Even August's Gloom," _Daily Sketch_, 16 August 1968.

The Provok'd Wife

Background

[1]Antony Coleman, "Sir John Brute on the Eighteenth Century Stage," _Restoration and Eighteenth Century Theatre Research_, 8(November 1969), 45.

[2]Coleman, pp. 42-43.

The Provok'd Wife (1963)

[1]This transfer added to the stature of the company founded at Oxford in 1961 by Elizabeth Sweeting and Iain Mackintosh. As a result of this success, Robertson became artistic director of the company. Shortly after his appointment as Director of Productions, the Arts Theatre, Cambridge, where the company played regularly, became the base of its activities until 1963.

[2]Milton Shulman, "Restoration Frolic, But It's Still Up-to-Date," _Evening Standard_, 25 July 1963.

[3]Gerald Barry, "At the Play."

[4]"Revival Lacks Vanbrugh Sparkle," _Times_, 25 July 1963, p. 15.

[5]B. A. Young, "The Provok'd Wife," _Financial Times_, 25 July 1963.

[6]Young.

[7]_Times_, p. 15.

[8]Young.

[9]See Background for fuller historical information.

[10]Shulman.

[11]_Times_, p. 15.

[12]Kenneth Tynan, "The Horrors of Marriage," _Observer_, 28 July 1963.

Intrigues and Amours (1967)

[1]"Harry H. Corbett with Clive Goodwin," in Acting in the Sixties, ed. Hal Burton (London: BBC, 1970), p. 39.

[2]Theatre Workshop was more successful with contemporary playwrights, giving to the public the works of Brendan Behan and Shelagh Delaney.

[3]A. V. Coton, "Fun and Games Made from Vanbrugh," Daily Telegraph, 25 May 1967.

[4]Milton Shulman, "Hands Off Vanbrugh!" Evening Standard, 25 May 1967, p. 4.

[5]Terry Coleman, "'Intrigues and Amours' at the Theatre Royal, Stratford East," Manchester Guardian, 25 May 1967.

[6]Ronald Bryden, "Split Second Farce in Action," Observer, 28 May 1967, p. 19.

[7]Shulman, p. 4.

[8]Corbett, p. 42.

[9]Bryden, p. 19.

[10]Coton.

The Provok'd Wife (1973)

[1]J. W. Lambert, Sunday Times, 17 June 1973, p. 35.

[2]Irving Wardle, "The Provok'd Wife," Times, 15 June 1973, p. 9.

[3]Lambert, p. 35.

[4]Wardle, p. 9.

[5]Wardle, p. 9.

[6]Lambert, p. 35.

The Confederacy (1951)

[1]"The Confederacy," Birmingham Post, 3 October 1951.

[2]"A Restoration Comedy," Times, 8 October 1951, p. B10.

[3]Birmingham Post.

[4]"Architect's Comedy," Birmingham Mail, 3 October 1951.

The Confederacy (1964)

[1]"Vanbrugh Celebration," Stage, 19 October 1964.

The Confederacy (1974)

[1]Also in repertory were Pirandello's Tonight We Improvise, not considered especially inventive in approach, and an outstandingly inept version of Oedipus with Michell in the title role and Diana Dors as Jocasta. Its one claim to notoriety was that at least it elicited outrage.

[2]Anthony Curtis, "The Confederacy," Plays and Players, 21(July 1974), 31.

[3]Curtis, p. 31.

[4]Douglas Watt, Daily News, 4 August 1974, p. 3.

[5]Benedict Nightingale, New Statesman, 7 June 1974, p. 810.

[6]Robert Cushman, Observer, 2 June 1974, p. 30.

X. CONGREVE

The Double Dealer (1959)

[1]For a lengthy, but rewarding, study of the original casts of Congreve's plays see Peter Holland, "Text and Performance (3): the Comedies of Congreve," in The Ornament of Action (Cambridge: Cambridge University Press, 1979), pp. 204-243.

[2]The Times critic found that the production shed additional light on the plays of Congreve: "He wrote them for the stage and not for the study . . . they are far richer in delight than the printed page, rich as that is." "The Double Dealer: A Restoration Review," Times, 16 May 1916, p. 4.

[3]Observer, 30 August 1959.

[4]W. A. Darlington, "Old Vic Show Complexities of Congreve," 25 August 1959, p. 2.

[5]"Modern Review Implicit: Congreve for the Collector," Times, 25 August 1959, p. 11.

[6]"Gusto and Polish in Congreve," Stage, 10 September 1959. The idea echoes the 1916 Times review which conceded that "A Congreve plot is of no more importance than the plot of a modern revue: it is

merely there as a string to hang the 'turns' together; only these 'turns' of his happen to be pure gems of art and wit and gaiety. . . . That the Restoration stage here hit upon a really vital form of art is clearly shown by the revival and vogue of that form on our 'variety' stage to-day." "The Double Dealer," Times, 16 May 1916, p. 4.

[7] Observer, 30 August 1959.

[8] Harold Hobson, "Morality is Not So Easy," Sunday Times, 30 August 1959, p. 17.

[9] Philip Hope-Wallace, "Old Vic Revives a Neglected Comedy: Congreve's 'The Double Dealer,'" Guardian, 28 August 1959, p. 5.

[10] In March the Comédie Française had appeared at the Princes Theatre in a Feydeau and Les Femmes Savantes by Molière. They proved themselves adept in both. The Feydeau showed the company in "a style of acting which has no other end than the display of its own virtuosity," while in the Molière they exhibited "the style proper to classic comedy." "Comédie Française Delight in Different Style," Times, 24 March 1959, p. 6.

[11] "Restoration Comedy Restored," Times, 8 September 1959, p. 14.

[12] Herbert Whittaker, "Old Vic at Home with Congreve," Globe and Mail [Toronto], 17 September 1959.

[13] Hope-Wallace, p. 5.

[14] Stage, 10 September 1959.

[15] Whittaker.

[16] Whittaker.

[17] John Trewin, Illustrated London News, 12 September 1959.

[18] "The Double-Dealer," Plays and Players, 10 (October 1959), 15.

[19] This traditional approach was argued in the 1916 Times review cited above. The reviewer found Lady Touchwood "a really tragic figure, and all the more welcome among the lighthearted crew because she gives you something, in Byron's phrase, 'to break your mind on,' something that strikes a deep, full note of passion amid the trills and roulades of wit."

[20]*Plays and Players*, p. 15.

The Double Dealer (1969)

[1]Harold Hobson, "This Side of Ecstasy," *Sunday Times*, 27 July 1969, p. 47. The other two plays were *The Country Wife* (Chichester) and *The Way of the World* (Old Vic).

[2]Frank Marcus, "War--Not Love," *Sunday Telegraph*, 27 July 1969, p. 12.

[3]Milton Shulman, "Reviving a Bit of the Immoral and Profane," *Evening Standard*, 23 July 1969, p. 15.

[4]"The Double Dealer," *Herald* [Boston], 11 June 1916.

[5]Ronald Bryden, "Views from Everest," *Observer*, 27 July 1969, p. 23.

[6]"The Double Dealer," *Stage*, 24 July 1969, p. 15.

[7]Philip Hope-Wallace, "The Double Dealer," *Guardian*, 23 July 1969, p. 6.

[8]John Barber, "Slow-Witted Husbands and Lascivious Wives," *Daily Telegraph*, 23 July 1969, p. 19.

[9]Clive Barnes, "Art of Congreve," *New York Times*, 7 August 1969, p. 29.

[10]Felix Barker, "Lost in a Maze of Treachery," *Evening News*, 23 July 1969, p. 11.

[11]Barber, p. 19.

[12]Irving Wardle, "A Play with Evil as the Mainspring," *Times*, 23 July 1969, p. 11.

[13]Wardle, p. 11.

[14]Marcus, p. 14.

[15]Bryden, p. 27.

[16]Wardle, p. 11.

[17]Wardle, p. 11.

The Double Dealer (1978)

[1]Pit, *Variety*, 4 October 1978, p. 98.

[2]John Barber, "Miraculous Revival is Laced with Subtlety."

[3] Benedict Nightingale, "In His Humour," <u>New Statesman</u>, 6 October 1978, p. 448.

[4] Peter Jenkins, "Nasty Stars," <u>Spectator</u>, 7 October 1978.

[5] B. A. Young, "The Double Dealer," <u>Financial Times</u>, 28 September 1978, p. 21.

[6] Bernard Levin, "The Quality of Mercer is Not Strained," <u>Sunday Times</u>, 1 October 1978, p. 39.

[7] Levin, p. 39.

[8] Robert Cushman, "Restoration House Party," <u>Observer</u>, 1 October 1978.

[9] Young, p. 21.

[10] Nightingale, p. 448.

[11] Barber.

[12] Irving Wardle, "Comedy with a Villainous Vein," <u>Times</u>, 28 September 1978, p. 10.

[13] Cushman.

[14] Michael Billington, "The Double Dealer," <u>Guardian</u>, 28 September 1978.

[15] Nightingale, p. 448.

[16] "There's a Chill Behind the Fun in this Dark English Comedy," <u>Daily Mail</u>, 28 September 1978.

[17] Levin, p. 39.

[18] Barber.

[19] Billington.

[20] Cushman.

[21] Nightingale, p. 448.

[22] Wardle, p. 20.

[23] Levin, p. 39.

[24] Nightingale, p. 448.

[25] Nightingale, p. 448.

[26] Levin, p. 39.

[27] Wardle, p. 10.

[28] Billington.

[29]Cushman.

[30]Wardle, p. 10.

[31]Jenkins.

Love for Love (1944 and 1947)

[1]John Gielgud, Stage Directions (London: Mercury Books, 1965), p. 65.

[2]Gielgud, p. 67.

[3]Gielgud, p. 67.

[4]Gielgud, p.70.

[5]James Agate, "The Legend of Ben," Sunday Times, 4 April 1943, p. 2.

[6]"Love for Love," Times, 9 April 1943, p. 6.

[7]Times, p. 6.

[8]Gielgud, pp. 70-71.

[9]William Hawkins, "'Love for Love' Bawdy but Brittle in Revival," New York World-Telegram, 27 May 1947, p. 30.

[10]Brooks Atkinson, "The New Play," New York Times, 27 May 1947 p. 30.

[11]Nathan Cohen, "A Sepulchral 'Love for Love,'" Daily Star [Toronto], 4 November 1967.

Love for Love (1965)

[1]Maureen Cleave, "Moscow Laps Up Our 'Love for Love' and Cheers," Evening Standard, 10 September 1965. Cleave noted that a Russian interpreter had been flown to England before the opening to study the script and insure that "what lewd remarks there are were faithfully and . . . accurately translated."

[2]J. W. Lambert, "The Theatre of Conscience," Sunday Times, 24 October 1965.

[3]Alan Brien, "Shelley All Too Plain," Sunday Telegraph, 24 October 1965, p. 14.

[4]E. Martin Brown, "A Look Round the London Theatre," Drama Survey, 5(Winter 1965-66), 88.

[5]Peter Lewis, "Love for Love," Daily Mail, 21 October 1965.

338

[6]Harold Hobson, "No Play for Puritans," _Sunday Times_, 2 January 1966. However, in an article, "The Legend of Ben," _Sunday Times_, 4 April 1943, p. 2, James Agate explored the ideas of Hazlitt and Lamb on "that most callous of sea-going monsters," and, agreeing with Lamb, he decided that "Ben is a piece of satire, a creation of fancy, a dreamy combination of all the accidents of a sailor's character." He cited the 1934 revival in which Roger Livesey "brought off to perfection the miracle of happy naiveté."

[7]"Restoration Comedy Restored," _Times_, 21 October 1965, p. 16.

[8]Lambert.

[9]Philip Hope-Wallace, "Love for Love at Old Vic," _Guardian_, 21 October 1965, p. 9.

[10]Thomas Lask, "With Olivier in the Cast, Can You Fail?" _New York Times_, 11 December 1966, p. D30.

The Way of the World (1948)

[1]W. A. Darlington, "London Letter," _New York Times_, 7 November 1948, sec. 2, p. 3.

[2]Darlington, p. 3.

[3]Darlington, p. 3.

[4]Darlington, p. 3.

[5]"The Way of the World," _Times_, 22 October 1948, p. 7.

The Way of the World (1953)

[1]Ivor Brown, "Gielgud," _Observer_, 7 June 1953.

[2]John Gielgud, _Stage Directions_ (London: Mercury Books, 1965), p. 104.

[3]Ivor Brown, "Fine Matters," _Observer_, 22 February 1953, p. 11.

[4]Kenneth Tynan, "Miss Rutherford's Chin Steals the Show," _Evening Standard_, 20 February 1953, p. 11.

[5]Philip Hope-Wallace, "'The Way of the World' Revival by Gielgud," _Guardian_, 20 February 1953, p. 5.

[6]Gielgud, p. 5.

[7]Brown, p. 11.

[8] Gielgud, p. 62.

[9] Hope-Wallace, p. 5.

[10] Cecil Wilson, "Gielgud Shares His Company's Glory," _Daily Mail_, 20 February 1953, p. 6.

[11] "The Way of the World," _Times_, 20 February 1953, p. 2.

[12] Brown, p. 11.

[13] Tynan, p. 11.

[14] "Margaret Rutherford, 80, Fey Comedienne, Is Dead," _New York Times_, 23 May 1972, p. 44.

[15] Tynan, p. 11.

[16] Brown, p. 11.

The Way of the World (1956)

[1] Derek Granger, "The Way of the World" _Financial Times_, 7 December 1956, p. 2.

[2] Milton Shulman, "Mr. Clements Loses His Touch," _Evening Standard_, 7 December 1956, p. 12.

[3] Granger, p. 2.

[4] Philip Hope-Wallace, "Congreve at the Saville," _Guardian_, 8 December 1956, p. 5.

[5] W. A. Darlington, "Kay Hammond Unsuccessful as Millamant," _Daily Telegraph_, 7 December 1956, p. 10.

[6] Shulman, p. 12.

[7] Granger, p. 2.

[8] Hope-Wallace, p. 5.

[9] Kenneth Tynan, "Second-Best Bed," _Observer_, 9 December 1956, p. 11.

[10] "The Way of the World," _Times_, 7 December 1956, p. 3.

[11] _Times_, p. 3.

[12] J. W. Lambert, "Plays in Performance," _Drama_, 44 (Spring 1957), 22.

[13] W. A. Darlington, "London Letter," _New York Times_, 7 November 1948, p. 3.

[14] Granger, p. 2.

[15]Tynan, p. 11.

[16]_Times_, p. 3.

The Way of the World (1969)

[1]Harold Hobson, "From Grace to Disgrace," _Sunday Times_, 4 May 1969, p. 53.

[2]John Gielgud, _Stage Directions_ (London: Mercury Books, 1965), p. 14.

[3]Frank Marcus, "Restoration and Demolition," _Sunday Telegraph_, 4 May 1969, p. 14.

[4]Ronald Bryden, "A Matter of Money," _Observer_, 4 May 1969, p. 27.

[5]J. W. Lambert, "Plays in Performance," _Drama_, 94(Autumn 1969), 22.

[6]Milton Shulman, "A Starr Lacking in Lustre," _Evening Standard_, 2 May 1969, p. 23.

[7]Eric Shorter, "Bold but Solid Style for 'The Way of the World,'" _Daily Telegraph_, 2 May 1969, p. 21.

[8]Bryden, p. 27.

[9]Shulman, p. 23.

[10]Geraldine McEwan had played for the National Theatre in farce (_A Flea in Her Ear_), experimental comedy (Maureen Duffy's _Rites_), comedy (Maugham's _Home and Beauty_) and in more serious roles (Brecht's _Edward II_ and Strindberg's _Dance of Death_). Her versatility and real comic expertise were undeniable. Surprisingly, Millamant was one of her more disappointing performances. Even more surprisingly, Maggie Smith, who was already established in Restoration comedy and would have been the natural choice for Millamant, was in the company at the time that the play was produced but was passed over. John Elsom and Nicholas Tomalin, _The History of the National Theatre_ (London: Jonathan Cape, 1978), pp. 216-17, briefly discuss the situation at the National at the time the production was mounted.

[11]Bryden, p. 27.

[12]Shorter, p. 21.

[13]Bryden, p. 27.

[14]The program, which gave a critical background to the performance, included brief quotations from Walpole, Hazlitt, Lamb, Macaulay and Meredith with extensive quotations from Norman Holland's The First Modern Comedies and Bonamy Dobrée's Restoration Comedy.

The Way of the World (1978)

[1]Peter Hepple, "The Way of the World," The Stage and Television Today, 2 February 1978, p. 11.

[2]John Peter, "John Barton Gets His Own Way," Sunday Times, 29 January 1978, p. 38.

[3]Benedict Nightingale, "The Way of the World," New Statesman, 3 February 1978, p. 161.

[4]Peter, p. 38.

[5]Irving Wardle, "The Way of the World," Times, 28 January 1978, p. 11.

[6]Peter, p. 38.

[7]Wardle, p. 11.

[8]Wardle, p. 11.

[9]Robert Cushman, Observer, 5 February 1978, p. 26.

[10]Peter, p. 38.

[11]Cushman, p. 26.

[12]Ned Chaillet, "The Way of the World," Plays and Players, 25(March 1978), 28-29. For additional material on twentieth-century Congreve productions see Kenneth Muir, "Congreve on the Modern Stage," in The Singularity of Shakespeare and Other Essays (Liverpool: Liverpool University Press, 1977), pp. 159-179.

On 1 August 1984 Maggie Smith played Millamant in the Chichester Festival Theatre's production of The Way of the World. The cast of Restoration veterans included Joan Plowright as Lady Wishfort, Michael Jayston as Mirabell, Sheila Allen as Mrs. Fainall, Sara Kestelman as Mrs. Marwood and John Moffatt as Witwoud. William Gaskill directed. The costumes were by Deirdre Clancey and the lighting by Andy Phillips.

Robert Warden, "The Way of the World," Plays and Players, No. 372 (September 1984), p. 30, praised the "austerity" of Gaskill's direction with particular attention to the understated "reformed rake" of

Jayston's Mirabell and the inventive stage business of Plowright's Lady Wishfort. Particular credit was given to the spontaneity of Smith's creation, for she approached her lines "not only as though they were written for her, but so you cannot guess what she will say." Unusually attractive was the partnership of the lovers as they captured the "underlying feeling that their proposals would at least try and succeed on a basis of affection." In mid-November the production transferred to the Haymarket in London.

XI. FARQUHAR

Love and a Bottle (1969)

[1] John Coggan, "Playhouse 'Moll' is Their Best Musical," Guardian Journal, 23 June 1966.

[2] Eric Shorter, "Plays in Performance," Drama, 94 (Autumn 1969), 38.

[3] Alan Addison, "Too Much for All Too Little," Morning Star, 9 May 1969, p. 2.

[4] Irving Wardle, "Swinging 1690's," Times, 8 May 1969, p. 12.

The Constant Couple (1967)

[1] Michael Billington, "A Theatre Prospect that Pleases," Times, 20 May 1967, p. 7.

[2] Irving Wardle, "A Well-Cast Version of Farquhar," Times, 30 June 1967, p. 8.

[3] Harold Hobson, "Wild Airs and Witty Fools," Sunday Times, 2 July 1967, p. 25.

[4] Ronald Bryden, "A Scotland All to Themselves," Observer, 2 July 1967, p. 19.

[5] Wardle, p. 8.

[6] Wardle, p. 8. West's roles for Prospect Productions included Dr. Johnson and Prospero. In 1969 he played Bolingbroke to Ian McKellen's Richard II and in the companion play of the company's tour, young Mortimer to McKellen's Edward II.

[7] Sunday Telegraph, 2 July 1967. In the 1943 revival by Alec Clunes at the Arts Theatre, Richard Wordsworth, the doyen of dirty old men, had, indeed, played Smuggler.

[8]"The Constant Couple," <u>New Statesman</u>, 7 August 1943.

[9]Valerie Grovesnor Meyer, "The Constant Couple," <u>Guardian</u>, 26 May 1967.

Trumpets and Drums (1956)

[1]The program of the production gives no credit, but a record, <u>Pauken und Trompeten</u> (Litera), recorded in East Berlin by the Berliner Ensemble and containing songs and scenes from the adaptation does credit three adaptors: Bertold Brecht, Benno Besson, who directed the production, and Elizabeth Hauptman.

[2]"Trumpets and Drums," <u>Times</u>, 30 August 1956, p. 4.

[3]Kenneth Tynan, <u>Curtains</u> (New York: Atheneum, 1961). p. 453.

[4]Berliner Ensemble program translated by Andrew LeBlanc.

[5]<u>Times</u>, p. 4.

[6]Albert Wertheim, "Bertold Brecht and George Farquhar's The Recruiting Officer," <u>Comparative Drama</u>, 7(Fall 1973), 181.

[7]<u>Times</u>, p. 4.

[8]<u>Times</u>, p. 4.

The Recruiting Officer (1963)

[1]On April 30, 1968, the National Theatre Company introduced the Brecht version of Marlowe's <u>Edward II</u> into the repertoire. There is a comparison between Marlowe and the German version in the program, but the director, Frank Dunlop, saw no need to apologize for his choice of the German play. However, the production was not a success and did not remain long on the stage of the Old Vic.

[2]William Gaskill, "Director in Interview," <u>Plays and Players</u>, 17(May 1970), 53.

[3]Alan Brien, "Alarums and Discursions," <u>Sunday Telegraph</u>, 15 December 1963, p. 10.

[4]Milton Shulman, "This Lusty Box-Office Hit Defies Time," <u>Evening Standard</u>, 11 December 1963, p. 4.

[5]George Farquhar, <u>The Recruiting Officer</u>, ed Kenneth Tynan (London: Rupert Hart-Davis, 1965), p. 61.

[6]Farquhar, p. 23.

[7]Bamber Gascoigne, "Army Game--1706 Version," <u>Observer</u>, 15 December 1965.

[8]For an even fuller treatment of the National Theatre Company's <u>The Recruiting Officer</u> see Appendix D and my article, "The Effects of Brecht's Techniques in the Berliner Ensemble's <u>Trumpets and Drums</u> on the staging of <u>The Recruiting Officer</u> by the National Theatre of Great Britain," in <u>Transactions of the Fifth International Congress on the Enlightenment</u> (Oxford: The Voltaire Foundation, 1980), III, 1440-1446.

The Recruiting Officer (1970)

[1]Michael Billington, "The Recruiting Officer," <u>Times</u>, 14 October 1970, p. 13.

[2]Pearson Phillips, "Foppish and Witty: But No Message," <u>Daily Mail</u>, 13 October 1970.

[3]Billington, p. 13.

[4]Phillips. In 1969, McKellen had scored a triumph for the company, as well as a personal success, in playing the title roles in <u>Richard II</u> and <u>Edward II</u>. It was likely that any of his subsequent performances would be viewed with keen critical attention.

[5]Billington, p. 13.

[6]Phillips.

The Beaux' Stratagem

Background

[1]Ivor Brown, quoted by Bryan Forbes, <u>Dame Edith Evans</u> (Boston: Little, Brown and Company, 1977), p. 127.

The Beaux' Stratagem (1949)

[1]"The Beaux' Stratagem," <u>Times</u>, 6 May 1949, p. 3.

[2]Peter Forster, "Plays in Performance," <u>Drama</u>, 19 (Autumn 1949), 6.

[3]<u>Times</u>, p.3.

The Beaux' Stratagem (1970)

[1] Winfred Blevins, "National's 'Stratagem' Mature and Brilliant," Herald-Examiner [Los Angeles], 20 January 1970.

[2] Blevins.

[3] Blevins.

[4] Irving Wardle, "Farquhar Restored," Times, 9 April 1970, p. 18.

[5] William Gaskill, "Director in Interview," Plays and Players, 17 (May 1970), 53.

[6] Milton Shulman, "Delicious Dance of Deception," Evening Standard, 9 April 1970, p. 11.

[7] Gaskill, p. 53.

[8] Wardle, p. 18.

[9] The opening of the play coincided with the awarding of the Oscar to Miss Smith for her performance in The Prime of Miss Jean Brodie. Ronald Bryden, "A Queen with Her Crown On," Observer, 12 April 1970, p. 28, noted the mixture of sentiment and aesthetic appreciation in the reception of her Mrs. Sullen:

> She entered quietly upstage as a previous scene ended down front, unobtrusive in a creamy silk dress of the same canvas-colour hue as René Allio's sketch book cut-outs of eigtheenth-century Lichfield. Few people realized she was there until she launched into her first line, "I think, Dorinda, there's no form of prayer in the liturgy against bad husbands." So that acknowledgement of Maggie Smith's night of nights last Wednesday had to wait til the Old Vic curtain fell on Farquhar's The Beaux' Stratagem, in a shy English flurry of strangled bravos.

[10] Wardle, p. 18.

[11] Bryden, p. 28.

[12] Bryden, p. 28.

[13] Frank Marcus, "A National Restorative," Sunday Telegraph, 12 April 1970, p. 28.

[14]B. A. Young, "The Beaux' Stratagem," <u>Financial Times</u>, 9 April 1970, p. 3.

[15]Wardle, p. 18.

[16]Young, p. 3.

[17]Wardle, p. 18.

APPENDIXES

Appendix A: <u>The Way of the World</u> (1924)

[1]"Congreve at Hammersmith," <u>Guardian</u>, 8 February 1924, p. 12.

[2]"Congreve at Hammersmith," <u>Morning Post</u>, 9 February 1924, p. 5.

[3]<u>Guardian</u>, p. 12.

[4]James Agate, "The Way of the World," <u>Sunday Times</u>, 10 February 1924, p. 4.

[5]<u>Morning Post</u>, p. 5.

[6]Agate, p. 4.

[7]<u>Guardian</u>, p. 12.

[8]"The Way of the World," <u>Times</u>, 8 February 1924, p. 8.

[9]<u>Morning Post</u>, p. 5.

[10]Nigel Playfair, <u>The Story of the Lyric Theatre Hammersmith</u> (London: Chatto and Windus, 1925), p. 184.

[11]Agate, p. 4.

[12]Sidney W. Carroll, "A Real Actress," <u>Daily Telegraph</u>, 18 February 1937.

[13]"The Way of the World," <u>Times</u>, 16 November 1927, p. 12.

[14]Hubert Griffith, "How to Act," <u>Daily Courier</u>, 7 February 1924.

Appendix B: <u>The Way of the World</u> (1976)

[1] Clive Barnes, "Phillips Staging a Mini-Miracle," <u>Globe and Mail</u> [Toronto], 10 June 1976, p. 15.

[2] John Fraser, "Maggie Smith as Cleopatra Saves the Day Again," <u>Globe and Mail</u> [Toronto], 10 June 1976, p. 15.

[3] Barnes, p. 15.

[4] Walter Kerr, "Maggie Smith Has Her 'Way' at Stratford," <u>New York Times</u>, 4 July 1976, p. 5.

[5] Audrey M. Ashley, "Acting Bright Spot in Long, Often Dull 'Way of the World ,'" <u>Citizen</u> [Ottawa], 8 June 1976, p. 76.

[6] T. E. Kalem, "Canada's Dramatic Lodestar," <u>Time</u>, 21 June 1976, p. 42.

[7] Kerr, p. 5.

[8] Kerr, p. 5.

[9] Kerr, p. 5.

Appendix C: <u>The Country Wife</u> (1936)

[1] "The Country Wife," <u>Guardian</u> 19 February 1924, p. 12.

[2] "The Country Wife," <u>Times</u>, 7 October 1936, p. 10.

[3] Richard Watts, Jr., "The Theatres," <u>New York Herald Tribune</u>, 2 December 1936.

[4] Brooks Atkinson, "The Play," <u>New York Times</u>, 2 December 1936, p. 34.

[5] Richard Lockridge, "'The Country Wife,' with Ruth Gordon Opens at Henry Miller's," <u>New York Sun</u>, 2 December 1936.

[6] Douglas Gilbert, "'The Country Wife' at Miller Theatre," <u>New York World-Telegram</u>, 2 December 1936.

Appendix D: <u>The Recruiting Officer</u> (1963)

[1] George Farquhar, <u>The Recruiting Officer</u>, ed. Kenneth Tynan (London: Rupert Hart-Davis, 1965).

[2] "The Recruiting Officer," <u>New Statesman</u>, 18 December 1943, p. 40.

[3]Philip Hope-Wallace, "'The Recruiting Officer' at the National Theatre," Guardian, 11 December 1963, p. 7.

[4]Farquhar, p. 97.

[5]Kenneth Tynan, "Rehearsal Logbook," Plays and Players, 13(November 1965), 17. Also published in George Farquhar, The Recruiting Officer, ed. Kenneth Tynan (London: Rupert Hart-Davis, 1965), pp. 12-16.

[6]Farquhar, pp. 127-28.

[7]Farquhar, p. 61.

[8]Farquhar, p. 71.

[9]Farquhar, p. 76.

[10]Farquhar, pp. 76-77.

[11]Farquhar, p. 87.

[12]Farquhar, p. 118.

[13]"And the Time of the Great Taking Over: An Interview with William Gaskill," Encore, 9 (July-August 1962), 22.

[14]Tynan, p. 16.

[15]Gaskill, p. 23.

[16]Tynan, p. 16.

[17]Tynan, p. 17.

[18]Hope-Wallace, p. 7.

[19]"Classic Related to the Modern World," Times, 11 December 1963, p. 17.

[20]Tynan, p. 30.

[21]T. C. Worsley, "The Recruiting Officer," Financial Times, 12 December 1963, p. 20.

[22]Tynan, p. 46.

[23]Hope-Wallace, p. 7.

[24]Tynan, p. 46.

SELECTED BIBLIOGRAPHY

HISTORICAL BACKGROUND

Ashley, Maurice. England in the Seventeenth Century. Vol. VI of The Pelican History of England. 3rd ed. Baltimore: Penguin Books Inc., 1971.
Compact history of the period from the reign of James I through the death of Queen Anne.

Fraser, Antonia. Royal Charles: Charles II and the Restoration. New York: Dell Publishing Company, 1979.
The history of the fortunes of Charles from birth to death. Brief but welcome attention to the theatrical climate.

Hill, John Christopher. The Century of Revolution 1603-1714. Edinburgh: Thomas Nelson and Sons, 1961.
Treating events from 1603-1714, the book approaches the decades from the viewpoints of economics, politics and the constitution and religion and ideas.

Trevelyan, George Macaulay. England Under the Stuarts. London: Methuen, 1949.
From the beginning of the century through the reign of Queen Anne. Annotations in the margin allow for handy quick reference.

BIOGRAPHY

Aston, Anthony. A Brief Supplement to Colley Cibber, Esq.; His Lives of the Late Famous Actors and Actresses. In An Apology for the Life of Mr. Colley Cibber. Edited by Robert W. Lowe. 2 vols. London: J. C. Nimmo, 1889.
Brief addition gives short biographies of players of the period. There is also a set of memoirs from the Bellchambers edition of the Apology (1822), which enlarges the biographies.

Borgman, Albert S. The Life and Death of William Mountfort. Cambridge: Harvard University Press, 1935.
This brief, scholarly life covers the activities and some of the theatrical history in which Mountfort was involved.

Forbes, Bryan. _Dame Edith Evans_. Boston: Little,
    Brown and Company, 1977.
        An authorized biography which highlights
    significant performances and events in a long,
    rich career.

Gildon, Charles. _The Life of Mr. Thomas Betterton_.
    London: R. Gosling, 1710.
        Deals with Betterton's theatrical activities
    with an emphasis on acting technique.

Highfill, Philip H., Jr., Burnim, Kalman A. et al, eds.
    A Biographical Dictionary of Actors, Actresses,
    Musicians, Dancers, Managers, and Other Stage
    Personnel in London, 1660-1800. Carbondale:
    Southern Illinois University Press, 1973-.
        Estimated to run to 16 volumes (10 are now
    available), the work offers pithy biographies of
    the careers of London theatrical folk of all
    ranks. Bonus: beautifully produced.

Jacob, Giles. _The Poetical Register: or, the Lives_
    and Characters of the English Dramatic Poets.
    New York: Garland, 1970.
        Brief biographies of playwrights who have become
    famous for "adorning their native language."

Langbaine, Gerard. _An Account of the English Dramatick_
    Poets. New York: Garland, 1973.
        Classic which combines traditional information
    and literary criticism. The lives and writings of
    many now unknown authors.

Lanier, Henry Wysham. _The First English Actresses_.
    New York: The Players, 1930.
        Brief account of some early actresses and the
    social background that ushered them in with
    portraits of Oldfield and Bracegirdle.

Lowe, Robert. W. _Thomas Betterton_. London: K. Paul,
    Trench, Trubner and Company, 1891.
        Vivid picture of the goings on during the time
    of the Restoration playhouses; emphasis on
    1635-1710.

Trewin, J. C. _Edith Evans_. London: Rockcliff, 1954.
        A brief study of Evans with emphasis on her
    technique in major roles.

Wilson, John Harold. _All the King's Ladies_. Chicago:
    University of Chicago Press, 1958.

Vivid account of the major actresses of the period with considerable theatrical information in a fluid style.

_____. Mr. Goodman the Player. Pittsburgh: University of Pittsburgh Press, 1964.
Account of and speculation about the racy life of Cardell Goodman.

THEATRE HISTORY

Avery, Emmett L. et al, eds. The London Stage, 1660–1800. 11 vols. Carbondale: Southern Illinois University Press, 1960–68.
Describes itself as a "calendar of plays, entertainments, afterpieces together with . . . contemporary comments compiled from playbills, newspapers and theatres of the period."

Baker, David E. et al. Biographia Dramatica. 3 vols. London: Longman, Hurst, Rees, Orme and Brown, 1812.
Historical and critical memoirs, anecdotes from the rise of the British stage to 1782.

Baker, H. Barton. History of the London Stage and Its Famous Players, 1576–1903. New York: Benjamin Blom, 1969.
Continuous, consecutive history of the rise, progress and changes in the stage from the foundation to the present with the principal dramatic events of the periods, the authors and the actors.

Boswell, Eleanore. The Restoration Court Stage, 1660–1702. Cambridge: Harvard University Press, 1932.
Describes the court theatres of the period and the productions. A chapter is devoted to the masque, Calisto, which brings into focus all the material by the description of a single court play. Documents.

Cibber, Colley. An Apology for the Life of Colley Cibber. Edited by B. R. S. Fone. Ann Arbor: University of Michigan Press, 1968.
Cibber's view of the theatre from the Restoration to 1733. Cibber describes his roles as playwright, actor and actor-manager of Drury Lane. Contains many significant portraits.

Doran, John. Their Majesties' Servants, or Annals of the English Stage. 3 vols. Boston: Francis A. Niccolls and Company, n.d.
   An account of the players from the Restoration period through Kean. The prologue is devoted to earlier history.

Downes, John. Roscius Anglicanus. Edited by Montague Summers. New York: Benjamin Blom, 1968.
   Downes's memoirs of almost fifty theatrical years from the opening of the theatre in Lincoln's Inn Fields to 1706 with copious explanatory notes by Summers on actors and productions.

Egerton, Thomas. Theatrical Remembrancer. London: T. and J. Egerton, 1788.
   A chronological account of events relative to the English stage from Rastall (died 1536) to 1787.

Genest, John. Some Accounts of the English Stage from the Restoration in 1660 to 1830. 10 vols. New York: B. Franklin, 1967.
   Stage history including: theatres, plays, players and theatre companies.

Hotson, Leslie. The Commonwealth and Restoration Stage. Cambridge: Harvard University Press, 1928.
   Deals with two periods. 1642-1660 talks about the players and the fate of the drama and the theatre during the interregnum. 1660-1704 describes the rise of the theatre. Documents.

Hume, Robert D., ed. The London Theatre World 1660-1800. Carbondale: Southern Illinois University Press, 1980.
   A collection of essays on various aspects of the theatre from players and playhouses to censorship.

Lambert, J. W. Drama in Britain 1964-1973. London: Longman, 1974.
   Brief survey of theatre activity of a decade with special emphasis on the major companies and a look at regional theatre, overseas theatre and the West End.

Langhans, Edward A., ed. Restoration Promptbooks. Carbondale: Southern Illinois University Press, 1981.
   Twelve complete promptbooks in facsimile and 150 oversized pages of commentary and interpretation.

Reaches significant conclusions about theatrical productions in London 1660-1700.

Loftis, John et al. The Revels History of Drama in English. Vol. V: 1660-1759. Gen. ed. T. W. Craik. London: Methuen, 1976.
    The survey has three broad divisions: social and literary context, theatres and actors, and plays and playwrights. The bibliography chapter is devoted to bibliographical essays.

Nagler, A. M., ed. A Source Book in Theatrical History. New York: Dover, 1959.
    A collection of documents and other basic material which help recreate the conditions under which plays were performed from antiquity through contemporary times.

Nicoll, Allardyce. A History of Early Eighteenth Century Drama, 1700-1750. Cambridge: Cambridge University Press, 1925.
    The early chapters particularly deal with audience, theatres, performers and the dramas of the period including early domestic models and foreign influences. Documents and a handlist of plays.

_____. A History of English Drama, 1660-1900. Vol. I, Restoration Drama, 1660-1700. 4th ed. Cambridge: Cambridge University Press, 1967.
    Looks at the evolution of the theatre, dividing the approach to drama broadly into tragedy and comedy with subheadings. A playhouse history, various documents and a handlist of plays complete the work.

Pepys, Samuel. The Diary of Samuel Pepys. Edited by Robert Latham and William Matthews. 11 Vols. Berkeley: University of California Press, 1973-83.
    Playgoing, gossip, criticism, sex. Pepys's unending saga of himself and his times.

Scouten, Arthur H. and Hume, Robert D. "Restoration Comedy and its Audiences, 1660-1776." In The Rakish Stage: Studies in English Drama, 1660-1800. Carbondale: Southern Illinois University Press, 1983, pp. 46-81.
    The essay reevaluates the evolution of the audience and gives substantial references for those who want to follow the subject along.

Southern, Richard. Changeable Scenery. London: Faber
    and Faber, 1952.
       Detailed account of movable scenes from their
    introduction at court through their development in
    the public theatres in the seventeenth and
    eighteenth centuries to the revolution in the
    theatre of the nineteenth century.

Summers, Montague. The Playhouse of Pepys. London:
    K. Paul, Trench, Trubner and Company, 1935.
       Deals with the rise of the Restoration theatre,
    the early dramatists, the men of "quality" and the
    minor dramatists from 1660-1682.

_____. The Restoration Theatre. London: K. Paul,
    Trench, Trubner and Company, 1934.
       From advertisements through the decoration of
    the stage, the players and the audience. There
    is an appendix on the Phoenix Society for the
    Production of Old Plays giving a description of
    its activities and listing its productions.

Wells, Staring B., ed. [Charles Gildon]. A Comparison
    Between the Two Stages. Princeton: Princeton
    University Press, 1942.
       The competition between the two companies at
    Lincoln's Inn Fields and Drury Lane as they vied
    for popularity with the fickle public is herein
    described.

Wright, James. Historia Histrionica, 1699. Rpt. New
    York: Garland, 1974.
       Brief account of the stage which focuses on the
    "ancient use, improvement and perfection of
    dramatic representations in this nation." Gives
    an idea of the evolution of the theatrical
    climate.

HISTORY OF THEATRES

Elsom, John and Tomalin, Nicholas. The History of the
    National Theatre. London: Jonathan Cape, 1978.
       The background: politics, money raising,
    rivalries, desire for achievement. Portrait of
    the building of the theatre.

Evershed-Martin, Leslie. The Impossible Theatre: The
    Chichester Festival Theatre Adventure. Prologue by
    Laurence Olivier. London: Phillimore, 1971.
       History of the theatre from the idea through the
    building to the opening night of The Chances.

Playfair, Nigel, Sir. <u>The Story of the Lyric Theatre Hammersmith</u>. New York: Benjamin Blom, 1969.
     An account of the founding of the theatre with copious references to actors and performances; a special chapter on <u>The Way of the World</u>.

Rosenfeld, Sybil. <u>The Georgian Theatre of Richmond Yorkshire</u>. London: The Society for Theatre Research, 1984.
     An account of the sixty lively years of this theatre which highlights its productions and players. Reopened in 1962, it is one of four eighteenth-century theatres remaining in England.

Williams, E. Harcourt. <u>Old Vic Saga</u>. London: Winchester Publications, n.d.
     The story of this most significant playhouse, its productions and performers.

STAGE HISTORY

Avery, Emmett L. <u>Congreve's Plays on the Eighteenth-Century Stage</u>. New York: Modern Language Association of America, 1951.
     Follows the stage reputation of his dramas from the early years through the age of Garrick and the decline of the plays. Appendix lists performances from 1700–1800.

Muir, Kenneth. "Congreve on the Modern Stage." In <u>The Singularity of Shakespeare, and Other Essays</u>. Liverpool: Liverpool University Press, 1977, pp. 159–179.
     Brief essay touches on eleven revivals from the first quarter of the century through 1969.

Taylor, Aline Mackenzie. <u>Next to Shakespeare: Otway's Venice Preserv'd and The Orphan and Their History on the London Stage</u>. New York: AMS Press, 1966.
     Detailed history of Otway's two tragedies from the opening performances through the early years of the twentieth century with a survey of the rise and fall of Otway's reputation.

ON ACTING

Betterton, Thomas [William Oldys or Edmund Curll]. _The History of the English Stage_. Boston: William S. and Henry Spear, 1814.
    Defines the rules of acting of Betterton's time. Should not be taken as a definitive verbal snapshot of Betterton at play, but some material may have been based on authentic notes.

Burton, Hal, ed. _Acting in the Sixties_. London: British Broadcasting Corporation, 1970.
    Interviews with, among others, Burton, Finney, Smith, Stephens and Tutin.

Farquhar, George. _The Recruiting Officer: The National Theatre Production_. Edited by Kenneth Tynan. London: Rupert Hart-Davis, 1965.
    The text used for the National Theatre production with stage directions and Tynan's "Logbook" of rehearsals.

Gielgud, John. _Stage Directions_. London: Mercury Books, 1965.
    Sir John writes about his major endeavors both on stage and as a producer, including a look at the Hammersmith season with its Restoration emphasis.

Gourlay, Logan, ed. _Olivier_. New York: Stein and Day, 1974.
    Actors, playwrights and directors talk about Olivier.

Seyler, Athene and Haggard, Stephen. _The Craft of Comedy_. New York: Theatre Arts Books, 1957.
    An exchange of letters. Good points on interpretation by archcomedienne Seyler.

CRITICAL WORKS

Brown, John Russell and Harris, Bernard, eds. _Restoration Theatre_. New York: Capricorn Books, 1967.
    Selected essays illustrating modern views of the writing, acting and comic style of the Restoration.

Dennis, John. <u>The Critical Works</u>. Edited by Edward
    Niles Hooker. 2 vols. Baltimore: Johns Hopkins
    University Press, 1939.
        The first volume covers the period 1692-1711 and
    is a series of essays and prefaces on literature
    and the stage that includes an answer to Collier's
    outburst.

Holland, Peter. <u>The Ornament of Action: Text and
    Performance in Restoration Comedy</u>. Cambridge:
    Cambridge University Press, 1979.
        Examines the nature of performance itself which
    includes the theatre, the actors, the audience,
    the staging and the text. Examines three examples
    of interconnection of text and performance with a
    relationship between the theatre and the comedies
    produced in two theatre seasons between 1691-93.
    The comedies of Congreve get special attention.

Hughes, Leo. <u>The Drama's Patrons</u>. Austin: University
    of Texas Press, 1971.
        An analysis of London's theatrical public from
    the days of Dryden to Sheridan investigating
    the relationship between playgoer and performer
    with an emphasis on the public's view of itself
    and the changes in taste, manners and morals.

Krutch, Joseph Wood. <u>Comedy and Conscience After the
    Restoration</u>. New York: Russell and Russell, 1949.
        Deals with the development of the dramatic
    tradition, drama and society and is particularly
    concerned with the Jeremy Collier controversy.

Milhous, Judith and Hume, Robert D. <u>Producible
    Interpretation: Eight English Plays, 1675-1707</u>.
    Carbondale: Southern Illinois University Press,
    forthcoming January, 1985.
        The work examines eight plays and offers deduc-
    tions based on six kinds of investigation from
    analysis of the original cast and scenery required
    for performance through discussions of modern
    critical opinion.

Sherburn, George and Bond, Donald F. <u>The Restoration
    and Eighteenth Century (1660-1789)</u>. Vol. III of <u>A
    Literary History of England</u>. 2nd ed. Ed. Albert
    C. Baugh. New York: Appleton-Century-Crofts, 1967.
        A chronological account of English literature
    including biographical, critical and historical
    sources.

Wilson, John Harold. _A Preface to Restoration Drama_. Boston: Houghton Mifflin, 1965.
    Compact and readable study of the theatre and theatre practices with a look at actors, audience and plays.

GENERAL REFERENCE

Laver, James. _A Concise History of Costume_. London: Thames and Hudson, 1974.
    From earliest times through recent high fashion.

Lowe, Robert W. _A Bibliographical Account of English Theatrical Literature from Earliest Times to the Present Day_. London: J. C. Nimmo, 1888.
    A combination handbook, dictionary and bibliography--somewhat idiosyncratic.

McAfee, Helen. _Pepys on the Restoration Stage_. New York: Benjamin Blom, 1916.
    Draws from Pepys's diary pertinent references to plays, actors, playwrights, audiences and theatres.

Roberts, Peter. _Theatre in Britain: A Playgoer's Guide_. New York: Pitman, 1975.
    A compact handbook for theatregoers with a reference section and theatre guide.

Finn, Christine: as Corinna, 173
Finney, Albert: 261; as Horner, 105; as Ben, 203
Fleetwood, Susan: as Amanda, 153; as Silvia, 255
Flutter, Sir Fopling: 77, 270; popularity of character,
    80; Ronnie Stevens as, 82; John Wood as, 85;
    Timothy O'Brien describes, 85-86
Garrick, David: as Jaffeir, 129; comments on Jaffeir,
    134; as Sir John Brute, 161, 164; plays Kite,
    Pearmain and Plume, 247
Gaskill, William: director of English Stage Company,
    123; director of The Double Dealer, 186-189
    passim; director of The Recruiting Officer, 186,
    250-254, 284-291 passim; influenced by Brecht,
    56, 251-252; influenced by Berliner Ensemble,
    56-57, 250-252; Richard Cottrell compared with,
    254-255; director of The Beaux' Stratagem, 57,
    262-269 passim
Georgiadis, Nicholas: designer of All for Love, 75
Georgian Theatre: 47; renovation, 81-82
Gibbon's Tennis Court Theatre: 4
Gielgud, Sir John: i, 44, 218, 271, 329-330n;
    production of Venice Preserved, 50,130-137 passim;
    season for Tennant Productions, 130; his Jaffeir
    compared with Scofield's Pierre, 134-137 passim;
        produces Love for Love, 197-202; as Valentine,
    199; defines style, 211-213; defines his approach
    to a text, 212-213; director of The Way of the
    World, 211-218 passim; as Mirabell, 216; on speech
    in the theatre, 222
Gilbert, Kenneth: as Ventidius, 76
Goodman, Cardell: 15; racy life, 73-74
Gordon, Ruth: 48; as Margery, 94, 281-283
Gostelow, Gordon: as Pinchwife, 100-101
Green, Dorothy: as Mrs. Marwood, 273
Grinling, Amanda: as Flippanta, 174-175
Grout, James: as Sir John Brute, 167
Guthrie, Tyrone: director of The Country Wife, 281
Gwyn, Nell: 32, 34
Haines, Joe: background,91; triumph as Sparkish, 91
Hall, Sir Peter: director of The Country Wife, 103-105
Hammond, Kay: as Melantha, 70; as Millamant, 219-221;
    as Mrs. Sullen, 261-262
Hancock, Sheila: as Lady Dunce, 125; compared to a
    comic Mrs. Siddons, 126
Hands, Terry: director of The Man of Mode, 83-87
    passim
Hardy, Robert: as Sir Harry Wildair, 56, 242
Harris, Rosemary: as Constantina 1, 63

Hart, Charles: 16, 31; Rymer's description, 60; as Antony, 73; as Horner, 90
Hauser, Frank: director of _All for Love_, 75-76
Haymarket Theatre: 129; Downes reports on progress, 170
Hazell, Hy: as Clarissa, 174
Heeley, Desmond: designer of _The Double Dealer_, 183; designer of _The Way of the World_, 222-223
Hepton, Bernard: as Antonio, 139-140
Herlie, Eileen: as Belvidera, 133
Holmes, William: as Sir Davy, 122
Houston, Donald: as Maskwell, 185
Howard, Alan: as Dorimant, 86-87
Hughes, Hazel: as Clarissa, 173; as Lady Wishfort, 223-224

Ingham, Barrie: as Lord Foppington, 154-155; compared with Sinden, 50, 154
Innocent, Harold: as Pinchwife, 96
Intrigues and Amours: Theatre Workshop, 165-167. See also _The Provok'd Wife_
Jacobi, Derek: as Foigard, 269
Jayston, Michael: as Young Fashion, 156-157; as Mirabell, 342-343n
Jeans, Ursula: as Lady Touchwood, 185
Jefford, Barbara: as Cleopatra, 75-76
Jevon, Thomas: as Fourbin, 122
Johnson, Richard: as Pinchwife, 105
Kay, Charles: as Clincher, 242
Kean, Edmund: unsuccessful as Jaffeir, 129
Kemble, John: as Jaffeir to the Belvidera of his sister, Mrs. Siddons, 129
Kestelman, Sara: as Lady Touchwood, 192-193
Killigrew, Thomas: 6-8, 13, 25, 31
King's Company: 7-8, 31
Kingsley, Ben: as Sparkish, 105
Knaup, Dieter: as Plume, 247-248
Knepp, Mary: description, 90; as Lady Fidget, 90
Kynaston, Edward: 31, 34; career, 69; as Harcourt, 90; as Lord Touchwood, 40, 180
Lang, Robert: as Petruchio, 63; as Scandal, 204, 224; as Mirabell, 224-225
Langham, Michael: director of _The Way of the World_, 222-225 passim
Leggatt, Alison: as Lady Plyant, 189; compared with Maggie Smith, 189
Leigh, Anthony: as Sir Jolly Jumble, 121-122, 129; compared with Nokes, 122; as Antonio, 129
Leigh, Elinor: 34; as Lady Wishfort, 207; Cibber describes, 207
Lindsay, Helen: as Lurewell, 242-243
Lisle's Tennis Court: See Duke's Playhouse

Phillips, Robin: director of The Way of the World, 278, 280
Pickup, Ronald: as Aimwell, 266
Plain Dealer, The: 322-323n
Playfair, Sir Nigel: 198, 261; director of The Way of the World, 213-214, 272, 280
Plowright, Joan: as Constantina 2, 63; as Margery, 93-94
Powell, George: drunk on opening night, 145
Porter, Eric: as Fainall, 217
Prospect Productions: 270, 332n; All for Love, 75-76; The Man of Mode, 47, 81-82; The Soldier's Fortune, 50, 122-123; The Provok'd Wife, 51, 162-164; The Confederacy, 52, 174-175; The Constant Couple, 240-243; The Recruiting Officer, 47, 254-255
Proud, Frank: director of The Provok'd Wife, 167
Provok'd Wife, The: 53, 141; plot summary, 157-159; background, 159-162; success of The Relapse leads to The Provok'd Wife, 159; rewritten in 1725, 159; Prospect Productions (1963), 51, 162-164; Intrigues and Amours (1967): adaptation by Joan Littlewood, 51, 165-167; Robin Phillips's Company (1973), 167-168
Queen's Theatre: 258; described by Cibber, 10-11
Quin, James: as Sir John Brute, 161, 164
Ravenscroft, Edward: 49, 112-117 passim; influenced by Molière, 112
Recruiting Officer, The: 230, 270; compared with The Soldier's Fortune, 118; plot summary, 243-245; background, 245-247; Trumpets and Drums (1956), 56, 247-250; National (1963), 56-57, 250-254; Prospect (1970), 57, 254-255; textual changes in Trumpets and Drums, 248-250; Trumpets and Drums influences Gaskill, 250-254 passim; alterations in National text, 252-253, 284-291; equalled or surpassed by The Beaux' Stratagem, 260; textual changes and various rehearsal techniques in National (1963) production, 41, 284-291
Red Bull Theatre: 4
Reid, Beryl: as Lady Wishfort, 227
Reid, Sheila: as Dorinda, 268
Relapse, The: 36, 53, 141; plot summary, 142-143; background, 144-146; Vanbrugh inspired by Cibber, 144; Cibber praises Vanbrugh, 144-145; Cibber compares The Relapse to his Love's Last Shift, 145; boosts Drury Lane, 146; Quayle production (1948), 51, 146-148; Virtue in Danger (1963), 50, 148-150; RSC (1967), 50, 150-153; RSC (1968), 50, 153-157; masque theme emphasized, 155; success of The Relapse leads to The Provok'd Wife, 159

Rich, Christopher: 8-11, 22
Richards, John: background, 114
Ritchard, Cyril: 271; as Foppington, 50, 56, 141, 147-148; Lowe compared with, 125; as Tattle, 201
Robertson, Toby: director of The Man of Mode, 82; director of The Soldier's Fortune, 122-123; director of The Provok'd Wife, 162-164 passim; director of The Confederacy, 174-175
Rochester, John Wilmot, Earl of: 32, 34; model for Dorimant, 79
Rogers, Mrs.: as Amanda, 36; protests too much about her chastity, 145-146
Routledge, Patricia: as Lady Fidget, 101
Royal Shakespeare Company (RSC): 47, 50, 270-271, 330n; in The Man of Mode, 47, 82-87; in The Relapse (1967), 51, 150-153; in The Relapse (1968), 51, 153-157; in The Way of World, 56, 226-229
Rutherford, Margaret: 271; as Lady Wishfort, 216-217, 220-221; compared with Edith Evans, 221
Ryall, David: as Squire Sullen, 268-269
Ryder, Thomas: emphasizes less civilized aspects of Sir John Brute, 161, 164
Sandford, Samuel: 34; tries to play a decent man, 37
Scofield, Paul: as Pierre, 134-137 passim; his Pierre compared with Gielgud's Jaffeir, 134-137 passim; compared with Webb, 139; as Young Fashion, 148; as Witwoud, 217
Seyler, Athene: as mother of Constantina 2, 63
Shadwell, Thomas: 49, 106; influenced by Jonson and Etherege, 106
Shaftesbury, Anthony Ashley Cooper, Earl of: 128
She Would If She Could: 322n
Siddons, Sarah: Sheila Hancock compared with, 126; as Belvidera, 129; with John Kemble as Jaffeir, 129
Sinden, Donald: 271, 331n; as Foppington, 50, 141, 148, 151-152; compared with Ingham, 50, 154
Smith, Maggie: 44, 271; as Margery, 49, 101-102; as Lady Plyant, 184; Alison Leggatt compared with, 189; as Mrs. Sullen, 57, 263-269 passim; as Millamant, 277-280 passim, 342-343n; as Silvia, 289; wins Oscar, 346n
Snow, Peter: designer for Intrigues and Amours, 166
Soldier's Fortune, The: compared with The Recruiting Officer, 118; plot summary, 118-120; background, 120-122; Downes reports, 121; as afterpiece, 122; Prospect Productions (1964), 50, 122-123; English Stage Company (1967), 50, 123-126; 1935 production, 123, 327n; compared with Venice Preserved, 139. See also Trumpets and Drums

of plot, 213, 225-226, 342n; 1953 Gielgud production compared with 1924 Playfair production, 213-214; Playfair Production (1924), 54, 225, 272-276; Stratford, Ontario (1976), 55, 277-280; Chichester (1984), 342-343n

Webb, Antony: as Pierre, 139; compared with Scofield, 139

Wenham, Jane: as Mrs. Marwood, 225

West, Timothy: 343n; as Smuggler, 242

Whistler, Rex: designer of Love for Love, 198

Wildair, Sir Harry: 270; attracts both actors and actresses, 32, 240; remains a significant character, 56; Wilks as, 239-240; described, 241-242; Hardy as, 56, 242

Wiles, Anthony: director of Epsom Wells, 110

Wilks, Robert: Cibber reports that he objects to playing Constant, 160-161; as Sir Harry, 239-240; success of The Beaux' Stratagem attributed to, 258; versus Powell, 258-259; Cibber describes, 259; Steele describes, 259; partnering with Oldfield, 260

Williams, Charles: as Roebuck, 233; Cibber describes his worth, 233

Wintershal, William: 31; background, 68

Wood, John: as Sir Fopling, 85

Wood, Peter: director of The Double Dealer, 189-194 passim; director of Love for Love, 202-204 passim

Wordsworth, Richard: 343n; as Antonio, 133

Wycherley, William: 48-49, 88-105 passim; compared with Ben Jonson, 103

Yarde, Margaret: as Lady Wishfort, 273

Zinkeisen, Doris: designer of The Way of the World, 218

Retta M. Taney is Associate Professor of English at Xavier University in New Orleans. She founded the Danaan Players in London, where she worked in fringe theatre for three years. She has written and delivered papers on Farquhar, Congreve, Etherege, Shaw, Synge, Tennessee Williams, John le Carré and Maggie Smith. Her two one act plays have been produced in New Orleans and at Cambridge University. Her first novel, The Masque of the Fox, is currently being rammed down the throats of Xavier students.